DEDICATION

This book is dedicated to the memory of two wonderful holy women, Sister Aine O'Connor, Sligo, Ireland and Sister James Patrick Kavanagh, Blauvelt, NY

A Sergeant Markie Mystery

THE CASE OF

TOO MANY

WIVES

Anthony Celano

1

<u>Big Ears</u>

THE LONG WHITE CANE AND DARK GLASSES that covered her eyes made it apparent that Mary Beth Carbone was visually challenged. Having lost her sight at an early age, the auburn-haired thirty-three year old had long adjusted to her situation. Of average height and slender, Mary Beth took pride in her ability to hold down a job and live independently in a city that could be dangerous at times.

It was just months away from the year 2000 and the world was caught up in the Y2K scare, which threatened computers and computer networks around the world. Throughout this ordeal Mary Beth remained unfazed. She continued to live alone in a one-bedroom apartment on East 5th Street in lower Manhattan. The building was located just a few houses from the 9th Precinct.

Living in such close proximity to the station house offered Mary Beth the opportunity to make friends with a number of the cops attached to the precinct, many of who made it their business to look out for her. There were times, particularly during the inclement weather, when the cops would drive her to her job. This came as a great relief to her parents, who lived nearby on Avenue A off East 2nd Street.

Mary Beth was employed full time at the Manhattan-based Wozenkroll Trucking Company. Because her daily commute to work was just a few train stops uptown, she made the trip without trepidation.

The entire office staff at Wozenkroll Trucking was working overtime on what turned out to be the most exciting evening of Mary Beth's life. As was often his practice when holding his employees late, Mr. Wozenkroll treated his workers to Chinese takeout.

At 7:00 p.m. the announcement was made that the food arrived. Mary Beth followed the flow of voices to the company lunchroom. After securing a seat at the long table, she listened attentively for her order to be called out by Mr. Wozenkroll, who was distributing the food.

"Who ordered the pork fried rice?" asked Wozenkroll, a wiry man in his late sixties.

"That's me," answered a husky female voice. "Let me have a Coke with it."

"Who gets the chicken chow mein?"

"Over here," shouted a woman with a distinct accent. "I'll take bottled water."

"General Tao's—" called out the owner of the company.

"That's me," voiced Mary Beth.

"Would you like a soda or a bottle of water with that?"

"Coke, please."

Mary Beth listened for the sound of the plastic container of food to be placed directly in front of her. She put her hand over the lid to feel the intensity of the heat on her palm.

"Wow, this is really hot," she commented.

"Yes, it is," replied the coworker sitting next to her. "The soda is at two o'clock," she whispered.

"Thank you," replied Mary Beth, reaching for the Coke. She carefully poured the beverage into a coffee cup she held in her hand. She stopped pouring when her index finger felt the chill of the cold beverage through the cup.

As 10:00 p.m. approached, Mr. Wozenkroll arranged for transportation to take his workers home. While everyone else accepted the ride offer, Mary Beth chose to decline. Her preference was to take the train. For Mary Beth, her refusal of the ride was validation of her self-reliance. Wozenkroll didn't insist—he understood.

Whenever Mary Beth traveled the streets, she remained attentive to the sounds around her. Being attuned to the level of noise allowed Mary Beth to determine how populated the streets were. A steady flow of pedestrian and vehicular traffic reassured her that people were nearby should she need assistance. Silence, on the other hand, represented an iffy unknown.

Mary Beth navigated the subway by counting her steps. She had long memorized how many steps it took to reach the bottom of the subway stairs. She also knew the number of steps it took to reach the turnstile.

Although Mr. Wozenkroll respected his employee's wishes, he nevertheless was concerned for her safety. Unbeknownst to Mary Beth, Mr. Wozenkroll took it upon himself to follow her to the subway platform. Because there was no longer a token booth clerk on duty at the 23rd Street station, Wozenkroll saw it as his obligation to do this. Once Mary Beth was on the platform, Wozenkroll was able to head home with a clear conscience.

As she waited for the train, Mary Beth sensed that she stood alone on the platform. She listened attentively for the sound of an oncoming train or some form of activity. As always, she kept her distance from the edge of the platform. In order not to soil the black business suit she wore, she was careful not to lean against anything.

After a while, two masculine voices could be heard entering the platform a short distance from where Mary Beth was positioned. As their conversation became increasingly more audible, she came to realize that two men were engaged in some type of disagreement. Their tone deteriorated into one of outright hostility. The harshness of the discourse was something Mary Beth wasn't used to. Confrontation, in her experience, was heard predominantly on television. Such a disagreeable exchange was exciting to a woman historically shielded from unfriendly behavior. Mary Beth's heart began to race as the conflict continued to escalate.

"Look, Professor, why don't you just smarten up and do what's good for you," said the more aggressive voice. "You know as well as me you're gonna give me what I want."

"I'll never pay what you're asking," the second voice adamantly stated.

"Oh, you'll agree to pay, alright," barked the extortionist confidently.

"You're never gonna see that kind of money from me!"

"What are you crying about? Ten grand a month is a drop in the bucket for somebody like you."

"Listen, I'd rather be dead than have to pay you off forever!"

"Oh, yeah?" came the heated response. "Then as sure as I live and breathe, you're gonna have to deal with both broads knowing about your double-dipping! Don't forget, there are laws, my friend."

Fascinated by their street dialogue, Mary Beth was all ears. Not wanting to miss anything, she inched closer to the men. As if listening in on an old-time radio drama, Mary Beth now slightly pitched forward, bursting with anticipation as to what would come next.

"Look, I'm willing to meet you halfway," said the shakedown victim. "How about you take a one-time, lump-sum payoff to go away?"

"No dice, Professor," replied the extortionist. "It's gotta be my way, or you'll face the consequences. You got plenty of money, so why don't you just agree to pay up."

"Why don't I just call the cops, turlet head?"

The word turlet resonated with Mary Beth. It reminded her of her Brooklyn-bred father, who was in the habit of saying turlet when referring to the toilet.

"Smarten up, will ya?" said the extortionist. "What good does talk like that do either one of us . . . or your women?"

"I don't like getting backed into a corner," warned the shakedown victim, now angrier. "When a man gets desperate, he does desperate things."

Mary Beth was surprised at how unafraid the extortion victim seemed to be. At this point she thought his voice was as equally formidable as that of the extortionist. She gulped as she waited to find out how things would further unfold.

"Listen, you *crazy* two-timing bastard," said the extortionist, an off-duty Philadelphia police officer who now took things to an elevated level. "You ain't in any position to puff up your chest with me. You got until tomorrow to come up with the first ten grand. If you don't, it's your funeral."

Unknown to Mary Beth, the extortion victim's body language was telling. The Professor stood his ground, his fists defiantly clenched in a ball. He was so worked up that two large veins protruded from his neck. The expression on his face was one of pure defiance.

Mary Beth began to hear what sounded like guttural growls coming from one of the men. Even in her darkness, Mary Beth was able to sense that heightened ugliness was imminent. Expecting things to get physical, she recoiled, inching back toward her original position on the platform.

Now triggered, the Professor opened his coat. With surprising speed he drew the concealed knife from the sheath that hung from his belt. Oblivious to the fact that there was another person present on the platform, the Professor attacked.

"I'M GONNA SHOW YOU WHAT CRAZY IS!" shouted the armed man as he suddenly stabbed the extortionist in the abdomen.

The cop from Philadelphia was too slow in sidestepping the blade that was thrust deep into him. He let out a shrill scream from the pain, followed by a series of low moans that eventually died out. The killer thought it best to make it seem as if a random robbery had taken place. The man with the knife quickly relieved the homicide victim of his gun, shield, wallet and cell phone.

Just as he was about to flee the subway, the Professor noticed Mary Beth, who stood cowering against the platform wall hoping to remain invisible. Trembling, she braced herself for the worst as she listened to the footsteps approach her.

"I'm blind," Mary Beth blurted out, alerting the murderer she was unable to see. She hoped her sightlessness would be to her advantage.

As the killer neared her, he could see Mary Beth's lips quivering. Noticing the dark glasses and white stick, he waved his hand in front of her face to gauge the extent of her disability. Mary Beth felt a slight breeze pass by her nose. When she didn't react, the killer was satisfied she couldn't see him. The Professor then fled the platform.

Mary Beth listened with relief to the sound of footsteps that grew fainter. She tapped her white stick in front of her as she proceeded in the direction of where the groans had come from. When she reached the body of the murdered man, she gently poked him with her stick. Receiving no response, she poked a bit harder. It felt as if she were jabbing into a marshmallow. Mary Beth raised the tip of her stick and touched it with her fingers. As she rubbed her fingers together she realized that the liquid she felt was likely blood.

"Sir, can you hear me?" she shouted down at the body.

When she received no reply, Mary Beth knew for sure that death rested at her feet. She began to make her way to the street to notify the authorities when she heard an approaching train about to enter the station. Relieved, she waited for the train to come to a full stop before calling out for help.

##########

WHEN THE UNIFORMED POLICE ARRIVED AT the 23rd Street subway station, it seemed evident to them that a robbery/homicide had been committed. The officers restricted access to the platform and notified the precinct squad detectives, who, after arriving, requested the presence of the crime scene unit. While forensic investigators processed the crime scene, the precinct investigators searched the platform and surrounding areas for clues.

Squad Detective Theodore Hart, a tall gray-haired man with a distinguished white mustache, remained at the scene with the forensic investigators. His partner, Detective Denise Boucher, was assigned to the homicide case.

Boucher, a neatly dressed single mom, took charge of the only witness. A swimmer in high school and college, the detective was noticeably broad-shouldered.

Excited over what had occurred, Mary Beth willingly accompanied Boucher to her office for the purpose of interview.

"Would you like some coffee, Ms. Carbone?" asked Boucher once they were settled in chairs.

"No—no, thank you."

"Did you call 911?" asked the detective after preparing a cup coffee for herself.

"No, I didn't get a chance to. The train pulled in before I got around to it. I think someone coming off the train must have made the call."

"Do you think anyone on the train might have seen anything?"

"I don't think so. The person who did the killing ran off around the same time I first began to hear the train."

"Do you think the motorman might have had a chance to see anything?"

"It's possible, I suppose, but I wouldn't know."

"Please tell me exactly what you saw, Ms. Carbone."

"Well, detective, I didn't actually *see* anything," replied the witness.

Boucher quickly realized her poor choice of words. Embarrassed, she began to restate her question.

"Excuse me, I meant to ask—"

"Don't worry—it's alright."

"Let's restart this," said the detective. "Why don't you just tell me what happened, Ms. Carbone."

"I was on my way home, waiting for my train when—"

"Do you always work this late?"

"Not as a rule; today was just an unusually busy day."

"I see. Please continue."

Detective Boucher began taking notes as Mary Beth conveyed what had occurred on the subway platform. The witness explained how two people, who she suspected to be men, engaged in a verbal dispute that escalated into a violent confrontation. She then provided a detailed account of the words that were exchanged to the best of her recollection.

"This sounds like the killer was being extorted by the deceased," commented the detective.

"That's exactly right," concurred Mary Beth. "The man killed was demanding monthly payments of ten thousand dollars."

"Do you have any idea who these men were or where they might have come from?"

"No, all I know is that the dead man called the other man Professor."

"Do you think he was a teacher?" asked Detective Boucher.

"I have no idea, detective."

"Did he sound educated, like a professor might?"

"Not really. Both men sounded about average. Well, actually, they talked kind of tough."

"I see. Do you think these men might have been anyone you may possibly know?"

"No, that's doubtful."

"Ms. Carbone, forgive me, but I have to ask you this question," said the detective. "Are you able to see anything at all?"

"No, I'm totally incapable of seeing."

"Can you make out shadows?"

"No, I've even lost the ability to see shadows."

Detective Boucher shrugged as if helpless. She concluded that Mary Beth was limited in her ability to further the investigation at this time.

"Thank you for your cooperation, Ms. Carbone," said Boucher, terminating the interview. "I'll drive you home now."

"Thank you, but you don't have to put yourself out. All you need to do is take me as far as the subway."

"It's no trouble. It's getting kind of late—I'll take you home," insisted the detective.

"Oh, there is one other thing I forgot to mention, Detective Boucher."

"What's that?"

"The murdered man called the other a crazy two-timing bastard. Things really got heated after that."

"In what way did things get more heated?"

"It seemed that the murdered man took offense at being called crazy."

"Did he sound crazy to you?" asked Boucher.

"Not really. But after that remark, he did sound like someone going off."

"Can you think of anything else you might have forgotten to mention?"

"No, I think you have it all now."

After taking the witness home, Detective Boucher returned to the crime scene to discuss the case with her partner.

"So what do you make of it, Teddy?" Boucher asked after filling in Hart about how her interview went.

"The deceased calling the killer a two-timing bastard suggests a romance angle," replied Hart.

"He called him a *crazy* two-timing bastard," clarified Boucher. "Being called a two-timer didn't seem to set him off, but according to the witness, being called crazy did."

"Are you thinking that the perp's a psychiatric case, maybe?"

"I see that as a possibility. Maybe that's why he was sensitive to being called crazy."

"Could be . . ."

"The only thing we have to go on is the name *Professor,*"

11

noted Boucher. "And how many professors do you suppose there are in the city?"

"I don't know," replied Hart. "So you don't see this as a straight-out robbery gone sour, right?"

"I don't think so—there's more to this."

"Technically, it's a robbery because his pockets were turned inside out. The victim has no wallet and no money on him."

"Why wouldn't the perp take his watch and ring if it were a straight robbery?" asked Boucher.

"That's a good question," conceded Hart. "Maybe he panicked. Let's see what the DOA's fingerprints tell us. Once we know who he is, maybe we'll have a direction to go in."

"Yeah, that'll help," concurred Boucher.

The detectives notified their squad commander, who was on vacation. After receiving his briefing, the detective lieutenant advised his detectives to conduct a canvass and to prepare an unusual, a report designed to notify the police hierarchy of any unusual occurrence. He also instructed them to check the surrounding precincts to see whether anyone had a line on someone by the name of Professor. Since things seemed under control, the lieutenant resumed enjoying his off-duty time with his family with a clear head. As directed, Boucher and Hart conducted their canvass in the vicinity of the train station. They were hoping to identify someone who could provide useful information. They had no such luck.

The detectives knew that it would take a long time before the homicide victim's fingerprints came back. They hoped the results would identify the body. The detectives next began contacting the surrounding precinct squads in an effort to identify someone called Professor. This proved fruitless.

"I think all we can do now is just wait for the prints to come back, Teddy," said Boucher.

"Yeah, we might as well call it a night," agreed her partner. "Tomorrow's another day."

##########

THE PROFESSOR HAD THE PRESENCE of mind to flee the homicide scene by walking out of the subway system as opposed to running out. Once on the street, he briskly proceeded to his place of business, an 8th Avenue storefront located just a few blocks north of 23rd Street. He was certain that the return trip to his bookshop didn't arouse suspicion.

For a man who just murdered a cop, the Professor did a remarkable job of maintaining his composure. Once sure no one was around on the street, he opened the front door to his shop. Upon gaining entry, he locked the door and pulled down the window and door shades. Now feeling insulated, he popped a couple of his calm-down pills before sitting at his desk.

The Professor closed his eyes and rested the back of his head against his chair. He allowed himself twenty minutes of idleness to give the pills time to work their magic. At the expiration of the allotted time, the first thing the Professor did was to take a moment to examine the dead cop's gun, shield, and wallet. After doing so, the Professor locked all these items in the small combination safe he kept underneath his desk. He'd deal with them at another time.

The Professor next examined his victim's cell phone. He noted that multiple calls were made to and from Ella, the Professor's Philadelphia-based wife. Oddly, the Professor wasn't surprised or particularly bitter over this. Ella's fidelity was a secondary concern. All that mattered to him at this point was not getting caught by the authorities.

The Professor's true interest in his second wife Ella rested

13

purely on her physical nimbleness. This made her unfaithfulness easier for him to cope with. As long as Ella remained available in Philadelphia to satisfy his needs, he could care less what she did with the rest of her time. Besides, he was in no position to say anything even if he wanted to. It would hardly be in his interest to admit to Ella that he knew of her involvement with the man he just killed.

Before leaving the bookshop, the Professor called his New York City-based wife Rebecca to let her know that he would be heading home to Brooklyn Heights shortly.

"I won't be long," he advised.

"Where are you? I was beginning to get worried," said Rebecca.

"I stopped to have drinks with a business acquaintance to discuss a potential opportunity. I know I should have called, but I didn't think I'd be this late. I'll be home in a half hour if not sooner. I'll grab a cab."

"What about eating?"

"I could eat something. Do you need me to pick up anything?"

"No, I have food at home. I'll fix something nice for you. It'll be ready by the time you get here."

After exiting the taxicab two blocks from his home, the Professor disposed of the dead cop's cell phone by dropping it down a Brooklyn sewer. After entering his house, he had tried to put the entire incident behind him as if it never occurred. Unable to do so, he turned in after eating.

Sensing he was tense, Rebecca sat on the edge of their bed. To soothe him, she began massaging the back of his neck. The treatment helped, but it didn't cure his woes. The Professor still carried the worry connected to the law possibly finding out that he murdered an out-of-town police officer. His sleep was uneasy that night.

14

2

Business As Usual

THE MANHATTAN BOOKSHOP WAS NOTORIOUS for its inconsistency when it came to hours and days of operation, so the Professor's absence went unnoticed. He only returned to work after concluding no one suspected him of involvement in the 23rd Street subway slaying.

The Professor always extended himself when it came to the needs of his customers. His willingness to exceed expectations enabled him to establish an unusually loyal client base. Since the location of his business was not far from the theater district, his clients included a number of theatrical people who worked and/or resided in the area. On occasion, some had need for a specific book or magazine.

The Professor was sitting behind the desk situated at the front of his shop. He was examining the condition of a novel he attained at the request of Sally Belle, a prominent Broadway actor. Once satisfied the book had minimal imperfections, he contacted Ms. Belle to advise her he was in possession of an excellent copy of *Trilby* by George du Maurier.

As the Professor awaited the arrival of Ms. Belle, he read portions of the book. Intrigued by the sinister Svengali, a character who exerted irresistible control over a young girl, he found himself absorbed in the tale he was reading.

The Professor barely looked up from his book when the Hell's Kitchen youths entered his bookshop. They were just two of the many boys from the West Side of Manhattan who came by to play the arcade games the Professor had hidden in the back room of his shop. These machines were installed not for the purpose of financial gain but rather to draw a young audience who would likely have an interest in the card tricks the Professor delighted in performing.

"How's it going, Professor?" asked one of the boys.

"Great, kid. You guys are gonna like the new machine I got coming in," advised the Professor.

"What kind of machine?"

"It's a shooting game with a rifle."

"Cool!"

"Go in the back and have fun. Before you go home, I'll show you my new card trick."

##########

WHEN THE DOOR SWUNG OPEN, the Professor looked up from his desk. A stylishly dressed woman of sixty with a mix of long silver and blond hair entered his Manhattan bookshop. Nicely figured, from afar she gave the appearance of someone much younger. Under her white raincoat she was attired in a celery-green jacket worn over a black, long-sleeved silk shirt. The combination was striking. Her jeans were form fitting and her heeled shoes red.

16

The visitor to the shop carried herself with great confidence. Her make-up was impeccably administered to a point where one would assume it was professionally applied. She stood before the desk with her feet positioned as would a model posing for a photo. Sally Belle was the epitome of an accomplished talent in the legitimate theater. The Professor couldn't help but wonder how she would be in bed.

"Good afternoon, Professor. How are you, darling?" greeted the visitor in a voice that oozed of fine diction. "Thank you for locating the book I've been seeking."

The Professor smiled warmly. "I scoured the country to locate this book, Ms. Belle," he exaggerated. "I'm glad to report that I haven't disappointed you."

"Wonderful!"

"You know, I was just reading about Svengali."

"Isn't the storyline fascinating? There has been some talk of bringing it to Broadway. That's why I so wanted a copy of the book."

"I remember seeing the movie on television."

"John was simply marvelous in that film. He captured the character Svengali wonderfully."

"John Berrymore?" asked the Professor.

"That's Baaa-ree-more, darling. He was a friend of the family, you know. I recall as a child of three or four sitting on his lap."

"Really?" the Professor asked as he placed the book in a bag for his customer.

"Oh, I was too young to really know him, but my father and he were quite friendly. Everyone in my family was taken by him," she confided. "Especially enamored was my father's sister, Lucille."

"So, he was a man of conquests."

"Oh, yes indeed. He was a very important man in his time. It was such a shame how he fell victim to drink."

"You'll have to tell me more about him one day, Ms. Belle," said the Professor, angling for some alone time with her.

"You really must stop calling me Ms. Belle, it's so formal. You *can* call me Sally, you know."

"Alright...Sally."

"It's a pity you're not available for the soiree at my home this weekend—you'd get to meet the Maestro. As a young violinist he appeared on stage with Barrymore. The dear man has consented to play for us Saturday evening."

"I'm sorry, but I'll be in my Philadelphia location that day. But my wife Rebecca intends to be there. If you invite me to the next one, I'd be glad to entertain your friends with my card tricks."

"That would be such a treat!" said Sally enthusiastically. "I am going to hold you to that, Professor. And be sure to wear that black cape you're wearing, I love the red velvet lining."

"You can bank on it."

"I so look forward to seeing your wife again. Rebecca is such a darling."

"She is, ma'am. I'm blessed and consider myself very lucky."

"Often, people are slow to appreciate how true a blessing a good mate is. Good day, Professor," said the actress, departing with her book in hand.

Twenty minutes after the transaction was completed, the two young boys emerged from the back of the shop to step up to the desk where Professor Extraordinarious sat.

"Hey, Professor, how about showing us that card trick?" asked one of the boys.

"Sure," said the Professor, who needed no coaxing. "I have a brand-new one for you."

The Professor reached into his desk drawer and pulled out his latest trick. Standing erect in his cape, he held up four aces in his left hand, the front of the cards facing the boys. Then he took the ace of diamonds in his right hand and placed it at the top of the remaining aces, positioning the card between the ace of spades and ace of clubs.

"Watch the ace of diamonds," said the business owner. "Keep a close eye on it."

Using his index finger, the Professor lightly tapped the top of the ace of diamonds downward three times into the hidden sleeve behind the ace of spades. As he tapped he uttered, "Going, going, gone!" With the diamond now safely tucked behind the spade, the Professor separated the remaining three cards to show that the ace of diamonds had vanished.

"How much does that trick cost?" asked one of the boys, impressed enough to want to purchase the magic trick.

Professor Extraordinarious laughed at the question. "How much do you have?" he asked jokingly.

The two boys left with the trick without having to pay anything for it. They also got their pinball money returned.

##########

REBECCA WAS RUSHING HER SON along so he wouldn't be late for school. She was proud her boy was attending one of the most exclusive schools. Her plan was for him to go on with his studies and receive the finest education possible. The goal she set was one that eluded both her and her husband.

The Professor sat at the kitchen table in their Brooklyn Heights home. He watched approvingly at how his wife interacted with their son. In Rebecca he had found the pinnacle of loyalty. In return, he gave her all that was within his power. She could walk or take a limo. It made no difference to him.

The fact the Professor was elsewhere half the time never strained the relationship he enjoyed with Rebecca. In terms of intimacy, his absences only served to spice up her physical desire for him. His return to the nest was often accompanied by new lovemaking techniques that she found to be a turn-on. Her excitement, in turn, went far in exciting him. Yet, even with this added passion, the willing Rebecca still didn't quite measure up to his other wife Ella in Philadelphia. When it came to the romance department, the double-jointed Ella was in a class by herself.

"Put a move on dear—it's getting late," said Rebecca to her teenage son.

"I got lots of time," said the boy, who was getting ready to head for school.

"C'mon now, listen to your mother, and step on it," said the boy's father.

"Alright, I'm going. Are you going to be home tonight, dad?"

"No, I'll be home Sunday."

"Okay, I'll see you when you when you get back," said the youth, who was used to only seeing his father three or four days a week.

"You have enough money on you?"

"Yeah, I do. I'll see you Sunday."

After the boy left for school, the Professor poured himself a second cup of coffee. "Ms. Belle is expecting you to attend her party, Rebecca. She's having entertainment."

"That's nice—what kind?"

"Some violinist is going to play. Supposedly he worked with John Barrymore."

"Who is he?"

"Barrymore was a famous actor," he replied. "He's probably

20

dead over fifty years."

"I wish you were going to the party with me."

"I'll definitely go next time. I promised her I'd do some of my card tricks for her friends. Sally was all over the idea."

"Oh, so now it's Sally, is it?" asked Rebecca.

"Not really. I still mostly call her Ms. Belle."

"I was thinking, do you think we should buy a condo in Philadelphia?" Rebecca asked. "I hate to see you trucking all the way over there to stay in a motel or sleep in the shop all the time."

"That's not necessary. I really don't mind. I'm used to it by now."

"Well, alright. Maybe at some point I'll go down to Philly with you so you won't be all by yourself."

"Don't worry about me. I'm able to get a lot of work done when I'm alone."

"But I've never even seen the bookshop in Philly."

"The store isn't in the best of areas down there. I'd rather you not go. I'd rather you come to the Manhattan store instead— that way I don't have to worry about you."

"I don't even know where the Philadelphia shop is. All I know is that you said it's not very safe."

"Don't fret, Rebecca. I'm never without my Bowie or Smith & Wesson survival knife. They'll keep me protected," assured the Professor. The last thing he wanted was to see Rebecca in Philadelphia.

"Alright, but please be careful."

"I've been thinking of maybe expanding again."

"Expanding to where?"

"I'm not sure yet. I'm thinking Florida, South Carolina, maybe even someplace out west."

"What about us?"

"Nothing is going to change. I'll work it into my schedule. Remember, I don't run my businesses in a traditional way. I'm at a point where I have the luxury of opening up at my convenience now. Besides, I could always hire someone when the time comes."

"What was it that Horace Greeley said?" she asked, letting out a sigh.

"Go west, young man, and grow up with the country," said the Professor, repeating the exact words of the founder/editor of the long defunct *New York Tribune*.

3

Professor
Extraordinarious

THE PROFESSOR WAS RAISED IN A DYSFUNCTIONAL BROOKLYN
HOME ruled by a street-hardened father. Partnering with a
mobster, Henry Harrison Blount Sr. eventually rose to be the
sole owner of a highly lucrative manufacturing firm in
Manhattan's garment district. Blount Sr. had every expectation
that his son would one day take over the business.

   When the teenage Henry displayed no interest in involving
himself in the rag trade, the patriarch was flabbergasted. He
couldn't fathom why his only son refused to enter into such an
established enterprise.

   "Women buy clothes!" explained the father, on numerous
occasions. "What the hell is wrong with you?"

   "I'm not interested, pop," was the son's stock reply.

   "Don't be a crazy turlet head!" said Henry Sr. nastily. "The

23

heavy lifting is long over—it's a sweet set up you'd have."

"I'm sorry, but I'm just not interested."

"If you wanna be a crazy turlet head your whole life, then go and be a crazy turlet head," bellowed the father in disgust.

The term turlet, a mangled version of the word toilet, was commonly used by past generations of working-class Brooklyn residents. Being repeatedly referred to as turlet head, crazy, and other unflattering adjectives by his father had a deep effect on Henry Jr. The impact of this ongoing verbal abuse caused Henry Jr. to evolve into a person with a rage festering within him. He housed an explosiveness that could surface at any time.

It took a particularly destructive outburst before Henry's parents finally acknowledged that their son had anger management issues. In response to being called a turlet head once too often, Henry snapped and heaved the family television out the window of his parent's eleventh-floor high-rise apartment. The recklessness of this act resulted in the arrest of the sixteen-year-old. Adhering to the order of the presiding judge, the parents sought professional help for their son.

The subsequent therapy and medication Henry received managed to stabilize his behavior. Regular sessions with a psychiatrist furthered efforts to keep him functioning within societal norms.

With Henry's anger now under control, one closeted condition stubbornly remained. His being oversexed was something he went to great lengths to conceal. Perhaps his fixation with the opposite sex had something to do with years of listening to his father's lecherous comments about the women who wore his special line of naughty apparel. Regardless of the causation factor, Henry Jr. developed into a person hopelessly consumed with sexual desire.

When it came time for college, Henry Jr. declined the

opportunity to further his education. Instead, he opted to travel the country so he could experience the sexual treats elsewhere.

Alone, he bummed his way, unrestricted and far from his home turf. While he might not have studied with co-eds, the experience nevertheless proved to be quite educational.

Upon Henry's return to New York City a few years later, he arrived with two newly acquired passions. Having worked for a while as an assistant to a knife maker in Boulder, Colorado, Henry Jr. became so fascinated that he became an avid collector of knifes. His other interest was in performing card tricks. This enjoyment stemmed from his friendship with a Kentucky carnival magician many years his senior.

Henry's parents were mortified by what they considered to be their son's unusual interests. His mother believed that the only hope for her son was for him to go into business for himself. As a result of the pressure applied by his wife, Henry's father reluctantly agreed to finance the son he still referred to as a turlet head in some kind of an entrepreneurial venture.

After some quibbling, it was agreed that Henry Jr. would open a small secondhand bookshop as opposed to his parent's preference of opening a rare bookshop. Henry disliked the term "rare books" because it seemed too hoity-toity for his liking. The one thing that all concerned agreed on was that a Manhattan location would be best.

With his father's backing, Henry opened a small storefront located on the west side of Manhattan. The business was a boutique enterprise that peddled secondhand books, magazines, and, on occasion, rare first editions. Henry Jr. worked hard, and to the surprise of his father, eventually turned the bookshop into a successful enterprise. He accomplished this by hanging out in the bars frequented by the theatrical crowd who worked, resided, and played on the west side. This socializing led to dalliances that that advanced his efforts to establish a client base.

In time, Henry was earning enough money to support himself, pay his bills, and finance his need for a multitude of sexual encounters. He also did well enough over the years to enhance both his knife and card trick collections. Far from abundantly wealthy, he was happy living a lifestyle that suited him.

Things changed for Henry after meeting Rebecca Merced, an attractive high school senior twenty years his junior. Rebecca had first entered the bookshop looking for a book on witchcraft. After several chats with Henry, a friendship was formed.

Rebecca began stopping by the bookshop after school on a regular basis. Finding Henry's talk of books, knives, and card tricks to be interesting, she soon gravitated to feelings of attraction. Rebecca experienced this transition to romance once the business owner began sharing tales of erotic gratification. Such talk caused the innocent Rebecca to tingle when in his presence. Hopelessly infatuated, she became his for the taking.

"Henry . . . I think I'm pregnant," announced Rebecca one afternoon.

"Are you sure?" asked the business owner, who could see the young woman was frightened. She wasn't alone in that feeling.

Once the pregnancy was confirmed, the bookshop owner stepped up to assume full responsibility. His offer of marriage not only startled Rebecca, but also stunned her parents, who were totally unprepared for such a situation.

The teenager had a difficult time convincing her parents that marriage to a man so much older was a good idea. As expected, Mr. Merced's first reaction after learning of Rebecca's pregnancy was one of extreme displeasure. To put it plainly, the plumber's helper wanted to wring Henry's neck. Fortunately, cooler heads prevailed.

When Henry formally asked for Rebecca's hand in marriage, his future father-in-law respected the gesture. The birth of a baby boy also helped ease some of the tension.

##########

YEARS LATER, THINGS TOOK an unanticipated turn for Henry after he purchased a few lotto tickets. The return on his investment was just under a staggering one hundred million dollars. As one would imagine, such a financial windfall did much to improve Henry's relationship with Rebecca's family.

Henry acquired a three-bedroom condo that overlooked the promenade in the prestigious Brooklyn Heights section of Brooklyn. He purchased fancy cars and jewelry, and he spoiled Rebecca and their son beyond reason. He also continued to spread his seed liberally wherever possible. This was a happy time for Henry. He only wished his parents had lived long enough to see his good fortune.

Now having the wherewithal to do whatever he pleased, Henry expanded his knife collection and routinely purchased the latest card tricks. It was at this point he started on a journey to reinvent himself.

With his penchant for card tricks in mind, he decided to project an aura of mystery. This hobby was one of the reasons he stayed in business after coming into his fortune. The bookshop provided him with a venue to show off his talent as a card wizard.

Henry grew a goatee to fit the role he chose to play. He then began to advertise himself as Professor Extraordinarious. He favored the odd-sounding name because he felt it had a certain mysterious ring to it. Henry took to wearing a black cape in order to ramp up his new image. His being tall and thin and having a hawk-like nose further contributed to the appearance he was looking to capture. He even changed the name of his business to The Professor's Used Bookshop.

########

AT THE AGE OF FORTY-SEVEN, Henry continued to indulge himself when it came to women. Thanks to the money he came into, his days of seeking out one-night stands on the sly were over. No longer did he need to prowl the city seeking willing women. His money would enable him to facilitate what he saw as a more convenient way to satisfy his needs.

The bookshop owner saw embracing a bigamous lifestyle as the solution to his desires. Having the financial wherewithal necessary, his plan was to establish homes with a number of strategically located wives.

After morphing into his Professor role, Henry opened a second bookshop, this one in Philadelphia. The location was opposite Diamond Joe's Italian Garden, a popular Philadelphia restaurant. Once the new entity was up and running, the Professor began splitting his time between Philly and his Brooklyn Heights residence. This two-state arrangement provided him the latitude to carry out the solipsistic scheme he conjured up.

In his ardent search for a second wife, the free spending Professor began frolicking with an assortment of women from Philly, all who differed in appearance from his wife Rebecca. The loyal Rebecca, who remained in the dark as to her husband's behavior, tolerated his frequent absences from home out of her love for him.

The Professor astutely reinforced his hold on Rebecca through frequent acts of generosity. He moved his in-laws close to where they lived in Brooklyn Heights. In addition to a new residence, Rebecca's parents were gifted a black Lincoln Continental to get around in. It pleased Rebecca greatly to see her family finally accept her husband. She grinned ear to ear after hearing her father state how a wonderful man like Henry was the perfect son-in-law.

When Rebecca's father passed away unexpectedly, the Professor took care of all the arrangements. His mother-in-law was so touched by this gesture that she began encouraging her daughter to have more children.

When it came to other women, the Professor kept his financial status a mystery. The only love interest who knew the exact extent and origin of his wealth was Rebecca. She was also the only person he truly loved.

4

Double-Jointed

Ella

PHILADELPHIA BORN ELLA CORNELL WAS THE ONLY CHILD of a single working mother stretched thin by the dual responsibility of raising a child and juggling a demanding career. The teenager took advantage of her unsupervised time throughout her high school years. The mischievous sort, she snuck out nights when her mother had business obligations, neglected her studies, and made every effort to appear older than she was. In her senior year, the teenager began bleaching her hair blond, drinking, and dressing suggestively. Her mother, having her hands full, agreed to Ella's demand to put college off for a year.

By now Ella had developed into a beautiful young woman who drew the interest of many men. One admirer who took notice was Elwood Brown, a manipulative rogue who everyone knew as Tootsie Roll. At twenty-five, the handsome six-foot Brown personified the bad boy. His unsavory reputation as a drug dealer was also the key to his allure. The sweet talker was the marijuana supplier to high school students looking to cop weed. For Ella, the abundantly confident Tootsie Roll represented a forbidden fruit that she found to be irresistible. The special attention he showered upon her was effective enough for Ella to become his girl.

After Ella's graduation, Tootsie Roll convinced her to move into the one-bedroom apartment he shared with a Siamese cat named Katana and Charles, a caged hamster. Ella's being double-jointed impressed Tootsie Roll. He viewed her flexibility in terms of an opportunity to expand his skullduggery. He put into motion a plan designed to profit off his young lover.

Efforts by Ella's mother to put an end to the relationship came to an abrupt halt after Tootsie Roll terrified the woman by threatening to burn her house down when she was sleeping. By this time Ella was viewed as too valuable a property for Tootsie Roll to let go of.

While Ella's mother was having discussions with lawyers about what to do with her now of-age daughter, Tootsie Roll continued to soften Ella up with a steady diet of flattery and false promises. He began expanding Ella's use of alcohol and introduced her to cocaine. Brown's purpose was to diminish Ella's resistance to the unsavory suggestion he intended to propose. When Ella balked at partaking in drug use, Tootsie Roll doubled down on the alcohol. Once she became dependent on drink, he introduced a carrot-and-stick form of control in their relationship. If Ella complied with his wishes, she was rewarded; if she didn't, the consequence was going dry.

Ella's alcohol weakness led her to oblige Tootsie Roll's demand that she service the men he began scheduling on an appointment basis. Charging a premium rate, Tootsie Roll shrewdly began promoting Ella as would a barker at a carnival. When pitching Ella he referred to her as Ella Spreadella, the double-jointed wonder. It proved to be an effective come on.

Prior to Tootsie Roll, Ella never thought of being double-jointed as something that could be turned into a profitable commodity. As Ella's appointment book began filling up, she grew resentful over the money she was realizing for her labor.

Things finally came to a head when Tootsie Roll broached the idea of Ella's accepting a role in a cheaply budgeted porno film. Ella declined the opportunity, fearing that such explicit exposure would reach her mother, who hadn't yet given up on her. Ella's resistance didn't sit well with Tootsie Roll, who countered her opposition with his hands.

This physical abuse, along with having to turn the bulk of the money she sold herself for over to Brown, led to her rebellion. Fearful of Brown's violent tendencies, Ella knew she couldn't just walk away from him without someone standing behind her.

Ella went to see the operator of the car service she used. After conveying her need of assistance in putting an end to her association with Tootsie Roll, she was put in contact with Richie Cadillac, the hidden owner of the car service. Since the mob-connected Cadillac disliked pimps anyway, a quickie in the back room of the car service secured the support she required.

Tootsie Roll soon found himself confronted on the street one night by two thugs who dragged him into an abandoned building. After pistol whipping him, they forced him to strip down. Before setting fire to his clothes, the goons advised him to stay away from Ella or else. Tootsie Roll, recognizing that he was out-muscled, felt it prudent to heed their warning.

With Tootsie Roll ousted, Ella, was now a free agent. Having limited savings, she managed to curtail her drinking and rely on her bedroom skills to get by. Looking at the bright side, there was satisfaction in knowing the money she made was all hers. At this point she no longer had a relationship with her mother.

##########

ELLA WAS SHOPPING IN A SUPERMAKET WHEN she first set eyes on Diamond Joe Ormento, the owner of Diamond Joe's Italian Garden. She was standing undecided in an aisle comparing two jars of sauce when Diamond Joe, a man nearing seventy, stopped pushing his cart to initiate a conversation.

"The good one is in your left hand," he said.

Ella turned to look at the stranger with the bushy salt-and-pepper hair. Unlike many men his age, he was robust and seemed powerfully built. He wore a black button-down short-sleeved shirt that fell outside his black slacks. A gold cross on a thick gold chain could be seen around his neck. The tattoo of a topless mermaid decorated his right forearm.

"This one is better?" Ella asked, raising the jar in her left hand.

As was her way, Ella spoke assertively. Experience taught her that most men would take a step back when up against a forceful woman, particularly one who was attractive.

Diamond Joe didn't respond to her question. He just stood there biting his lip as he evaluated her. His failure to speak caused Ella to repeat her question. When the stranger again remained mute she looked at his ears for signs of a hearing aid. When Ella saw none, she began to lose patience.

"What's the matter with you, are you deaf, or don't you understand English?" she asked, sounding perturbed.

"Eh, sure I do," Joe replied calmly in a soft voice. A faint smile could be seen on his face.

The man's confident demeanor caused Ella to reevaluate him. She now took notice of the expensive watch and pinkie ring he

33

wore. Once attuned to the jewelry, Ella saw the door of opportunity ajar. Turning on the charm, she smiled broadly.

"Could you *please* help me pick out the best sauce?" she asked sweetly.

The senior citizen's amused look became more pronounced.

"Sure thing, honey," replied Joe.

It was no mystery to Diamond Joe that Ella was out to play him. The restaurant owner had more than his share of experience with such women. As it turned out, their meeting proved to be fortuitous. Diamond Joe was a strong believer in hiring pretty young girls to work in his eatery. He saw Ella as someone who could draw customers to his restaurant.

"You work?" he asked, handing her the best sauce on the shelf.

"Sometimes . . ." replied Ella.

"You cook?"

"Do I cook?" she asked, taken aback by his bluntness. "Yeah, I can cook. What, you want me to cook for you?"

"No, I don't need you to cook for me, I'll show you how to cook right," he answered confidently. "How about you come to work for me?"

"Work for you where?" she asked, stepping back from him to get a fuller look. At this point she suspected the old man might be working his own angles.

"In my place of business, where do you think?"

"What place?" she asked skeptically, thinking he was referring to his home.

"Diamond Joe's Italian Garden, that's my place," Joe declared proudly. "I'll put you on as a waitress and teach you how to cook on the side."

"Get outta here, that's not *your* place . . ."

"I'm Joe Ormento!" he declared. "Everybody calls me Diamond Joe."

Ella was aware of the reputation Diamond Joe's Italian Garden enjoyed. She now definitely viewed Diamond Joe as a potential sugar daddy. "How much money are you gonna pay me?"

"I pay my people good, ask anybody."

Taking into account that she was estranged from her mother and her funds were running low, Ella took the job. She saw it as a sure-fire way to get close to the restaurant owner.

As it turned out, Diamond Joe went on to take a sincere interest in Ella. Since he and his wife were childless, he told people that he was a father figure to the much younger woman. The truth in this statement would be debatable.

In some respects, Diamond Joe was good for Ella. Exhibiting great patience, he devoted time to smoothing out some of her rough edges. When he realized her weakness for drink, Diamond Joe made sure to monitor Ella in order to restrict her alcohol consumption.

The arrangement didn't escape the watchful eye of Mrs. Ormento, a jealous woman determined to keep things wholesome at the restaurant. With Diamond Joe's wife always on the alert at the eatery, the green-eyed Ella was soon discouraged in her pursuit of her intended sugar daddy.

With Joe unattainable, Ella began flirting with men who dined at the restaurant. The added attention netted her a number of male followers, one of whom was Professor Extraordinarious, who owned the bookshop across from the restaurant.

The Professor, who often ate dinner at the restaurant, was immediately charmed by Ella. He soon began taking all his meals at Diamond Joe's when in Philadelphia. After establishing himself as a big tipper, the bookshop owner was treated well at

Diamond Joe's. The restaurant owner made it a point to make a big fuss over the Professor whenever he came in.

"Ella, make sure you're *extra* nice to the guy who owns the bookshop," directed Mr. Ormento.

"Sure, Joe, I'll treat the Professor like he owns the place," replied Ella.

Ormento did a double take. "Don't treat him that good," corrected the owner, waving his index finger from side to side.

The Professor really caught Ella's attention once she noticed that he dined at the restaurant with a number of different women. Wanting to know more about the owner of The Professor's Used Bookshop, Ella exhibited her interest. She complimented the Professor on his whiskers, claiming to find them fascinating. She also pretended to enjoy the card tricks he performed for her. Encouraged by this, the Professor began eating at the restaurant alone. He then started making inquiries as to Ella's marital status. When word got back to Ella that the Professor was asking about her, she stepped up her game.

"So, are you going to tell me what your real name is?" she asked one evening at the restaurant.

"I'm Professor Extraordinarious."

"C'mon, what kind of name is that?"

"It's a magical name."

"Okay, Merlin, have it you way, Do you live in Philly?"

"Sometimes I stay in Philly, and sometimes I'm in New York."

"New York City?"

"I have another bookshop in Manhattan."

"Oh, now I am impressed. Are you married?" The Professor found her question pleasing. It was proof of her interest in him.

"No, but I wouldn't rule it out if I met the right person."

"I feel exactly the same way," said Ella, flashing a smile as she stared into his eyes.

Ella embarked on a campaign of bumping into the Professor outside the restaurant. These were strategically orchestrated meetings that were welcomed by the Professor. In time, a for-pay romantic relationship was established. This arrangement didn't escape the eyes of Diamond Joe Ormento.

"You like this guy, Ella?" Diamond Joe asked her one day.

"He'll do, Joe. You don't mind, do you? We're both single and over twenty-one, you know," she joked, testing the waters.

"It's none of my business what you do," he said.

The smile Ella displayed was sincere. *Old shrivel-dick is a pretty good guy,* she thought. "You're alright, Joe," she said fondly.

When the Professor expressed a deeper interest in her, Ella was up front with the Professor. With their sexual intimacy a regularly scheduled affair, she was able to speak plainly.

"Look, Professor, I have to be honest," she said. "I like you, but I'm not in love with you. I want to hook up long term with someone who can take care of me—and I'm not talking just dinner and a movie."

"I know what you want, Ella, and I got no problem with that," said the Professor. "Don't worry, I could afford you."

His candidness was something Ella found surprising. "Are you being honest about that?"

"Of course I am."

"You mean to say you aren't in love with me?" she asked point-blank.

"I care for you enough to ask you to marry me," he replied.

"Why do you want to marry me?" she asked, stunned by his proposal. "You *do* understand that I *don't* love you?"

"You're a special talent."

"So we understand each other?"

"I think we understand each other perfectly. The wedding ring I offer you will come with whatever else you want." Ella looked at the Professor as if she were seeing him for the first time. She was about to ask him if he was crazy before changing her mind.

"I know what you're thinking, Ella. There is no need for you to worry about me," he assured her. "I'm no turlet head."

"I never thought that of you."

"I'm serious about this, Ella. I have enough money to accommodate you in every way."

"How much do you have?"

"Enough. Tell me what you want."

"I want a new car."

"Done, what kind of car?"

"I want a house."

"Sure—we'll go partners on one, and I'll throw in an allowance that you'll have trouble spending."

The Professor made it clear he was willing to pay plenty to have her as his wife. In Ella, unlike his New York wife Rebecca, he found someone he could explore unspeakable desires with. When the Professor again proposed marriage, Ella readily accepted. Her glee was such that the Professor caught her struggling to maintain a straight face. The two wasted little time in making it official. The following morning, they flew to Las Vegas to tie the knot.

From the Professor's perspective, everything was going beautifully once he purchased a home and settled into a regular routine in Philadelphia. Ella, however, eventually began dwelling on one major drawback. The Professor turned out to be a man with a taste for sexual perversions that even she found to be too much. Even his giving Ella whatever she wanted was unable to offset this turn off. Frustrated, Ella began to express her disinterest.

"Can't you put this on speed dial once in a while?" she asked her husband one evening when she was not in the mood for a

38

lengthy engagement.

"I can't help myself." replied the Professor. "I just can't get enough. How about we try—"

Doesn't this bozo ever run out of ideas? The last thing Ella wanted was more exposure to the Professor's creative side. It was something she dreaded.

##########

WITH NO LACK OF AVAILABLE MEN in Philadelphia, Ella soon found other suitable partners that were more to her liking. With a husband who spent half his time out of town, arranging trysts wasn't a problem. Since the financial aspect was a key component of her relationship with the Professor, Ella was allotted enough to meet whatever expenses her extra marital affairs came to.

Whenever her husband was away, she'd be sure to stop by Diamond Joe's to have dinner. Saying hello to Joe and catching up was one of the things she enjoyed doing. While she never got along very well with Joe's wife, she did maintain a solid platonic friendship with Joe.

"I wish you luck," said the restaurant owner when Ella was having dinner. "It's nice that you come back to see me."

"Don't worry, Joe, I'll be eating here all the time," assured Ella.

Diamond Joe smiled affectionately. When he noticed his wife watching him from afar, the smile on his face quickly disappeared. "Uh-oh," he said, as he saw her coming his way.

"What's wrong, Joe?"

"Shhh . . . tra moglie e marito non mettere il ditto," he whispered, advising never to interfere between a husband and wife. Not versed in Italian, Ella had no idea what he was talking about. When Mrs. Ormento arrived at the table her look wasn't

39

pleasant. "What?" asked Joe, raising his right hand up. "I just asked her how she was making out with her sauce."

"What do you care how her sauce is?" barked Joe's wife, her back to Ella. You should worry about your own sauce!" she added, before storming off.

"What's her problem?" asked Ella.

"She always been jealous," replied Joe. "Pay her no attention."

Diamond Joe later approached his wife in the restaurant's kitchen. "Why would you do such a thing like that?" he asked. "Now she's not gonna come back maybe . . ."

The restaurant owner's wife shook her head slowly. "Too bad," said Mrs. Ormento. "You know what my mother used to say?"

"What?"

"Buona liberazione per la spazzatura male!" Translated, the words meant good riddance to bad rubbish.

##########

PROFESSOR EXTRAORDINARIOUS COULD BE FOUND IN THE Philadelphia bookstore only a few hours a day. The rest of his time in Philadelphia he spent at home in the love nest he purchased for himself and Ella. Unbeknownst to him, he was fiddling while Rome was about to burn.

Bored with married life, Ella was secretly beginning to think of an exit strategy. She mulled over the possibility of having a baby, feeling that the presence of a little one would ensure a larger settlement when it came time to divorce. Ella later dismissed the idea after considering the work involved in raising a child.

After a while Ella realized that the first thing she needed to do was ascertain how much money the Professor was actually worth. Efforts to pump her husband as to his financial affairs were met with resistance. It was a topic the Professor simply refused to discuss.

"What's the big secret?" asked Ella over dinner one night.

"It's not a big secret. I know how much I got."

The reply became the Professor's standard response. He had no intention of ever telling Ella that he was a huge lottery winner. His will was going to reflect that his entire worth was to go to his first wife Rebecca and their son. It was to be his gift to a loyal woman and wonderful child. The Professor's only regret about the will he prepared was that he wouldn't be around to see Ella's reaction when it was read.

"But what if something were to happen to you?" asked Ella.

"Nothing is going to happen to me," replied the Professor.

"But how will I know what I'm entitled to if something does? Where's my security?"

"Relax, Ella, I keep telling you, I'm no turlet head. My attorney will see that you get everything that is coming to you."

"I don't even know who your attorney is!" protested Ella.

"Ella, don't you trust me? If you don't, then we may have a real problem here."

"Alright, whatever you say," she said, pouting.

Since the Professor didn't want to upset the arrangement, he agreed to sign over his half of the Philadelphia house to her. He also began talking about buying her a condo in Fort Lauderdale. These gestures appeased Ella for the time being.

Judging by her husband's spending, Ella was certain the Professor was very wealthy. In one respect, she considered herself fortunate that the Professor spent half his time in New York. His absences enabled her to see other men.

Things went this way until Grady came along. Closer to Ella's age, Grady O'Lang entered Ella's life unexpectedly. His presence awakened her emotions. Ella hadn't figured on falling in love with, of all people, a Philadelphia police officer—it just happened. He possessed the very ingredient that could melt Ella's heart and collapse her façade of strength.

##########

THE PROFESSOR WAS WAITING FOR ELLA in the living room of their home. He nervously fingered his ear as he checked his watch for the time. Feeling stiff after his long drive from Manhattan, he began stretching to loosen up. His own flexibility was important if he were to take advantage of his wife's exceptional freedom of movement. Adding to his excitement were the mental comparisons he'd make between his wives.

The Professor was at fever pitch by the time Ella walked through the front door. He sprung to his feet, hell-bent on having her. Having just returned from the hairdresser, Ella was less than enthusiastic about her husband's amorous intentions. After being taken in his arms, she began fending off his pawing.

"Hey, take it easy," she protested. "What did you just get out of jail?"

"I've missed you," replied the Professor, undeterred.

Pulling her head back out of range, Ella looked up at the ceiling. The expression on her face could have been construed in many ways. Perhaps it could be described as a look of great tolerance—or maybe one of disgust would be more appropriate. Some might even perceive her look as a sign of anguish. This was the tough part of being the Professor's second wife. Rebecca, his first wife, was spared this side of the bookshop owner.

##########

THE TWO WOMEN THE PROFESSOR married didn't have the slightest inkling as to his mental history. His need for medication to manage his anger remained a closely guarded secret. The Professor informed each spouse that the pills he took were to control a rare medical condition.

Since things seemed to be working out well for him, the Professor began seriously considering taking on a third wife. The lady he had in mind was Concetta Piatelli Bryant, a counterwoman at the Manhattan pharmacy where the Professor renewed his prescriptions.

It started innocently enough with small talk. Whenever the Professor went to pick up his supply of medicine, they chatted casually for a few minutes. It was only after Concetta expressed an interest in seeing the card tricks he often spoke of that the Professor began seeing her in an amorous light. As they conversed, she came to learn of the Professor's knife collection. A gun enthusiast, she genuinely found his talk of knives interesting. The synergy that existed between the two was simply too powerful for the Professor to ignore.

Concetta was flattered when the Professor became flirtatious. While she declined his attempts to take her out, she did nothing to discourage his advances. She appreciated the attention.

After the unexpected job-related death of Concetta's husband, an iron worker, she had a change of heart concerning the Professor. Believing he was unattached, she began taking her own steps to open the door to a relationship.

"Do you like going to the movies, Professor?" she asked as she removed his change from the register.

"I love going to the movies."

"Have you seen *Saving Private Ryan*? I'm dying to see it!"

"Well, let's go see it then."

Hitting it off from the very start, the two just got along well. Their close proximity in age meant they saw many things from a common perspective. Concetta's being a bit on the plus side added to her physical appeal. Since his two wives were thin, Concetta represented a welcomed variation. She was a change of pace, so to speak.

The widow had always been enamored with the thought of one day living her life out west. Now, with the insurance money she received in connection with her husband's accidental death, she could afford to do so. She envisioned herself amid western music, ranches, and cowboy hats along with spur-wearing, bow-legged men galloping along on horses.

Concetta chose the "The Italy of America" as the ideal place to live her life. Where else but Arizona could she find such scenic mountain regions that reminded her of Italy? The question was whether or not the Professor would feel the same way.

5

Shady Grady

GRADY O'LANG LIVED WITH HIS GRANDFATHER IN A SMALL
APARTMENT in Philadelphia above his grandfather's pool hall.
Since the older man owned the building, Grady lived rent-free.
Most days he could be found in the pool room honing his skills
with a cue stick. His ambition at one time was to be a champion.
However, Grady fell short of acquiring the skill necessary to
meet this goal.

Years of practice made Grady proficient enough to earn a few
bucks by hustling less-talented players for small stakes. While
he lacked the aptitude of someone like fellow Philadelphian
Willie Mosconi, a former pocket billiard champion, Grady did
manage to run off seventy consecutive balls playing straight
pool on one occasion. While achieving this difficult feat
enhanced his notoriety at the pool hall, it did nothing to
brighten his financial future.

Grady's grandfather eventually decided the time had come for
a heart-to-heart talk with his grandson at the dinner table.

"You're pushing thirty years old and still treading water," said the grandfather. "Isn't it about time you went out and got a regular job? You can't depend on me to support you forever."

"I know. I'll start looking next week," replied Grady.

"I'm serious, Grady. I ain't getting any younger. If something happens to me, then what? You'll be shit out of luck!"

"Nothing is gonna happen to you, Gramps."

"Will you leave him alone already?" said Grady's unmarried aunt, who always cooked their dinner on Sunday. She lived alone in the top floor apartment. "He said he'll start looking next week, didn't he?" The aunt, who had always been protective of her late sister's son, was looking to short-circuit a potential argument.

"You stay out of this!" barked the grandfather. "You're part of the problem I got over here with this bronco!"

"I'm NOT the problem, you—"

"Will you two please stop bickering?" shouted Grady.

"Listen to me," said the grandfather, lowering his voice. "You see those guys who come around the pool hall? Well a lot of them are retired city workers collecting pensions—and they all got good health benefits. That could be you one day if you smarten up. Keep doin' what you're doin' and you're gonna end up like me—workin' until you drop dead."

Grady had to admit that hustling pool wasn't going to cut it as a lifetime career. He decided to take his grandfather's advice.

"You win, Gramps. Square business, I'll look to take a civil service exam."

"Now you're making sense, kid. I know that they got the cop test coming up."

"Okay, I'll file for it."

"Good. I got just one other thing to say."

"What's that?"

"Do yourself another favor and ease off the gambling. If you don't stop with the betting, job or no job, you'll wind up without a pot to piss in. You're a good-looking kid, so go find yourself a nice girl and settle down."

"He's right on that point," injected the aunt, supporting her father. "A lot of the girls around here ask me about you—"

"I know, I know," said Grady, "how about we stop with the lecturing and finish eating?"

##########

GRADY O'LANG FOUND THE PHILADEPHIA POLICE ACADAMY to be quite demanding. The arduous routine left him no time to devote to vices. By the time he graduated, he had a little money in the bank and lived alone in a neat one-bedroom apartment. Unfortunately, within a year after receiving his patrol assignment, his gambling weakness had reentered his life.

The pull of the Atlantic City casinos proved to be too powerful a temptation for Grady. Once his savings were exhausted, he began living paycheck to paycheck. Money became so tight that Grady was compelled to cut costs. The first step he took to conserve funds was to move into a studio apartment in a seedy section of town, where he remained for years.

At thirty-seven Grady was still working on patrol in uniform. By this time the uniformed officer was in the habit of gambling while working his shift. When he ran out of money he'd replenish his losses by creating opportunities with motorists who committed traffic violations.

A chance car stop ultimately put Grady on a destructive path of no return. He pulled over a late-model green Jaguar that neglected to come to a full stop at a stop sign. His purpose in stopping the vehicle was not to enforce the law. On the contrary, he pulled the car over in the hope of receiving a bribe.

"Let me have your license and registration," said the officer firmly, disappointed to see that a young woman sat behind the wheel of the Jaguar. *Shit, a women driver*, he thought. *They never come across with any money.*

"What did I do?" asked the motorist, fishing in her purse to produce the requested documents. Far from timid, Ella looked the cop in the eye as she handed over her license and registration. The driver displayed a confidence that was rarely exhibited by someone pulled over by the law.

"You're supposed to come to a full stop at a stop sign, lady," said Grady crisply, "not slow up and drive through it. It's looks like I *might* have to write you up."

The word might made Ella suspect that the officer was interested in her personally. Since Grady was a handsome, well-built man, she was amenable to his attention.

"What's the big deal, handsome?" she asked flirtatiously. "There was no harm done. You don't *really* want to give me a ticket do you?"

"I could forget it . . . *if* I was so inclined. Now out with the insurance card," he ordered.

Ella, not used to being commanded, complied.

"Ms. Blount, what do you think we can do about this?" asked the officer. He was sending out a feeler, hoping that Ella would catch on and offer him money.

Ella was appalled. With other cops she only had to flutter her eyes to get out of a ticket. "Well, what do you suggest I do?"

"You're not giving me a reason why I should let you go."

"Give me one why you shouldn't," countered Ella.

Seeing that he was getting no place fast, Grady lost patience. "Just because you're easy on the eyes don't earn you a pass with me. I need an incentive, sweetheart," he stated plainly.

Ella's attention was now drawn to the officer's gun, handcuffs, and the Sam Browne black leather belt his holster hung from. "Oh . . ." uttered Ella softly, feeling intimidated. Ella perceived abundantly confident men as masterful, particularly when they were on the nasty side. "Allow me to thank you," she replied, as she reached for her wallet.

From Grady's vantage point he was mostly impressed by the bankroll Ella flashed. The new Jaguar and the jewelry Ella wore also influenced him in terms of her desirability. Grady took Ella's money and invited her to meet for coffee at the end of his shift.

########

IT WASN'T LONG BEFORE THE INFLUENCE OF GRADY'S domineering personality controlled Ella. To her, he was a force she found addictively intoxicating. Contrary to her other dalliances, she was willing to follow the Philadelphia cop blindly.

Grady's hold over Ella was remarkable. Instead of expecting him to do the things she wanted, as she normally would, she was willing to do the things that pleased him. As someone not used to being an afterthought, Ella nevertheless was motivated to please the Philadelphia cop.

Ella's permitting Grady to dictate the terms of their relationship gave him such a voice that he even had a say in how *they* should spend the allowance that was allotted to her by husband, the Professor. This translated into Ella floating whatever gambling expenses her lover incurred.

In need of money to pay his rent, Grady was waiting impatiently for Ella at his studio apartment. Tired of having to deal with a pestering landlord, he was foul-tempered.

"Where the hell is this bitch?" asked the Philadelphia officer aloud as he paced the floor of the small space he lived in.

Grady let out a sigh of relief when he heard the lock to the front door turn. It was Ella letting herself in with the spare key he gave her. Along with her arrival came the relief money he desperately needed.

"It's about damn time. What kept you?" he asked, rising from his chair.

"I came over as soon as I could," replied Ella. "I thought my husband was never going to leave the house." She sounded almost childlike as she explained herself.

Seeking his approval, Ella passed Grady an envelope containing cash. She then snuggled up to him. In response, Grady enveloped her waist with his arms. Behind her back he began thumbing through the money she had given him. She rested her head on his chest with her eyes closed as he counted quietly to himself.

"Did your old man go back to New York?" he asked, after pocketing the money.

"No, he goes back tomorrow."

"Where is he now?"

"He's at work. I passed by the bookshop to make sure he was there before coming here. I thought he'd never leave the house.

"What was the tie up?"

"What's always the tie up?" she asked. "He wanted me."

Pausing, an unpleasant look crossed Grady's face. "I hope you accommodated him."

"I told him I wasn't feeling well. I could never be with him when I'm waiting to see you, Grady."

"You know, you're really stupid sometimes," barked Grady harshly. "Don't you realize that you gotta keep him happy? What are you trying to do, derail the gravy train?"

"Don't worry, Grady, he's not going anyplace until I'm good and ready to cut him loose." Her words came out very formidably, like the Ella of old.

"That's my girl," said Grady approvingly. Ella felt as if a star had been placed at the top of her test paper. The Philadelphia cop took Ella by the arm and led her toward his unmade bed. "Did your old man say anything when you asked for money?"

"Not a word," Ella relied proudly. "He's knows he has to pay if he wants to play."

"What a chump! Get over here," he demanded, pulling her toward him.

"So soon, Grady?" she asked elfishly.

After they finished making love, the two returned to conversing.

"I've been thinking, Grady."

"Thinking about what?"

"Maybe I should just divorce the Professor. We'll try and get all we can get out of him. As things stand, if he ever gets wise, he may not be willing to be very generous."

"How much has he got?"

"I don't really know."

"Then how can you look to divorce him?" asked the Philly cop. "We gotta know what he's got so we know what to ask for."

"I know that he's gotta have plenty."

"Sure he does, but we can't underestimate his worth."

"You're right."

"I know I'm right. Let me tell you something—I can't help but smell a rat. Why is he so secretive about his money?"

"That's just the way he is."

"I'm telling you, he ain't being totally on the level. Do you think he could be dealing drugs?"

"Believe me, if the Professor was into dealing drugs, I'd know it. Not a chance of that."

"If you can't find out what his bankroll is, maybe I could."

"How are you gonna do that?" asked Ella, perking up.

The Philly cop thought for a moment before replying. "I'm gonna have to do something."

"You *can* do something?" asked Ella hopefully.

The wheels were now turning in Grady's mind. "Leave it to me, baby. I'll take some time off and find out what your old man's worth."

"What are you gonna do?"

"I'm gonna tail his ass. I'll probably have to spread some money around, though. Can you get your hands on more cash?"

"I can. How much do you want?"

"I'm thinking that a couple grand might do the trick."

"No problem. I got that much home."

"Then just leave it to me," said Grady, now regretting he asked for so little. "Get me the money, and I'll find out where he's got the treasure buried."

A big smile came over Ella's face. She loved Grady's macho confidence. Her eyes sparkled as she gazed into the eyes of the man capable of ruling her.

##########

GRADY PARKED HIS POLICE CAR BY THE fire hydrant in front of The Professor's Used Bookshop. Having only seen Ella's husband once from afar, he was there to get a better look at him. Appearing very much the cop in his police uniform, the Philadelphia officer pulled down his hat before entering the bookshop.

Shoulders back, the officer stood erect as he visually scanned the premises. Grady was surprised to see how small the shop was. Satisfied there were no customers inside the location, Grady looked down at the proprietor, who was seated behind his desk.

"May I help you, officer?" asked the Professor, looking up from his chair.

What is it with this guy's black cape and those whiskers? Grady wondered.

"Has anyone come in today trying to sell you any books?" asked the cop.

"What kind of books?"

Grady wasn't prepared for the question. "Uhh . . . biographies, autographed first editions," he replied.

"No, no one has come in here selling anything along those lines," answered the Professor, relieved that the officer's interest had nothing to do with him. "Why do you ask?"

"There was a burglary, and books like that were stolen." The officer noticed several blue and red decks of cards stacked on a shelf directly behind the desk. Being a gambler, Grady became inquisitive.

"What's with all the cards?"

"I perform magic tricks. Here, let me show you one."

The Professor removed four aces from a desk drawer and proceeded to show Grady the vanishing ace trick. "Did you like that one, officer?"

"Yeah, that was pretty neat." *For a twelve year old!* Grady thought.

"Here, take the cards home with you, compliments of Professor Extraordinarious."

"Thanks," said Grady, who took the gift.

"Wait a minute," said the Professor, let me show you another one before you go."

"Not now. I have to run down those stolen books."

When Grady returned to his patrol car, he examined the four aces that were given to him. After seeing the ace with the built-in pocket, he shook his head thinking, *a sneaky bastard like this has to be up to something.*

When Grady got home that day, he left the cards atop a mantelpiece before going to the refrigerator for a cold brew. With his beer in hand, he opened his calendar book to check his work schedule. He called up the station to seek permission to take off the following week. His leave request was granted, making it possible for him to devote the time necessary to shadow the Professor.

6

A Secret No More

SOME MIGHT ARGUE THAT GRADY O'LANG WAS a criminal in the purest form. Those of a more generous nature would characterize him as simply a weak man who succumbed to the temptations his profession offered. Either way, O'Lang used his position as a cop to support his gambling addiction.

Although O'Lang was without a strategy, the Philadelphia officer remained confident in his ability to determine the wealth of the Professor. His only plan was to shadow the Professor when he left Philadelphia and then rely on his wits.

Grady sat in his car near the entrance to the highway that led to New York City. He listened to the radio and chain-smoked cigarettes as he awaited word from Ella, whose job was to notify him that her husband left the house. Once Grady received the heads-up, he'd be on the lookout for the Professor's white BMW. If no call was forthcoming, it would mean the Professor likely changed his plans and wasn't going to New York City after all.

While Grady waited he compartmentalized the two thousand dollars Ella had given him for expenses. He put seven hundred in his front pocket for easy access. This cash was held together in a silver horse-head money clip. Another seven hundred was placed in the money section of his wallet. The remaining cash was folded and hidden behind the only credit card he had in his wallet. That money was for gambling.

Unsure of how long he'd be in the car, Grady took two sardine sandwiches, several bottles of water, and, in the event nature called, a huge empty plastic jar that once housed pretzels. When his cell phone rang, the Philadelphia police officer jumped up in his seat.

"He just left," alerted Ella.

"Okay, I'm on it," said Grady in a clipped way. "I'll call you once I know something."

The Philly officer diligently waited for the Professor to come into view. Once the rolling surveillance commenced, Grady was relieved to see that the Professor drove cautiously, remaining within the speed limit. It came as a surprise when the Professor exited the highway at the first exit.

"Why the hell is he getting off here?" Grady asked aloud.

The Professor pulled into the parking lot of a diner just off the exit. He went inside and then emerged from the eatery after a few minutes without indication that he purchased anything. After returning to his vehicle he continued on to New York City.

He must have tapped a kidney, thought Grady, figuring the Professor needed to use the restroom.

Once in Brooklyn Heights, the first stop the Professor made was at a bank close to his home. As was his routine, he withdrew cash. Grady jotted down the address of the bank on a pad he kept in the car.

Unaware that he was being shadowed, the professor then

proceeded to a nearby florist, where he purchased two dozen roses. This stop caused the Philadelphia cop to wonder where the Professor was going with the flowers.

Smelling the roses as he walked, the Professor casually returned to his vehicle. He drove to a parking garage where he dropped off his BMW. With the flowers in hand, he headed home to see Rebecca, his first wife.

Grady parked his vehicle a short distance from where the Professor lived. After briefly stretching his legs, he got back into his car and prepared for a long wait.

After two hours the Philly cop observed the Professor emerge from his building carrying half the flowers he entered with. Accompanying him was a much younger woman and a boy. Grady followed the three on foot to a nearby address. The Professor entered the location alone with the roses, coming out a few minutes later empty-handed. With him was an older woman with short, curly, silver hair who took the arm of the youth as they walked. Now a foursome, the Professor and his party proceeded to a restaurant for dinner.

"Look at this shit," said the Philadelphia cop to himself. Amused, he was imagining Ella's reaction after he reported back to her. *Ahh, maybe they're his sister and mother*, thought Grady, giving the Professor the benefit of the doubt.

At the conclusion of their meal, the dinner party walked to the older woman's home. After she entered her building, the remaining three returned to their own residence. After Grady witnessed the Professor holding hands with the younger woman as they walked, he believed the bookshop owner was with his mistress. When it became obvious that the Professor was likely tucked in for the night, Grady returned to the restaurant.

The Philadelphia officer scanned the restaurant for a friendly looking face. He settled on the bartender, a dark-haired, olive-skinned man of middle age. Grady walked over to where he stood behind the bar. Placing a twenty-dollar bill on top of the bar, he pushed the currency toward the bartender.

"What's your pleasure?" asked the bartender.

"Some information," replied the Philly cop.

The bartender was taken aback. He found such a request to be quite unusual in the venue where he worked. Grady picked up on the bartender's puzzled look.

"I got an additional half a yard with your name on it," said Grady, displaying a fifty-dollar bill between his fingers, "*if* you answer a few simple questions."

That did the trick. "Sure . . ." replied the bartender scooping up the twenty that was left on the countertop.

"A little while ago, a man with a goatee was in here eating with a young woman, a kid, and an older lady. They sat at that table over there," said Grady, pointing to where the Professor and his family had eaten. "He had on a blue sport jacket and a white shirt."

"I know who you mean. What about him?"

Grady nodded. "What can you tell me about him?"

"He's a regular who comes in here with his family a lot."

"His family?" asked Grady, sounding surprised. "Who exactly were those people with him?"

"He was with his wife, his son and—"

Grady interrupted the bartender midsentence. "Hold it a second. Are you telling me he's married with a kid?"

"Yeah, and the old lady is his mother-in-law."

"Are you sure about that, my friend?"

"Sure I'm sure. His name is Henry. He owns bookstores."

"Does his wife have a name?"

"Yeah, her name is Rebecca."

"What about the older woman?"

58

"I don't know her name."

"And the kid is Henry's son?"

"Now you got it."

"Here, take the fifty, you earned it. Do us both a favor and keep our little talk under your hat."

After the Philadelphia cop found lodging for the night in a hotel, he went for something to eat. He waited until midnight before heading out to do more investigating.

Grady incentivized the overnight doorman where Rebecca's mother lived to confirm the information he received from the restaurant bartender. Satisfied he had put in a productive day, Grady returned to his hotel room. Once comfortable in the privacy of his bed, he telephoned Ella in Philadelphia.

"I've been waiting to hear from you," she said after answering the call. "So did you find out anything?"

"Plenty, baby."

"What did you find out?"

"You ain't gonna believe this. . ."

"Believe what?" asked Ella.

"It's like this, baby—you got some competition in New York."

"What competition?"

"The Professor's been playing house over here."

"Get outta here!" Ella declared abruptly.

"I'm telling you the truth, Ella."

"That bastard's got himself a girlfriend in New York?"

"Don't underestimate the old Professor, baby doll. He's not a guy to be restricted."

"What do you mean?"

"Your hubby's got himself a whole other family in New York."

Stunned by the revelation, Ella's mouth dropped. "You've gotta be kidding me . . ."

"No joke—he's got a wife *and* a son. I even saw him with the mother-in-law, who's not all that much older than he is."

"Are you sure, Grady?"

"Yeah, I'm sure. Moneybags is a friggin' bigamist!"

"That son of a bitching turlet head!" said the peeved Ella, using the term frequently voiced by the Professor. "I can't believe it!"

"Believe it, baby. As far as I can tell, they're one big happy family over here in Brooklyn."

"That lousy two-timing son of a bitch!" she shouted into the phone, not caring how hypocritical she sounded.

"I can't believe that clown was able to put something like this over on you," added Grady, rubbing it in.

Being made a fool of was the one thing that Ella couldn't tolerate. She displayed her dark side quickly.

"I'm gonna make that bastard pay in spades! He's not getting get away with pulling this shit on me."

"Take it easy, baby. Before you do something stupid, let me finish what I started over here. I'll find out how much he's worth, and then we'll figure out the next move. Give me a couple of more days."

"You're right, Grady," agreed Ella. "But I swear, he's getting his ass handed to him. I want every penny of his money that I can get my hands on!"

"You'll get your due—don't worry about that. I'll get back to you as soon as I know more. Just leave everything to me."

Ella let out a deep breath. "Alright...do you promise to call me tomorrow?"

"Sure, I'll keep you posted," he answered.

##########

THE FOLLOWING MORNING Grady O'Lang rose early, wanting to

get an early start. Since he had never been in Brooklyn Heights before, he decided to spend some time exploring the neighborhood. He stopped in a deli to pick up a container of coffee and a buttered bagel. Seeking a place to sit down and eat his food, he came to discover the scenic view the Promenade offered while walking along the pedestrian walkway.

Grady sat on a bench facing the Brooklyn Bridge and industrial waterfront. Gazing beyond the water at the impressive Manhattan skyline, he got to thinking of all the things he had been missing out on. *That's all gonna change once me and Ella get our teeth into the Professor's bankroll*, thought the rogue Philadelphia cop. The notion of "me and Ella" then began to linger in his mind. The more he pondered it, the sound of "me and Ella" just didn't sit right with him.

At 9:00 a.m. the Philly cop walked to the bank the Professor had visited the day prior. He assumed the bank to be the best place to get an understanding of what the Professor was worth.

Grady still hadn't worked out exactly how he was going to go about approaching those employed at the bank. He briefly considered identifying himself as an out-of-town police officer on official business. He nixed this after taking into account that bank policy would likely require a subpoena for the information he sought. That left him only two options—he'd have to either bribe or con someone who was working at the bank.

Grady was going to rely on bribery to elicit the information he was after. He entered the bank to find   someone who seemed to be pliable to such an overture. After identifying someone who looked like he could be compromised, Grady stepped outside thinking that he'd make his move at lunchtime.

Grady's strategy changed after he noticed a uniformed police officer standing post opposite the bank. Appreciating the leverage that usually went with being a hometown police officer, he arrived at what he believed could be the perfect solution to his problem. Adding to the appeal of the idea was its being cost effective. After coming up with a cover story, Grady proceeded to solicit the New York officer's assistance.

"How's it going, officer?" he asked, flashing his Philadelphia police shield. "I'm on the job in Philadelphia."

The New York cop wasn't satisfied with the glimpse of the badge O'Lang flashed. "Let me see that tin again." The officer checked the out-of-town cop's credentials. "How are you doing?" he asked, once satisfied.

"To tell you the truth, I'm not doing so great. I've been trying to get something done here without much luck."

"Are you here on official business?" asked the officer on the beat.

"No, I only wish I was," answered Grady. "I'm here on a personal matter that I could use some help with."

"What's the problem?"

"I'm trying to do a little due diligence for my kid brother," explained Grady, "but I'm not sure on how to accomplish that here in New York. My brother's involved in a business deal with some fat cat around here. They're gonna be opening a steakhouse in South Jersey. This guy is putting up the money, and my kid brother is supposed to run the place."

"What's wrong with that?"

"Nothing—the only problem is that my brother has to quit his job to go in on this proposition. With four kids, he can't afford to take chances. If the restaurant flops, he'll be sucking wind."

"Well, all businesses have a risk factor," commented the uniformed officer.

"We know, but here's the rub. This guy wants my brother in on the deal bad. So bad, that just in case the joint flops, he promises to carry my brother until he gets another job."

"What more can you ask for?" asked he beat cop.

"Nothing more, *if* the guy is being on the level. I need to find out if he actually has the funds to do what he promises if push comes to shove."

"I see."

A thought came to O'Lang after noticing that the New York officer displayed a Marine collar insignia above his police shield. He seized the chance of establishing a commonality by pretending to be a former Marine himself.

"You were a jarhead?" asked the Philadelphia cop, pointing to the Marine insignia.

"You bet."

"So was I."

"I'm Jerry Moogan," said the uniformed cop, adjusting his receptiveness. "What's your name, brother?"

"Grady O'Lang."

The Philadelphia officer knew enough about the Marines to bluff his way through a conversation. After discussing military life, the men got down to the business at hand.

"So what can I do to help you?" asked the officer.

"All I need is to get one question answered."

"What?"

"How much money this guy has in that bank across the street," said Grady pointing to the bank. "Do you have any juice over there?"

"What's the guy's name?"

"Henry Harrison Blount."

"How do you spell that?"

"B-L-O-U-N-T," advised Grady.

"Stand by. Let me see what I can do."

The uniformed officer entered the bank and spoke to a young female teller who, after a brief conversation, directed him to the branch manager.

"May I help you, officer?" asked the manager.

After apprising the manager of his need, Officer Moogan was denied access to the information requested.

"Are you sure about that?" asked the officer, who was used to getting his way when in uniform.

"I'm sorry, but it's against bank policy to give out that kind of information. Unfortunately those are the rules."

"I'm sorry too," replied Officer Moogan, expressing regret. "But rules *are* rules, aren't they?"

"Thank you for understanding."

"You know, I have this post steady."

"I've never noticed."

"Yeah, I pound this beat Monday through Friday on the day shift."

"Well, by all means, come in for coffee whenever you want. You're also welcome to use the facilities."

"That's very considerate of you, sir. And if there's ever a problem here on your end, I'll be outside at the ready to make it go away for you."

"That's sounds like a win-win to me, officer."

"Does it?" asked the officer, using a different tone. "The funny thing about rules and problems . . . they can come and go."

"I don't follow you," said the confused manager.

"Have you ever seen those two guys who work the three-card Monte game around here?"

"I haven't seen them in a long time, but I know who you mean. What about them?"

"You haven't seen them because of me," declared the New York cop. "They're around—just not on *this* block in front of *your* bank. And do you know *why* that is?"

"No, tell me why."

"Because of *my* rules—it's not permitted."

"I appreciate that, officer," said the bank manager, who wasn't sure where the conversation was going.

"I'd hate to see them set up shop right outside the bank here. Your bank would be an attractive place for those guys . . . you know, people with money going in and out all day."

The manager was finally beginning to get the message. "Hold on a second, they can't be permitted to set up here," said the manager. "Their presence would discourage my customers from banking here."

"Yeah, that would be a problem," said the cop, "wouldn't it?"

"I don't understand."

The officer assigned to the post then raised his eyebrows and shrugged. "Everybody has to be someplace—and in front of your bank can be as good a spot as any."

"What exactly are you saying?"

"I'm saying exactly that if they decide to set up shop outside, I have no cause to move or arrest them unless I personally witness their breaking the law. I can't be expected to break any *rules* now, can I?"

"You could tell them—"

"I could now, now couldn't I?"

The manager, looking to avoid a headache, provided the information the police officer requested. The beat cop then returned to where Grady O'Lang was waiting.

"Tell your brother he's got nothing to worry about. Blount is loaded. The guy in the bank told me he was a hundred-million-dollar lottery winner."

Grady's tongue began to lick his lower lip. "How much?"

"According to the bank manager, he took in a hundred million clams. He owns a business over in Manhattan and everything. Here, take this," said the officer, writing down the Professor's

Manhattan business address and entity name. "I'd say that your brother's got himself a real good partner."

The cop from Philadelphia never dreamt the Professor was worth that much money. "I *know* how to thank you for your courtesy, but I don't want to insult you," said Grady, treading carefully. "Would it be alright for me to . . . *thank* you?"

"Nah, that's not necessary. We're brothers, so we gotta stick together. If you want to do something for me, send a few Philadelphia Police patches to me at the precinct."

"You got it. Thanks," said Grady, who conspicuously dropped a hundred-dollar bill to the floor. He then winked and continued on his way.

########

ELLA RUSHED TO THE TELEPHONE when she heard it ring. She was glad to find out it was Grady reporting in.

"How did you make out?" she asked. "I couldn't sleep at all."

"Relax—I'm on the case. I *always* deliver," bragged her lover. "Now hold on tight, because this is gonna rock your little boat."

"What now?" Ella asked, not knowing what else to expect.

"The old Professor could afford himself a harem. He's worth a hundred million bucks!"

The phone went silent on Ella's end. She placed her fingers to her lips as the staggering number sunk in.

"Ella?"

"C'mon, don't be a turlet head—don't do this to me . . ." she stated, finding the information unbelievable.

"This is square business, baby. I got the scoop straight from where he banks. For all we know, he could have more stashed elsewhere."

"Just wait until I get my hands on him back here in

Philadelphia! I'll nail his ass to the wall! I'll—"

"Take it easy, baby. We have to play this smart. I'll handle this for you." Grady's words soothed Ella, tempering her aggressive instincts.

"How much do you think I can get from him?"

"I don't know for sure, but it's gonna be plenty."

"Should I go look for a lawyer, Grady?"

"No, why should you pay a lawyer if we can work something out without one? Don't forget, he's a bigamist. We got him by the short hairs, so don't do anything until I get back."

"But . . ."

"I said sit tight," he insisted. "If need be, I'll find the *right* lawyer for you when I get back to Philadelphia."

"Are you coming home now?"

"Give me another day or two over here in New York. Let's see what else he does."

7

Looking Out For Number One

GRADY O'LANG WENT DOWN TO THE HOTEL BAR for a drink. He felt that ascertaining the wealth of the Professor was all the entitlement he needed to justify rewarding himself. As he reached for his money to pay for his drink, seeing the wad of cash in his hand brought upon him the urge to gamble. Midway through his cocktail, the pull of his addiction proved too potent a temptation to resist.

"Why not?" said Grady. "I earned the right."

"Are you ready for another one?" asked the man behind the bar, thinking he was summoned.

"Yeah, once more," answered Grady, downing the rest of his drink. "Are any tracks around here open tonight?"

"Yonkers Raceway is open," replied the bartender.

"Do they run the flats or the trotters?"

"It's harness racing." The bartender picked up on Grady's lack of enthusiasm. "If you're not crazy about trots, tomorrow you could go to the Big A. They run the flats at Aqueduct Raceway."

"How far away is it from here?"

"It's in Ozone Park, Queens, less than an hour by car."

Flush with the remaining money Ella fronted him, Grady headed for Aqueduct the following day after breakfast. Arriving in plenty of time for the first race, he purchased a racing form and a cup of coffee. He then settled into a seat overlooking the track. After reading up on the opening race selections, he placed twenty dollars across the board on Ramrod Lover at six-to-one odds. After winning the race, the ecstatic gambler relocated to a small bar at the track where he studied the entrants in upcoming race.

In the next race, things continued to break Grady's way. Having made some money, he switched from coffee to bourbon. The consumption of two bourbons caused him to begin questioning Ella's loyalty. Grady worried that an influx of great wealth might very well alter Ella's feelings toward him. Realizing that his position was one without guarantees, he worked himself into a desperate state of mind.

Once I broker an agreement between Ella and the Professor, I got no assurance of being taken care of,
Grady thought. *The first time I piss her off, I could be out!* The more the cop thought about it, the more convinced he became of his vulnerability. "I gotta look out for me!" he declared as he rose from his seat.

Grady checked his money. Since he could no longer concentrate on anything other than his unwarranted suspicion of Ella, he left the track.

"If that tramp thinks she's gonna double cross me, she's in for a rude awakening," he railed to the windshield as he drove.

"She's not getting the chance to leave me high and dry!"

Consumed by his paranoia, Grady drove to the Professor's Manhattan bookshop with extortion in mind. In his agitated state, Grady began nervously consuming breath mints two at a time. By the time he reached his destination, he had gone through two packs.

The Philadelphian was resolved to not just broker a deal for Ella but also to feather his own nest by independently shaking down the Professor. The question became how much to demand. One thing was set in stone: the Professor was going to pay plenty.

##########

WHEN GRADY O'LANG ENTERED THE Professor's Used Bookshop in New York City, he did so with a revised strategy. It was near closing time when the Philly cop found the bigamist seated at his desk, reading a 1901 copy of *Collier's Weekly*. The business owner looked up from the oversized periodical he was holding. Not recognizing the Philadelphia cop, the professor flashed a friendly smile at his visitor.

"May I help you, sir?" asked the Professor.

Grady didn't find the Professor's lack of recognition unusual. He was used to people not recognizing him when out of his police uniform. The fact that they met only once prior, in another state, contributed to the Professor's failure to remember Grady.

The officer visually scanned the small shop. He could see that the interior of the business was arranged exactly like the one in the City of Brotherly Love. Grady looked with interest at the deck of cards atop the owner's desk.

"You don't remember me, do you?" asked Grady.

"I beg your pardon?"

"Don't you recognize me?"

The Professor looked closely at the man before him. "Now that you mention it, you do look familiar."

"Philadelphia?"

The Professor's air of casualness ceased. He looked at his visitor closely in an endeavor to place him. Still unable to make the connection, he inquired accordingly. "I'm sorry, but I just can't recall where we might have met. Were you a customer in my Philadelphia shop?"

"I'm the cop who asked you about the stolen books."

The Professor was now immediately able to place Grady. "Of course—that's right. I remember you now," advised the Professor. You look very different out of uniform. What brings you to New York City?"

"You do."

The Professor's expression suddenly abandoned all pretense of amicability. "I do?" he asked, now wary. He sensed the officer's presence meant trouble.

"You know, Professor Extraordinarious . . . or, do you prefer to be called Mr. Blount?"

The Professor's suspicion of trouble was now actualized. Grady's tone smacked of a problem being imminent.

"What do you want?" asked the Professor, not responding to the question concerning his preferred title.

"It's not about what I want, Professor," replied Grady smugly.

"It's more about what I can do for you."

"Talk English . . ." said the Professor, losing patience.

"Relax, Professor, I'm willing to keep your secret."

"What secret?"

"C'mon, Professor, you don't have to play it close to the vest with me. After all, we're both men here. Actually, you should consider me a fan. I'm impressed by what you were able to pull off. Holding down two wives is nothing to sneeze at."

"I don't know what you're talking about."

"Alright, let's stop with the games. There are laws against committing bigamy. In New York, you're looking at a felony rap, back in Philly, you're facing a misdemeanor. Need I go on?"

Unable to voice a credible defense for his great deception, the Professor remained silent for a moment before speaking. "So, what's your proposition?" he finally asked, point blank.

"Look, let's approach this practically. It's in nobody's interest to make a federal case out of this. After all, what's the real harm, when you get right down to it?" Grady's apparent understanding provided a ray of hope for the Professor. "This doesn't have to be a police matter, now, does it, Professor?"

"I would hope not," replied the Professor grimly.

Grady felt that he was making headway. "I'm not looking to create a headache on the home front for you, Professor, especially since you have a kid in New York."

"Look, I'm listening, so get to the point. What do you want?"

"I'm here to help you, Professor. Your wife Ella knows all about what you got going here in New York. She knows about the wife, the kid, and your lotto score."

"You told her, I suppose. Why didn't you come to me *before* you told her?" asked the Professor.

"Never mind the questions—the point is she knows, and she ain't happy about the situation."

"If she already knows, then how can you possibly help me?"

"I'm here to tell you that she's out for blood. She's gonna squeeze you like a lemon, my friend . . . and maybe even still rat you out," explained the extortionist. "You know how vindictive some women could be. Anyway, I could prevent all that."

"You could broker a settlement with her in Philly?"

"I could, *if* we go that route."

"What other route is there?"

Grady shrugged, before answering. "Look, I could deal with Ella and influence the negotiation in your favor to get her to accept less. But first, you and I would have to come to an understanding as to my fee."

"How much are we talking about?"

"I'm thinking we can be like partners ... say something to the tune of ten grand a month."

"*Partners?*" asked the Professor in a louder voice, disturbed by the term.

"Don't get excited, Professor, that's only the first option."

"Well, I'm telling you right now, I'm not looking for any *partners.*"

"Alright then, have it your way," said Grady calmly. "We'll go to plan B."

"Which is?"

"Since Ella wants out of the marriage, why not accommodate her . . . and I'm talking about a permanent exit."

The Professor wasn't thrilled at what Grady was suggesting. However, at this point he was open to discussion. "How much is that gonna cost me and what exactly happens to Ella?"

"I'm not a pig, Professor. Give me a one-time, lump-sum payment of, say, a half million dollars."

"I pay that in return for what?"

"My getting rid of Ella for keeps," answered Grady coldly.

"By keeps, you mean—" The Professor ran his index finger across his throat rather than say it.

"Correct."

The notion of murder caused the Professor to gulp. "I'm gonna need to think this over."

"That's fine," said the extortionist. "I know this is distasteful to you, Professor. I feel the same way about it. But we have to look at this practically if we don't want to hurt your wife and kid in New York. Let's face it, when you come right down to it, what's the big loss? Ella is . . . well, you *know* what she is."

The Professor nodded as though Grady were getting through to him. "I still need time to mull this over," he said. "This is something that requires thought."

"Look, go get yourself a couple of drinks and something to eat. That'll give you plenty of time to think my proposition over. I'll meet you back here in front of the bookshop at, say, 9:45 p.m."

When the two men later regrouped they resumed their conversation. The Professor advised Grady that he needed more time to think about it. He indicated he wanted to sleep on the matter. Once he made that clear, the Professor began walking toward the subway. Grady followed alongside him.

"Where are you going, Professor?" asked the Philadelphia cop.

"I'm going home—I'm gonna need more time. I have to sleep on this."

"Where's your car?"

"I took the train," replied the Professor.

"Listen to me, my friend," began the Philly officer, as he continued to walk alongside the extortion victim. "What I'm offering you here is a good deal. Look, if it's the money, I'll even take a little less maybe."

"It's not the money."

"Then what is it?"

The Professor was hesitant to admit what was behind his apprehensiveness. The fact of the matter was, even with her infidelity, the Professor didn't want to lose Ella. "You wouldn't understand," he answered.

"Use your head," said Grady. "What choice have you got in this? Either you play ball, or Rebecca of Sunnybrook Farm and

74

the cops get wised up," threatened Grady, using a harsher tone.

"Leave Rebecca out of this!" the Professor shot back, clearly angered.

Seeing he touched a raw nerve, Grady resorted to a softer tone. "Look, I know you're uptight over this, Professor. But hostility ain't gonna advance us. Look at the proposition like it's a business expense. It's not like you don't have a boatload of money."

The Professor didn't want to hear any more. At this point, he only wanted to get away. He turned to address Grady,

"I *told* you, I need more time to think about this," said the Professor, stepping up his pace. "Let's talk in a couple of days."

"Remember something: if I tip off the cops, you're gonna have to deal with Ella, that whore you married."

The Professor didn't answer. He just walked faster. The Philadelphia cop picked up his own pace to keep up. They continued their back and forth as they made their way down the steps of the train station and onto the platform. Neither man realized that for one of them, the 23rd Street station would be the last stop.

8

Heads Roll

IT CAME AS A SURPRISE TO DETECTIVE BOUCHER when she learned that the fingerprints of the subway homicide victim matched that of a Philadelphia police officer. Because the homicide of a law enforcement officer was big news, Boucher expected political and media attention. What she failed to realize was the uproar connected to tardiness when it came to making department notifications. While she immediately notified the Philly authorities that one of their officers had been murdered, she procrastinated in conveying that message to her squad commander.

Things began to percolate when the police commissioner of the Philadelphia Police Department reached out to New York City Police Commissioner John Randolph.

Randolph, furious at being caught flat-footed, had no knowledge of the homicide. With no other choice other than to wing it, he danced around his Philly counterpart's questioning.

"Don't worry, we're pulling out all the stops on this," assured

Commissioner Randolph. "Our best detectives are on the case."

"Do you have any witnesses?"

"Errr . . . we're talking to a number of people as it stands. I expect my daily update shortly. Let me get my briefing, and I'll call you back with the latest developments."

"Thanks, John," said the Philadelphia executive. "Whatever resources you need from my end is yours for the asking. That includes manpower."

"We got it covered for now," replied Randolph confidently. "My people are out there shaking the bushes as we speak. I'll keep you posted."

After hanging up the phone, Commissioner Randolph looked up at the office ceiling. The rolling of his eyes made it clear he was annoyed. *Does everybody have their head up their ass around here?* Randolph picked up the phone to call Chief of Detectives Harry McCoy.

"Hey, Harry, what am I supposed to do, read about this Philly cop in the obituaries?" asked the irked Randolph.

"What are you talking about, John? What Philly cop?"

"The off-duty Philadelphia cop who got himself clipped!"

"Where was this?"

"How the hell am I supposed to know if no one tells me anything? It happed on some subway platform in Manhattan."

"This is news to me, Commissioner. I didn't get any notification of this," replied McCoy. "Are you sure it happened within the five boroughs?"

"Don't ask *me* questions, Harry—I'm asking *you*! I just got a call from the Philly police commissioner asking me what's being done. "I'm sure I'll be getting a call from the mayor's office. Get a handle on it, and get back to me."

"Will do, boss."

"And Harry, remember something. I don't need to be looking

like an asshole in front of City Hall. If that happens, I'll be embarrassed, maybe, but some people are gonna be gone!"

"I hear you, John. I'll get to the bottom of this asap."

"Just make sure that you have good people working on this."

Chief McCoy called Lieutenant Wright into his office. After being apprised of the situation, the lieutenant shook his head. "This cop killing is news to me as well, Chief, but not surprising."

"What do you mean not surprising?"

"We haven't been getting the same caliber of investigators in the squads that we once did. Even a lot of the squad commanders leave a lot to be desired."

"That's another story," replied McCoy, who didn't want to get into it. "Right now we need to get a line on this homicide. I have to report back to the commissioner, so get me some particulars. I want Markie and Von Hess pitching in on this case."

Wright began making calls, eventually identifying the squad in question. After getting the facts to date on the subway homicide from Detective Boucher, the precinct detective who caught the case, his next call was to the precinct squad commander to give him a heads-up that trouble was brewing.

When Lieutenant Vernon O'Mara received a call at home from police headquarters, he knew there was likely some kind of problem. After being informed by Lieutenant Wright that the police brass blew a gasket, he asked what the problem was.

"The chief was put on the carpet by the police commissioner over the Philly cop homicide," advised Wright.

"What Philly cop homicide?"

"You don't know about the Philadelphia cop who got stabbed on the subway?"

"That guy was a cop?"

After being brought up to speed, the precinct squad commander knew there would be repercussions.

78

"How steamed are the Gods?" asked O'Mara.

"Chief McCoy told me the police commissioner was livid," replied Wright.

"I distinctly told my detectives to notify me of any new developments," fibbed the squad commander.

"Well, I guess they missed the memo."

"Tell McCoy I'll give Boucher and her partner a good reaming."

Lieutenant Wright shook his head after hearing his fellow lieutenant's proposed remedy to the problem. "I'm afraid that might not cut it," he advised.

"So I'll give them both a five day rip."

"Whatever, I just wanted to tell you what you're up against."

Lieutenant Wright hung up the phone knowing that writing up a couple of detectives wasn't going eliminate O'Mara's problems. When he conveyed the homicide details to Chief McCoy, the chief in turn posted the police commissioner, who by now was out for blood.

"So all they got is a blind witness right now, Harry?" asked the police commissioner.

"That's it, Commissioner."

"You assigned Markie and Von Hess to this?"

"It's done, John."

"There are lessons to be learned here, Harry. I want you to see to it that an example is made so that there isn't any repeat performance. The people in the squads need to know that I'm no afterthought."

"How many vacation days do you want them banged for?"

"No, taking time away ain't enough. I want the squad commander out of the bureau altogether and the detective transferred to another borough."

"You can count on it, Commissioner."

Shortly after this conversation, a telephone message to

Boucher's squad was sent from the office of the chief of detectives. It communicated that, effectively immediately, the squad commander in question was transferred forthwith to uniform patrol in the 44 precinct in the Bronx. The message further stated that Detective Boucher was transferred to the 84 Squad in Brooklyn North.

The Grady O' Lang homicide was subsequently reassigned to Boucher's partner, Detective Teddy Hart. Hart was directed by the chief of detective's office to work the case in conjunction with Sergeant Al Markie and Detective Oliver Von Hess.

##########

THE DISPIRITED DETECTIVE BOUCHER was emptying her locker when Markie and Von Hess arrived at the precinct squad. Her downturned mouth made it clear that she was disgruntled over the sudden transfer she received. Boucher was about to transport the last of her belongings to her car when she was approached by the sergeant.

"I'm Sergeant Markie from Police Headquarters," said the sergeant, introducing himself.

"We've been expecting you, Sarge."

"You knew we were coming?"

"Yeah, news travels fast. We received a call right after the transfers came down. You just missed Lieutenant O'Mara. He came in to pack up his things."

"Both of you got transferred?" asked Markie, who was unaware of the movement.

"Yeah, I'm going to the 84 Squad in Brooklyn North."

"Did you have any say in that?"

"No, they just transferred me."

"Where did the squad commander go...home?"

"You'll probably find him in Duffy's around the corner."

"What is he drowning his blues over a transfer?"

"He's been on the job thirty-something years, Sarge, so he's had it. He's putting in his papers."

"Where did they end up sending him?" asked Von Hess.

"He got flopped back to uniform and sent to the Bronx. Teddy Hart is assigned to the case now."

"Is Hart around?" asked Von Hess.

"He just stepped out for a minute. He'll be back shortly. The homicide folder is on his desk," advised Boucher, pointing to Hart's desk.

"If we have any questions, we may be reaching out to you. Are you okay with that?"

"No problem, Sarge."

The investigators from headquarters sat at a desk to read over the case folder. Markie read the reports while Von Hess took notes as directed.

"It looks like we caught a bad break right off the bat, Ollie," noted Markie.

"What's that?"

"It seems the only witness is blind."

"At least there was someone there when the homicide went down," said Von Hess, looking at the bright side. "Where do you want to start?"

"Let's find out if anybody in this precinct knew the Philly cop," said the sergeant. "Then let's talk to some of the people he worked with in Philly. Maybe somebody could tell us what he was doing here in New York in the first place."

"I'll get the ball rolling, boss."

"Start with the precinct roll call people, Ollie. Have them attach a note to the roll call on every shift. I want the sergeant turning out the troops to ask if anyone knows anything about this murdered cop."

"No problem. I'll stop by the community affairs office too."

############

THE COMMUNITY AFFAIRS OFFICE was located on the first floor of the precinct. The person assigned to community affairs had over twenty years in the department, all of which were spent in the same precinct. It was his job to schmooze with the residents, businesses, politicians, and community groups operating within the confines of the command.

Detective Gil Constantine's competency in the position he held was good enough to earn him a promotion to second grade detective. Tall and deeply tanned, Constantine presented a dapper appearance. The salt-and-pepper mustache he sported was of the neatly trimmed variety that didn't travel beyond the corners of his mouth.

"How can I help you, Sarge?" asked the detective cheerily.

Based on his relaxed demeanor and the way he voiced those few words, Markie could tell he was a good fit for the position he held. The detective was clearly smooth.

"Do you know anything about the cop that was murdered on the 23rd Street subway platform?" asked Markie.

"I haven't any of the details. All I know is that there was an out-of-town cop murdered there."

Constantine's easy manner was an indication that he'd been removed from the street for a very long time.

"Do you know of anyone in the precinct who goes by the name of *Professor*?"

"That sounds familiar, but I'll have to get back to you on that, Sarge. I'll ask around. Let me have your number."

Good to his word, the community affairs detective contacted

Markie a short time later. He advised the sergeant that there was a proprietor of a used bookshop in the precinct who called himself Professor Extraordinarious.

"What can you tell me about him?" asked Markie.

"From the things I'm hearing, he's a bit of a character."

"In what respect is he a character?"

"Don't get me wrong, there haven't been any complaints about him. It's just that people are saying that he's a little odd. He's got a pointed goatee and sits around in his bookshop wearing a black Dracula cape. The word is that he likes to show off card tricks when he's not selling his books."

"Let me have the address of his business."

Armed with the requested information, Markie and Von Hess were about to leave the office when Constantine called them back.

"Hey, Sarge, there is one other thing."

"What's that?"

"This guy the Professor is also supposed to be a knife buff . . . and it's my understanding that the cop was stabbed to death."

9

Branching Out

MARKIE AND VON HESS could see inside the Manhattan bookshop by looking through the front glass from the sidewalk. The Professor was so absorbed in conversation with a woman who was close to his own age that he never noticed the faces peering in. Their smile-filled interaction made it obvious the two were smitten with each other.

"Get a load of the two lovebirds, Ollie," commented Markie.

"What do you make of those whiskers and that black cape? I'd be scared of him if I were her," commented Von Hess.

"They do make him appear kind of sinister," replied the sergeant. "I'm going inside to see what gives."

"Do you want me to go in with you, Sarge?"

"No, I got it."

Markie entered the bookshop and began browsing. He went unnoticed by the Professor, who was occupied showing the woman his vanishing ace card trick.

"Going, going, gone!" said the Professor as he held up three of the four aces he originally had.

"That's a wonderful trick, Professor!" said Concetta Piatelli Bryant. "What do you call it?"

"I call that one 'The Vanishing Ace,' Connie," replied the Professor. "Talk about vanishing, you know, I'm going to miss you a lot," he said very seriously.

"I'll miss not seeing you as well, Professor," she replied, "but if I don't make the move to Arizona now, I never will."

"I understand, but now that we've become really good friends, I hate that you're leaving."

"Well, we could still be good friends," she said, with a twinkle in her eye. "I won't be that far away. I'm only going to Arizona."

The professor let no grass grow under his feet. He seized what he viewed as an invitation to visit. "I'll come visit you."

"Wonderful! My new place is very roomy. Since I don't really know anyone there, I'd really look forward to the company."

"I've been considering opening up another bookshop somewhere. Maybe Arizona is as good a place as any."

Concetta's face lit up. "That would be so great!" she said excitedly. "You'll love it there!"

"Why don't I come and see you in a couple of weeks? You could help me find a proper location for a bookshop."

"Wonderful!" Concetta jotted down her new address and telephone number on a piece of paper. "Promise to come?"

"*That's* something you can bank on."

"Until Arizona," she said.

Markie took in all of their conversation as he pretended to be reading a book that actually interested him. He purchased the book before leaving.

"What's the story, Sarge?" asked Von Hess, who had been waiting outside patiently.

"This guy is a player. Did you see that lady he was talking to?"

"Yeah . . ."

"The Professor's got something going with her. She's moving to Arizona and he's going out there to spend time with her.

"Maybe we better talk to this guy before he goes, Sarge."

"We got time. He's not going anyplace for a couple of weeks. Let's do some homework on him before we sit him down."

What is that a poetry book you got there, Sarge?" asked Von Hess, noticing that the sergeant was leafing through the pages of the book he purchased.

"Yeah, I always liked poetry ever since I was a kid in school. I remember when I had to memorize Walt Whitman's, *O Captain! My Captain!*"

"I remember reading that poem years ago."

"Want to hear it, Ollie?"

##########

THE FOLLOWING DAY THE INVESTIGATORS heard from Detective Constantine. Constantine advised that a police officer in the precinct had information that could further the investigation. Von Hess asked Constantine if he apprised Detective Hart, the precinct case detective, of this. Constantine advised that Teddy Hart was in court making an appearance on another case.

Arrangements were then made for Von Hess and Markie to meet with the officer. Upon arriving at the precinct they came to learn that the cop in question was the precinct summons man, whose primary responsibility was to write parking tickets.

"Community affairs said that you have some information for us," said Markie.

"I think so," said the summons man. "At roll call the sergeant said something about that Philadelphia cop homicide. I

86

remembered tagging a car with Pennsylvania plates not far from the subway station where the cop was murdered, so I went back to where I wrote the ticket. The car was still there with the tag under the windshield wiper. When I checked the plate, it came back to the murdered cop."

"Good job," said Markie, respecting the officer's initiative.

"Where's the car now?"

"It's still out on the street."

"Where exactly on the street is it parked?"

When the officer provided a vehicle description and location, the investigators looked at each other.
The dead cop's vehicle was parked in close proximity to the Professor's bookshop.

"Let's get over there and give the car a good search, Ollie."

The search of Grady O'Lang's vehicle proved to be fruitful.

"Take a look at this pretzel jar, Sarge."

"What about it?"

"It's filled with piss. The only time I've seen a piss jar that size was during a long surveillance."

"He might have been shadowing the Professor," noted Markie.

"Maybe . . . hey, here's something," advised Von Hess, holding up an address written in ink.

"That's it, just an address? No name?"

"Yeah, that's all—just an address."

"Let's take a ride over to Brooklyn and check it out."

"Maybe we should touch base with Detective Hart later as a courtesy," suggested Von Hess.

"Yeah, do that," agreed Markie. "We might as well keep him in the loop, it's his case. And one other thing . . ."

"What's that?"

"Remind me to write an attaboy letter to the precinct captain for that summons man. He did a good job by showing initiative and should be recognized for it."

##########

THE NEXT INVESTIGATIVE LEAD CAME A SHORT TIME later while the investigators were en route to the Brooklyn address. The information came from a surprising source. This time it was Detective Boucher who reached out to Markie. The tone of her voice over the phone suggested that she had something important to convey.

"Sarge, it's me, Detective Boucher. I got a lead regarding the Philadelphia cop homicide," she advised. "I already filled in Teddy Hart."

"I thought Hart was supposed to be in court."

"His case got adjourned. He's back at the squad."

"What have you got?" asked Markie.

"You're not going to believe this," she began.

"Try me."

"I just came from a bank with one of my new partners over here in Brooklyn Heights," began Boucher. "We were there to investigate a forgery matter. After we finished interviewing the branch manager about the forgery, he started bitching about the man on post. He said the MOP had given him a hard time."

"What kind of hard time?"

"The man on post was leaning on him for information about one of the bank clients. He wanted to find out how much money the client has."

"So?" asked Markie.

"So this: the branch manager said the cop wanted the information to give to a Philadelphia cop. The person they were checking into was Henry Blount. The bank manager said that Blount was a big-time lotto winner who owns The Professor's

Used Bookshop in the city."

"Where's the bank?"

Detective Boucher provided the sergeant with the address of the bank in question. It matched the address the investigators found in the Philadelphia cop's vehicle.

"Is the beat cop around now?"

"Yes, he's working."

"Hang on to him until we get to the precinct," advised Markie.

"Is this something that calls for a notification to internal affairs, Sarge?"

"No, no, no, sit tight." said Markie. "We don't need them spooking the cop before we get to him. I want to hear what he has to say."

"Are you sure?"

"Listen, Boucher, they got a one-track mind over there in internal affairs. Sometimes their priorities are out of whack."

"What's up?" asked Von Hess once Markie got off the phone.

"We just caught another break," advised the sergeant. He then filled Von Hess in on the recent developments. "Do you have a photo of the homicide victim?"

"Not on me."

"Then let's go to Manhattan and get one. Then we'll come back to Brooklyn, I want to show the beat cop the picture," advised Markie. "See if Von Hess wants to come along."

When Von Hess walked into the precinct squad he found Hart at his desk. "The sergeant said that if you're free, you can come along with us, Teddy," advised Von Hess after getting the photo.

"No, you don't need me. Besides, I just got back from court and got plenty to do around here to keep me busy."

"It's your baby, Ted. We're just here to assist you," reminded Von Hess.

"I know that, Ollie. But I kind of like the feeling of being a squad commander."

"I don't follow you . . ."

"The squad commander sends his detectives to do the work."

Von Hess laughed. "I forgot that you've been around the horn like me, Teddy. There ain't a lot that excites us anymore."

"Ain't that the truth," concurred Hart. "Just keep me in the loop so I can clue in my new squad commander."

Markie and Von Hess proceed to the Brooklyn Heights precinct to talk to the beat officer. After hearing the story firsthand about how the officer helped a Philadelphia cop at the bank, Von Hess produced the crime scene photos.

"Yeah, that's him," said the uniformed officer as he looked at the photos.

"You say that he wanted to know how much money a guy named Henry Blount had, right?" asked Von Hess, double-checking what he was initially told.

"That's right."

"Did he tell you *why* he wanted to know that information?"

"Sure he did. He said he had a brother who was entering into a business deal with Blount."

"And you got the information for him," said the sergeant.

"That's right, Sarge," answered the officer.

"Why would you do that?"

The officer stiffened. "He was a Marine like I was, Sarge. Is there anything wrong with helping another Marine?" he asked.

"Take it easy," said Markie. "I was just curious."

"How much money did Blount have?" asked Von Hess, getting the conversation back on track.

"I was told by the bank's branch manager that he had about a hundred million dollars. Blount hit the long ball with a lotto ticket." Von Hess reacted by letting out a slow whistle.

Markie could only imagine what inducement was used to

90

make the bank manager provide such information. As is sometimes the case, he took the precaution of avoiding the possibility of opening a can of worms. He let the matter drop.

"Thanks for stepping up," said Markie, dismissing the officer. Markie turned to Detective Von Hess. "You know, Ollie, this Boucher deserves a lot of credit for sticking by the case after she was bounced out of her command."

"I agree, Sarge. A lot of people would've been too bitter to have lifted a finger."

"I respect that. Boucher is a team player," said Markie. "Give her a courtesy call and let her know how we made out here."

Von Hess got Detective Boucher on the telephone and posted her as to where they stood with the case.

"I didn't expect a call, but thank you," said the surprised Boucher. "Do I need to notify internal affairs?"

"Hold on a second," said Von Hess, cupping the phone before turning to address Markie. This kid's a broken record, she's still asking about internal affairs, Sarge—"

"Tell her just to make a memo book entry that she notified me," instructed Markie. Von Hess relayed the message.

"That's it?" asked Boucher.

"That's it," replied Von Hess. "Let me ask you something— how would you rate the witness in this case?"

"She's really good. The only problem is that she can't really identify anyone because she can't see."

"Her lack of vision may be something we can work around," said Von Hess. "She was willing to cooperate, right?"

"Oh, yes, definitely."

"Ollie, ask her how she's making out with the new squad commander," interrupted Markie.

"The sergeant wants to know how your new squad commander is."

"Tell him that he's a sweetheart."

"She says he's very good, Sarge," relayed Von Hess.

"Ask her about her commute."

"The boss wants to know how the new place is travel-wise."

"Tell him it sucks."

"She says it's not very convenient, Sarge." Markie just nodded, and then signaled Von Hess to cut the call short.

"I'm gonna give Teddy Hart a call and let him know how we made out, Ollie."

After Markie finished talking to Detective Hart, Von Hess posed a question. "Was the new boss pleased, Sarge?"

"What new boss?"

"I'm talking about Teddy. He says that the way things are working out, he feels like a squad commander who is giving us the work to do."

"He said that?"

"Yeah, but he was just kidding," added Von Hess, not wanting to give Markie the wrong impression. "Teddy's a good guy."

Markie thought about Hart being a good guy for a couple of seconds before responding. "He's a good guy alright," he finally said, "and he makes a good point."

10

Shepherd Fish

FISHNET MILLIGAN WALKED THE STREETS of Manhattan, savoring each deep breath of fresh air he took into his lungs. Every painless step he took was evidence enough for him to rid himself of doctors, nurses, and any restrictions connected to his healing. The former detective had no time for medical distractions. Feeling invincible after having eluded death once, he now lived for the moment.

Fishnet, who had been recently released from rehab, strolled into Macy's 34th Street store with his girlfriend, Wayna Garcia. His pockets were filled with the money he netted from the police fundraiser that was held in his honor the evening prior. As the survivor of a wild gun battle that nearly killed him, he was considered by many in law enforcement to be a celebrated hero. Fishnet couldn't agree more with their assessment.

Fishnet handed Wayna enough cash to shop with. He did this not out of largesse but rather to free himself of distraction while he traveled to his far-off world of make believe. Lagging behind, he mentally relived the prior evening. He happily recounted each of the accolades he received by those connected to his former profession.

The party in his honor was held in a hotel on a police payday. An upstairs suite was rented by a law enforcement-friendly businessman to accommodate the dice and blackjack games that could be counted on to add to the coffers nicely. Those who didn't gamble spent money on fifty-fifty raffle tickets, drank liberally, ate, and socialized in the hotel party room. It had been a night of smiles, giggles, and back pats.

Fishnet felt the pack of cigarettes in his pocket. It caused him to break into a wide grin as he remembered how he acquired the smokes. At the party he had spotted a vacated table where a sport jacket hung off the back of an unoccupied chair. As party goers danced and mingled, Fishnet took a seat at the empty table. After discreetly rifling the pockets of the sport jacket, he walked away with an unopened pack of Marlboro cigarettes. Stealing the cigarettes pleased him as much as receiving the money that was raised in his honor. Taking what didn't belong to him had always been one of the things Fishnet enjoyed doing.

"I'm starting to get hungry. Do you want to get something to eat?" asked Wayna, pulling Fishnet out of his daydream.

"Huh?"

"I'm hungry—let's eat."

"Sure, we can get something," replied the former detective. "I know a nice place we can go to in the theatre district."

"How far away is it?"

"It's not too far. C'mon—the walk will do us both good."

When they arrived at the restaurant, Wayna was impressed. Her experience eating out at pricy restaurants was limited.

"This is a very nice place, Fishnet," said Wayna.

"Stick with me, kid, and you'll see how the other half lives."

"Do you really know the owner here?"

"Yeah, I know him. I worked in this precinct for a couple of years when I was a cop in the bag," advised the former detective. "I made an impression on him back then, and he's been good to me ever since."

"What do you mean by in the bag?"

"It means working in uniform. What do I have to, explain everything to you?" he asked.

Fishnet withheld the details as to *how* his familiarity with the restaurant owner came about. The truth was that after being charged for a meal, Fishnet launched a campaign to discourage people from dining at the restaurant. He'd pull over restaurant patrons for minor traffic violations at every opportunity. After issuing a ticket, he'd conclude the interaction by conveying that the restaurant had a history of being infested with bedbugs. As anticipated, the restaurant owner came to realize the upside to keeping Fishnet happy. Fishnet never had to pay for another meal at the eatery.

"Oh, before I forget to tell you, they know me here as Fishnet. So, here it's okay to call me that. But whenever we meet new people, be sure to remember to call me by the new name."

"What is it again?"

Fishnet let out a deep breath of frustration. "Shepherd . . . Shepherd Fish."

"Don't worry, I'll remember," Wayna assured him.

Fishnet noticed that two mature women at a nearby table seemed to be staring at him. Instinctively, even though he was seated, he glanced down toward his zipper to make sure it was closed. Seeing that he was appropriately covered, he stared back at the women. He broke into a broad smile after noticing they seemed to be expensively attired. The smile he flashed was politely returned by both strangers.

"What are you grinning at?" asked Wayna,

"Those two antiques over there are checking me out."

"Do you mean the older ladies in the corner?"

"Yeah, they look like they're rolling in money. I'm gonna find out if they're worth my time."

"How do you intend to do that?"

"Leave it to me."

Fishnet summoned the waiter to his table. "Let me ask you something, pal. Those two women over there in the corner—do you know them?" he asked.

"Do you mean Ms. Belle and Ms. Hatton?"

"I'm asking *you* who they are."

"Oh," said the waiter, a delicate man in appearance. "The woman sitting closest to the door is Sally Belle. The other woman is Estelle Hatton."

"Sally Belle, the woman who acts in plays on Broadway?"

"Yes, sir."

"Well, how about that. She was a hot number in her day."

"I would say so, sir," agreed the waiter.

"She doesn't show up in many movies, does she?"

"You'll rarely see her on the screen. She appears mostly in stage productions," corrected the waiter in an uppity sort of way. He was an aspiring actor with a great appreciation for the legitimate theater.

"What's the story with the other one?"

"Ms. Hatton is a highly regarded agent."

"Thanks," said Fishnet, finding out all he needed to know.

"What are you thinking?" asked Wayna, seeing that Fishnet suddenly became pensive.

"I'm thinking those two old crows are worth cultivating. Go over and ask for an autograph."

"Why? I don't want their autograph."

"Just go over there, and then I'll pull you away from bothering them. It'll give me an excuse to meet them."

"I feel funny doing that," replied Wayna. "Why can't you go?"

"Because I'm the guy who is supposed to be Shepherd Fish, remember? I'll make my entry by apologizing for *you* being rude and interrupting their eats."

Before the issue was settled, Mr. Nellie rose from her seat and proceeded in the direction of the restrooms. Fishnet, seeing this as an opportunity, rose from the table.

"Never mind—I'll handle this myself," he said, abruptly stepping away from his seat.

The former detective followed the actress to the rear of the restaurant. He waited patiently for her to emerge from the restroom. When she did, she made it easy for Fishnet by initiating a conversation with him.

"Please accept my apology for staring at you earlier, sir. You probably already know why we were so interested in you."

"Not really."

"It's your remarkable resemblance to the king, of course."

"What king?" Fishnet asked, unclear as to what she was talking about.

"Really, now—you must realize that you're the spitting image of Clark Gable."

Fishnet chuckled. He had forgotten how much he looked like the famous actor. "Oh, yeah . . . well, to tell you the truth, I do get that a lot."

"Gable was simply a divine specimen. He was *all* man."

"I guess I'll have to take that as quite a compliment."

"By all means, do. You simply *must* meet Estelle. She was the one who first noticed you."

"No problem—I'd love to meet her. You're Sally Belle, right?"

"Yes, you recognize me? How very flattering that is."

Wayna watched in awe as Fishnet accompanied Sally Belle to her table. She couldn't believe that he'd abandon her and accept a stranger's invitation to sit down.

"Estelle, say hello to . . . oh, excuse me," said Sally, turning to Fishnet. "I forgot to ask your name."

"I'm Shepherd Fish."

"Shepherd Fish, how delightful a name you have! Mr. Fish, please say hello to Estelle. Perhaps you've heard of her—Estelle Hatton, the theatrical agent? Estelle is well regarded by just about everyone of importance in the theater."

"Including you, darling," pointed out Estelle. "I'm pleased to meet you, Mr. Fish," she said, extending her hand upward. She was expecting it to be kissed.

Fishnet was immediately drawn to the two rings that adorned Estelle's fingers. Despite the lure of the gems, he couldn't bring himself to kiss the back of her hand. He found Estelle's protruding blue veins unattractive. Instead of bringing her hand to his lips, Fishnet opted to just shake and nod politely.

"You know, Sally, it's absolutely incredible how much he looks like Gable," said Estelle, continuing to cling to Fishnet's hand as she spoke. "You have no idea how some of our friends would be impressed by your likeness, Mr. Fish!"

"You folks knew Clark Gable?" asked Fishnet.

"Yes, of course," answered Sally. "It was late in his life, naturally, and I was quite young then."

"Oh, yes, quite, quite young," added the agent, amused by her client's comment.

Estelle still hadn't released Fishnet's hand. Her lingering grip was meant to convey her interest in him. The red wig Estelle wore dominated her head to a point where it drew attention to her small facial features. Her prominent leathery wrinkles were the results of far too much sun. Estelle reminded the scheming Fishnet of a prune.

"I've just had a brilliant idea, Estelle!" announced Sally.

"What, darling?"

The actress turned to address Fishnet. "Mr. Fish, I'm giving a soiree over at my home, and I'd love for you to join us. It would be such fun to see the look on the faces of my other guests when they set eyes on you. You must say yes! Bring along whomever you like, of course."

"It would be my pleasure," said Fishnet, graciously accepting the invitation. For the conniving ex-detective, things could not be going better.

"Isn't that wonderful, Estelle?" asked Sally.

"Simply marvelous!" agreed Estelle. "Are you involved in the arts, Mr. Fish?" she asked, finally releasing his hand.

"No, I'm not. I've had a near-death experience, so now I live to do only good," replied Fishnet, who then went on to tell of his being shot in a gun battle while attempting to apprehend a notorious organized crime killer.

The two women sat in awe as Fishnet articulated the incident. Glued to their seats, they wanted to hear similar tales. They were mesmerized by the former detective, who went on to convey a litany of embellished crime fighting anecdotes. He remained with his new friends until their car arrived.

"I'll see you at my soiree!" said Sally, giving a slight wave from the open window of the car.

After they drove off, Fishnet remained on the street to smoke. "Hoo-ray, I'm going to a swa-ray!" he said, as he fired up a cigarette.

"Since when do you smoke?" asked Wayna, who emerged from the restaurant to remind Fishnet that she was there.

"I've been smoking since I was twelve. I just took a break

because I was sick. Now I'm all better."

"Smoking will put lines in your face," warned Wayna.

Fishnet looked at the youthful Wayna. He gently placed his fingertips to the side of her cheek affectionately. He took a second to admire the smoothness of her flawless skin. He began to wonder if she'd ever end up looking like a prune.

11

Party Time

THE MAESTRO, AN OCTOGENARIAN, waddled when he walked. A stocky man, his body shifted from side to side with each step he took. His thick, white walrus mustache along with his sparse, stringy hair and black bowtie gave him a cartoonish look.

The musician, who was attired in a black suit, prided himself on presenting what he felt to be a dignified appearance. This effort was undermined whenever he neglected to button his suit jacket. Failure to do so revealed a belt that could be seen crossing his white shirt an inch or so below his breasts. Some might have likened him to a penguin.

People appreciative of the arts respected the Maestro primarily for his musical brilliance. In recent years the elderly violinist earned his living by giving violin lessons to aspiring musicians who could afford his pricy rates. Those signing up for his services tolerated his no-nonsense, task-master approach because they knew they were being tutored by a genius.

Notorious for his passion, it wasn't unusual for the sharp-tongued Maestro to permit his temper to surface. Distracting him with idle chatter while he worked his bow or referring to his instrument as a fiddle were offenses that were sure to extract his nastier side.

The Maestro arrived at the front door of Sally Belle's West Village townhouse carrying a wooden case that contained a German-made John Juzek violin. He stood tapping his foot impatiently as he waited for someone to answer his ring. When Pascal, a man of forty-eight, opened the door, the Maestro's eyes widened. The two shared a long history. The Maestro had first introduced Pascal to Sally Belle many years prior. The musician never quite forgave himself for making the introduction that led to the defection of his then-boyfriend.

The Maestro noticed some of the changes in Pascal. The black pencil-line mustache he sported was now spotted with some gray. His hair, which he wore plastered back with a high part, was graying at the temples. Most apparent was Pascal's having put on a few pounds around the middle. Then there were those sideburns that came to a point just below the hollow of his ears. The Maestro wondered what that was all about.

Particular when it came to his clothing, Pascal was attired in tan slacks, a white shirt, and navy blue sport jacket with gold buttons. The paisley ascot covered his fleshy neck.

"Maestro!" blurted Pascal with great enthusiasm. "It's so wonderful to see you again, my dear friend. Welcome to our humble abode." Pascal then raised his finger to summon one of the help that was hired for the evening.

"Inform Madame that the Maestro has arrived," he instructed. "Allow me to take your case, Maestro."

"Don't bother, Pascal, I'll be playing soon," said the musician dryly. "You're looking well—how have you been?"

"I've been simply wonderful!"

"What have you done to your sideburns?"

"You don't like them?"

"They are rather . . . *different*," replied the Maestro.

"I like being different," said Pascal.

"How is Sally?" asked the Maestro, not going there.

"She's as beautiful as ever. She's full of energy—bridge, dinner out most evenings, it's hard for *me* to even keep up with her."

"Hmmmm," muttered the Maestro, who was not exactly thrilled to see Sally's paramour so happy. "That's nice."

The Maestro entered the large living room where guests were already conversing in small groups over cocktails. Everyone in attendance was dressed very stylishly. Surveying the area he entered, he spotted the hostess sipping a drink on the other side of the room. Wasting no time, he proceeded in her direction. Before he reached Sally Belle, he was greeted by Estelle Hatton, who on this evening wore a blond hairpiece.

"Maestro! " she said, raising her hand to be kissed.

"Estelle, my dear, you look wonderful as a blond," said the aged violinist, taking her hand. He bowed slightly and gently kissed the back of her hand, oblivious to the protruding blue veins that had repulsed Fishnet.

"Thank you, darling."

"Pardon me, I'll return to you soon. I must make my presence known to our hostess," said the Maestro, politely excusing himself.

"Of course, we'll catch up later."

"The Maestro is here!" shouted Sally enthusiastically upon seeing the violinist. "Thank you so much for joining us!"

"Anything for you, my dear," he replied, releasing her hand after kissing it.

"Pascal, darling," summoned Sally, "see that the Maestro gets some red wine." She then turned her attention to her guest's violin case. "I see you came prepared . . . I've been *so looking* forward to hearing you play for us."

"It will indeed be my pleasure to entertain you and your friends."

"By the way, I've a surprise for you this evening."

"You do?"

"Yes, indeed I do, darling. I've invited a special guest that I simply must introduce you to."

"A talent?" he asked.

"Well, I wouldn't exactly say that, but then again, you may find him to be so. He'll definitely be of interest to you."

"You've tickled my curiosity—who is it, my dear?"

"You'll see . . ."

"Oh, come now. Stop with this playfulness. Who is it?"

"You're going to have to wait, Maestro," answered Sally, quite amused with herself.

"Very well, have it your way," groused the musician. "Sometimes I feel I'm getting too old for such levity."

"Now, now, Maestro, be patient. I suspect that my guest will return you to your youth."

In another section of the room, Rebecca Blount, the Professor's first wife, was engaged in a cordial conversation with a retired married couple. She listened attentively as the wife spoke of their professional dancing career.

"We received our first big break on the *Arthur Murray Show*," advised the slender, blue-haired woman. "It was Arthur's wife who gave us our chance. She put us on their television program, which was quite popular then."

"Arthur Murray was the dance instructor, wasn't he?" asked Rebecca, who was far too young to remember the show.

"That's right."

"Is he still alive?"

Oh, no. He's been gone awhile, but Kathryn just passed away only a few months ago. They lived in Honolulu, you know."

"I didn't know that."

"Anyway, after that appearance, we were in demand. We were on all the big television shows. Isn't that right, dear?" she asked, looking at her gaunt, bald-headed husband.

"What did you say?" he asked, adjusting his hearing aide.

"I said that we performed on television."

"Oh sure, Ed Sullivan, Perry Como, Dinah Shore, we were on all of those big shows. Como was a really good guy."

"And don't forget Arthur Murray."

"Yes, that's right. Mr. Murray was the first to put us on."

"Not Arthur—it was Kathryn who gave us our first chance," corrected his wife. "*She* was the one who noticed us." Rebecca nodded and smiled politely after this clarification was made. "Arthur was more the businessman, you know."

As this was being discussed inside the townhouse, Fishnet

Milligan and Wayna Garcia stood outside at the front door. Before ringing the doorbell, Fishnet gave his girlfriend last-minute instructions.

"Listen, once we're inside, remember to call me Shepherd."

"I'll remember," answered Wayna. "You reminded me a hundred times already. I'm not stupid, you know."

"Hey, cut it out!" barked Fishnet. "I don't need you giving me grief before we even get inside the dump." Wayna let out a deep breath. She was beginning to realize just how difficult Fishnet could be at times. "Go on, ring the bell, will ya?"

As they waited for someone to come to the door, Fishnet gazed at the building. His mind soon drifted into his fantasy world, where he saw himself as the master of the magnificent townhouse he was about to enter. Wayna the maid was in the process of serving 5:00 p.m. cocktails.

"What's taking them so long to answer the door?" asked Wayna, interrupting Fishnet's fantasy. Seeing his confused look concerned her. "Are you alright?" she asked.

"What?" barked Fishnet, annoyed at being distracted.

"They're not answering the door."

"So ring the damn bell again," he said abruptly.

"What are you snapping at me for?"

"Alright, alright, just don't forget to call me Shepherd when we get inside. I don't want anything to go wrong tonight."

"Don't worry, Shemp," Wayna replied, intentionally trying to agitate him.

Fishnet wasn't amused. "C'mon, cut the crap, will ya? This is serious."

Fishnet patted his hair as he awaited someone to come to the door. He had slicked his hair back and manicured his mustache to make his likeness to Clark Gable stronger.

"Oh my, Madame wasn't joking," commented Pascal when he finally answered the door. He was immediately taken by Fishnet's uncanny resemblance to late movie star. "You, sir, are most certainly the spitting image of Gable. Welcome."

Inhaling a whiff of the potent aftershave Pascal had on caused Fishnet to size him up from head to foot. The term "our humble abode" gave Fishnet pause. If Pascal was the man in Ms. Belle's life, that meant he'd be around all the time. This presented a potential barrier that might stand in the way of the former detective's plans.

Fishnet's mind again strayed. This time he saw himself armed with a sword, issuing a challenge to Count Pascal, the continental nobleman. The outcome of their duel would determine the winner of the heart—and assets—of Sally Belle.

"You are most certainly the spitting image of Clark Gable," repeated Pascal, this time in a louder voice.

"Everyone says that," said Wayna. "Isn't that right, *Shepherd*?" she asked, giving Fishnet a sharp elbow.

"Uh, yeah . . ." replied Fishnet, totally unaware of the preceding conversation.

"I'm Pascal, sir. I can only imagine how wonderful it must be to have such a strong resemblance to such a monumental icon."

"I do, alright," replied Fishnet, who now returned to the present. "I'm Shepherd Fish, and this is Wayna."

"It's my great delight in meeting you both," said Pascal, who then gently took Wayna's hand to kiss.

It irked the former detective that Pascal kissed Wayna's hand with such aplomb. *What a smoothie this slippery bastard is,* thought Fishnet. *He's gotta go. I won't get a cup of coffee out of the old lady with pretty boy in the picture.*

"Please come in," invited Pascal. "All of our guests have been anxiously expecting you."

After the guests entered the house, Pascal immediately called for everyone's attention.

"ATTENTION EVERYONE!" he shouted. Fully aware of the Maestro's huge ego, he intentionally made this announcement to irk his former lover. "LET ME HAVE YOUR ATTENTION! OUR VERY SPECIAL GUEST HAS ARRIVED."

Fishnet displayed a forced smile. *Just listen to this mook,* he thought. *He's talking like I'm some freak show attraction!*

The approach of Sally did much to take the former detective's mind off Pascal.

"Thank you so much for coming, Mr. Fish," said Sally softly.

"Allow me to introduce you to the others."

"Certainly," answered Fishnet.

"Please, everyone welcome my very special guests, Mr. Shepherd Fish and Ms. . . . . I'm sorry, dear, what was your name again?" asked the hostess, addressing Wayna.

"Wayna Garcia."

"Of course—*and* Ms. Wayna Garcia, please make them feel at home. And no folks, Clark Gable hasn't risen from the grave."

All eyes were now on Fishnet, who was being evaluated as if he were a Picasso painting.

"The resemblance is uncanny," said one partier, who only knew the movie star from films.

"Clark had bigger ears," said someone who had worked on a picture Gable did late in his life.

"He's a little taller than Gable was," commented another.

The big fuss being made over Fishnet didn't sit well with the Maestro. The violinist, who felt snubbed, was under the impression that he was to be the featured attraction.

"How nice to see you again, Mr. Fish," said Estelle Hatton. The agent took his hand, latching on for an extended period.

"Nice to see you too, Ms. Hatton." replied the former detective politely. It was clear to him that Estelle had amorous intentions. *Jesus, now she's got on a blond rug—and a long one yet!* Fishnet thought. *I wouldn't be surprised if she's got a tattoo on her ass.*

Ms. Hatton smiled. She was glad Fishnet remembered her name. It didn't take long for the ex-detective to find a place for Estelle in Fishnetland. He designated Estelle the official witch of his other world. Fishnet stretched his neck to put his lips close to Wayna's ear.

"Where did she park her broom?" he asked.

"Be nice, *Shepherd*," whispered Wayna.

"Mr. Fish and I are *old* friends," Estelle could be heard announcing to the others present, stretching the truth. "Isn't that right, Shepherd?"

"Yes, indeed we are," said Fishnet, going along with the lie.

While Fishnet had zero interest in Estelle, he had different intentions with Sally Belle. Although Sally was substantially older than him, her trimness and facelifts did much in terms of maintaining her appeal. He could envision himself getting romantically involved with the actress as long as it would further his path to riches.

Ms. Belle asked Fishnet to recount his police career. This was the opportunity he was looking for. His narrative included an embellishment of the police cases he worked, his getting shot, and his subsequent miraculous recovery. He held his audience in the palm of his hand with his past exploits of daring. Fishnet gradually eased his way into speaking about what he referred to as his current calling.

"Well, my new job requires a different kind of courage. I've dedicated myself to helping those who have started their life at a disadvantage," he said.

Fishnet went on to expand upon what he described as his enlightened career. Armed with photos of an indigent little girl from overseas, he passed them around for the guests to view.

"Oh, my!" said Sally, upon viewing the photos. "This poor child . . . did you photograph these yourself?"

"I did—on my last trip," he lied.

"Please tell us how we could be of assistance?" asked the hostess.

Fishnet flashed the warm smile he had been practicing for months. "The best way to help is financially."

Fishnet's con worked perfectly. The optical incentives he produced were successful in loosening the purse strings of those at the party. The photos he used as bait were those he received from Hope, the certified nursing assistant who had taken care of him when he was in rehab. A genuinely caring person, Hope was another unwitting victim of the former detective. Fishnet induced Hope to write home to her relatives in Haiti asking for genuine photos of desperate cases in need of support. The well-intentioned woman was under the impression that Fishnet sincerely intended to send money overseas.

When he finished pitching to the group, Fishnet began to work the room, speaking to the party guests individually in an effort to get them to make donations. Much to his chagrin, every time he began to speak one on one with Sally, Pascal interrupted his flow by joining their conversation. This was further incentive for Fishnet to cancel Pascal.

Off in a corner of the room sat the Maestro, who was waiting to be called upon to entertain. The elderly musician was feeling neglected. He didn't appreciate taking a secondary role to a former civil servant whose claim to fame was surviving a gunshot to the head. With his violin at the ready, the Maestro continued to wait while tapping his foot nervously. He was less than cordial when he was approached by Wayna.

"Hi—I'm looking ahead to your playing this evening," said Wayna, creating a reason to engage the Maestro in conversation.

"At some point I assume I'll be asked to begin, my dear," he replied, adding, "before breakfast, hopefully."

"Would you like to buy a raffle ticket?" she asked. "The money will be sent overseas to the needy."

"What are you raffling off?"

"We're putting up a brand-new Cadillac."

"Sorry, but I don't drive," said the Maestro, who abruptly relocated to another section of room. The musical genius wasn't one to part with his money easily.

The scheme to raffle off a car was Fishnet's idea. He had taken a photo of the vehicle with the sole intent of presenting it as the grand prize—in a rigged drawing with a phantom winner.

While Wayna continued to work her side of the room, Fishnet did the same elsewhere. This time the object of his scam was Rebecca, the Professor's wife. Fishnet was drawn to Rebecca after noticing the impressive necklace she wore.

"Hi, I'm Shepherd," he said, introducing himself.

Rebecca was in awe at Fishnet's striking resemblance to Gable. "I'm Rebecca, I admire the work you're doing."

"Thank you. That's a beautiful piece you're wearing."

"Thank you—it was a present from my husband."

"You're fortunate to have such a generous husband."

"Yes, he's wonderful. After having heard you speak of your exploits, I've come to the conclusion that you've lived the most fascinating life of anyone I've ever known," she added.

"Well, let's say I've been fortunate. Is your husband here?"

"No, he is out of town on business."

"What business is he in?" probed Fishnet.

Before she could answer, Ms. Belle had Pascal call for quiet so the Maestro could be introduced.

"ATTENTION EVERYONE, LET ME HAVE YOUR ATTENTION, PLEASE!" shouted Pascal, quieting the room. "As you all know, we have a special treat in terms of entertainment this evening. Our dear, dear friend the Maestro is going to play for us. Music, Maestro, please?" sang out Pascal.

Fishnet's attention was once again drawn to Pascal. *Again with this guy*, he thought. *I'd like to piss in his martini!*

The violinist bowed and commenced playing something from Mozart. As others settled in to listen to the music being played, Fishnet whispered to his girlfriend that she should position herself at the back of the room far away from where the Maestro played. Once everyone was focused on the Maestro, he slipped away unnoticed, making his way to the second floor.

Fishnet began exploring the upper floor of the house. He was looking to see what was available for the taking. Entering Ms. Belle's bedroom, he opened the jewelry box that rested atop her dresser. Removing two expensive necklaces, he slipped the valuables into the side pocket of his jacket. He came upon an idea regarding Pascal after discovering five thousand dollars in cash, all hundred-dollar bills, inside an envelope in Sally's dresser drawer.

110

Fishnet immediately slipped the money into his pocket. After using his hankie to wipe down the jewelry box and everything else he touched, he made sure to leave the dresser drawer slightly ajar. He was confident that the execution of his plan would remove the halo over Pascal's head. All he needed to do was find where Pascal kept his things.

Fishnet discovered that Pascal had his own room. He searched it until he found something that fit his purpose, a red pocket square with the name Pascal stitched into it. Fishnet placed one of Sally's bracelets in the pocket of one of the suits that hung in Pascal's closet. He then dropped three hundred-dollar bills on the center of Pascal's bed. After again wiping his fingerprints off whatever he touched, Fishnet returned to Sally's bedroom. He dropped Pascal's pocket square on the floor, not far from the dresser drawer that he looted minutes earlier.

Satisfied with how he set the stage, Fishnet discreetly returned to the party with his pocket filled with booty. He took a seat at the back of the room next to his girlfriend. As the crowd listened attentively to the Maestro's music, Fishnet slipped the money and bracelet he stole into Wayna's purse. Feeling in high spirits, he gave his girlfriend's hand an affectionate squeeze.

After the Maestro finished playing his final selection of the evening, Fishnet approached him.

"How about playing 'Sweet Georgia Brown?'" he asked, wanting to hear the theme song of the Harlem Globetrotters.

"*That* is not my music," replied the Maestro rather snobbishly.

"What is it, too tricky?"

"Hardly," replied the Maestro, who, after hearing this, prepared to leave the party.

Before the evening ended, Fishnet collected donations from everyone except the violinist. The collected checks were made payable to the former detective's newly established Fish And Give Corporation.

##########

THE MORNING FOLLOWING THE PARTY, Sally rose from bed later than usual. Pascal, who was already shaved, showered, and dressed, sat downstairs reading the morning newspaper. His relaxed demeanor and the silk smoking jacket he wore presented the picture of contentment.

As he sipped orange juice, Sally rose to straighten out her room. She went to the jewelry box on top of her dresser to return the jewelry she left overnight on the nightstand beside her bed. She did this without noticing anything missing from the box. It was only when she saw that her dresser drawer wasn't fully closed that she became curious. Neatness being her way, she would never leave a drawer anything short of closed flush. Inspecting her things inside the drawer led her to realize that someone had stolen the envelope that contained her spending money.

Sally hastily rushed to her closet to put on a bathrobe. After doing so she noticed Pascal's pocket square on the floor. She immediately picked up the telephone to summon Pascal to her bedroom. After hanging up his cell phone, Pascal gazed up at the top of the staircase that led to the second floor and frowned. He disliked being disturbed when reading the morning newspaper.

"Now what does she want?" asked Pascal under his breath, as he rose from the chair.

When he entered Sally's bedroom he could see that the woman of the house was fretting over something.

"Sally, dear, what's wrong?" he asked, feigning great concern.

"Are you missing anything?"

"Missing what, Sally?"

"Missing money perhaps?"

"No, I don't think so."

"Go and check your room, Pascal."

After doing as he was told, Pascal returned after a couple of minutes. "Everything is fine," he advised, puzzled as to what was wrong.

"Are you sure you aren't missing any money?"

"Why, no—"

"Well I am!" she said, clearly annoyed, "five thousand dollars, in hundred-dollar bills!"

"Strange you should say that."

"What's so strange about it?"

Pascal removed three hundred-dollar bills from his wallet. Sally's eyes widened after seeing the large denominations. "Where did you get those bills? I never gave them to you," she said.

"I was about to tell you, but you cut me off, dear. I *found* these three hundred-dollar bills on my bed last night. I assumed you left them for me."

"You found *just* three?" she asked skeptically.

"You left more?"

"What do you mean, did I leave more?" she asked, seemingly astonished at the question. "I didn't leave you anything!"

"I don't understand . . ." voiced the perplexed Pascal.

"What about this?" Sally asked, producing Pascal's pocket square.

"That's mine, of course," he said after examining the accessory. "Where did you get it?"

"I found it on the floor of *my* bedroom, where you weren't invited into last night. I'm missing all the spending money I keep in my envelope, Pascal."

"I don't understand any of this."

"If you needed money, Pascal," she said sternly, "you should know that all you needed to do was simply ask me."

Pascal was highly insulted at her insinuation. "You suspect *me* of taking your money?" he asked, his outrage quite evident.

"Well, the evidence does seem to point in your direction."

"You know, you must be getting feebleminded, Sally. Why on earth would I admit to finding money if I stole it?"

Being told she was feebleminded was devastating to Sally's ego. "I have no answers for you, Pascal, *or money* to give you! But, I do know one thing—I'm not *feebleminded* enough to forget that I've been supporting you for years!" Her remarks were meant to hit home hard.

Pascal took it without responding. Ms. Belle went directly to check her jewelry box. After realizing that things were missing she turned on Pascal viciously.

"Who are you spending money on and giving *my* jewelry to?"

"Sally! How could you disrespect me like this! After all we've been to each other—"

"Don't flatter yourself, Pascal. You're nothing to me, and never were! I can tolerate a lot of things, but a sneak, a thief, *and* a cheat, never! The Maestro warned me about you years ago! I should have listened to him."

"How could you listen to ravings of an insignificant old man?" Pascal countered angrily, raising his voice. "He never forgave my leaving him for you."

No words voiced would have been sufficient for Sally. Her mind was made up. She convinced herself that Pascal looted her room because he needed money to further some affair he was having.

"Who have you been dallying with, Pascal?" asked Sally.

"Oh, stop it!"

"Tell me!"

"But Sally, dear, can't you see that someone has orchestrated all of this to make me look bad. How can you be so blind?"

There was more to Sally's pain beside the missing money and jewelry. Being sensitive to their age disparity, she anguished over the thought that Pascal betrayed her in favor of a woman who was likely younger

"Were you in my bedroom last night or not?" she asked, looking to catch Pascal in a lie.

"Just to kiss you good night, like always. You were asleep."

"You weren't ever in this room alone?"

"No. What's happening to us?" he asked.

"Five thousand dollars is missing from my drawer, Pascal, and more in jewelry. That's what's happening!" she reminded.

"So you seriously think I took your money and property?"

"Who else is there to suspect?"

"How dare you, Madame!" shouted Pascal, who took great umbrage at the accusation. From this point on their conversation really got ugly.

When Pascal began making hurtful remarks about Sally's age and the creases along her stomach, there was no tempering the row. Furious, the woman of the house rushed to Pascal's room and emptied the contents of his dresser onto the bed.

"I want you out of this house now!" she raged.

"Will you please try and control yourself, Sally" said Pascal, now worried that Sally was serious about his leaving.

Sally Belle wasn't in a listening mood. She went to the closet and tossed Pascal's suits onto the floor. Feeling something inside one of the jacket pockets, she looked to see what it was. When she discovered her jewelry, her rage seemed to strangely subside.

Sally returned to her own bedroom in silence. With all the coldness she could muster, she picked up the phone next to her bed and called her lawyer. Pascal, who followed behind, couldn't believe his ears when he overheard the instructions Sally gave to her attorney.

"Send people to my house right now, Marvin," she said stone heartedly. "I want this bastard I've been living with out of here immediately!" At this point Pascal knew he was in for hard times.

##########

SALLY BELLE WAS TOO EMBARRASSED TO REACH OUT to any of her friends. For years they had warned her that the age difference between her and Pascal would eventually become an issue. She couldn't bring herself to prove them right. Convinced that Pascal had taken up with another, she was in dire need of a sympathetic ear. The actress turned to the Clark Gable lookalike, Shepherd Fish, for comfort. Believing him to be a good man, she was sure he'd listen without casting judgment.

Fishnet wasn't totally surprised when Ms. Belle telephoned him advising that she wanted to see him about something important. Fishnet rose to the occasion without hesitation, immediately agreeing to meet the distressed woman at her townhouse.

"We had a terrible row," confessed the actress, as she and Fishnet sat in her living room. "He said such dreadful things to me, Mr. Fish."

"Please, call me Shepherd," said Fishnet in the most soothing voice he could muster. "What did this scoundrel say?" he asked. Zeroing in on her ample bosom, he began wondering how Sally looked underneath her clothing.

"He made remarks that are simply too painful for me to repeat."

Fishnet nodded. "I understand your pain. But try and tell me—what did he do and say that hurt you so?"

"Pascal called me . . . an *old* crone!" she said, struggling to keep it together. "He then made the cruelest remarks about my—oh, what's the difference."

A seemingly sympathetic Fishnet placed his hand gently atop hers. "I understand."

It was clear to Fishnet that for all her success, affluence, and seeming sophistication, Sally Belle was still emotionally vulnerable. Once recognizing her need, Fishnet morphed into a shark sensing blood. He held her close, providing the comfort she required.

"I've never been any good alone, Shepherd. Pascal's presence in the house was security for me."

"At a big cost," reminded Fishnet, as he brushed his thumb against the back of her neck.

"I know, but peace of mind is well worth . . . the expense."

At this juncture Fishnet ceased listening. As the words flowed from Ms. Belle's mouth, he continued to work his thumb to assure her. As he did this his mind transported him to his fantasy world. In that make-believe sphere, he now had full run of the townhouse. He designated the basement as a banishment zone to house Sally's friends. Arthur Murray's husband-and-wife dance team, Estelle Hatton, Pascal, and the rest of the geriatric set he met at the soiree were down below. They sat in rocking chairs to form a large circle. In the center was the Maestro, playing the peppy song *Just Because* on his violin as his audience dunked their Graham crackers into their warm milk. The only exception to the underground hootenanny was the Professor's wife Rebecca. Fishnet filed her for future reference under the heading of unfinished business.

"Do you think I should call the police?" asked Sally once she tired of lamenting her state of affairs. She thought it odd that she received no response. "Shepherd, are you alright? MR. FISH—"

When Fishnet came out of it, he cleared his voice. "I beg your pardon—I was just thinking this thing through," said the former detective, quick on the rebound. Could you repeat what you said?"

"Do you think I should call the police on Pascal?"

"No, no, no, Sally. The police can't do much for you in a case like this. Besides, do you *really* want to see Pascal jailed?"

"No, of course I don't. So you think I should forgive Pascal?"

"I don't advocate that by any stretch of the imagination. The hard work is already done. You've given him his walking papers—don't look back."

"Just cut him off completely?"

"You now know he's a thief—do you really want someone like that back in the house?"

Sally shrugged, unsure of the answer to his question. Sensing she was weakening, Fishnet reached into his pocket for the pictures from Haiti. "There are more deserving causes to support," reminded Fishnet, pointing to the photos.

"I know . . ."

"Why make life easy for the wicked?" asked Fishnet. "Don't worry, Sally, I'll stand by you. You'll not be alone."

"Thank you," Shepherd, "this is so reassuring to know."

"So tell me, on another note, what are the things you like to do for fun?"

Ms. Belle smiled sweetly when Fishnet took her hand in his. She closed her eyes and thought of Clark Gable as he proceeded to massage the back of her hand. The cunning manipulator had

118

succeeded in getting her attention.

##########

THE PROFESSOR KISSED REBECCA on the forehead before assuming his seat at the breakfast table. When it came to his first wife, he was used to being treated royally. Everything was to his liking. She poured his coffee, buttered his toast, and poured syrup on his pancakes. The Professor tried talking Rebecca into taking on full-time domestic help, but she wouldn't hear of it. All she would accept was the services of a weekly cleaner.

"Do you need anything, Rebecca? I can give you more."

"You've already given me flowers *and* money! Are you trying to spoil me?"

"Here, take some more," said the Professor, handing his New York-based wife cash. I stopped by the bank when I got back. I want you to go and buy yourself something."

"You know you really shouldn't be doing this all the time."

"Spoiling you is what gives me my greatest pleasure. Besides, what good is having all this money if I don't spend it on someone I love?" His line was corny but effective.

"Do you want juice?"

"No thank you. Hey, you forgot to tell me how the Sally Belle party went."

"It was okay, although most everyone there was pretty old."

"Did the guy play the violin?"

"Oh my, yes, the Maestro played wonderfully. He's an odd-looking little old man, but in a cute way."

"I never met him. Who else was there?"

"There was this ex-police detective who was *very* interesting."

"What police detective?" the Professor asked, perking up. As would be expected, the bigamist was sensitive to any contact with the law.

"He's a friend of Sally's. He spoke about his career in law enforcement."

"Did you talk to him?"

"I did, just briefly."

"Did he ask you a lot of questions?"

"Not really. Why would he do that?"

"That's what detectives do, don't they? Ask questions?"

"I suppose so. Anyway, he's no longer a detective."

"So what did he have to say?" pressed the Professor.

"He told a story of this shootout he was in. He was left in the street for dead after being shot in the head. Can you imagine anyone getting shot in the head and living to talk about it?"

"That does sound pretty amazing."

"He was totally paralyzed and then somehow later regained his form. He said it was a miracle that he came through."

"So what does he do now?"

"As a result of his near-death experience, he's devoting the rest of his life to helping poor people all over the world. He raises money to send overseas to the needy."

"That's nice of him," said the Professor, who secretly questioned the credibility of all he was hearing.

"I think so," agreed Rebecca.

"What's the name of this turlet head anyway?"

"Why are you calling him a turlet head? You don't even know him, so why are you so negative?"

"Who's being negative?"

"It sounded like you were. His name is Shepherd Fish."

The Professor let out a laugh. "Now that's an appropriate name, because his whole story sounds fishy!"

"You think this is a scam?"

"I can't see Ms. Belle knowingly bringing anyone into her home who is disreputable. But I could see her being naïve enough to be snookered. How much did you give him?

"What makes you think I gave him anything?"

"Because I know how you are. How much was the check? Whatever it is, I'm not going to mind."

"I wrote him a check for one thousand dollars."

"Alright, that's not so much. It could have been worse," said the Professor.

"But let me tell you the best part. Everybody was amazed at how Mr. Fish looks so much like Clark Gable. That was why Sally invited him to the party in the first place."

"This story gets better all the time," laughed the Professor. "Let me have some more pancakes. I do better on a full stomach."

12

Getting Close To Sally

ATTENDING SALLY BELLE'S PARTY EXPOSED FISHNET to the sort of company that would have been difficult to penetrate for someone coming from his background. Having been granted access to the affluent celebrity and the crowd she associated with fueled his motivation to take advantage of them.

More than ever, Fishnet stereotyped artistic people of means as being a compassionate lot. According to his perverse thinking, such good-heartedness made people soft—and thus vulnerable to bilking. With this mindset reinforced, the ex-detective continued to invent overseas hard-luck stories designed to tug at heartstrings. His plan was to use these concoctions of woe to guilt his targets into making charitable donations. Fishnet saw his formula as a foolproof scam that would enrich him.

Sally Belle was preparing to go downstairs to the first floor of her townhouse, where Fishnet was waiting patiently. Having just finished her bubble bath, she put on a robe and poured what was left of her pitcher of water into a wine glass. Sally then sat before a mirror meticulously applying her makeup.

As Sally beautified herself, Fishnet seized the opportunity to explore the first floor of the townhouse in search of something valuable to pilfer. His hunt netted him a gold cigarette case that was found deep inside a cranny within a roll-top desk. Believing the item to be of value, he slipped it into his pants pocket.

In another cubby hole inside the desk, Fishnet came upon a vintage Waterman orange ebonite fountain pen. As he was examining the pen, he heard Sally's pleasant sing-song voice calling down to him.

"I'll be a few more minutes, Shepherd," she happily advised. "Help yourself to a pick-me-up if you like."

"Take your time, Sally, I'll help myself" he shouted up the stairs with equal geniality as he tucked the pen in his jacket pocket. He chuckled at his own remark.

Fishnet couldn't imagine what Ms. Belle was doing that took so long. However, her tardiness was welcomed because it gave him additional time to look for other items worth taking.

Hearing the sound of the turning of a lock, Fishnet's attention was suddenly drawn to the front door. He was surprised to see that it was Pascal letting himself in. The two men looked at each other, both
wary at the other's presence.

Pascal seemed to be wearing a sad expression. It was a poor-me type of look that gave the impression of his carrying the burden of the world on his shoulders.

"Oh, it's you, Mr. Fish," said Pascal, finally. "Am I correct in assuming that Madame is upstairs?"

"*Madame* ain't around," replied Fishnet, looking to discourage the uninvited visitor.

"She isn't? Why, where is she?"

"She's out having her toes shellacked," answered the former detective curtly. Seeing it was only the banished Pascal, the ex-detective didn't temper his slangy way of saying things.

"I beg your pardon?" asked Pascal, who was puzzled by the answer he received.

"She's out—I don't know when she'll be back."

"It's urgent that I talk to Madame."

"Save your breath, Pascal," advised Fishnet. "You'll be doing yourself a favor."

"What do you mean?"

"Sally left orders concerning you—she said that you're out." The former detective had no desire to encourage the reemergence of his competition.

"I'm out?"

"Yeah, she made that clear. She figured sooner or later you'd be back sniffing around."

"I beg your pardon?" asked Pascal, unconvinced Sally would be so crude.

"Let me give it to you short and sweet, my friend. In sum and substance, Madame said *scram.*"

"Madame would never say any such thing," said Pascal, raising his voice in way that made it clear he was taking a stand. "I *insist* on talking to Madame!"

Fishnet puffed his chest, taking on an aggressive bearing. He stood erect to his full height with his shoulders back. "Don't get your shorts on backward, pal. Face the facts—it's the ballgame for you."

124

"Who are you to speak for Madame? Do you realize who I am?"

Fishnet scoffed at the question. "Yeah, I know who you are," he replied. "You're a sponge who went dry," said Fishnet harshly. "What do you need, a friggin' diagram? You had a good run, but now it's over, so keep walking. Be grateful you lasted as long as you did."

"How dare you—"

"Don't dare me, pal," warned Fishnet. "Go find yourself another meal ticket. Try Estelle Hatton, she probably hasn't gotten any in twenty years."

Pascal ignored the suggestion, remaining adamant in wanting to talk to Sally. "I'm not leaving this house until I speak to Madame!" he said, drawing a line in the sand.

Seeing Pascal's declaration as a challenge, Fishnet took a step closer to him. The menacing look on the face of the former detective was one he spent years perfecting. It was designed to frighten. Pascal flinched when Fishnet suddenly held up his right fist menacingly.

"Do you see this, my friend?" asked Fishnet, shaking his fist under Pascal's nose. "Shove off before I let one fly."

"How . . . how dare you threaten me!" said Pascal, his voice faltering. "I am Madame's—"

Fishnet was through talking. "You ain't a pimple on a Madame's ass!"

The former detective took Pascal by the collar of his shirt and walked him to the house entry point. In one quick motion, Fishnet whipped Pascal through the open door. The ejected Pascal hit the sidewalk hard, landing on his tailbone. Not used to such manhandling, Sally's former lover was shaken. The pain stemming from the stinging ache in his tailbone was evident on his face. Pascal looked up at Fishnet from the ground, hoping that there wasn't more punishment coming.

"Listen to me carefully, asshole," said Fishnet coldly. "If you come back here again, you'll be making the same exit . . . only next time from an upstairs window."

Absent the capacity to retaliate, Pascal slowly rose to his feet. Saying nothing, he straightened his clothing and walked off slowly. The thought crossed his mind to call the police. He dismissed that idea after considering the potential for scandal. A scene would ensure his never reconnecting with Sally.

"Did I hear voices down here, Shepherd?" asked Sally when she finally came down from the upper floor.

"I was just talking to some salesman who came to the door. You know, I was thinking, Sally, you may want to change the door lock."

"Is that really necessary?"

"I think so, if you want to avoid the chance of uninvited guests coming around, if you get my drift."

"Oh well, I suppose you're right."

Fishnet watched Ms. Belle as she walked about. He gave her credit for how physically nimble she was. In all the times he saw Ms. Belle rise from a sitting position or bend, she did so with relative ease. He once again began to wonder what she would be like under romantic circumstances. *I'll bet she purrs*, he thought. *But then again, she could be a screaming scratcher.* With this thought in mind, he began to drift to his other sphere, a world in which he could customize performance to his liking.

"What are you thinking about, Shepherd?" asked Sally. "You look so distant."

"Oh, what was that you said?"

"I asked what you were thinking about."

"I was just thinking of how you navigate your way about with the ease of a high school girl," said Fishnet.

126

Sally smiled, finding his comment amusing. "The key is to remain active. I make it a rule to go up and down those steps as many times as I can in a day," she explained.

Fishnet pointed to the bookcase where a framed autographed photo of a woman was displayed.

"Is that a picture of your mother?"

"No, that's not my mother. It's Nora Bayes. Ms. Bayes died shortly after that picture was taken."

Fishnet read aloud the inscription on the photograph.

To Claudia, my dearest friend:
Wishing you all the best,
with love and best wishes always,
Nora Bayes.

"Who is Claudia?"

"Claudia was my grandmother. The two were good friends."

"Nice," said Fishnet, not knowing what else to say.

Sally could tell that Fishnet was unaware of who Bayes was. "Nora composed the song '*Shine on Harvest Moon*,'" advised Sally, adding, "few people would remember her today. Her husband wrote '*Take Me Out to the Ballgame*.'"

"That's pretty impressive," said Fishnet, who found the information somewhat interesting.

"Shall we go, darling?"

"Let's," said Fishnet. "Grab a wing." He then politely extended his elbow.

The actress took pride walking arm in arm with a robust younger man with the looks of a famous movie star. While Pascal had been impressive eye-candy at one time, his being past his prime now made Sally feel old. Her aging phobia was one of the reasons she enjoyed being the youngest among her friends. Such company served as her fountain of youth.

The actress was having good thoughts as they strolled. "Shepherd, are you seriously involved with Ms. Garcia?"

"Wayna?" asked Fishnet. "Oh, no, not at all. We were never *that* way," he lied. "The kid had a substance abuse problem, so I took her under my wing until she could make it on her own."

Sally smiled. "I'm glad, I do want us to be *good* friends."

Fishnet was delighted to hear this. It served to verify what he suspected. With Pascal out of the picture, he was being considered as the man to fill the vacancy in Sally's life.

"Don't worry, Sally, you and I have too much in common not to be *good* friends."

"Do you really feel that?" she asked.

"I sensed it right away. We two are very similar."

"How so?" she asked, surprised by the comparison. Her stemming from affluent circumstances in comparison to his made his statement seem odd.

"We're both givers," said Fishnet with a straight face. Besides, I'd rather spend time with you more than anyone."

Glad to hear this, Sally smiled. "I feel exactly the same way."

Fishnet thought the time was right to make another pitch. He stopped walking and reached into his pocket. "Take a look at these," he said, producing several tear-inducing photos of an unfortunate small child. "May I tell you about this sad case?" he asked.

13

Squirt The Pervert

MITCHELL EMERY LIVED WITH HIS OLDER brother in the three-story, two-family Brooklyn home they grew up in. The Sunset Park property was bequeathed to them by their grandmother, who assumed responsibility for raising the siblings after the untimely death of their parents.

The sixteen-year-old Oswaldo was six years older than Mitchell, his grandmother's favorite grandson. Oswaldo was sensitive to what he considered being overlooked. As a result, the older sibling regularly bullied the much-smaller Mitchell. Aware of this mistreatment, their grandmother went to extreme lengths to protect Mitchell. Out of concern for his wellbeing, she insisted the younger brother sleep in her room at night. This only intensified the friction between the brothers.

Oswaldo was twenty-two when their grandmother entered the early stages of dementia. At this point, having graduated college and working for a construction firm, the older brother declared himself the head of the family. It was a role he filled in the fashion of a tyrant.

Oswaldo assigned the teenage Mitchell the responsibility of taking care of their grandmother. This commitment came at the cost of Mitchell's education and interpersonal skills. After dropping out of high school and relegated to caregiver, Mitchell found himself socially awkward and virtually friendless.

At home, Mitchell spent leisure time playing cards with his grandmother. Rummy, which had been a favorite card game of theirs, eventually degenerated to a point in which the elderly woman began shouting *bingo* every time she paired a card.

Complicating Mitchell's advancement was Oswaldo's tagging him with the nickname of Squirt. At just sixty-two inches, there was nothing more hurtful to Mitchell. This largely contributed to the animosity Mitchell felt for the six-foot Oswaldo.

Oswaldo, an ambitious man, dreamed of owning his own business one day. After the death of their grandmother, the older brother wasted no time in broadening his authority in the house. Ignoring that Mitchell held a half share in the property they inherited, Oswaldo restricted his brother to a second-floor bedroom. Mitchell, who was at this juncture mentally unbalanced at times, reluctantly abided by this arrangement to avoid conflict with the domineering Oswaldo.

The one thing the brothers found themselves in agreement on was that the top-floor apartment should be rented to a solo occupant. A divorced retired fireman fit that bill perfectly.

Due to his limited education, Mitchell's employment opportunities were meager. He eventually secured a job in a century-old factory, where his duties consisted of operating an old freight elevator.

An avid walker, in his off time Mitchell would visit bars, some of which were located several miles away from his home. Never successful at making a new friend, after a few drinks he'd go home to watch television in his room. During the commercials he'd turn to an adult magazine he kept at his bedside to stare at his romantic ideal, a nude model he referred to as Page Thirty-Seven, after the page number her nakedness graced.

Mitchell's resentment of Oswaldo heightened after his older brother opened his own business. Curious of where the money came from, Mitchell grew suspicious at seeing his brother dressed in yet another expensive new suit.

"Is that another new suit, Oswaldo?" asked Mitchell.

"You bet, Squirt," answered the older brother. "Why?"

"I'm just wondering."

"Well, don't," said Oswaldo tartly.

Since the older brother was drawing a fee for managing their finances, he could well afford new clothes. Between that, his business, access to the inherited money, and the apartment rental, Oswaldo enjoyed the fruits of a healthy income. Ballgames, going on dates and weekend getaways had become part of his active lifestyle. Eventually there came a point where the envious Mitchell finally broached the topic of his due with his brother.

"I want to know what I'm entitled to," said Mitchell, returning home one evening after consuming several beers.

Oswaldo was taken aback by the question. "What's all this sudden interest about, Squirt?"

"I just want to know about my end of the money."

"What's to know?" asked the older brother. "I got you covered. You're entitled to half of everything—the house, the rental income, and the money we inherited. What else is there to know, Squirt?" Oswaldo asked snippily.

"What does it all come to?"

"I don't know off hand, I gotta figure it out."

"Where is all this money you spend coming from, Oswaldo?"

"I work hard for what I got, Squirt!" replied Oswaldo, displaying a flash of anger. "So back off, and don't forget that I'm a businessman who makes good money. I don't ride on a friggin' elevator all day."

"But we were left money to share . . . and what about my half of the rent money?"

"What half of the rent money? You're forgettin' that I'm the guy paying the bills around here. Where do you think the money comes from to run this house?"

"What about the inheritance?"

"Look, I already told you, I got you covered, Squirt. I invested the money in things you'd never understand."

"Like what?"

"Oh, please—I haven't got a lifetime to smarten you up," said the older brother dismissively, walking off. "I got a date."

Mitchell sulked in his room after the disagreeable exchange. For solace he turned to Page Thirty-Seven.

"What's so special about Oswaldo?" he asked the photo. "He's nothing special—all he's got is a few inches over me and money . . . half of which is *mine!*"

As Mitchell looked at the naughty pictures in the magazine, he noticed that the surroundings of the photographed models were plush. It caused him to further recognize the importance of money if he aspired to gain the attention of someone like Page Thirty-Seven.

There's only one way for me to get ahead, he thought. *With Oswaldo around, nothing will ever change.*

Mitchell slept that night resolved to do away with his brother. He saw such a drastic measure as the only solution. With few things to distract him, he had all the time necessary to come up with a plan of execution. Having read an article about subway casualties, Mitchell arrived at a clever way to do away with

Oswaldo.

Since Oswaldo liked basketball, for his birthday Mitchell surprised his brother by giving him one of the two tickets he purchased to a Knicks name at Madison Square Garden.

"Happy birthday, Oswaldo," said Mitchell.

"This is for me?" asked the surprised older brother. "You've never given me a birthday gift before, what's the hitch?"

"Yeah, well, I was thinking that maybe it's time we try and get along better. I got a ticket for me too. We can go together, if that's okay with you."

"Maybe that's a good idea, Squirt," said Oswaldo, shrugging his shoulders.

On the way home after the game, amid the crowded 34th Street subway platform, Mitchell listened for signs that the train was coming in. When he heard what he was listening for, he turned to address Oswaldo.

"Let's get closer to the edge of the platform so we can get in a car," suggested Mitchell. "Maybe we'll get a seat if we're the first ones in the door." Oswaldo nodded. The brothers then worked their way to the edge of the platform.

As the train approached Mitchell pretended to stumble over the newspaper he intentionally dropped. Thrusting himself forward, he pushed forcefully with two hands into his brother's back, causing Oswaldo to fall onto the track. Oswaldo's thundering scream could be heard echoing throughout the station as he stood paralyzed in the path of the oncoming train. It wasn't a pretty sight. With the death of Oswaldo also came the death of the name Squirt.

The tearful statement Mitchell made to the authorities was short and sweet. He explained that after tripping, he attempted to break his fall by grabbing onto his brother. To the investigators it seemed to be a plausible explanation as to how

Oswaldo fell onto the tracks. Since so many people were on the platform, they discounted foul play. Mitchell's assassination strategy turned out to be brilliantly executed.

Mitchell was pleasantly surprised to learn that, in addition to what was due him, he also gained Oswaldo's portfolio. All in all, enough revenue was available for Mitchell to do many of the things he wanted to do. He began visiting a gentleman's club, where size only mattered when talking in terms of a bankroll.

The attention Mitchell received from the women at the club turned out to be a form of therapy. As long as he remained a spender, he was fawned over by the staff. This diet of feminine attention boosted his confidence around the opposite sex to the point of occasional arrogance. No longer an introvert, he freely began making overtures to any woman he found appealing.

Aside from this social outlet, Mitchell took up a new hobby. He began collecting postwar Lionel trains. Now having full run of the house, he decided it would be fun to construct a town for the powerful Lionel locomotive to travel through.

##########

THE PRESIDENT OF THE BLOCK ASSOCIATION WAS a community activist who kept abreast of every development on her street. She could usually be found at the helm of any organization she took an interest in. In her professional life she was a public high school principal.

While walking by the home of Mitchell Emery the block president saw something visually disturbing. The sidewalk in front of the Emery house was in dire need of repair. Noticing this need for repair caused her to take a closer look at the front of Mitchell's building, where she soon discovered several other eyesores. She brought her observations up at the next block association meeting held at her home.

"That house is degenerating into an absolute nightmare," she declared. "Permitting such deterioration to continue only serves to devalue our own properties."

"Who lives there?" asked one of the homeowners.

"Mitchell Emery. You must know him—he's the short man at the end of the block."

"Oh, now I know who you mean. Is anyone friendly with him?"

"He's a loner," chimed in another neighbor.

"Maybe he just doesn't have the money for repairs," voiced yet another property owner.

"I doubt that very much," replied the block president. "That house must be long paid for. And I know he rents the apartment upstairs, so he's collecting rent."

The end of the meeting resulted in all agreeing that representatives, headed by the block president, should have a word with Mitchell Emery. The following evening a trio of neighbors led by the president appeared at Mitchell's door.

Mitchell came to the door after the third ring. His delay in answering the bell was due to his playing with his electric trains. The track for the train was extensive. It ran throughout the entire first floor of his home. When running his train, Mitchell pretended to be Casey Jones, the Illinois Central Railroad engineer who sacrificed his own life to save passengers.

Mitchell's neighbors were surprised to see him come to the door wearing an engineer's hat. The conversation between the neighbors took place in front of the house. It was a cordial discussion that ended with Mitchell readily agreeing to address the house repairs in question.

"Hmmm...he seemed awful agreeable," commented the block president to the neighbors who accompanied her. "I just can't help feeling that there is something creepy about him."

14

Wedding Bells

WHILE MARKIE WAS INVESTIGATING THE HOMICIDE of the Philadelphia police officer, his girlfriend Alley devoted time to organizing their wedding. Alley, who worked full time as a bartender at Fitzie's, was leafing through a 1999 planner in search of an appropriate wedding date. When she reached the month of March she paused, thinking the day prior to St. Patrick's Day might be suitable. Alley's immediate thoughts were that they could marry locally and then go on their honeymoon immediately afterward. Her only reservation was that she'd be missing out on working one of the busiest days in the bar business. She decided to forego the advantage of working on a fun day that usually came with generous tips.

New Orleans was one destination considered. The future bride saw great fun partaking in that town's festive atmosphere on that special day of green beer, corned beef, and cabbage.

Her second consideration was a shipboard wedding ceremony. The idea of enjoying cocktails and finger food with guests followed by the couple staying aboard to sail off on their honeymoon someplace was also appealing.

As usual, Alley was early reporting for work that afternoon. She stopped at a deli to pick up something to eat prior to her evening shift at the Fitzie's bar. The owner was bartending when she arrived. As was his custom, the former old school prizefighter was holding court. Half a dozen customers gathered around the customer's side of the rail to listen to one of Fitzie's stories of the squared circle. The daytime crowd that frequented the bar looked forward to these tales of the ring almost as much as the beer they consumed.

"You're just in time, Alley!" said Fitzie, after noticing her entrance. "Come around the bar by me and listen to this. They want to hear about the Dempsey-Willard fight again."

Alley took her place next to Fitzie, who was positioned in front of the oil painting of former heavyweight champion Jack Dempsey, the topic of his narrative. After proclaiming his familiar opinion that the Manassa Mauler was the greatest of all heavyweights, Fitzie recounted his often-told story of Dempsey's title winning bout.

"Dempsey took the title off the Pottawatomie Giant in Toledo, Ohio, on the Fourth of July in 1919 . . ." began the bar owner.

Fitzie was about to recount the fight round by round when he was interrupted by a customer.

"What were the odds for the fight?"

"The champion was a six-to-five favorite. Willard was a giant of a man for the times, something like six-six and two hundred and fifty pounds," advised the saloon owner. "Now will ya stop interrupting me?" he asked.

Fitzie went on to tell of the battering Jess Willard took in the first round. Hearing his account, one would have thought the bar owner had actually been sitting ringside. Only a couple of those listening were aware that a ten-thousand-dollar wager at ten-to-one odds was placed by Dempsey's manager on the outcome of the fight. The manager, Doc Kearns, had bet boldly that Dempsey would score a first-round knockout.

"It was so hot that day in Toledo that Bat Nelson, the old lightweight champ, took off his clothes and jumped in the lemonade vat!" told Fitzie.

"Go on," said one skeptical imbiber, voicing disbelief in the lemonade story.

"It's the truth, so help me" swore the bar owner. Fitzie raised his right hand as if taking an oath. "You could look it up. The lemonade concession went for a thousand bucks, which was a lot of coin in 1919."

"Did you drink any of the lemonade?" The question drew howls from those in attendance.

"Very funny," replied Fitzie stiffly.

A distinct cackling drew Alley's attention to a very short, slope-shouldered man who had been partially hidden in the crowd of men. She frowned at seeing the man she nicknamed Little Creepy.

Alley had a true dislike for this particular customer, a relative newcomer to Fitzie's place. Her distain for him intensified each time she saw him. Alley tried to ignore his annoying habit of staring at her while she worked. The customer only added to her irritation when he began taking vulgar liberties. Most revolting to Alley was when he licked his lips whenever their eyes met. This lecherous conduct only served to enhance her animosity toward the man she viewed as a creepy pervert.

Physically, although short, the offensive customer had a powerful upper body that would usually be associated with a much larger man. Much of his muscularity stemmed from his work as the freight elevator operator at the Pristine Rose

Laundry. The opening and closing of the ancient commercial elevator was a rigorous endeavor. Due to his diminutive stature, Little Creepy had to jump up to reach a thick leather strap that hung off the top half of the elevator door. He'd then have to muster the strength to pull down hard for the top to meet the lower half of the door. This task required a good deal of physical ability. The repetitive nature of the work resulted in chiseling the physique of the elevator operator.

Once Fitzie concluded his storytelling, Alley began performing her duties. Things soon got ugly as she served Little Creepy a drink. He latched onto Alley's hand when she placed a mug of beer down before him. As she struggled to break free from his grip, Little Creepy began slurping. The sight of this behavior freaked Alley out. She shouted loudly, "CUT THE SHIT!" Her outburst caused the offensive bar patron to immediately release his hold on her. Fitzie, now aware that something was amiss, made his way over to where Alley stood.

"What's the problem over here?" asked the former fighter.

"You better keep this bastard away from me, Fitzie," said Alley. "If you don't, I'm gonna crack a bottle over his head!" she threatened angrily. Alley then stormed off to the other end of the bar where there were other customers.

"What the hell did you do to her?" asked the bar owner, turning to the source of the trouble.

"I didn't do a thing! I was just trying to be sociable."

"Well don't be so *sociable*!" barked Fitzie. "Just leave her the hell alone, or take your business someplace else!"

"Sure—I'm not looking for trouble," answered the harasser. "I meant no harm. She just reminds me of someone I know," added Mitchell, referring to Page Thirty-Seven.

After a while Mitchell resumed staring at Alley from afar. This caused her to again complain to Fitzie.

"Look Fitzie, you can't have this little son of a bitch coming in here anymore," Alley said to her boss. "I just can't concentrate on my work with the little creep around!"

"What's the problem now?"

"He just gives me the creeps!"

"What's he doing?"

"The little creep keeps staring at me like I'm a piece of meat. I'm telling you, there is something wrong with him—he's some kind of a pervert."

"Well, Jesus. There ain't no law against looking, is there?"

Alley saw Fitzie's response as disappointing. "Fitzie, I'm trying to tell you that this man is a sicko. He licks his chops every time I happen to look his way."

"I ain't got time for this shit," exclaimed Fitzie, having heard enough. "You go give him a drink on the house," said the business owner. "I want to see for myself what he does."

"Okay, you watch him. When I place the drink in front of him he'll do something."

"Alright, don't get excited. Just go get the drink."

"Ugh! How would you like his greasy, slimy hands touching you?" asked Alley before walking off to fetch the drink.

"Always with the dramatics," muttered the bar owner under his breath.

Alley walked over to where the annoying customer was standing at the bar. "This is on the boss," she said coldly.

The man who disgusted Alley smiled and nodded. "You remembered what I like to drink," he commented happily. His broad smile revealed crooked teeth that added to his lack of appeal.

"Yeah, I remembered," Alley replied.

Little Creepy then added to his list of offensive acts. After taking a sip of beer, he opened his mouth wide while extending his mouth organ to the fullest. He then began to rapidly wiggle his tongue from one side of his mouth to the other. After a number of lateral wiggles, he began to dart his tongue forward as would a lizard. Alley turned to look at Fitzie. She wanted to confirm he observed these crude acts.

"This guy really is friggin' nuts," the bar owner whispered to Alley after calling her over to where he was.

"That's what I been trying to tell you!"

"Sit tight and relax. He's gonna be bounced out of here on his ear in ten minutes."

"I hope so," she replied. "Don't say anything to my boyfriend about this, okay?"

"Don't worry about a thing. This ain't a job for Markie," advised Fitzie. "I'll handle it."

Fitzie went to where the local loan shark was regularly stationed at the front of the bar.

"I need a favor, Peanuts," said Fitzie.

"What's up?"

"You see that little shit over there?" asked Fitzie, pointing out the offensive man. "He's some kind of pervert who needs a good bouncing. I don't want him in here again ever."

"You want him taught a lesson?" asked the money lender looking for clarification.

"Yeah, that's the idea. He needs to learn a *good* lesson."

"I'll have it emphasized," said the loan shark with a wink.

When Fitzie walked off, Peanuts made a call on his cell phone to the social club he frequented a couple of blocks away. Within fifteen minutes the problematic man was met at the bar by two husky men in their mid-twenties. One of the men was toting a pitching wedge. The golf club was sufficient inducement for the disrupter to go along with the men quietly.

When the bruisers returned to the bar, they reported back to

Peanuts. Peanuts then shot Fitzie a thumbs-up to convey that the problem was rectified.

Fitzie acknowledged the message with a nod. He then advised Alley that Peanuts and his two associates were to have drinks on the house. He added it was unlikely that Little Creepy would be coming around the bar anymore.

When Alley went over to the three men to take their order, she noticed blood on the shirt of one of the huskies. It was clear to her that someone was the recipient of a beating. Being a decent person, she couldn't help feeling a small degree of remorse that the situation came to this.

Alley never mentioned the incident to Markie. She was afraid her boyfriend would react violently to the situation. The last thing she wanted was for the sergeant to get in the kind of trouble that could jeopardize his job and pension. If that were to occur, she knew her wedding plans would be off the table.

Alley grossly underestimated her disturbed admirer. He was a man that couldn't be discouraged by a beating. Unbeknownst to Alley, Mitchell Emery was a stalker who had been taking pictures of her in and out of the bar for over a week.

##########

WHEN MITCHELL FINISHED PLAYING with his trains, he prepared to retire for the night. He looked into the mirror above his dresser to check out his facial healing. The injuries inflicted on him as a result of his visit to Fitzie's were substantial enough to require stitches and bandaging.

His infatuation with Alley Cat was such that a few scars weren't going to keep him from his love interest, a woman who he likened to Page Thirty-Seven in his porno magazine.

On top of Mitchell's dresser were two cameras, one of which

was in the form of a watch he purchased from a spy store. Taped to a wall were three photographs taken of an unaware Alley while at her place of employment. One picture was a full face shot, the second was of Alley's ample bosom, and the third was taken as she leaned down to pull beer out of a case stored under the bar. Thanks to slipping jeans, the photo captured part of the thong she wore. Mitchell climbed into bed hoping that he would have a pleasant dream of Alley.

##########

THE LAUNDRY WHERE MITCHELL WORKED was located in a very old building that came complete with a
loading dock for delivery trucks. The bustling enterprise boasted a workforce of over one hundred employees from diverse backgrounds, the vast majority being the laundry's blue-collar worker bees. These employees wore white uniforms as they performed their duties in a gruff work environment riddled with questionable behavior.

The creaky old building contained many areas for employees to sneak off on unauthorized breaks to   smoke, drink and do other inappropriate things. The general feeling among supervisors was that as long as the work went out and no one complained, it was easier to just look the other way.

When not being used to transport people and goods from floor to floor, the freight elevator served as Mitchell's private office. Between runs he sat in a weathered easy chair inside the elevator. A small shelf housed his portable radio. Next to the radio was a small jar of Vaseline. Taped to the wall over the shelf was the photo of a woman that he readily identified to people as *his* girl. The woman was Markie's girlfriend.

Most employees who used the elevator understood Mitchell's

having an easy chair, a radio, and a picture of his purported sweetheart in the elevator. Why he kept a jar of Vaseline on hand was a mystery to all but a few.

"What happened to your face, Mitch?" asked one of the employees who entered the elevator on her lunch break. She was a petite woman around Mitchell's age who was even shorter than he.

Mitchell, who was sitting in his chair, waved his hand dismissively without responding to the question.

"What floor?" he asked, rising from his chair.

The passenger had a crooked mouth as a result of a stroke. She watched in awe as Mitchell's shoulder muscles puffed up as he pulled down the strap to close the elevator doors.

"Who is the woman in the picture?" asked the passenger.

"My girl," replied the elevator operator. "How far do you want to go?"

"All the way," she replied, suggestively.

15

<u>Jealous Lover</u>

AFTER RECEIVING NEWS THAT her daughter was getting married, Alley's mother wasted no time in suggesting that the newlyweds honeymoon in London. The matriarch emphasized to her daughter how appropriate it would be to welcome her new son-in-law into the family. The one thing that gave Alley pause was the cost connected to visiting England. While she was in favor of the idea, the future bride wanted to hear Markie's thoughts prior to committing.

"Al, what do think about our going to London for our honeymoon?" asked Alley over breakfast. "My mother wants to officially welcome you to the family."

"Over in England?"

"They'd really love to see us over there. My mother is getting on in years, and I haven't been home in a very long while."

Alley's long absence from home activated the sergeant's tender side. Casting expense aside, he thought going to London would be the right thing to do.

"Sure, Alley. It's your wedding," he replied.

"It's not *my* wedding—it's *our* wedding," reminded Alley.

The sergeant quickly realized his poor choice of words. "Of course it's our wedding. All I meant to say was that I want things to be exactly the way you want them to be," Markie explained. Since he'd been down the marriage path before, he felt it only fair for Alley to dictate terms this time around.

"Will it fit into our budget?"

"Don't you worry—we'll make it fit."

The delight in Alley's seventy-six-year-old mother's voice was unmistakable when she was given the news. Pleasing her distanced mother was hugely rewarding for Alley. When it was time for her to report for work, she couldn't have been in better spirits. She could be heard humming the Village People's long ago hit, "In The Navy", as she began her journey to Fitzie's.

Alley's joyous thoughts of visiting home kept her from paying close attention to her surroundings. She failed to notice Mitchell Emery standing behind a car on the opposite side of the street, photographing her. A pronounced zoom lens was affixed to the camera carried by the man she dubbed Little Creepy.

Mitchell clicked away as Alley walked along the street, capturing every aspect of her on film. The photos were important to Mitchell because they memorialized his obsession from every angle. He wanted to capture Alley's every physical particular. Her facial expressions, body form, and the way she stood were all of equal importance to him. He craved to know what he couldn't confirm visually. Birthmarks and moles hidden by clothing were of interest to him, as were items contained in her pocketbook.

Starting at her head, Mitchell snapped his way down her torso to her feet. He photographed her while walking as well as standing still at crosswalks. Every new position her body assumed was bagged. These photographs of Alley were used to paper the walls along the train route he erected at home.

##########

AFTER RETURNING HOME FROM WORK, MITCHELL donned his engineer's cap. Before activating the Lionel electric trains, he checked to make sure that everything along the route was in order. It satisfied him to see that the photo display of Alley that graced the walls was coming along nicely. Mitchell slipped onto the high stool in front of the transformer. It was a section of the room he referred to as Alley Station in honor of the woman he was enamored with.

"All aboard," he shouted, after turning on the transformer that activated the train.

"Paper, mister?" asked Mitchell, giving life to the newsboy figure who stood in front of the plastic depot building.

"Not now, son," he answered for the grandfatherly figure that stood near the newsboy.

Before advancing the train, Mitchell took a moment to place smoke pellets in the powerful engine. Once in motion the train traveled along the track that rested on plywood tables and ramps. The train passed through Alleytown, which occupied most of the first floor of the building, at a steady pace.

Mitchell visually followed the train as it made its way along the track. The train passed a plastic water tunnel, trestle bridges, streetlights, barns, farmhouses, and factories, among other things. Anyone observing would have to appreciate the artistry connected to the intricate detail that the freight elevator operator put into creating a toy town and transportation system. When the train finally returned to Alley

Station, he flipped the off switch and hung his cap on a doorknob.

After dinner Mitchell began having the urge to see Alley. Being unable to show his face inside her place of employment, his access to her had become restricted. The infatuated stalker tried to find solace by going to bed early. After awakening at 2:00 a.m., Mitchell experienced difficulty going back to sleep. After much twisting and turning, he gave up trying. With Alley still on his mind, he rose from his bed and got dressed.

Tossing caution to the wind, Mitchell went to Fitzie's on the chance that he might find Alley alone in the bar. He foolishly believed he could make amends and convince Alley that his love was sincere. It was wishful thinking.

When Mitchell arrived at Fitzie's he crept up to the front window of the bar. Standing at an angle to prevent detection, he peeked through the glass. The stalker saw Alley behind the bar servicing just a handful of customers. Repositioning himself to the opposite side of the street, he decided to wait for Alley to finish her shift.

An hour later Alley exited the bar on the arm of a man who had been seated at the end of the bar. The arm she clung on to was that of Sergeant Markie. Alley's not being alone put Mitchell at a disadvantage. Unable to do anything, with a grim face he watched the couple drive off in Markie's car.

With the curiosity of a jealous lover, Mitchell made his way to Alley's residence. Once arriving he saw the car Alley entered parked on the block of her home. Mitchell was unable to bring himself to leave. He assumed a sitting position on the front steps of a nearby building that gave him a good view of where Alley lived. He looked up at the windows that faced the street. Considering the time, he figured that the apartment with the light on belonged to Alley. He went into a slow burn when no one left the building after the lights went off.

########

MARKIE LISTENED ATTENTIVELY AS ALLEY explained how wonderful their London honeymoon was going to be. The detective sergeant sat up in bed, smiling in an agreeable way as her words flowed. It made him happy to see her joy.

"It's going to be so great," Alley enthused, throwing her arms around Markie. She then unleashed an affectionate barrage of clipped kisses that overwhelmed the sergeant.

"Hey—back off, will ya? You gotta give me some time for my batteries to charge."

"Since when do *you* need more time?" she asked coyly. "Are you staying, luv?"

"No, I'm heading back to my apartment," advised Markie. "Since I'm paying rent I might as well spend some time there."

"Shall we have another go-round before you leave?" she invited. Markie stayed longer than planned.

########

THE LONGER MITCHELL WAITED for Alley's guest to leave her apartment, the angrier he grew. As his frustration elevated, so did his desire for revenge. Mitchell checked his watch. Seeing he had ample time before having to go to work, he rushed home to get a can of spray paint.

Upon his return to Alley's house, Mitchell was happy to see Markie's car still parked on the street. He began to vigorously shake the paint can. After looking about to make sure no one was in the area, he scrawled across the front window glass of

149

Markie's car a very incriminating message in bold, black lettering:

"STOP BANGING MILLIE SANCHEZ!"

Satisfied that the stage was set for a tumultuous exchange between Alley and her friend, Mitchell removed himself a distance away. He assumed a position where he could keep his eye on the car without being seen.

When Markie emerged from Alley's apartment he was stunned to see the graffiti message on his car. Furious, he returned to his girlfriend's apartment in a rage.

"What's wrong, Al?" asked Alley.

"Look out the damn window and you'll see what's wrong!" shouted the sergeant, unable to contain his anger.

Alley went to the window and stared town at the street. "I don't see anything . . ."

"You got any nail polish remover around here?"

Alley removed a small bottle of the solution from her pocketbook. "Here," she said, handing the bottle over.

"Is this all you got?"

"I have another bottle in my drawer."

"Go get it," said Markie in a huff.

"What's the problem?"

"Some asshole just marked up my car with paint, *that's* the problem!" answered the Sergeant.

Wanting to see what the big hullaballoo was over, Alley hastily threw something on and followed Markie down to the street. When she saw the message printed across the front windshield she stiffened. The man she referred to as Little Creepy accomplished his goal of creating conflict between the couple.

"Who is Millie Sanchez, Al?" asked Alley in an accusatory tone.

"How should I know? I don't know any Millie Sanchez."

"Well, somebody obviously thinks you do!" said Alley, stomping off to her apartment.

Watching Alley storm off caused the sergeant to fire the bottle of nail polish remover down on the ground to release his anger. After taking a few minutes to calm down, he returned to the apartment in an effort to explain his innocence to Alley.

"Look Alley, this is one of two things," Markie began. "Either this asshole got the wrong car or it's an out-and-out frame up."

"I find it hard to believe there is another bomb on the road like yours," she said snippily.

"Then I'm being framed."

"Why would anyone want to do that to you?" she asked.

"How should I know? But, I'll tell you one thing—if it is a frame, it has to be someone we both know."

"Why is that?"

"Because whoever it is wants me to look bad in your eyes."

"But who would do such a thing?" asked Alley, who had calmed down a bit.

"Have you had an ex-boyfriend sniffing around you lately?"

"Oh, *please*," she replied, dismissing the notion. Alley never even considered Mitchell Emery.

########

AT MARKIE'S REQUEST, DETECTIVE OLLIE VON HESS arrived at Alley's residence with an ample amount of graffiti remover. After reading the message left on Markie's car, he shook his head disapprovingly.

"Only a real son of a bitch would do something like this, Sarge. You got any idea who could have stooped this low?"

"I'm clueless, Ollie. But I'll tell you one thing, if I ever find out who the rat bastard is you'll be booking me for assault."

"What did Alley have to say about it?"

"What do you think? She's pissed off at me. She thinks I'm cheating on her with this Millie Sanchez."

"Are you?"

"NO!" shouted the sergeant. "I don't even know anyone by that name."

"What are you gonna do to convince her?"

"I'm not sure what I can do. I already gave her my wallet to go through to help convince her. I even promised to show her my credit card charges when the bill comes!"

"I suppose you can't blame her."

"I don't blame her at all, Ollie. I wouldn't believe me either. Let me tell you, if I ever get my hands on the bastard who did this, it'll be just too bad."

"It might just be the prank of some dumb kid."

"Nah—what have I got to do with kids?"

"Maybe you were just randomly selected?"

"Whatever—c'mon, we gotta get goin' on the windshield so we can get to work on time."

Mitchell watched from a safe distance as Markie and Von Hess scrubbed the graffiti off the sergeant's car. Seeing the men toil gave Mitchell satisfaction. Aside from the inconvenience he created for the perceived competition, Mitchell hoped his act of mischief would put an end to the relationship that he believed stood in his way.

Checking his watch, Mitchell saw it was nearing time to report for work. He headed to his job before Markie and Von Hess finished the laborious task of removing the inflammatory words off Markie's car.

##########

MITCHELL COULD BE SEEN YAWNING EXCESSIVELY throughout the day while navigating his freight elevator. Listening to talk shows on his transistor radio was some help in keeping him awake. One host, known for giving relationship advice, was taking calls from the listening audience. After fielding a series of questions, the host received an inquiry that interested Mitchell.

"I have feelings for a woman who lives in my building, but I'm not sure if she would be interested in me," voiced a caller. "How do you suggest I proceed?"

"You need to go after what you want," advised the radio host. "Introduce yourself, and ask her if she'd like to join you in an activity. Remember to respect her decision if she expresses no interest. Nothing ventured, nothing gained, you know."

The advice provided by the talk show host made an impression on Mitchell. *That's it! I've been too crude*, he thought, realizing his past behavior lacked polish. *I was communicating wrong!*

"You're right," announced Mitchell, speaking to the radio.

As the elevator operator navigated his up-and-down route, he began to think of alternative ways of conveying his intentions to the women he obsessed over. He decided it would be a good idea to start humbly. *This time I'll get off on the right foot,* he thought.

Mitchell's plan called for his expressing remorse over his past behavior. Once securing forgiveness, he intended to ask her to join him for coffee. Or, depending on how things went, dinner.

Mitchell intended to spare no expense in preparation for this overture. Wanting to make a good impression, he decided to improve his grooming by getting a haircut and shaving. He even purchased a new set of threads..

If I can get her to the house to see the city I built in her honor, she'll flip, thought Mitchell. *It'll flatter her to death!*

When Mitchell got home after work he donned his engineer's cap, revved up his electric locomotive, and fed it a couple of smoke pellets. As the toy train journeyed through Alleytown, a feeling of tremendous confidence came over him. He likened himself to the powerful locomotive that he watched pull the trains. There was no doubt in his mind that his next encounter with Alley would have a positive outcome.

Exhausted from a lack of sleep, Mitchell skipped dinner and went to bed after running his train. His last thought was of Alley before slumber came.

16

<u>Brooklynese</u>

MARY BETH CARBONE WAS ON THE telephone talking to her father. As was sometimes the case, their conversation evolved into a disagreeable one. Their clashing centered on Mary Beth's determination to participate in the Grady O'Lang homicide investigation. Unfortunately, her efforts to persuade her father that it was her duty to cooperate with the authorities fell on deaf ears. Mary Beth's frustration led her to reach for the pack of cigarettes and ashtray she kept out of sight in a drawer.

"I can't understand why the hell I can't get through to you, Mary Beth," said Mr. Carbone, in his unmistakable voice of annoyance. Mary Beth exhaled the smoke from her cigarette loudly enough to be heard at the other end of the line. "Are you smoking over there?" asked the father. "What did I tell you about that?"

"No, I'm not smoking," she lied, shaking her head.

"Don't tell me that—I know you're smoking!" said Mr. Carbone, raising his voice. "Don't you remember what smoking did to your grandfather?"

"He was eighty-nine . . ."

"That's not the point!"

"I'm not a baby, dad. Look, I really have to go."

"Wait a minute, your mother wants to talk to you," he said, passing the phone to his wife.

"I don't know why you're not listening to your father," said Mrs. Carbone, after taking the phone from her husband. "Why get yourself mixed up in a murder if you didn't have to?"

"Because I was there, that's why."

"Oh, come on, Mary Beth," scoffed the mother. "You never make it easy, do you?"

"But I already told you, Ma—I'm a witness."

"How on earth could *you* be a witness?"

"I *heard* everything that happened."

"Can't you appreciate the risk? Your father is about to jump out a window—that's how upset he is with you."

"He'll get over it, ma."

Mrs. Carbone cupped the telephone and turned to her husband. "This damn kid is as thick as shit!" she whispered to her husband. "She gets that from your side!"

"Give me that phone," said Mr. Carbone, reaching for the receiver.

"Keep your head. Otherwise she'll only be more stubborn," his wife warned before passing the phone.

"Mary Beth," began Mr. Carbone taking a deep breath, "let me ask you something. Why can't the cops figure this thing out without dragging you into it? That is their job you know."

"I don't know, dad," she answered, letting out a big sigh. All I could tell you is that the detectives called me and said they needed me."

"When they come to the house, just tell them you don't

156

remember anything too clearly," advised the father. "Be vague . . . you know, tell them that after thinking it over, you can't be sure of anything."

"I can't do that," Mary Beth stated firmly, as she ground out her lit cigarette in the ashtray.

"And why is that?"

"Because I know what I heard on that platform."

"What the hell are you talking about? How in the hell can you be sure who said what?"

"I can identify their voices."

"This kid is driving me nuts," said Mr. Carbone, throwing up his hands in disgust. He passed the phone back to his wife. "I give up. You talk to her, I'm going to the turlet."

"What on earth did you say to your father, Mary Beth?"

"I didn't say anything. Look, Ma, I have to go. I'll call you."

"Alright, Mary Beth, this is getting us nowhere," conceded the mother. "Just please be careful. You don't know what kind of person you're dealing with."

"But he'll be in jail—"

"Oh, don't be so naïve, for Christ's sake," said Mrs. Carbone, in a flash of anger. "There is no guarantee of that! Can't you see how the cops are using you? You're handicapped, and that's gonna gain them points with the jury."

Being reminded of her situation was painful to hear for Mary Beth. It was a topic her family usually tried to avoid using. The sting was enough to put an end to their conversation. "I have to go," said the daughter, "I'll call you tomorrow."

"I'm sorry, dear," said Mary Beth's mother, realizing the hurt she caused. "Why don't you stay with us until this mess is over and done with? Your father is retired now, so he'll drive you to and from work. Will you at least think about that?"

"Okay, I'll think about it. But I really have to go now. Bye, Ma."

###########

THE INTERVIEW WITH MARY BETH CARBONE was one that Markie and Von Hess intended to enter into carefully. They remained in the car for a minute to chat prior to going inside her building.

"Do you suppose she lives alone, Ollie?" asked Markie, who sat in the passenger seat of the unmarked police car.

"I don't know, Sarge. She rides the train by herself, so it would seem she's plenty independent. She very well might live alone."

"I can't imagine myself in that situation."

"You'd adapt, Sarge. You'd have to."

"I suppose. I wonder what happens when she dreams. How do you think that works?"

"She's gotta dream like everybody else—"

"I'm not questioning her ability to dream, Ollie. I'm thinking about her not being able to visualize anything."

"Maybe she was able to see at one time. Anyway, I don't think we better ask that question."

Markie smirked at the very suggestion. "It's not likely that I will. C'mon, let's go in and talk to her."

Mary Beth lived on the first floor of her building. Immediately after hearing her bell ring, she went to the intercom.

"Who is it, please?" she asked.

"It's Detective Von Hess," answered the detective.

After being buzzed in, the investigators proceeded to her apartment. When they got there, they found the witness standing in the doorway, waiting to let them in.

"Detective Von Hess?" called out Mary Beth when she no longer heard their footsteps.

"Ms. Carbone?" asked Markie.

"Who are you, sir?" the witness asked, not recognizing

Markie's voice.

"It's alright, Ms. Carbone—"

"Oh, Detective Von Hess, you are here."

"Yes, I'm here. Thanks for taking the time to see us. I'm with Sergeant Markie to talk to you about the subway incident."

"I'm pleased to meet you, Sergeant. Come on in—I've been expecting you."

Markie and Von Hess followed the witness into her apartment. Both men were impressed by her meticulous appearance. They were also surprised to see how confidently she navigated her well-maintained home.

"Can I get you gentlemen anything?" asked Mary Beth.

"No thank you," advised the sergeant. "We won't be taking up too much of your time."

"You can take all the time you need—I'm home this evening. Tonight is my off night."

"It's your off night?"

"Yes, I go to my fitness club three nights a week." Mary Beth picked up on their sudden silence. "You shouldn't be so surprised," she said.

Markie was glad she couldn't see how his face reddened due to his embarrassment. "Well, I'm not . . ."

"Working out at my gym is one of the things I have control over. Like this apartment, it's a safe environment."

"Mary Beth," said Markie, addressing the business at hand, "can you tell us what you remember about what happened on the subway platform that night?"

Ms. Carbone provided the details surrounding the Grady O'Lang homicide as she initially stated them to Detective Boucher. She repeated her account without contradiction.

"Do you think you'd recognize the voice of the man who was called the Professor if you heard it again?" asked Von Hess.

"I think so, Detective Von Hess," she answered. "I'm very adept at recognizing voices," she quickly added. "I had no problem recognizing your voice, and we only spoke once."

"That's true, ma'am, you didn't," replied the convinced detective.

Markie posed the next question. "Was there anything unusual about the killer's voice? Perhaps a lisp or stutter?"

"Now that you mention it, there was definitely one thing that I vividly recall about how he spoke. It was something I didn't think of until later, after I spoke to Detective Boucher."

"There was?" asked Markie, perking up. "What was that?"

"It was the way he pronounced the word toilet. He said it the same way my father does."

"And how is that?"

"They both say *'turlet'* instead of toilet. To this day my father says he took the car for an *erl* change instead of an *oil* change."

"That's very interesting," said Von Hess.

"You have no doubt that the homicide victim called the other man a two-timer, correct?"

"Yes, that's right."

"Thank you, Mary Beth. You've been a great help."

"You're welcome. Are you sure I can't get you anything?"

"Next time, right now we have to get back on the job. We'll definitely be in touch."

Once back in the car the detectives discussed the interview they conducted. Markie was feeling pretty good about the case at this point.

"I think we're looking at a winner with this case, Ollie."

"This smacks of some kind of love angle we got here."

"Well, Professor Extraordinarious does seem to like the women."

"That he does, Sarge. Do you think it's time to talk to the

160

district attorney's office?"

"Let me post Lieutenant Wright before we take that step, Ollie."

"And the case officer," reminded Von Hess.

"That's right—you can clue in Teddy Hart."

As they were driving Von Hess suddenly slowed up the car. When he came to a full stop, the sergeant wondered why.

"What happened?" asked the sergeant.

"See that guy who just came out of the double-parked Toyota, Sarge? He's going toward the deli."

"The man in blue work clothes, right?

"Yeah, he's one guy I have to settle up with. This may end up in a pinch."

"Go ahead, knock yourself out."

Markie wondered what the motorist had done to cross Von Hess, who was usually not the sought to seek revenge. The detective never let on to Markie that the man who came out of the Toyota had made a false accusation against him nine years earlier, after Von Hess arrested his son for pouring a can of beer into a mailbox.

When the owner of the Toyota emerged from the deli, he saw Von Hess standing by his car. It took a moment for him to focus on the detective.

"You're parked illegally," advised Von Hess, sounding very official.

"So it's you," declared the motorist, now recognizing the detective.

"Let me see your license and registration," ordered the detective.

"Here," said the man, producing one of the documents.

"Where's the registration?"

"My registration is in the car."

"Get it."

The man entered his car to retrieve the document from the glove compartment. After doing this he closed the door and hurried away from the vehicle. From where Markie sat in his car, it seemed to him that the man was intentionally distancing himself from his vehicle. Now suspicious, the sergeant exited his car to check the interior of the motorist's Toyota. While Von Hess examined the paperwork, Markie observed a looped leather strap protruding from underneath the driver's seat. Thinking it was a blackjack he pulled the strap forward. After confirming his suspicion he left the deadly weapon where he found it and walked over to where Von Hess was.

"What, are you looking to shake me down now?" asked the owner of the Toyota, addressing Von Hess.

Hearing this, Markie directed the detective to check out the car. The motorist stood flat footed with his mouth agape as Von Hess walked to the vehicle.

When Von Hess returned he did so with his handcuffs in one hand and the blackjack in the other. From the perspective of Von Hess, arresting the motorist avenged the slight he received years earlier. Both investigators considered the bust to be one of those little satisfactions that come along in police work from time to time.

17

A Package Deal

HAVING ELIMINATED THE COMPETITION PASCAL presented, Fishnet's path to Sally Belle was now unfettered. Attuned to the sympathetic nature of the actress when it came to a sad story, he initially viewed her strictly in terms of being a prime candidate to bilk. Once it became apparent that his offerings of affection were being well received, the former detective set his sights on a broader agenda.

Fishnet amended his scheme to include an emotional component. His expanded intent called for his winning her heart in the belief that if he accomplished this, there would be no limit to his financial betterment.

As Fishnet saw things, he had several factors working in his favor. Since Sally was well north of her sweet spot in terms of age, he believed that she'd likely be receptive to the amorous advances of a younger man. Secondly, aware of the appeal raw masculinity could generate, he saw himself as standing alone in comparison to the men he met in Sally's circles. Lastly, his resemblance to Gable made him the prize, a trophy that would make Sally the envy of her friends.

Cognizant of the effect that flattery had on people, Fishnet commenced to liberally compliment Sally in and out of her presence. This was a major part of his blueprint to seduce the actress.

As Fishnet got closer to Sally, he came to learn that she was actually Sally Eunice Belletower, the daughter of the late Archibald Belletower. Her father, referred to in the press as Highball Archie, was the playboy son of Maurice St. Johns Belletower, founder of the mammoth Belletower International Holdings (BIH). The Belletower family, long synonymous with old New York money, was one of the wealthiest of families.

When Fishnet became aware of Sally's heritage he researched the family. Once he found out that Sally's interest in the conglomerate made her one of the richest women in the country, he became determined to be officially part the empire.

One of the things that baffled the former detective was why such an affluent woman lived so modestly. Sally's having no household help or driver on a regular basis was beyond comprehension. Equally puzzling was her seeming lack of interest in the business. He chalked this phenomenon up to Sally's love of her profession taking precedence.

Fishnet saw the opportunity of a lifetime before him. Revising his plan once again, his new focus was to now marry Sally. He had no intention of settling for the short end of the stick.

Now entering his world of fantasy, he did so as Sally's husband. Along with this status came a English valet named Wilson that attended to his everyday needs. Wilson shaved him, drew his bath, and set out his clothing. When Fishnet felt like smoking, Wilson was there to provide the light. When his shoelaces needed tending to, it was Wilson who got on one knee.

The most enjoyable segment of this particular fantasy came during the final reel. The finale always featured Sally Belle in her final moments.

Fishnet's mental photoplay had him bedside as Sally awaited the grim reaper's house call. The breathing of the actress came with a labored rhythm. A haunting dirge could be heard in the background. Sally's rhythmic gasps were prolonged as she struggled to live on Fishnet touched Sally's forehead gently as the ultimate silence was closing in.

"Don't fight it, dear," purred Fishnet. "It's time—it's all a part of living." The ex-detective then began to hum as Sally transferred to a better place.

##########

THE MORE SALLY'S FRIENDS COMMENTED about Fishnet's striking resemblance to Gable, the more leverage he had with the actress. Fishnet came up with a way to highlight just how hot a commodity he was. He'd convince Sally to host another party at the townhouse, only this time, the gathering would be theme-based. The theme would be one designed to showcase his desirability.

"Sally, why don't we throw a *Gone with the Wind* party?"

"Do you mean a costume party, Shepherd?"

Fishnet nodded enthusiastically. "Think of what a hoot it would be—I could go as Rhett Butler, and you could go as the stunningly beautiful Scarlett O'Hara!" The suggestion that Sally pose as the young and vibrant Scarlet O'Hara was too irresistible a temptation to dismiss.

"What a fun idea!" said Sally. "Let's do it!"

Sally spared no expense in preparing for the evening. The period costumes she and Fishnet wore were of a professional caliber. A make-up person was hired to fine-tune their resemblance of Vivian Leigh as Scarlett O'Hara and Gable as Rhett Butler. Sally even called in someone to doctor the interior of the townhouse so it was dressed to replicate Tara.

Fishnet, as Rhett Butler, worked the room with just the right mix of flirtatiousness and charm. The costume party went as the crafty former detective figured it would. By the end of the night, Sally was inundated by friends who voiced lofty accolades regarding Fishnet's magnetic attractiveness. The cunning conniver's desire for physical intimacy was now assured.

##########

ONCE FISHNET AND SALLY BECAME BEDMATES, his quest to lure the actress to the altar began advancing nicely. Then, out of the blue, an unexpected obstacle appeared in the form of an unlikely source. Fishnet never counted on Sally's longtime friend, Estelle Hatton, having the influence she had. The connection between the women was one that ran far deeper than he ever imagined.

Sally and Estelle had been lovers for decades. The two turned to each other for comforting during both the fair and foul periods in their lives.

Due to her affinity for the late Clark Gable, Estelle placed Fishnet on her bucket list. A determined woman, Estelle wasn't one to be shy about going after what she wanted. When she got around to unabashedly making her intentions known to Fishnet, he was appalled.

The two were sitting on the couch drinking wine at Sally's townhouse when Estelle made her first overture. Not wanting to jeopardize the strides he had made with Sally, who was busy doing something on the second floor, Fishnet did his best to discourage Estelle's advances. As she began inching closer to him on the couch, he adjusted his position to further their distance. Fishnet, at this point, remained in the dark as to the relationship of the two women.

"Relax, darling," said Estelle, with a look of amusement on her face. "Sally and I are both *very* fond of you, Shepherd," she advised, placing her hand atop his.

Fishnet pulled his hand away and glanced at the top of the stairs, afraid that Sally might be coming down the steps. Relieved that she wasn't, he nervously gulped his wine.

What a bitch this one is, thought Fishnet before speaking. "Look Estelle, Sally and me are getting along real good," informed Fishnet. "We have something very special going."

Estelle smirked. "You don't need to convince me of that, darling. Only someone special gets to have their photograph displayed on top of the baby grand," she said, pointing to Fishnet's photograph on the piano next to her own. "By the way, you should know that Sally and I share *everything*, including men," she added, batting her eyes. She then once again placed her hand atop his. "*Pascal* understood that," she added, referencing Sally's former live-in lover.

"Pascal? What exactly are you trying to tell me?"

"Oh, come now, Shepherd, are you that naïve?"

Fishnet took great exception to Estelle's suggesting that he was naive. Taking it as an insult, he fought off a great urge to set her straight. Focusing on the red wig Estelle wore on this day, his thoughts became wicked. *I'll show you how naïve I am, I'll rip that friggin' rug off your head and shove it up your ass!*

Fishnet took a deep breath before responding to Estelle. "Easy, Estelle," he said, "you're moving way too fast for me." Fishnet feared that Estelle was liable to upset the applecart that he had put great effort into constructing. "Besides, I thought

Sally was supposed to be your friend."

"She is, darling," replied Estelle. "And by the way, isn't Ms. Garcia supposed to be yours?"

"Wayna and I have always been just friends," he lied.

"Of course, dear, and Sally is *my* very *best* friend . . . and continues to be."

Talk about treacherous—just listen to this bitch, thought Fishnet. "Look, Estelle, this conversation is kind of awkward."

"You don't understand, Shepherd. Sally and I have never limited ourselves. We're *very* agreeable when it comes to these things. You could say that we're exceedingly open-minded."

"Are you saying Sally would approve?"

"Approve?" asked Estelle, bursting forth with laughter loudly. "I'm sorry, but I find that very rich. I didn't mean to laugh."

"What the hell is so funny?" asked Fishnet, who only wished he could send Estelle sailing down a flight of stairs.

"Why of course she'd approve, silly. Actually, I'm surprised that she hasn't already mentioned to you that we three need to get together one evening."

"I think I could use a drink," said Fishnet, finding the conversation hard to take in.

The idea of being sandwiched between the two women wasn't something he relished. As he glanced at Estelle, all he could imagine was odor of liniment as opposed to the fragrance of perfume.

In the time it took to pour a stiff scotch for himself, Fishnet did some quick calculating. If what he was being led to believe was accurate, then Estelle just might have juice enough to sabotage his efforts to marry Sally Belle. Taking a hardy slug of his drink, he accepted that he might have to take one for the team.

"Would you like some more wine, Estelle?" he asked, forcing himself to smile.

############

FISHNET SOON FOUND HIMSELF meeting the needs of both Sally and Estelle. To his surprise, his participation in these bedroom romps actually advanced his progress with Sally, who now saw him as the perfect fit for her lifestyle. When Fishnet finally got around to broaching the idea of marriage, Sally didn't dismiss his offer from the realm of possibilities.

"Perhaps it would be best for you to just move in, Shepherd," suggested Sally, as they returned home from the theater.

"I'll pack tonight," Fishnet replied without hesitation.

His only reservation rested in the belief that if he were successful in wedding Sally, he'd be saddled to Estelle as well. As far as the ex-detective was concerned, such an arrangement translated into his having too many wives.

############

THE ROW GOT UNDERWAY ONCE FISHNET began packing his belongings. At first Wayna Garcia thought her boyfriend was joking when he informed her that he was moving out of their apartment. Seeing his things actually going into a suitcase woke her up to the reality of the situation. Blindsided by Fishnet's sudden decision to leave, Wayna sought answers.

"Why are you doing this?" she demanded to know. "What have I done?"

"You didn't do anything, Wayna. This is something that I just gotta do," answered Fishnet.

"But why are you leaving me?"

"I already told you—it's time for me to move on."

"But where are you going?"

"What difference does it make where I go?"

169

"What difference does it make?" asked the astonished woman. "What about me?"

"I'm sorry, but you just don't fit into my plans at this point."

"I don't fit into your plans!" Wayna screeched. "Don't I *mean* anything to you?"

After letting out a deep sigh, the former detective ceased packing. He turned to face Wayna as he replied to her question. "Sure you do, but I got a shot at marrying Sally Belle. Do you know what that means?" he asked. "It means the opportunity of a lifetime."

"Marry Sally Belle!" replied Wayna, who stood stunned. "You must be crazy," she finally said, unable to comprehend how Fishnet could leave her for such an older woman.

"Don't take it personal, Wayna. She means nothing to me. This is all business," explained Fishnet.

"But she's so old . . ."

"She ain't all that old."

"Oh, please!"

"Look, just face it—I'm moving on."

"Do you really think that's all there is to it?" asked Wayna, who resented being dumped. Her tone was now aggressive.

"Will ya stop with the dramatics already? I'm going, and that's it. Be a big girl and suck it up."

"She's got to be over seventy!" Wayna roared, exposing her temper. "You're NOT leaving *me* for *her*!"

"First off, Sally's only sixty. For seconds—I'm gone!"

"I don't give a damn how old she is!" screamed Wayna, who began looking for something to throw at him.

"Will you relax? It's nothing personal against you. I just got a better deal with Sally. She'll take good care of me until I figure a way to grab it all. Once that happens, maybe I'll ring you up."

"Ring me up? She'll take good care of *you?* What about

somebody taking care of *me*?"

"What do you want me to tell you, Wayna? Our ride has come to an end. We had a good thing going for a while, but it's time to turn the page."

In response, Wayna picked up an ashtray and threw it, just missing Fishnet's head.

"Jesus! Calm the hell down and get real, will ya?"

"I am getting real, you son of a bitch!" she bellowed, reaching to take his clothes out of the suitcase he was packing.

"Back off!" said Fishnet sternly, now prepared to take the gloves off. "I'm traveling first class now, and I ain't sticking around in the steerage section just to hold your hand!" he said nastily, shoving her away from the suitcase.

"Where am I supposed to go? What do I do?"

"You're a CNA, you got a job. I didn't sign anything saying I adopted you, you know."

"Where do I live?"

"Go back and live with your aunt. Or stay here if you want. The rent is cheap. Hey, I'd even be willing to come by to visit you once in a while if you want company."

"You can't get away with this—I'll tell everyone about you!" shouted Wayna, the rage causing her eyes to seem like they were dancing.

Fishnet flashed Wayna a menacing glare meant to intimidate. She reacted with equal aggression.

"I'm not afraid of you," she declared. "Save that look for somebody it'll work on."

Wayna's bold response pushed Fishnet over the edge. He reacted by violently slapping Wayna across the face to silence her. He then removed the licensed revolver he carried on his hip. Fishnet pressed the cool steel barrel of the gun against the wall of her nose. Now terrified, Wayna's eyes bulged. She realized that Fishnet was far more dangerous than she ever previously imagined. At this point there was no denying that the former detective was capable of murder.

"Listen to me, bitch. If you get in the way of my plans, you're gonna find yourself underground," he threatened. "Here's what you're gonna do, you're gonna go back home to Paraguay or Ecuador or wherever the fuck you came from," he ordered.

Convinced Fishnet would carry out his threat, Wayna agreed to return to the land of her birth. After Fishnet gave her some travel money, he watched her pack her things in preparation to leave the apartment. Before she walked out the door, Fishnet made her pen a note to her father advising that she was tired of living in the United States and was coming home immediately. Fishnet then placed the note in an envelope, sealed it and had her address it. His final words to Wayna were a reminder that if she didn't go back home, the next mail her father would receive would be a box containing her head.

Fishnet, who always walked on the dark side to begin with, had drastically changed for the worse after surviving his shooting. After his brush with death, rather than appreciate life as most would, he placed little value on it. His attitude had become one of here today and gone tomorrow. Murder, if one could get away with it, had become an appropriate means to achieve a desired result. The former detective had every intention of carrying out the threat he made against Wayna had she not complied with his demand that she leave the country.

##########

SALLY BELLE SAT AT HER BABY GRAND PIANO, PREPARING FOR what she liked to refer to as a command performance. She loosened her fingers by tickling the ivories while humming.

172

While she warmed up, Fishnet fixed himself a cocktail. With his drink in hand, the former detective took a seat on the couch. To anyone looking, Fishnet couldn't seem more at home.

Since moving into Sally's townhouse, Fishnet had no difficulty assuming the role that Pascal once held. Since he was roughly the same size as Sally's former lover, he inherited the wardrobe Sally had purchased for the ousted Pascal, who departed her home with little more than the clothes on his back. Fishnet was quite at ease attired in Pascal's white shirt, beige slacks, maroon ascot, and blue smoking jacket. The only thing missing in his outfit was the cigarette holder Sally permitted Pascal to take with him when he was hastily removed from the townhouse.

"What are you going to play for me?" asked Fishnet.

"What would you like to hear?"

"Surprise me."

"No, tell me what you want to hear, Shepherd. I select what I play and sing to you all the time," she
said, pointing to Fishnet's photograph atop the piano. "Now *you* tell me—what is your preference?"

"How about you play that song you sang in that big show you did, Sally?"

"Which one do you mean?"

"The waltz, you know the one, that real oldie that I like.

"Oh, you mean this one,'" she said as she began playing. "I sang this when I appeared in *Paper Thin*."

"No, that's not the song. The other old one you sang—the one that never fails to put me to sleep."

"Oh, now I know the one you mean," she said, "here you go." Sally then began playing Leo Friedman's 1909 hit song, *Meet Me Tonight In Dreamland*.

"When you play and sing, I feel as if I'm worlds away, immersed in wonderful thoughts," said Fishnet.

Fishnet wasn't exactly being untruthful. As Sally began warbling the ancient ditty, Fishnet closed his eyes. Soon he drifted off to his imaginary dimension. In the dreamland world he created, his scenarios were always satisfying. The former detective got a great hoot out of hanging Estelle out of an upper-floor window by her ankles. Her squealing caused him to giggle.

"Are you laughing at my singing?" asked Sally.

"What's that you said?" he asked, returning to reality.

"What's so funny?"

"Nothing—I wasn't laughing. I just got emotional. I was touched by how beautifully you sing that song."

"Oh, Shepherd—you can be such a sentimental dear sometimes."

After thirty minutes of entertaining Fishnet musically, Sally needed a break. During this intermission, Fishnet steered the topic of their conversation to Pascal.

"You shouldn't keep neglecting to amend your will, Sally," said Fishnet.

"What do you mean?"

"Do you really want to provide for Pascal, after what he did?"

"Oh, I suppose not. I'll get to it," she replied dismissively.

"Remember what they say, never put off . . ."

"I suppose I will have to get that dreadful ingrate removed from the papers. I promise to get around to it soon."

"You have no obligation to Pascal. He's gone from your life. Remember, to give to the needy *and* worthy is divine," said Fishnet, sticking to the pious Shepherd Fish image he cultivated.

"I know, dear," she acknowledged. "You just keep reminding me of that."

"I've come to live by those words. It's the only way to be. "

Touched by Fishnet's feigned goodness, Sally smiled softly.

"Do you like watches?"

"Sure I do."

"I have a Hamilton watch in the safe that belonged to my father. It's a Glenn Curtiss, and very rare. Would you like to see it?" Fishnet nodded.

When Ms. Belle returned with the gold watch, Fishnet placed it on his wrist. He looked down at the vintage piece with admiration.

"You can wear it whenever you like," she offered. "You know, Pascal was simply mad over this watch. He asked me to give it to him several times."

"Thank you, Sally. I'll cherish this watch forever."

Surprised at Fishnet's assumption that the watch was a gift, Sally paused before responding.

"Well, I suppose if you *really* like it, I'll give it to you—someday perhaps."

"Thank you—I love it!" Fishnet stepped in close and pulled her toward him affectionately. "And now we have other business to attend to."

"Aren't you the naughty one . . ." came her response.

18

A Guest Of The West

WHILE ELLA AWAITED WORD in Philadelphia from Grady O'Lang concerning his progress on the Professor, she kept herself busy by going shopping. Wanting to please her police paramour, she went out looking for something she thought O'Lang might like. She settled on a charcoal sport jacket and a black silk shirt for her lover.

After the passing of another day, Ella began to anticipate Grady's return. Wanting to look her best for him, she had a manicure and pedicure and got her hair done. By the following evening, after still not hearing from Grady, she began to grow concerned. Ella responded to her distress by calling the Philadelphia cop's cell phone every thirty minutes. When her messages went unanswered, she didn't know what to think.

Something must have gone wrong in New York, she thought.

There is no other explanation for his not calling me.

With only the worst of scenarios circulating in her mind, Ella worked herself up into a state of near panic. She coped by doing things she believed would help calm her down. When chain-smoking cigarettes no longer eased her condition, she turned to alcohol, a vice proven to be destructive to her wellbeing.

Finding limited comfort with moderate alcohol intake, Ella increased her consumption. The physical cost connected with her excessive drinking became evident within days. Looking into the bathroom mirror, Ella instantly regretted what she was doing to herself. Her face was bloated, and the bags under her eyes were pronounced. The once-fine lines on her brow were now noticeably deeper. Ella had become unsteady of hand, which hampered her attempts to conceal these unflattering imperfections with a heavy application of makeup. Her efforts at improvement backfired, only creating a grotesque appearance similar to the Baby Jane Hudson character, as portrayed by Bette Davis, in the movie *Whatever Happened to Baby Jane*?

Giving up, Ella continued to drown her troubles in drink. There were periods in which she either passed out or dozed off in a chair. During one of these sleeping sessions, the ringing of her telephone awakened her. In her excitement to get to where she left her cell phone, she tripped over a foot stool. Rising uninjured, she managed to make it to the phone in time.

"Hello?" Ella asked in a decidedly hoarse voice. She was disappointed after realizing that the person on the other end of the phone was that of her husband, the Professor.

"Ella?" asked the Professor.

"Oh, it's you," she answered, making no effort to conceal her disappointment. "What do you want?" Her slurring voice alerted the Professor that she wasn't right.

"Are you okay?" he asked. "Have you been drinking?"

"You woke me up," she curtly answered.

It was an odd situation for Ella. Remembering well Grady's instructions, Ella fought hard to suppress her urge to call out the Professor on his bigamous behavior. At the same time, her husband held his tongue concerning Ella's relationship with the man he murdered on the train platform.

"I have some bad news for you, Ella," said the Professor.

Wanting to hear what the Professor had to say, Ella began striking the side of her head with the heel of her hand to shake off the cobwebs.

"What's the bad news?" she asked, fearing it had something to do with Grady. Ella raised her chin as she steeled herself in preparation for what was coming.

"I won't be coming home at all this week. I have some businesses to attend to out of town that'll take about a week."

Ella let out a deep breath of relief. She then snickered, not caring about her husband's absences. After taking a second deep breath, she inquired as to the type of business the Professor was involved in.

"I'm thinking of opening up another bookshop."

"You're opening another bookshop....where?"

"Arizona."

"Arizona?"

"Don't worry—little will change. My shops don't need me there every day."

Worrying about the Professor was the last thing on Ella's mind. "Send me a postcard," she said sarcastically.

"Don't be like that—"

"I gotta go. I'm not feeling too great right now."

Ella hung up the phone rudely. She didn't want to engage a husband she had no affection for. Since he didn't mention it,

Ella assumed that the Professor was unaware that he had been under Grady's surveillance. She took this as a good sign.

On the Professor's side of the equation, he never mentioned he was aware of her suspected dalliances with Grady O'Lang. How could he after having killed the Philadelphia cop?

Still consumed with thoughts of Grady, Ella decided to go his studio apartment on the outside chance that he'd be there. Before preparing herself to go out, she decided on having a hefty drink as a bracer. It proved to be one too many. Before collapsing on the sofa, her last words were, "The hell with the two of them!" She was referring to the Professor and Grady.

##########

SINCE THERE WAS NO APPARENT POLICE blowback in New York City, the Professor felt reassured. Without the police displaying an interest, the bookshop owner felt confident he was home free concerning the murder he committed. This peace of mind made for an enjoyable evening with his first wife Rebecca in Brooklyn Heights.

Their son was out with his friends, leaving the couple to themselves. They chatted pleasantly as they sat in front of the television watching the evening news.

"Don't you want a piece of the apple pie I made?" Rebecca asked. "It's your favorite."

"If you went to the trouble of making it, then certainly I want it," her husband replied cheerily. "Let me get it."

"Stay put. I'll get it," volunteered Rebecca, aiming to please the man she genuinely missed.

After Rebecca cut the pie, she put a piece on a plate with a fork and handed it to the Professor. To Rebecca, catering to her husband wasn't considered obligatory—it was something she wanted to do for the man she adored.

As a teenager, Rebecca's initial attraction to the much-older Professor stemmed in part from her belief that he needed someone to take care of him. He was quite convincing in his claim to the young girl that he had a health issue. He concocted this fabrication to explain away his dependency on the medication he took. Because of Rebecca's tender age at the time, stepping into a care giving role was welcomed because it made her feel grown up. Her thirst for adulthood at the time was an exploitable desire that the Professor capitalized on.

"This is the best apple pie you've ever made," declared the Professor enthusiastically.

It was simple recognitions such as this that the Professor used as a weapon of manipulation. Since he realized that Rebecca thrived on receiving his approval, gestures of gratitude were used to control her. Often the Professor would express his thanks with thoughtful gifts. Such considerations fed the engine that propelled her extreme permissiveness. Without such latitude, the Professor would never have been able to pursue his bigamous ways.

"Absolutely delicious," praised the Professor, after finishing his pie. "Do you want to go for a walk before we turn in?"

"No, I'll clear the table and do the dishes," replied Rebecca.

"Alright, I'll help you."

Shortly after they cleaned up, Rebecca announced that she was preparing for bed, stepping into their bedroom.

"I'll be right in," said the Professor, anxious to be with her.

There was a distinct scent of perfume in the air when the Professor entered their bedroom. The sweet-smelling fragrance was meant to convey Rebecca's desire for intimacy.

"I forgot to tell you about Sally Belle, dear," said Rebecca afterward, as they sat up in bed to read.

"What about her?"

"She broke up with her boyfriend Pascal."

"No kidding? What happened?" asked the Professor, surprised at hearing this.

"Apparently he stole money and jewelry from her," explained Rebecca. "She ended up throwing him out of her house."

The Professor found the news surprising. "How did you find out about all this?"

"She told me. I happened to call her to belatedly thank her for inviting me to her party, and then after
a while, she let it out."

"She's still an attractive lady. She'll have no problem finding a replacement."

"You must be psychic. You should have heard her gushing about her new man!"

"She found someone already?"

"Yes, apparently she's been spending a lot of time with that ex-detective she invited to the party," Rebecca said.

"Who is he again?"

"The former cop, Shepherd Fish—I told you about him. You remember, I wrote the check to his organization."

"Oh, that's right, now I remember. If Sally's smart, she'll tread lightly with that guy."

"Why do you say that?"

"There are lots of men and women out there looking to hitch their wagon to a good thing," advised the Professor.

"You mean like I did?" Rebecca joked.

"No, you did me the favor."

"Mr. Fish didn't seem that type to me, and I can usually tell."

The Professor snickered at his wife's statement. "Ah, what the hell difference does it make anyway?"

"What do you mean what difference does it make?" asked

Rebecca, surprised at her husband's comment.

"At her stage of the game, if he can make her happy, that's all that matters."

"Well I think it's despicable if he isn't being sincere with her."

The Professor shrugged. He had no counterargument to offer. "I suppose so," he stated, now ready to change the subject. "You know, I'm gonna miss you while I'm gone."

"I'll miss you too, dear. Do you think your business will take the full week?"

"Probably, but then again, you never know how things with the other side can go."

###########

THE PROFESSOR'S INTENDED THIRD WIFE had little difficulty starting anew in Arizona. As a strong woman, Concetta was inclined to think positively. As a healthy, unattached lady able to live comfortably thanks to her late husband's insurance policy, she saw herself as someone with a bright future.

Although Concetta remained loyal throughout their marriage, many of her interests ran contrary to those of her late husband. Conditioned at an early age to seek security, the man she married offered the peace of mind that came with earning a decent living. But that was yesterday. Today, her thoughts were on living in the west, owning a gun, and greeting people with a robust, 'Howdy, partner!'"

The move to Arizona was a giant leap toward attaining the lifestyle she always yearned for. At an early age, Concetta developed a fondness for cowboys. Her infatuation began after reading Riders Of The Purple Sage by Zane Grey. From that point on, her dreams consisted of riding, roping, and shooting. While her friends were enamored with Elvis and the Beatles, she took a shine to cowboy actors John Wayne and James Arness. For Concetta, it was all about rodeos, ranches, and bucking broncos. She always maintained that if she had the power to change anything, she'd have lived life as the famed sharpshooter Annie Oakley.

Concetta rose early the day the Professor was expected to arrive. She looked at herself in the mirror with approval of the newly purchased western-style outfit she had on. The long-sleeve plaid shirt she wore went well with her wrangler style jeans and brown boots. Deciding against donning a Stetson indoors, she left the white hat conspicuously resting atop the six-hook cherry wood rack that was located by the front door. A visitor couldn't help but notice it. The widow smiled happily as she gazed at the Winchester that hung over the fireplace. She was satisfied with the stage she set.

##########

THE PROFESSOR RENTED A CAR at the airport when he arrived in Arizona. On his drive to Concetta's house, he was surprised to see a road sign advising people not to shoot from their vehicles. *This really is the wild west,* he thought.

When he arrived at the front door of his latest love interest, the Professor was greeted with a warm welcome. He found Concetta's open arms as an indication of better things to come.

"Howdy, partner," she said enthusiastically. The gleam in her eye oozed of such happiness that he could tell that she really was glad to see him.

"Howdy," he replied, with equal energy. "Look at you—you look absolutely wonderful!"

The widow smiled graciously as she accepted the compliment that she happened to agree with.

Concetta took the Professor's hand and led him into the house. After first noting the Stetson, he spotted the Winchester that hung over the fireplace. He seized the opportunity these talking points presented.

"When you're out plugging varmints with that rifle, do you wear the brim of that Stetson up or down?" he asked jokingly.

"Usually I don't look to shoot 'em. I prefer to rope 'em and then hog-tie 'em, partner!" she replied, playing along.

After catching up a bit over refreshments, the Professor excused himself to go to his car. When he returned, he was carrying a gift-wrapped package.

"What have you got there?" Concetta asked.

"I brought you something I thought you might find interesting," he said. "Here, this is for you."

She took the package and immediately opened it. The unwrapping revealed a book about the old west.

"Oh, this is so sweet of you!" Concetta said, smiling broadly.

"I thought you would find it interesting. You mentioned to me that you like to read about the west."

"I do," she said, leaning toward him to kiss his cheek. "Well, I just so happen to have a gift for you too."

"What's that?

"I'm cooking dinner for us this evening."

"You don't have to do that. Let me take you out to eat."

"We can do that tomorrow."

Aside from the obvious physical attraction, the Professor actually enjoyed conversing with someone in line with his own generation. Their synergy became more apparent over the course of the time they spent together. They discussed political, economic, and social issues without stepping into the pitfall of having contrary perspectives.

Yet even with all the chemistry between the Professor and Concetta, his efforts to share her bedroom was inexplicably met with rejection. Although Concetta had already given herself to the Professor on prior occasions, she didn't want to create the impression that she was easily his for the taking.

The Professor was relegated to spending the night alone in the guest room. He let it go, figuring Concetta had her reasons.

Undaunted by his disappointment, the following morning the Professor continued to enjoy the company of his Arizona love interest. They spent the morning hours after breakfast venturing out in quest of an acceptable venue for the Professor's third bookshop. There came a point when they stopped for a cold beverage at a local bar.

Over their beers, the Professor asked Concetta if she ever considered remarrying.

"Maybe someday," she replied wistfully. "My husband hasn't been gone all that long. Why do you ask?"

"Just curious," he answered.

"Take it from me, marriage is the solution when you lose a spouse. I remarried after my wife passed, and I can attest to it," injected a man who sat not far from them. "How long have you been widowed?" he asked.

Concetta smiled politely before answering. "Almost a year now," she replied.

"And you're not dressed in black?" asked the stranger in a shocked way.

Concetta didn't know if she should take the man seriously. "You honestly think I should be wearing black?" she asked.

"No, of course not, he was just joking," said the Professor, who called for the bill. After paying the bar bill, he and Concetta moved on.

"Do you know what that guy was?" asked the Professor once

outside.

"Let me guess—a turlet head?" she answered, using a term she often heard him use.

"Very good!" he replied with a chuckle.

The Professor pursued Concetta ardently throughout the rest of the day and into the evening. When he wasn't violating her personal space, he was sweet talking her. That night the Arizona widow invited the Professor to spend the night with her in the master bedroom. The time they spent together left her dreaming of a wonderful future with the new man in her life. She had no inkling she was slated to be number three in the bigamist's collection of wives.

19

The Trail Leads To Philadelphia

WITH HIS EYE ON A SUSPECT in the homicide of Grady O'Lang, Markie had Von Hess conduct an in depth background investigation on Henry Harrison Blount. From their office in police headquarters, Von Hess began by delving into the suspect's business interests. His research identified the Professor as the owner of two bookshops, one operating in New York City and the other in Philadelphia.

Lacking a date of birth for Blount, Von Hess ran his name through the New York State Department of Motor Vehicles. This resulted in his amassing a list of people with the suspect's identical name that possessed a driver's license. Working his way down the roster of names, Von Hess identified all registered vehicles, past and present, linked to each name on the list. In doing this the detective discovered a vehicle that was linked to the Professor's Manhattan business address. This connection provided Von Hess with a date of birth for the suspect. Subsequent research resulted in Von Hess concluding that the Professor was consistent in the use of his name and date of birth.

Armed with this information, the detective conducted a criminal history check on Blount which revealed the Professor's arrest that occurred many years prior.

"How are we making out?" asked Markie, looking for an update as to the progress made.

"I got him positively identified, Sarge," advised Von Hess.

"Did you come up with anything good?"

"Yeah, I think so. He took a felony pinch years ago for reckless endangerment."

"Did you get the details?"

"I was just about to pull the old arrest report, Sarge."

"Okay, after you do that, go downstairs to the photo unit and get his arrest photo," instructed Markie."

After Von Hess completed these tasks, the investigators regrouped in Markie's office.

"This is definitely our boy, Sarge," advised Von Hess, handing Markie the arrest photo of the Professor.

Markie examined the photo. "Jeeze—he's just a kid in this picture. What was the charge again?"

"He was booked for reckless endangerment."

"What's the story with the pinch?"

"Apparently he got a hair up his ass during a beef with his old man. He ended up tossing the family
television out of a high-rise apartment window."

"Ohh . . . then he's gotta be some kind of a nut case," commented Markie. "Only a guy with a screw loose would do a crazy thing like that."

"Yeah, he must be a bedbug," concurred Von Hess.

"Did anybody get hurt?"

"No—he got lucky in that respect."

"He probably forgot to take his friggin' medication that day," assumed Markie. "What else?"

"He drives a new BMW and apparently lives in Brooklyn Heights with Rebecca Merced Blount. They own the place."

"That's it?"

"No, he also owned a place in Philly. According to the property records there, he owned that house with a woman named Ella Cornell Blount. He later sold it to this Ella for peanuts."

Markie was curious about the Philadelphia property transfer. "Why would he transfer ownership of a property? What do you make of that, Ollie?" he asked.

"It could be some kind of settlement, Sarge."

"All this shit is starting to make some kind of sense to me, Ollie," said the sergeant. "Do you remember what the witness on the subway platform said? You know, about the Professor being unfaithful."

"Yeah," replied Von Hess, "She said that the homicide victim called the Professor a two-timer."

"That's right. I'm just wondering about the relationships regarding these women."

"Are we Philly-bound, Sarge?"

"We're definitely going to Philly. But before we go, I want to take a ride over the bridge. Let's hit the post office and then take a look at the suspect's home address in Brooklyn Heights.

Markie and Von Hess proceeded to the post office covering the Professor's residence in Brooklyn Heights. Their purpose was to interview the letter carrier who delivered the mail to the suspect's residence.

The investigators met up with the carrier while she was on her route. As a result of their interview, the investigators verified that Henry Blount and his wife Rebecca both received mail at the Brooklyn Heights address. The letter carrier conveyed that the family seemed to be a very nice one, mentioning that the couple had a boy living with them. The letter carrier had no recollection of seeing any mail coming to the home from anyone named Ella Blount. She also didn't recall delivering mail from Philadelphia.

"Let's check the courts in Philadelphia before we head out, Ollie. Maybe we can come up with something that ties the victim to these people."

"Righto, Sarge."

"Once that's done, we'll saddle up and do some poking around in Philly."

###########

WHEN VON HESS CAME UP DRY IN his Philadelphia criminal, civil, and bankruptcy court research, the investigators set out for the City of Brotherly Love. Their first stop was to consult with the Philadelphia Police Department to see if they had any information on Henry Harrison Blount, aka Professor Extraordinarious. They were told nothing they weren't already aware of.

When the investigators inquired about Grady O'Lang, they were informed that the murdered cop possessed a clean record with the Philadelphia Police Department. At their request, they were put in contact with several of Grady O'Lang's work peers. Through them they learned of Grady's prowess with a cue stick. They further established that the deceased cop was a degenerate gambler prone to borrowing money from coworkers. However, no connection was established linking the dead cop to the Professor or Ella Blount.

"Where to now, Sarge?" asked Von Hess once they regrouped.

"Let's go take a look at the bookshop."

Around lunchtime, Markie and Von Hess arrived at the Philly bookshop. Peering through the window of the closed business, the investigators could see that the interior of the shop was a replica of the Professor's Manhattan location.

"I guess the Professor likes to keep things uniform, Ollie," noted Markie. "This joint looks just like the one in Manhattan."

"I don't see how this guy manages to jump like a frog between here and New York all the time," commented Von Hess.

"Never mind that—with all his money, you gotta wonder why he would work at all."

"Maybe he does it to get out of the house."

"I don't get it," said Markie with a sigh. "There has to be more to it than that. I'm getting kind of hungry—how about you?"

"I could eat," answered Von Hess.

"Let's go sit down in that Italian place over there."

The investigators were soon seated at a square table in Diamond Joe's Italian Garden. While the red-and-black checkered cloth table coverings seemed basic, the rest of the restaurant was above par. The detailed woodworking along the walls was elegant. The tables were a comfortable distance apart, and the bar, although small, was fully stocked. A waitress in her early forties soon came by to take their order. Although attractive, it was the black beauty mark on her chin that made her stand out as memorable.

"I'm Marie," she said, introducing herself. "Can I start you gentlemen off with a cocktail?"

"Let me have a Coke, please," said Von Hess.

"You don't want a little wine with your meal?" asked Markie.

"Nah, soda is fine with me."

"Let's have a drink . . ." insisted the sergeant.

"Would you like to hear the specials?" the waitress asked after taking their drink order.

"What do you recommend?" asked Markie as he looked over the menu.

"That depends—how hungry are you?" replied the waitress.

"We could eat."

"Then I recommend the rigatoni with our Sunday gravy. It comes with pork, sausage, and a huge meatball."

"What do say to that, Ollie?"

"It sounds good to me."

"Can I start you off with a salad?" asked the waitress.

"Yeah, oil and vinegar," advised Markie.

"Oil and vinegar," echoed Von Hess.

Midway through their meal the owner of the restaurant stopped by their table. As was his custom with unfamiliar faces dining at his restaurant, Diamond Joe Ormento introduced himself. Ormento engaged in the customary chitchat that occurs between a business owner and new customers."

"You're gonna like my meatballs. They're the best around, you can ask anybody."

"I'm sure they are," said Von Hess. "This is a nice place you have here."

"Thanks," said Joe, "enjoy your meal." He then walked off, only to return to their table when they were midway through their meal. He inquired as to how their food was.

"Your food is great," complemented Markie, "especially the meatballs."

Diamond Joe smiled and nodded approvingly. "Marie's treating you good?"

"She's great," replied Markie. "Can I ask you something?"

"Go ahead and ask."

"Who owns the bookshop across the street?"

"*Il Professore.*"

"That's right, the Professor. Do you know him?'

"I know him good. He's not around all the time though."

"Do a lot of cops go to the bookshop?" questioned Von Hess.

"What do you mean?" asked the restaurant owner, who suddenly grew leery after mention of the word cops. "Why are you asking me?"

Markie identified himself to the restaurant owner as a New York City detective sergeant on business. He then fabricated a reason as to why he was being so inquisitive. The cover story the sergeant invented was that they were working on a New York City hit-and-run case. Markie claimed that someone took the Professor's license plate down at the scene, adding that they were hoping the Professor witnessed the incident.

"He ran somebody over?"

"No, no, no, he didn't run anybody over," emphasized the sergeant. "He was just there on the scene."

"Who told you he saw something?" asked Diamond Joe.

"We don't know who—the information came in as an anonymous tip."

"I'm sure he didn't see a thing. His eyes ain't so good," said the restaurant owner, looking to protect the Professor.

"Is that so?" asked Markie, now viewing Diamond Joe in a different light.

"Sure. He's not gonna be open for business today."

"How do you know that?"

"Because I ain't seen his car parked on the street. If you want, I can call his wife Ella. She used to work for me over here."

Markie was taken aback by the unexpected revelation. "What did you say his wife's name was?" asked the sergeant.

"Ella."

"Not Rebecca?"

"Where did you get Rebecca from?" asked he proprietor. "His wife is Ella, not Rebecca. I should know, she used to work for me over here."

"My mistake," said Markie. "Do you have a number for Ella?"

"*Aspetta*," said the restaurant owner, telling Markie to wait. "I'll call her for you."

"No, you don't have to do that—just give me the number. We'll call her up later."

"Whatever you say," said Diamond Joe, shrugging his shoulders.

"Thank you, and let me tell you again, these meatballs are really great. Aren't they, Ollie?"

"They're the best I've ever had," replied Von Hess on cue.

"That's what everybody tells me," said the restaurant owner.

After the authorities left the restaurant, Diamond Joe reached out to Ella to give her a heads-up that the New York authorities might be reaching out to her.

"What do the cops want with me?" asked the hung-over Ella.

"It's no big deal," replied Diamond Joe, passing on the information he was told by Markie.

##########

MARKIE TELEPHONED HIS OFFICE OVER at headquarters. He instructed the detective who answered the phone, Detective Silverlake, to check the Professor for a New York marriage record. Silverlake, who worked directly for the chief of detectives, wasn't happy to be put to work. His job was basically to answer the phones and do the chief's bidding.

An hour later the sergeant received a call from Silverlake verifying that the Professor had been legally married to his first wife Rebecca for years. Markie then had Silverlake conduct the same check in Philadelphia regarding Ella. Silverlake later reported back that he found no evidence of a Philadelphia marriage.

At this point Silverlake was asked to look into other areas of the country. Aware that Las Vegas was a notorious venue for matrimony, Silverlake began his research there. After ascertaining that the Professor married Ella in Las Vegas, he reported back to Markie. The authorities were now sure they were dealing with a bigamist.

##########

STILL ADHERING TO GRADY O'LANG'S INSTRUCTIONS, Ella tried to remain patient while waiting to hear from him. Frazzled after being alerted that the New York police were sniffing around Philadelphia, she found remaining idle challenging. Since Grady still wasn't returning her calls, she became more reliant on alcohol as a way to cope.

Ella was on a rollercoaster that took her in and out of the various stages of drunkenness. During her more sober periods, she contemplated calling the Philadelphia Police Department to find out whether Grady went back to work. She never acted on this impulse, knowing her lover would be furious if he ever found out she had been checking up on him.

Ella wasn't in the best of form when her phone began ringing. Before answering the call she happened to look out her front window. The two men in suits standing in front of her house looked like cops to her. One of the men was on his cell phone. When Ella didn't answer her ringing phone, she saw the man outside put his phone in his pocket and walk toward her front door.

Joe must have given them my number, Ella correctly assumed. *Why would he do that?"*

"It seems like no one is home, Sarge," voiced Von Hess, after ringing the bell. His voice carried far enough to be heard by Ella in her house.

Sarge? Thought Ella, now certain the men were cops.

"I guess we'll have to wait," said Markie. "C'mon, let's sit in the car and get comfortable."

As the investigators walked to their vehicle, they heard a voice coming at their rear. It was Ella, who finally came to the door.

"Who are you looking for?" she shouted from her doorway. Her voice was raspy, her appearance not the best.

"Are you Ella Blount?" asked Von Hess.

"Who are you?"

"I'm Detective Von Hess," said the detective, flashing his badge. "This is Sergeant Markie. We're from the New York City Police Department. Are you Ella Blount, ma'am?"

Ella pulled both sides of the housecoat she was wearing tightly together and tied the belt. She nodded at the detectives and began running her fingers through her hair in an effort to appear more presentable.

"She's looks half in the bag," whispered Markie as they returned to the front door.

"Can we come in and talk to you for a minute, ma'am?" asked Von Hess politely.

"What's this all about?" asked Ella, who was beginning to feel discomfort in her stomach.

"It's about your husband, Henry," advised Markie, cutting to the chase. "We have some information that you may be interested in knowing."

"He's out of town. What about him?"

"Can we come in?"

Like a cat whose curiosity had been stimulated, Ella's interest had to be satiated. "Okay, come on in."

"Thanks." Once inside, the detectives took seats in the living room.

"You want a drink?" asked Ella.

"No, thank you," replied Von Hess.

"We'll I could use a pick-me-up," she said.

The detectives couldn't help but take notice of Ella's poor condition. Her scratchy voice, the ashtrays filled with cigarette butts, and the bottles of scotch scattered about spoke volumes.

"You're legally married to Henry Harrison Blount, correct?" asked Von Hess.

"Yeah, that's right. Why?"

"Do you have proof of that?"

"Of course I got proof. What do you think I am?"

"Just his wife, that's all, ma'am."

"You want to see the marriage certificate?" she asked.

"If you don't mind, we would like to see it."

"Why should I mind? It's all legal," she added. "But what's all this about? He ain't dead, is he?"

"We'll be glad to explain once you produce the proof, ma'am. We just need to be sure."

Ella went to a drawer and removed a tin box containing papers, one of which reflected documentation of her Las Vegas marriage to the Professor.

"Here, look for yourself," she said, handing the certificate of marriage to Von Hess.

"Very good. Thank you," said the detective.

After reviewing the documentation, Von Hess nodded to the sergeant, indicating all was in order.

"Who has seniority?" asked Markie.

"Based on this dated document, Brooklyn came first, Sarge."

"So are you two going to tell me what this all about?" asked Ella, finding their conversation confusing.

"I'm sorry to inform you that your husband is a bigamist, ma'am," informed Markie.

"So tell me something I don't know," said Ella with a smirk. "I heard all about the bastard's wife in New York."

The detectives were surprised to hear this. "You knew? How long have you been aware of this?"

"I've known long enough."

"How did you find out?" asked Von Hess.

"I have my ways," she replied, taking a sip of her drink.

"How about you just tell us how you came to find out?"

"He was followed. How do you think I found out?"

"You followed him?"

The second Mrs. Blount hesitated before responding. "Yes, I did," she answered, rubbing her forehead in an effort to clear her head.

"What made you do that?" injected Markie.

"I had my reasons," she replied, again being evasive. "Besides, that's my business."

"Ms. Blount, I find it hard to believe that *you* followed your husband," said Markie. "Did you hire somebody to follow him?"

"*No,* I didn't hire anyone to follow my husband," she replied snippily. "Now are you through?"

"Why don't you just tell us who did the following?" asked Von Hess calmly.

Ella let out a sigh of frustration before replying. "I need another drink," she said. After fortifying herself, she turned to the detectives. "What was that last question?"

"Who followed your husband?"

"A friend of mine did," she replied, forgetting to continue with her earlier resistance.

"A friend named Grady O'Lang?" asked Markie point blank.

Ella looked as if she had been struck by a thunderbolt fired by Thor himself. Now befuddled, her inability to think clearly left her at a loss for words.

"Was it Grady who tailed your husband?" pressed the sergeant.

Still confused, Ella swallowed hard without answering. Finally, she replied. "Will you just leave me alone and get out of here?"

"I will as soon as you answer my question. Was it Grady who followed your husband?" insisted Markie. His firmness made it clear he wasn't going away until he got an answer.

"Alright, already! Grady found out for me."

"Was Grady more than just a friend?" questioned Von Hess.

"What business is that of yours?" asked Ella. After several passing seconds, the detective's use of the word *was* registered with Ella. "Now wait a minute, where is Grady? Did something happen to him?"

"We aren't here to judge you, Ms. Blount. All we want to do is arrive at the truth," said the detective. "Please, just be upfront with us. What exactly was your relationship with Grady?"

Ella cleared her throat, but she remained mute. She shook her head to indicate she had no intention of discussing her relationship with the Philadelphia cop. After a pause, she returned to her own line of questioning.

"Where is Grady? Are you going to tell me or not?"

"It's not pleasant for me to tell you this, Ms. Blount, but you'll have to find out sooner or later," stated Markie. "Grady O'Lang was murdered on a Manhattan subway platform."

Ella was ill prepared for the devastating news she received. She reacted by collapsing into a living room chair. When the sobbing ceased, she looked to fix herself another libation.

Once Ella's grief was under control, the questioning resumed. Now in a weakened state, she admitted that Grady was her lover. She unfurled the entire scheme that led to the surveillance of her husband.

"So you and Grady planned to shake your husband down," summarized Von Hess.

"That's not true! I just wanted to settle up with him . . . but first I needed to know how much he was worth. Once I found that out, I'd know how much we could ask for."

"Who is your attorney?"

"Well, we hadn't reached that point yet."

"So you were totally unaware that Grady intended to extort money from your husband?"

"Is that what he was doing?" asked Ella, who possessed no knowledge of O'Lang's independent plan of extortion.

"It seems that way. Did your husband have suspicions about you and Grady?"

"Of course not," she said dismissively.

"Where did Grady live?" asked Von Hess.

"Not too far from here."

"Do you have access to his apartment?" asked Markie.

"I have the key to his apartment."

"Would you mind taking a ride over there with us?" asked the sergeant. "You should probably turn in the key to the police."

"I suppose so," agreed Ella, exhaling deeply. She didn't care one way or the other at this point.

Markie contacted the Philadelphia authorities before entering Grady's apartment. The only item of interest found in the apartment was the vanishing ace card trick.

"Did *you* give Grady this card trick, Ms. Blount?" asked Markie.

"No, he must have gotten it from my husband. He was a nut for card tricks." Markie seized the cards for future evidence.

"Did my husband kill Grady?" asked Ella.

"It may be a good idea to secure legal representation, Mrs. Blount," advised Von Hess without answering the question. You may have to fight for your due in court."

"Did he kill Grady?" she repeated.

"We're still investigating," replied Markie.

"I'll have to call *someone*." Ella stated in a melancholy way to no one in particular. "Am I in some kind of trouble?"

"No ma'am."

##########

ON THE DRIVE BACK TO NEW YORK, Markie had Von Hess pull off to the side of the road. "Take a look at this, Ollie," he said, "I want to show you something."

Once the car stopped, Markie pulled out the four aces trick he took from the dead man's apartment.

"I think we may have something here, Ollie. See these four aces," said the sergeant, showing the face of the cards to Von Hess. "Watch how I make an ace vanish." Markie then performed the card trick that culminated with two of his fingers tapping down on the vanishing ace as he said, "Going, going, gone!"

"That one would only fool the kids," commented Von Hess.

"This was the same trick I saw the Professor show that lady in the bookshop that day."

"You mean the one who was moving to Arizona?"

"Yeah, that's the one."

"What next, Sarge?"

"Let's go back to New York," instructed Markie. "I want to voucher these cards. After that, we need to go talk to an ADA."

201

20

Big Plans

THE PROFESSOR FOUND THE AREA SURROUNDING an Arizona museum to be a worthwhile site for a third bookshop. He felt that a used book offering geared to complement what was on display at the museum would likely draw the interest of those visiting the cultural establishment.

"What do you think of my opening a bookshop near the museum, Connie?"

"Oh, I don't know too much about that," Concetta replied, not having much of an interest in such things. "If you're optimistic that it could work, it probably would," she added, wanting to show some support of the Professor's judgment.

"Maybe I'll have to put some more thought into this," he advised, finding her response not very encouraging. "So tell me, what goes on in Tombstone?"

"A lot goes on there!" she replied enthusiastically. "They say that it's supposed to be a wonderful tourist attraction. They even put on live shows there."

"I always wanted to visit Tombstone."

"So have I! Tombstone used to be Apache territory."

"No Pawnees?"

"No, no Pawnees," answered Concetta, who was surprised at his question.

"What about Comanche? The Lord of the Plains was considered the most dangerous Indian tribe."

"How do you know so much about such things?"

"I watch all the Gunsmoke reruns on television," answered the Professor honestly. "What do you say to our taking a ride over to Tombstone?"

"Yes, lets—I've always wanted to visit Boot Hill!"

The Professor laughed at her enthusiasm over visiting a graveyard. "Alright then, let's head over there."

Concetta's face lit up. Her broad smile and squinting eyes further expressed her delight. Within the hour they were off to be entertained by people pretending to be gunslingers and prospectors as they enacted the old west for the tourist crowd.

After taking in Tombstone both agreed that it was indeed a fun place. "What should we do now, Connie?"

The widow stepped closer to the Professor, causing him to slightly stiffen. "Maybe we should stay the night," she provocatively suggested. "Do you think you would like that?"

The Professor didn't have to be asked twice. That night, after having satiated his needs, he sat up in bed thinking about importing a mail order wife from other another country.

The following morning, after again witnessing the reenactment of the shootout at the OK Corral, they were off to a movie studio and theme park in Old Tucson. As they traveled in the car, they listened to western tunes on the radio. When Concetta began singing along, the Professor came to realize how fine a voice she had. It was a talent he had been previously unaware of. As the transplanted New Yorker warbled, the Professor was thinking of how good a fit Concetta was going to be as his third wife. Once they were settled into a home and routine, he intended to focus on identifying husband-seekers from foreign shores.

##########

ONCE MADE AWARE THAT GRADY O'LANG was dead, Ella knew she needed to maintain long-term sobriety. To accomplish this end, she needed support. Ella decided to seek the assistance of Diamond Joe Ormento, the one person she considered to be a true friend. It was reassuring for her to know that he'd listen without resorting to admonishment or casting judgment.

When Ella telephoned Ormento at his restaurant, she was hoping the restaurant owner's wife wouldn't pick up the phone. Fortunately, it was Diamond Joe who answered the call.

"Diamond Joe's Italian Garden, what's your pleasure?"

"Joe, it's me," said Ella, sounding desperate.

"Who?" Ormento asked, not recognizing the croaky voice.

"It's Ella."

"Ella, what's wrong?" he asked. "What are you sick?"

"I got problems, Joe. I really need your help."

"What happened? Those detectives busted your husband?"

"No, Joe, I just need somebody strong like you with me now. Could you come over?"

Diamond Joe looked around the restaurant for signs of his wife before answering. Not seeing her, he replied. "Sure, I'll be over in a little while. You're home, right?"

"Yeah, I'm home, Joe."

"Sit tight."

"Where are you going?" asked Ms. Ormento as she saw her

husband preparing to leave the restaurant.

"I have to go see somebody," he relied vaguely.

"Like who?"

"Never mind who," he snapped, walking toward the door. "My business is my business."

"Is that so?" she asked, her defiance evident. Ormento reacted to her question by just shaking his head. The gesture sufficiently conveyed his feelings.

When Ormento arrived at Ella's house, he was shocked at her poor appearance. "What did you do to yourself?" he asked, upon seeing her. "You look terrible!"

"I know I do, Joe. I'm a wreck."

"You gotta eat something, Ella. Sit down and I'll fix something for you," he said, heading for the kitchen.

"No Joe, I'll eat later."

"No, first you eat. While you eat, we'll talk."

Diamond Joe got right to work and prepared a breakfast consisting of a cheese omelet, two prunes, toast, and a piece of pound cake. He poured Ella orange juice and put on a pot of coffee. When all was on the kitchen table, he took a seat opposite her at the table. They spoke as Ella ate.

"So what's wrong?" asked Ormento.

"I need you to help me stop drinking, Joe."

"I thought you quit already. What happened?

Ella confided to Joe the entire situation involving her affair with the Philadelphia cop. She was also forthright as to her unhappiness with the Professor.

The restaurant owner remained detached as he listened to her narrative. However questionable the details of her conduct, they didn't seem to faze Diamond Joe. What did make an impression on him was the Professor being a bigamist.

"*Che Palle!*" remarked Diamond Joe in a low voice.

"What?"

"I said what a balls he's got!" replied Joe, in an almost admiring way.

"Oh," commented Ella, attributing his reaction to his being a typical male.

"Your husband's got a lot of money, right?"

"Yeah, he does, but I didn't know how much. That was the problem."

"You don't know what he's got?"

"Now I do, he's worth about a hundred-million."

"Get the hell out of here..." blurted Joe.

"Grady found out and told me."

"So what do you wanna do?"

"Let me finish the story, Joe—the New York cops told me that Grady was murdered on a subway platform."

"Murdered!" declared Joe with emphasis. "What happened?"

"He was stabbed."

"And they think your husband killed him?"

"The New York cops aren't saying that for sure, but I know that bastard must have done it. He always carries a knife."

"That's no-good if he did kill the cop," said Diamond Joe, who shook his head as he began to mull things over.

"What should I do, Joe?" asked Ella, looking at him through hopeful eyes.

"You gotta get your hands on the money, that what you gotta do."

"How?"

"Don't worry. Diamond Joe's gonna fix everything."

The confidence behind Ormento's words made Ella feel a little better. "What are you gonna do?"

"First, I'm gonna dry you out. You have to go on the wagon."

"But what do I do about poor Grady?"

"Don't give that guy another thought. He's gone, so he doesn't count no more. *Capisce?*"

"I understand," she replied softly. Ella knew that the words expressed by Ormento while hurtful, were practical.

"Right now we have to think about this son of a bitch you married."

"The cops . . ."

"Eh, the cops—now I know why they came here to Philadelphia. They think your husband killed your boyfriend . . . and maybe he did."

"So what do I do?"

"How do you feel about your husband now? Does he deserve any consideration?"

"I hate him, Joe."

"That's good. The primary thing is the money. I'm gonna call my friend Sammy."

"Who is Sammy?"

"He's a smart lawyer. He'll fix everything, that's for sure."

"You're calling him now?"

"Yeah, then I'll go see him." Ormento telephoned the lawyer at his office.

"Hello, Joe," greeted Samson Bello as he reached for a cigar from the mahogany cigar box that sat on his desk. "What can I do for you?"

"I got a question, Sammy. If a rich man is married to two women at the same time, who is it that gets the money when there's a divorce?"

"That could be complicated, Joe. Let me ask you something, how much money are we talking about?"

"The husband's got a hundred million." Sammy's eyes widened at hearing the amount of money involved.

"Is your friend the first wife?" asked the attorney.

"She's the second wife."

"Too bad, it's the first legally married wife that's in the best position."

"Is there anything we can do?"

"Sure there is. Why don't you come by the office, we got things to talk about."

"Okay, I'll be over."

"And Joe, find out when the husband is around."

"What did he say Joe?" asked Ella, after Joe got off the phone.

"He said that son of a bitch husband of yours is gonna pay," lied Diamond Joe.

"But Joe, I haven't enough money of my own to pay any lawyer."

"What are you worrying about money for? You'll pay me back when you collect."

"Thanks Joe, I owe you for doing all this. I'll never forget it."

"Ahh, come on, eat some more food. You still look terrible."

"You'll stick by me until I pull myself together?"

"You bet I'm gonna stick. Oh, before I forget, you gotta find out when your husband is gonna be around."

##########

WHILE ELLA, DIAMOND JOE, AND SAMSON BELLO were conspiring about how to get their hands on his fortune, the clearheaded Professor was enjoying himself in Arizona.

Unaware of the plotting taking place in Philadelphia, the Professor saw no reason not to extend his stay in Arizona and push forward his plans to marry a third time. The Professor decided to notify his two wives that he would be away longer than expected. He telephoned them in order of their importance to him.

"Hello, Rebecca, it's me. I'm afraid it looks like I'll be away longer than anticipated."

"How long are you going to be?" asked his disappointed first wife.

"I'll be here maybe another week or so. I think I found a location for the new bookshop. I'm gonna need to hang around to look at a couple of more places before I decide."

"Where in Arizona are you?"

"I'm looking at a small storefront not far from a museum," he answered, not pinpointing his location.

"That sounds wonderful—but aren't you neglecting your other shops?"

"I got it covered. Any calls to the shop(s) are forwarded to my cell phone."

"I miss you, Henry."

"I miss you too. How's the boy?"

"He misses his father, but other than that, he's doing okay. I told him you'd take him to the wrestling matches, so that made him happy."

"Good thinking. Let me go now—I'll call you tomorrow. Love you."

The Professor's next call was to his second wife, Ella. Their conversation ran similarly.

"So when exactly are you coming home?" asked Ella.

"In about a week," answered the Professor.

"What day?"

"I'm not sure yet."

"Well, make sure you call me as soon as you know."

"Why?"

"I have a surprise for you," replied Ella, thinking fast. "You know . . . what you wanted."

Her ploy worked in generating an excitement in the Professor.

When he hung up, he was so anxious to return east that he came close to rearranging his schedule.

The Professor never really felt any great love for Ella. What he did feel, and continued to feel, was great lust. Ella's physical allure was so compelling that her involvement with Grady O'Lang was diminished to the status of a forgivable transgression. All that mattered to the Professor was to maintain his relationship with Ella in Philadelphia. If need be, the Professor was willing to purchase a vacation condo for her in Florida. He believed this would go far in influencing his second wife to stay put.

Once his notifications were made, the Professor resumed devoting his attention to Concetta. By now he had become an experienced hand at reeling in women by fulfilling their dreams. In the case of Concetta, the path he needed to follow was simple. A couple of horses and a small ranch would net him all she had to offer.

Things began to heat up nicely as the Professor and Concetta sat outside under the Arizona sky after having dinner.

"A penny for your thoughts," Concetta said as she watched the Professor gaze upward at the sky.

"I was just thinking of how beautiful it is out here."

"It really is, isn't it?"

"I think so."

"Could you ever see yourself moving out here?"

"I could . . . if I knew I had someone to come home to."

All that remained for Concetta to do after a week of hugs, giggles, and boudoir fireworks was to figure out where they were going to have their rootin-tootin', high-falootin' Arizona wedding. Concetta began her planning immediately after the Professor began his journey to New York.

21

Tell-Tale *Turlet*

THE POLICE COMMISSIONER INVITED Chief of Detectives Harry McCoy to have dinner with him at Sparky's Pub in Gramercy Park. The two men, friends since their police academy days, regularly got together when their schedules permitted. Upon their arrival at the restaurant, they were graciously welcomed by the owner, Sparky Farrow. Farrow, a great supporter of law enforcement, took great pride in knowing the two police department heavyweights.

After finishing their meal, Commissioner Randolph felt like smoking a cigar. For special customers, Farrow granted access to the tiny rear yard of the restaurant. Two circular wooden tables and eight chairs were there to accommodate the privileged few.

"We're going to the backyard," announced the police commissioner to their waiter. "We'll take our coffee and dessert out there."

"I'm afraid you can't go back there this evening."

"I can't?" asked the police commissioner, taken aback at being denied access. "Are both tables taken back there?"

"No," said the waiter, who was uneasy in admitting that there was an open table in the yard.

"Hey Sparky," called out Randolph, signaling the owner to join him at his table. "I can't go in the yard to smoke a cigar?" he asked, sounding surprised.

The owner, smiling nervously, hesitated before answering. "No, of course you can go outside, Commissioner."

"C'mon, Harry, the yard awaits us," announced Randolph, rising from his seat.

In the yard, seated at the occupied table, were three men having pre-dinner drinks. The commissioner, whose eyes met with the men, could tell by the unpleasant look on their faces that they felt intruded upon. Since the threesome appeared to be the polished, affluent sort, Randolph prepared himself for a showdown of egos.

The commissioner, an aggressive man when it came to such situations, drew first blood by removing a large cigar from his suit jacket. Oblivious to the dirty looks he was receiving, he fired up his cigar. He then began purposely blowing smoke in the direction of the other table, assuming it would likely disturb those seated there. Seeing he was getting a rise from those he was antagonizing, he doubled down.

Randolph took out a second cigar and handing it to Chief McCoy. "Go on and light up, Harry," encouraged the commissioner, intentionally speaking loud enough to be heard by those at the other table.

Repulsed by the cigar smoke, the occupants of the opposing table rose in unison from their seats and left the yard, opting to dine indoors.

"What do you make of that?" asked Chief McCoy.

"They don't like cigar smoke," replied the commissioner, who was now blowing his smoke skyward.

"It's unbelievable how some people are, John. The bastards would have no problem if we smoked a joint back here."

"Screw 'em, Harry," said the commissioner curtly. "There's no plus to having the biggest dick if you don't show it once in awhile. You gotta let people know who leads the band."

After lighting up his cigar, Chief McCoy began taking short, hard drags. The smoke McCoy released was not done in the relaxed fashion of the commissioner—McCoy seemed to be spitting the smoke from his mouth, as though angry. McCoy, insecure over never having graduated college, saw the men who departed the yard as pompous elitists who would never accept him as an equal.

Police Commissioner Randolph, on the other hand, was the polar opposite of his dinner companion. An overachiever, Randolph was astute when it came to things like the value of his power. He understood that the loftier one was in the societal pecking order, the more meaningful it became for them to remain in his good graces. As the town's top cop, those in the highest net-worth bracket had to come to him to get their way on certain matters. Whether it was their need of a carry permit for a gun, the enforcement of a law, or the closing of a street, Commissioner Randolph was the man with the authority to make it happen. His was a position that commanded respect. Had he chosen to, Randolph could have probably sat at the same table with the men opposed to cigar smoke, held them captive in conversation, and smoked all the cigars he wanted.

"I'm planning some promotions around Christmas up and down the ranks, Harry. Is there anybody you want to take care of?" asked the commissioner. "I got some special assignment money to hand out."

"What slots are open?"

"I can give you lieutenant's money for two sergeants, captain's money for a lieutenant, and up four people to second-grade detective."

"Is there any first-grade money?"

"No, not this time around. I'm also appointing about a dozen cops to third-grade detective. All the other promotions are coming off the civil service test list."

"Let me talk to my division captains, John. I'll ask them if there is anyone worthy. Do you need the names right away?"

"No, we have plenty of time."

"How about we do Sparky a solid? I think he has a relative that's a detective."

"Good idea, go ask him."

Chief McCoy left the table to seek out the owner of the restaurant. Their subsequent conversation went far in smoothing out any ruffled feathers created over the yard skirmish. McCoy returned to Commissioner Randolph quite pleased with himself.

"Sparky's got a detective nephew up in Riverdale," advised McCoy. "He's a third grader with five years in grade. Sparky flipped when I told him a contract is in to promote the kid to a second grader."

"What's the nephew's name?"

"Gerard Farrow."

"Sparky better remember this when it comes time to pay the bill," said Randolph.

"Don't worry, John. You know Sparky's good like that.

"On another note, what's happening with the Philadelphia cop homicide?"

"That's looking real good," answered the chief. "According to Lieutenant Wright, Markie has his arms around this one tight.

An arrest should be coming down sooner rather than later."

"So what was it all about?"

"It had to do with extortion."

"The Philly cop was getting extorted?"

"No, it was the other way around."

"Oh, beautiful," said Randolph. "The police commissioner in Philly is gonna love hearing this."

########

MARKIE AND VON HESS MET WITH Assistant District Attorney Zoe Taylor Wiggins at her Manhattan office. Having worked well with Wiggins on a past case, a comfort level existed that made it easy to seek her guidance. The investigators explained to the prosecutor the particulars of the Grady O'Lang homicide.

"You've got a case here," advised Wiggins. "What do you need from me?"

"Legal advice on how we intend to proceed," replied Markie. ""Suppose we secure a tape-recorded telephonic conversation between the suspect and a detective," began the sergeant, "then I transcribe that tape recording word for word and have the same detective make five identical recordings using five other men, giving us a total of six identical conversations."

"Go on," answered the prosecutor.

"If our witness, after listening to the six tapes, makes an ID, is that the same as a line up with a witness who could make a visual identification?"

The ADA pondered the question before answering. "I want to say that it probably is."

"So it's enough of an identification to make an arrest, then?" asked Markie, looking for a clarification.

"Let me say this. The evidence would be stronger if your

witness made the identification after hearing a *live* voice, as opposed to a telephonic one."

"Got it," said Markie.

"Had the witness initially heard the perp's voice telephonically, then it would have been a different story, perhaps. But since that wasn't the case, a tape-recorded identification might appear weak in court," explained the prosecutor.

"What if we did it both ways?" asked Von Hess.

"That would certainly work," replied the ADA.

"Then that's what we'll do," declared Markie. We also got an eye witness, the victim's husband. He was present at the time of the crime. Once we nail down the voice ID, we'll pick up the suspect and put him in a regular line up."

"Sounds like a solid game plan."

"Thanks Zoe," said Markie, rising from his chair to leave the office.

"Good luck. I look forward to our victory drink after the trial."

"Let's just hope this perp doesn't look to take a piece of you in court like Everett Skidmore," injected Von Hess, referring to the deranged serial killer in the Case of the Cross-Eyed Strangler.

After they left the DA's office, the detectives returned to police headquarters. When they arrived, they were called to a meeting with their boss, Lieutenant Wright.

"The police commissioner was asking the chief questions about the Philadelphia cop homicide," informed Wright. "What's happening with it?"

Markie apprised the lieutenant that he and Von Hess had conferred with an assistant district. He then conveyed his strategy.

"So, the prosecutor is on board?"

"They're with us one hundred percent, Loo."

"What happens if your witness is unable to make the voice identification?"

"I guess we'll just have to figure out another way."

"What time frame are we looking at?"

"I don't see this case going on very much longer. Barring any unforeseen circumstances, I'm figuring a week or two, tops."

Wright nodded. "Don't forget to keep the squad detective who caught the case in the loop," he instructed. "There's no sense in alienating anyone."

"No problem, Loo. We've been posting Detective Teddy Hart all along. He's good with us running with the ball."

"Chief McCoy wants you to involve Silverlake in this," directed Wright. "The old man feels it'll do him good to get out from behind that desk and do a little police work."

"You got it. You know, there is something I'd like to bring to the chief's attention."

"What is it?"

"Detective Boucher."

"Who is that?"

"She's the detective who originally caught the case—the one the chief flopped to Brooklyn North."

"Oh, her," said Wright, remembering the detective. "She's lucky she didn't end up back in uniform like her squad commander. What about her?"

"She was a big help in furthering this case, Loo—*after* she got bounced to Brooklyn."

"She was?"

"Yeah, she was."

The lieutenant looked suspiciously at Markie. "What's your interest in her?"

"I got no personal interest, Loo. I'm just saying . . ."

"I'm not bothering the chief with that bullshit, Al. Don't

217

worry, she'll live and get used to Brooklyn."

##########

DETECTIVE VON HESS RETURNED TO THE OFFICE after establishing that The Professor's Used Bookshop was open for business. After going over the notes he prepared, the detective attached a recording device to a special phone that prevented caller identification.

"Ready to go, Sarge," advised Von Hess, once the stage was set.

"Okay, Ollie, let's get this show on the road. Go get Silverlake."

Detective Silverlake, who had been recruited to place the telephone call into The Professor's Used Bookshop, was less than enthusiastic.

"I don't know why the chief wants me involved in this," complained Silverlake. "Doesn't he realize that I might end up having to testify in court? Who is gonna pick up the phone around here and run his errands?"

"You better go ask the chief that question," advised Von Hess.

"Ahhh, what's the use of crying about it? What do you want me to say to this guy, Ollie?" asked Silverlake.

"First thing is to make sure that you got Professor Extraordinarious on the line," advised Von Hess. "Once you do that, just engage him in conversation. It doesn't have to be all that lengthy."

"What am I supposed to talk to him about?"

"Here, I got it all written out for you," said Von Hess, passing Silverlake a sheet of paper containing the talking points. "You start off asking him if he buys comic books. Tell him you got old Mad Magazines, Superman comics, that kind of thing."

"What if he says he has no interest?"

"What he says makes no difference. I want you to try and get into an argument with the guy."

"What kind of argument?"

"Anything that'll piss him off will do. We're looking to capture him angry on tape."

"Okay, Ollie, I get it," said Silverlake. "When do you want me to do this?"

Von Hess looked at Markie for an answer to the question.

"Showtime," announced the sergeant.

Von Hess rose from his seat to shut the door to their office. He gave Silverlake the number to the bookshop and passed him a legal pad containing the words he was to use in heading the tape recording.

"First thing you do is head the tape," advised Von Hess, turning on the recording device.

Reading off the legal pad, Silverlake headed the tape. The detective dictated his name, rank, and shield number. He then dictated the time, date, telephone number he was about to call, and who he was calling. Detective Von Hess then shut off the recorder. He took a second to label the tape, "Detective Silverlake-Henry Harrison Blount Conversation."

"Okay, you're on, Silvie," said Von Hess. "Remember, you're shooting to get into a beef with the guy."

"No problem, but before we start, I got just one question."

"What is it?"

"Taping this call is within the guidelines, right?" asked Silverlake, who was rusty when it came to legalities.

"Perfectly legal," replied Markie. "New York is a one-party state. As long as one party to the conversation consents to the taping, everything is good."

Once Silverlake nodded in the affirmative, Von Hess activated the recording device.

"The Professor's Used Bookshop," announced the male voice that answered the ringing phone.

"Let me speak to Professor Extraordinarious?" said Detective Silverlake, reading off his script.

"You're speaking to him. How can I be of service to you?"

"You're Professor Extraordinarious?"

"That's right, I'm the Professor. What can I do for you?"

"You don't sound much like a professor," said Silverlake, straying from the script. Winking, he exchanged smiles with Von Hess.

"Yeah, well . . . what do you need?" asked the Professor, trying not to express annoyance.

"I've got a bunch of Superman comics from the 1950s that I'm looking to unload. Is that something you'd be interested in?"

"Maybe," informed the Professor, not appearing too anxious.

"What do you mean?" asked the detective, raising his voice. "You're a used bookshop, right?"

"I'd be willing to take a look at your collection. Let's make an appointment."

"I have to make an appointment to see you? Are you kidding me, or what? What are you, a dentist?"

"No, I'm not a dentist. Do you want to meet or not?"

"I'll come by on Saturday—"

"We won't be open on Saturday."

"Aw, what kind of a shit joint are you running over there?" asked Silverlake, egging the Professor on.

"Hey, do you want to do business or not?"

"No, I'm calling you because I'm lonely," said Silverlake, further provoking the Professor.

The Professor's patience reached the limit. "I'll tell you what, why don't you take Superman and stick him where the sun don't shine!" shouted the Professor into the phone. "Take your business someplace else."

"What? How about I just come over there and put my foot up your ass?"

"Why don't you do just that? I'm here all day, *TURLET HEAD*!" screamed the Professor, abruptly slamming down the phone.

After the investigators listened to the tape recording Detective Silverlake turned to Von Hess to see how he did. "Is that what you wanted?" he asked, proud of himself.

"You did outstanding," praised Von Hess, patting Silverlake on the back. "I'll transcribe the tape and prepare a script. You're gonna have that exact phone conversation with five other detectives. We'll tape record each one of them.

"You mean I gotta do this five more times?" asked Silverlake.

"Yeah. Ain't life a bitch?" said Von Hess.

"I'm not used to heavy lifting, Ollie. My primary responsibility is the cocktail run for the chief."

"You can go back to your desk. We'll call you when we're ready, Silvie," advised Markie. "Nice job."

"You gonna let the old man know how I came through for you, Sarge?"

"You bet. You hit a home run on this," advised Markie.

"We really did, Sarge. It couldn't have gone better. We even captured the word *turlet* on tape," pointed out Von Hess.

"Let's get the other taped conversations made up," instructed Markie, "and hope Mary Beth can make a telephonic identification."

22

Riding The Rapids

FISHNET'S MARRIAGE TO SALLY BELLE marked what he considered to be among his greatest triumphs. It mattered little to him that every decision pertaining to the wedding had rested totally with Sally. All he cared about was making their union official so that he'd be sitting at the doorstep of a fortune.

Fishnet smiled broadly as he accepted the congratulations of those select few who received an invitation to the wedding. The affair was held at the Lambs, the first theatrical club in America. Fishnet always enjoyed going to the Lambs ever since Sally first took him to a cocktail party there and introduced him to a few celebrities.

Among those sharing in the wedding joviality was Sally's legal representative, Marvin Butterworth. Butterworth, an elderly man with a suspicious nature, had gone directly from high school to law school, which was possible at one time.

For years the attorney enjoyed a mutually beneficial relationship with Sally's accountant, who was tasked with paying all bills. Since neither professional interfered in the business of the other, when it came to receiving payment for their services, each was promptly compensated without question. Their submission of inflated invoices and acts of double billing were not uncommon practices.

Butterworth had been skeptical regarding Fishnet's motives from the onset. To no avail, he did all that was within his power to persuade Sally not to marry the ex-detective. Feeling threatened at the time, Fishnet promptly went on the offensive.

Whenever Butterworth was within earshot, Fishnet began asking Sally if she ever had an audit conducted concerning her financial affairs. He made it a point to amplify the many instances of grand larceny that he investigated when serving as a detective. This proved to be a wake-up call for Marvin Butterworth, who soon reversed his position and began embracing Fishnet as a welcomed addition to the fold. With an understanding reached, Butterworth represented another smiling face at the wedding celebration.

##########

IT DIDN'T TAKE LONG FOR THE NEWLY MARRIED COUPLE to reveal themselves for who they really were. Once a marital routine was established, it became clear to Fishnet that Sally Belle was going to be more difficult to handle than he'd initially imagined. Once Sally began to make demands on him, Fishnet reacted by tuning her out and entering into his fantasy world. Not accustomed to being disregarded, Sally addressed his lack of attention. Interrupting Fishnet's fantasies only compounded the tension.

Whenever her husband reacted testily to her intrusions, Sally was fast to remind him of his place in their marriage. Well attuned to the attractive lifestyle she was affording Fishnet, Sally felt little need for humility in ruling the roost.

During these rough patches, Sally couldn't help but reflect on how much more suitable her former lover had been. Unlike Fishnet, Pascal was perfectly content assuming a secondary station in their relationship. Even with Estelle, who Sally loved dearly, when it came down to it there was no question as to who held the power.

From Fishnet's side of the equation, he entered into the marriage considering Sally nothing more than a bridge to take him to the riches he thirsted for. She was a means to an end, no more, no less. Fishnet's failure to recognize Sally's formidability was his error. It was something that should have been vividly clear to him by the ease she displayed in banishing Pascal from her life.

Exasperating the situation for Fishnet was Sally's friend/agent Estelle Hatton, who took to acting like Fishnet's second wife. Fishnet reached the breaking point when Estelle began asking him to run errands.

If these two think I'm gonna let them walk around in my pants, thought Fishnet, *they're in for a rude awakening!*

The straw that finally broke the camel's back came when Sally asked her husband and not Estelle to leave the room during a discussion she was about to have with her attorney. Being excluded from the meeting with Butterworth irked Fishnet to no end. He stewed as he realized just how entitled Estelle seemed to be.

I'm gonna find a way to torch that wig....with her head in it! Fishnet thought, as he stared angrily at Estelle. In this very moment, Sally's offended husband decided he needed to devise a strategy that would correct his misery. Fishnet devoted himself to conjuring up a homicidal scheme that would set him free—and place him in control of Sally's wealth.

Until a plan was finalized and executed, Sally's husband was determined to tough it out and go along with things as they were. One reoccurring unpleasantness he endured involved his being called into service to help entertain Estelle Hatton.

"But she just stayed over with us last week," complained Fishnet to his wife.

"That's something we don't keep track of in this house," pointed out Sally. "Estelle is always a welcomed guest."

"But she snores like she's sawing wood—"

"That's quite enough, Shepherd."

"Alright, forget about it. I'll sleep with ear plugs."

"I hardly find that remark amusing," said Sally, annoyed that her husband was being disrespectful of Estelle. "Have you plans for tomorrow?" she asked, switching subjects.

"I'm not sure yet."

"I've noticed that you've been neglecting your calling. When was the last time you've helped those unfortunate people you promised to help?"

Fishnet let out a deep breath before recklessly lashing out. "I've been too busy making friggin' beauty parlor appointments for you and Estelle!" barked Fishnet, forgetting himself.

"How dare you speak to me in that tone!" Sally said sharply, in a way that was rarely publicly aired. The cutting edge to her voice was warning enough for Fishnet to back off.

"I'm sorry, Sally," he answered, aware that he pressed the envelope. "I'm just feeling a little overwhelmed."

"If things have become too tedious, perhaps we need to take on an assistant, dear."

"No, that's alright. I can handle things," he said, not wanting to crowd the field with people who might stand in the way of his unsavory plans.

"Oh, by the way, Estelle thought it would be great fun if you dressed up as a fireman when she comes over. You still have time to pick up a costume at Bakerfeld's."

"Are you joking, Sally?"

"No, dear, I'm quite serious. She wants you to pretend to be saving us from a burning building. We'll be passed out from the smoke, of course, and you'll be able to have your way with us. We're both fascinated by role playing, you know."

"Do I need to wear the hat in bed?" Fishnet asked, as if an employee assigned a task by his boss.

"That would add a nice touch."

When Fishnet went to pick up the uniform, the counterman at Bakerfeld's asked him if he needed an axe to go along with the outfit. Fishnet declined the offer. He didn't trust himself.

########

BEFORE FISHNET COULD ACTUALLY ENACT ANY MURDEROUS PLAN, he needed to first induce Sally to include him in her will. In order to accomplish this, he knew that he had to commit himself to doing everything in his power to make Sally happy, and that included being good to Estelle.

Once Fishnet began toeing the line to become her ideal husband, Sally saw fit to amend her will. The adjusted document called for ten percent of her fortune to be distributed among several charities. The remainder was to be split between her husband and Estelle.

"That's a lot of money to leave to those other charities, Sally," commented Fishnet.

"But why would you think that, dear?" asked Sally. "Half of that ten percent is going to your charity."

Fishnet just shrugged and answered, "I'm just saying. Anyway, the arrangements are more than generous, Sally. I'm sure Estelle's happy."

Marvin Butterworth made no effort to discourage his client from leaving everything to her charities, her husband and Estelle. What he had no way of knowing was that by Sally's signing off on her will, she was also signing her own death warrant.

The following morning Fishnet ramped up his efforts to devise a way to become a widower. As he thought things through, his mind drifted to his other world of pure fantasy. He saw Sally atop a horse in a remote area. Her hands were tied behind her back, and a noose hung from a nearby tree. Fishnet snugly affixed the noose around Sally's neck. Then, stepping back, Fishnet removed a cigar from his pocket. After lighting up, he took a long drag before casually drawing his revolver to fire a bullet in the air to spook the horse. Fishnet nodded approvingly as Sally kicked furiously as she dangled from the rope that held her off the ground.

##########

WHEN FISHNET MENTIONED TO HIS WIFE THAT he was going to make an appointment to have his teeth cleaned, Sally insisted that he use her Manhattan-based dentist. Sally's claim that her dentist was the finest in all of New York was hardly impressive to Fishnet. To Sally, everyone she engaged was the best at their craft.

"Does he take insurance?" he asked.

"Insurance?" asked Sally.

"Yeah, I have a dental plan with the police department."

"Oh, well, don't worry about that. My dentist always sends the bill to my accountant. He'll take care of it. Just let the dentist's office know we're married when you make your appointment."

Fishnet, doing as he was told, could hardly contain his outrage when the receptionist addressed him as Mr. Belle. After Fishnet had his mouth X-rayed and teeth cleaned, the dentist was summoned to examine him. The doctor was a man of about fifty who seemed to be, in Fishnet's estimation, someone who was pretty sure of himself.

"I see you had a root canal years ago," said the dentist.

"Yeah, I did, many years ago."

"Who did this work?"

"Dr. Steinborn. He's over in Brooklyn."

"You were lucky. He did a very good job."

Steinborn is still in business and charges half of what you get, thought Fishnet as the doctor examined his mouth. *What the hell am I doing here with you?*

"How is Ms. Belle doing?" asked the dentist as he worked. With his mouth open, all Fishnet could do was grunt. "I wasn't aware that she got married. Congratulations," said the dentist as he poked around in Fishnet's mouth. "You have one tooth in need of repair. I can take care of it now if you like."

"Go ahead and fix it," said the patient once the instruments were removed from his mouth. *Why not,* he thought, *the wife is footing the bill.*

As the dentist worked, Fishnet passed the time envisioning ways to do away with Sally. He was mindful that regardless of how clever he orchestrated the demise of his wife, he'd still likely be suspected of foul play due to the inheritance.

It'll have to be a double tragedy," thought Fishnet. *I'll take out both Sally and Estelle at the same time—that'll throw the law off for sure. They'll see no motive for me clipping the two of them.*

Fishnet put together a homicidal plan while still in the

dentist's chair. His mind drifted off, picturing himself with Sally and Estelle, chatting happily on their drive to the Lehigh Valley in Pennsylvania. He lured them there with the thrills of whitewater rafting. The rocky rapids would be the culprit recruited to snuff the life out of them. Sally and Estelle sat in the car, all smiles, as they traveled to their doom.

"You two are going to love it," said the soon-to-be assassin

"Do you really think we should give this a whirl?" Sally asked Estelle.

"Certainly, Sally. It'll be loads of fun," replied Estelle.

"You don't think it'll be too rough, do you Shepherd? I don't swim, you know."

"Don't you worry about a thing, Sally. I'll be right there with you. Think about it—after today, you two girls get to brag how you rode the rapids!" he enthused. "Next time we'll invite the Maestro!" he joked.

When they arrived at their destination, everyone donned a wetsuit. Once near the water Fishnet jockeyed to be the last raft in the pack of whitewater rafters. He looked around to make sure the rescuers in their kayaks were far off. As they approached a huge rock, Fishnet grabbed both Estelle, also a non-swimmer, and his wife. The trio toppled over the side of the raft and into the rapids. He guided the women to two large boulders where they held on for dear life . . .

"I'll be just a minute longer," announced the dentist, snapping Fishnet out of his fantasy.

When Fishnet returned to the present, he soon dismissed the whitewater death scene as being too complicated. The time of year, the weather, life jackets, and too many other variables posed problems. He'd have to come up with something easier.

Fishnet turned his thoughts to what he'd do *after* he killed the women. *Maybe I'll plant them somewhere near that Barrymore guy or, better yet, Clark Gable!*" he thought, giving himself a chuckle.

"All finished," said the dentist. "Give your wife my best."

"Will do," answered Fishnet, rising from the dental chair.

On his way home from the dentist Fishnet confirmed his belief that the whitewater scenario wouldn't work. He identified additional flaws in that method of execution. It made no sense to run the risk that the rapids presented. The power of the water might pull the women away from him before he got to kill them. Then there was the chance of their screams drawing attention or their putting up a good physical resistance.

"The hell with the whitewater," he said aloud. Disappointed, Fishnet returned to the drawing board, thinking of alternative ways to commit murder.

23

Cocktail Time

THIS WAS THE FIRST TIME DETECTIVE TEDDY HART responded to a job t the 23rd Street subway station since the homicide of Grady O'Lang. When he arrived he observed a group of people clustered around a police officer at one end of the platform. Making his way through the crowd toward the officer, he noticed that there was an unconscious person the floor.

"What have you got?" asked the detective.

"A train hit him," replied the officer, pointing to the body.

Detective Hart stooped down to get a closer look at the man in need of medical attention. Hart noticed that the contour of the injured man's shaved head was not unlike that of a light bulb. The detective found it odd that there was no blood, considering the depression at the back of the man's skull.

"How the hell do you get whacked in the back of the head by a train?" questioned Hart, who was looking up at the officer for an answer. The officer shrugged without replying.

Detective Hart put his face close to the face of the man on the floor. The whiff of air he inhaled made it clear that the injured man had been drinking, confirming his suspicion of intoxication.

Based on the statements of those who saw the incident, Hart gathered that the man with the dented head was definitely struck by an oncoming train. Due to conflicting accounts as to exactly how it happened, the detective concluded that the man either staggered into the train, or, while looking down the track in the wrong direction, was struck from the rear as the train pulled in.

The emergency medical technicians who arrived on the scene were uncertain as to the injured man's chances of survival. Before they removed him to a hospital, Hart recorded identification information obtained from the man's wallet. The detective then returned to his office where he proceeded to notify a family member as to what had occurred.

Feeling hungry, Detective Hart stepped outside to a nearby deli to pick up a tuna salad sandwich and soda. He was seated at his desk having his lunch when the phone rang. He wiped his mouth clean before answering the call.

"Detective Hart speaking, how may I help you?"

"It's Ollie Von Hess."

"Hey, Ollie, what can I do you out of?"

"Are you busy?" asked Von Hess.

"Not overwhelmingly. What's up?"

"We're going to see that witness in the Philly cop homicide."

"You're talking about the blind woman?"

"Yeah, we want to do that voice identification we spoke of. Are you available to come along?"

"Uhhh, I suppose I am, answered Hart. "I just caught an accident case where the guy may be going out of the picture, but there is nothing to do until he snaps out of it or dies."

Markie stood near Von Hess as he conversed with Hart. "Is he gonna come along, or what?" the sergeant asked impatiently.

"We're all set, Sarge. Teddy's in."

"Tell him to bring along the homicide folder."

"Teddy, the sergeant wants you to bring along the homicide folder."

"No problem," acknowledged Hart.

"Do you need a ride?"

"I'm good. I can pick you guys up if you want."

##########

MARY BETH CARBONE WAS in a good mood. She was at her station at Wozenkroll Trucking when she heard the footsteps of her boss nearing her. Mr. Wozenkroll tended to slightly drag his right foot when walking. This made recognition a dead giveaway for someone like Mary Beth, who was highly attuned to such things.

"Are they here already, Mr. Wozenkroll?" she asked cheerily, before the business owner could identify himself.

"Not yet. I just wanted to tell you that you can use my office when the detectives arrive," said Wozenkroll, who could never figure out exactly how his employee always knew when he was approaching.

"Thank you. That's very thoughtful of you."

"No problem. When they arrive, I'll circle back to let you know."

"Can I ask you something, Mr. Wozenkroll?"

"What is it?"

"My parents think I shouldn't get involved in a murder investigation. As you know, they're terrible worriers. I'm curious to know your thoughts."

Wozenkroll raised the palms of his hands upward as he

replied. "As a good citizen, I think it's your civic duty to cooperate with the police. As a parent, if you were my daughter, I'd have to go along with your folks."

"You know something, Mr. Wozenkroll, you're a lot like my father. Me, I'm the opposite. I'm going to cooperate to the fullest."

"I'm not surprised," replied Wozenkroll with a laugh. "You're in the same bracket as my daughter, Sheila. She doesn't listen either. You both have a mind of your own."

########

DETECTIVE HART PARKED HIS CAR outside of police headquarters. He sat patiently waiting for Markie and Von Hess to leave their office. To pass time he began thumbing through the Grady O'Lang crime scene photos. He paused after reaching the full body shot of the stabbing victim lying in a horizontal position on the floor of the subway platform.

"What a waste," uttered Hart sadly, shaking his head over the Philly cop's tragic end. He returned the photos to the homicide folder when he saw Markie and Von Hess approaching.

"I'll get in the back seat, Ollie," said Markie after reaching the vehicle.

"Hey, Teddy, how's it going?" asked Von Hess, after getting in the front seat.

"Good, Ollie. How are you, Sarge?"

"Good," replied Markie. "Do you know where we're going?"

"Yeah, you want to go to Wozenkroll Trucking."

"Did you bring along the homicide folder?"

"Yeah, I was just looking at the crime scene photos. What a shitty way for a cop to wind up."

"He was no cop," replied Markie coldly. "He was just another

234

crook who managed to worm his way on the job," he added bitterly. The sergeant's remark was met with silence. "It looks like you're gonna crack this one, Teddy," Markie said after a long pause, breaking the lull in conversation he created. "Since this is your pinch, I figured it would be best for you to witness the identification. It'll keep things simpler in court."

"That makes sense, Sarge,"

When the detectives arrived at their destination, they were directed to the office of the owner. Mr. Wozenkroll, in anticipation of their appearance, had taken a few minutes to neaten his office.

"I'm Wozenkroll," said the owner to introduce himself.

"Hello, sir," said Markie. "I'm Sergeant Al Markie."

"We've been expecting you. You men can conduct your business in the privacy of this office."

Wozenkroll's office was a large room that contained a desk, a cushioned chair, and a weathered burgundy leather couch. The cuts in the leather proved that the couch had been in service for years. A round table and four chairs occupied part of the room.

"Make yourself comfortable," said Wozenkroll. The investigators took their places at the table. "Before I get Mary Beth, I have a question for you men."

"Of course," answered the sergeant, "what is it?"

"Is Ms. Carbone facing any danger as a result of her involvement in your investigation?"

"They'll be no danger to the witness," replied Markie confidently.

"Are you sure?"

"I'm sure."

"If there *is* any indication of danger, I'd like to be notified. I'd want to put security precautions in place here."

Wozenkroll seemed like a decent man to Markie, the type who

worried about his employees. "Don't sweat it, Mr. Wozenkroll. You'll be the first to know if we suspect a problem."

"This isn't some sort of organized crime thing," injected Von Hess. "Don't be concerned about anyone coming around."

"Thank you," replied the business owner. "That makes me feel better. You know, I have an obligation to my other employees."

"We totally understand.. Can we see Mary Beth now?"

"I'll go and get her." Mary Beth was at her station when her boss approached her desk. "The detectives are here, Mary Beth. They're in my office, waiting to talk to you."

"I'm ready, Mr. Wozenkroll," said Mary Beth.

By the time Mary Beth entered the office, Von Hess had already set up the tape recorder that was in his attaché case.

"Hello, Ms. Carbone, have a seat. We'd like you to listen to these recordings."

"Alright, Sergeant," replied the witness, as she began feeling for a chair.

The men in the room looked at each other in silence. Having recognized Markie's voice, a man she hardly knew, was impressive.

"Here we go," said Von Hess, taking her arm gently as he guided her to a chair. 'Let's see if you can recognize any of the voices on the tapes you'll be hearing."

"Thank you, Detective Von Hess."

Mary Beth listened attentively to all six recordings. She asked for a certain section on the recording to be replayed—the part where the word turlet was spoken. After hearing the six voices say that word once again, she came to a decision.

"I've heard enough," advised the witness.

"So what's the verdict, Ms. Carbone?" asked Detective Hart. "Do you recognize any of the voices?"

"I'm sorry, who is speaking?" asked the witness, not

recognizing the voice.

"I'm Detective Hart."

"I think I do, Detective, but I just can't be one hundred percent sure."

"Which one do you think you recognize?"

"This second recording sounded *very* familiar to me."

"Familiar from where?" asked Von Hess, seeking a clarification.

"Number two sounded like the voice on the platform."

"The voice of the homicide victim or the assailant?" questioned Markie.

"Number two sounded like the voice of the man who committed the murder."

"On a percentage basis, how sure are you?"

"I'm ninety percent certain, but not one hundred percent."

"Fair enough, Ms. Carbone. Thank you," said Markie.

"What happens next, Sergeant?"

"We'll be in touch. We're going to need your cooperation just one more time. Is that okay with you?"

"Of course it is, Sergeant. I'll be available."

"Actually, you might find what we're cooking up to be fun," advised Markie, trying to present a brighter picture than what actually existed.

"I always enjoy having fun."

The remark touched home for Markie, who empathized with the visually challenged woman. "Do you need a ride home?" he asked after checking his watch.

"No, I'm perfectly fine taking the subway, thank you."

Something in Markie made him feel that he needed to do something special for the witness. "Seeing that it's nearing the end of the day, how about we all stop off for a drink someplace?" suggested Markie. "You wouldn't mind stopping would you, Teddy?"

"Certainly not," replied Hart. "Are you buying, Sarge?"

"You can forget that. How about you, Ollie, are you in?"

"I could go for a cold one," answered Von Hess.

"Ms. Carbone," said Markie, "it looks like you're the only holdout. What do you say?"

"You've twisted my arm, Sergeant," answered Mary Beth happily.

As Markie figured, Mary Beth was thrilled at the prospect of hanging out with the detectives. The war stories and banter she would hear over drinks would make for a memorable evening for her, which is what the sergeant wanted to accomplish.

"You sit tight, Mary Beth. We'll be back for you in a bit. We just need to go off duty and get our private cars," said Markie. "We'll regroup here in about an hour."

"You could ask your boss if he wants to join us," suggested Von Hess.

"I don't think Mr. Wozenkroll drinks," said Mary Beth, being less than truthful. She didn't want to share this special time with anyone else.

24

Making The

Rounds

PRESSURED BY DIAMOND JOE TO SPEED THINGS UP, Ella promised the Professor that she had something special waiting for him in Philadelphia. As expected, the news excited the Professor to where it was all he could think about. His second wife had known just what to say in order to lure her husband back to Philly. When it came to his sexual inclinations, she knew that the Professor would be incredibly weak in the face of temptation. Simply put, the bookshop owner was akin to a dope addict in need of a fix.

Intending to cut short his Arizona visit with Concetta, the Professor booked a flight back to New York for a brief stay with Rebecca. After that, he'd be off to Philadelphia to collect on his promise from Ella.

"When are we going to make plans for our wedding?" asked

Concetta, as the Professor got his things together to pack.

"You can start the process while I'm back east," replied the Professor.

"Are you sure your business in New York can't wait?"

"Unfortunately, I can't put this off. You know how it is—when opportunity knocks, I have to jump."

"What kind of opportunity is it?"

"I can pick up a very rare first edition," he lied. "It's one I have been trying to get my hands on for years for an overseas buyer."

"You have buyers overseas?" asked the impressed Concetta.

"I've got just a few. This one is an old friend," fibbed the Professor.

"When will you be returning?"

"I'll be back next week for sure. I'm sorry, but as I told you, traveling is a big part of my business."

"I know. I just didn't think you would be leaving so soon."

"I'll tell you what—while I'm away, why don't you look for those horses we spoke about?"

Concetta brightened. "Do you really want me to?"

"Yep, and while you're at it, keep your eye out for a small ranch with a corral to put those horses in. We'll call our new place . . . the Concetta Homestead."

"The Concetta Homestead!" she gushed.

"When I come back, we'll take that trip down the altar. How is that?"

The thought of her own ranch, complete with horses, put to bed all of Concetta's pouting. "What color horse do you want?" she asked, temporarily forgetting about their wedding plans.

##########

THE PROFESSOR ARRIVED at his Brooklyn Heights home a couple of hours before noon. After taking a nap, he cleaned up and intended to take his family to dinner.

"Where's the boy, Rebecca?" he asked, looking for their son.

"He staying over at my mother's tonight."

"Why?"

"She's been helping him with his Spanish. It'll be just us two."

"Where do you want to go eat?"

"I thought we'd just stay home tonight."

"Fine by me," said the Professor.

Rebecca snuggled up close to her husband on the loveseat that stood in front of the television.

"I glad you're home," she said softly. "What does your schedule look like this week, honey?"

"Tomorrow I'll be at the bookshop for a few hours, and then I have to rush off to Philadelphia," he advised.

"But you just got home . . ."

"It's one of those things, Rebecca. You know how it is. I have a great opportunity to purchase a very rare first edition that I don't want to miss out on. I'm going to have to horse trade on this one, so I'm gonna need time to wine and dine the seller," he fibbed.

"I understand," she stated, respecting that his work came first. "But you'll come right back home once that's done, right?"

"Yes, definitely, I should be back in a couple of days. After that, it'll be off to Arizona."

"How do you ever expect to maintain this crazy schedule? It isn't healthy."

"I don't mind it. But to be honest, I'll probably have to start looking to take on some help."

"I would think so."

"Either way, I'll be home a little less, at least for a while," advised the Professor. As expected, Rebecca's face dropped at hearing this. "You know, Rebecca, I could never do this without your understanding."

"But honestly, Henry, do we really need to be putting ourselves through all this? We certainly have enough money. Why on earth are you killing yourself?"

"A man has to work, Rebecca. You'd lose respect for me if I just loafed around all day. Besides, working is in my blood. It's what keeps me up."

Rebecca found his remark amusing. "Don't I keep you *up*?" she asked elfishly.

The Professor smiled. "Why do you think I come home?" Rebecca responded with a playful poke. "So what are *your* plans for tomorrow?"

"Since you'll be away, I'll think I'll give Sally Belle a call to see if she has time to get together for lunch. She mentioned several times that she wanted to take me to the 21 Club. She said they have a special dining room and passageway in the basement or something like that."

"That sounds like a fine idea. You should do that, send her my regards." A thought then came to the Professor. "What do you think of my being away for a month and then home for two?"

"What do you mean?"

"I talking about my schedule, maybe I can work it out that way.

"How can that possibly work?"

"I'll figure a way." The Professor was thinking that by spending such an extended period of time in Arizona and Philadelphia he'd be able to meet other potential wives in Utah and Ohio.

##########

THE PROFESSOR WENT TO HIS MANHATTAN BOOKSHOP AFTER having breakfast with Rebecca. On his way he began to think about the private investigative agency that operated just a few blocks from his office. The thought of hiring a gumshoe made sense to him in light of what Ella had been up to in Philadelphia.

The Professor didn't particularly care what Ella did in his absence as long as she was there for him when he wanted her. However, he did care about the possibility of another shakedown by one of her lovers. The Professor decided to inquire about hiring someone to shadow his second wife.

"What can I do for you?" asked the former cop who now was now working as a private investigator. He was a soft-spoken, middle-aged man who wore glasses.

"I need someone to follow my wife," replied the Professor. "She lives in Philadelphia."

"That's no problem. But an out-of-town job is gonna cost you a few more bucks, and we work off a retainer."

"No problem," said the Professor. "You also do background checks, right?"

"Yeah, we do."

Besides the money, what else are you gonna need?"

"I'll need a description, a photo of her, and her car plate if she's got a car. When are you looking to start this?"

"I'm not exactly sure. I'll let you know. Don't you want to know why I want her followed?"

"That's your business, sir. I mean, you can tell me if you want, but I don't need to know."

"Okay, I'll get back to you."

After arriving at his bookshop, the Professor collected his mail and assumed a seat at his desk. He took a moment to go through a military themed magazine he subscribed to in search of knives that might make an interesting addition to his collection. Finding nothing to his liking, he next began to retrieve the telephone messages that were left for him. After returning calls, the Professor sorted his mail and paid whatever outstanding invoices existed. His final task at the office was to familiarize himself with the new card tricks he received in the mail. As he was doing this, three boys entered his shop.

"Hey, Professor, where have you been lately?" asked one of the youths.

"I've been traveling, son," answered the Professor. "Go on in the back and play the machines."

"Is that a new knife, Professor?" asked one of the other boys, spotting the blade he carried on his hip.

"It sure is," the Professor answered, placing his hand on the brown leather sheath that housed his knife."

"What is it, a brass knuckle knife?"

"They call it a trench knife. Go play the game. I'll show you guys how to use it later."

25

A Thrilling Adventure

DETECTIVE VON HESS TELEPHONED MARY BETH at work to ask whether she'd be willing to accompany the investigators in the field. She jumped at the chance to participate in what she considered a thrilling adventure.

"I can definitely make myself available," advised the receptive witness.

"That's great, Mary Beth," said Von Hess.

"When are you going to need me?"

"Let's figure on our picking you up at work today at some point," replied the detective. "We just need to make sure our suspect is around."

"I'll have to talk to my boss—"

"We already spoke to him. You've got his blessing. Mr. Wozenkroll is a very understanding man."

"He said it's alright?"

"Yeah, he's totally okay with it."

"What do you need me to do?"

"When we come to pick you up, our first stop will be at headquarters to change your appearance," advised Von Hess. "We're gonna dress you up in a wig, a pair of glasses, and some padding to fatten you up."

"You want me disguised, like an undercover narc?" she asked, her heart beginning to race at the very thought of her role.

Von Hess was amused by the question. "You could say it's something along those lines. Are you game?"

Mary Beth gulped before replying. "Of course I'm game!" she declared, tickled at the thought of engaging in what she perceived as cloak-and-dagger activity. "And after I'm in costume, what then?"

"You and a detective are going to visit six businesses. The detective will engage a man in conversation at each location. All you have to do is listen carefully to their voices."

"Do I have to say anything?"

"You don't have to say a word. All you have to do is listen to the conversations and see if you recognize any of the voices. Do you think you can do that?"

"I definitely can do that. But how can I conceal my . . . limitations?"

"Don't worry about that," answered Von Hess. "As long as you hang onto the detective's arm, walk confidently, and follow his lead, it'll be fine.

"When did you talk to Mr. Wozenkroll?"

"Sergeant Markie called him up and got his approval."

"He didn't mind giving me the time off?"

"The sergeant said Mr. Wozenkroll loves you, so there wasn't a problem. Hopefully, we'll get together later today."

The chance of working with the detectives had Mary Beth's adrenalin working overtime. Feeling the need to share her excitement with someone, she called her parents. It might not have been the wisest of decisions.

"Are you totally out of your mind?" shouted Mr. Carbone into the phone upon hearing the news.

"No, I'm not out of my mind. I'm doing the right thing."

"What's the name of these cops?" asked the upset father. "I'm making a complaint against them!"

"Don't you dare!" she said emphatically.

"They're not getting away with using you to do *their* work. I just won't have it!"

"What's the problem now?" asked Mary Beth's mother as she approached her husband's side.

"Listen to this crap. The cops want to put her to work in the street with them—and she wants to go along with it! Can you believe it?"

Mary Beth's mother had long resigned herself to the pointlessness of arguing with her daughter when her mind was made up. "Let it go," she said, shaking her head. "Just let it go."

"Let it go? What the hell are you talking about?" the husband asked his wife, surprised at her response.

"Can't you understand? You're not going to change her mind."

From her end of the line Mary Beth was able to overhear the conversation of her parents.

"Just which side are you on?" shouted her father. "You show less sense than your daughter!"

"I don't like this anymore than you do, but Mary Beth is a grown woman who can make her own decisions!" yelled the mother, having the last word on the subject. "Now get off the damn phone and leave the girl alone."

"Here, then, you talk to her," said the upset father, handing his wife the phone. "That's it—I'm done talking. I just can't deal with turlet heads anymore!"

##########

ONCE THE DETECTIVES ASCERTAINED THAT THE Professor was working in his Manhattan bookshop, they reached out to their witness. Von Hess picked up Mary Beth at her job and transported her to police headquarters where her appearance was doctored to make her unrecognizable.

While Von Hess attended to having the witness disguised, Sergeant Markie contacted Detective Teddy Hart. He advised the detective that he wanted him directly involved in the voice identification for the purpose of consistency. As the arresting officer, Hart would be able to testify in court to both the telephonic and live identification.

"She needs a couple of wrinkles," said Markie upon seeing Mary Beth after her makeover.

"Do you think so?" asked Von Hess.

"Definitely, she still looks way too pretty. The suspect might remember her."

The addition of the wrinkles sufficiently altered Mary Beth's appearance to meet Markie's approval. After passing the sergeant's inspection the witness and Detective Teddy Hart took to the streets.

"Relax, Mary Beth," said Detective Hart, as they walked arm in arm. "There's nothing to worry about."

"I am a little nervous," whispered Mary Beth as she clung to the detective.

"There's nothing to be nervous about. Just hang on to me and walk with confidence. When I start talking, you start listening."

"What if I recognize the voice?"

"If you pick up on the voice, just play it cool and say nothing until we're alone outside," instructed the detective.

The Professor's Used Bookshop was the last of the six businesses they visited. Detective Hart and the witness arrived at the bookshop just minutes after the departure of several local youths. The Professor had been showing the boys the knife he carried. The business owner looked up from his desk when the couple entered the shop. Smiling pleasantly, he greeted the visitors to his bookshop.

"Hi," said the Professor politely. "Are you folks in the market for anything specific?"

"I'm looking to purchase autographed biographies," advised Detective Hart. "Do you carry those?"

"I really don't focus on autographs. You might find some books here that are autographed—I don't really know. You'll have to look for yourself."

"I'll have to come back another time for that. I have another question—are you the landlord here?"

"No, I'm not."

"Do you know where I can find the landlord?"

"Is there a problem?" asked the Professor.

"No, no problem. I'm in the business of heating," explained Hart. "I want to offer the landlord an opportunity that might save him money on his heating bill."

"Weillgold Management manages a bunch of the buildings along the avenue," informed the Professor."

"What kind of heating system do you have here—gas?"

"No, we got *erl*."

"You got a restroom here I could use?"

"I can't help you," replied the Professor. "Try the McDonald's around the corner—they got a turlet."

Mary Beth dug her nails in Detective Hart's arm after hearing the word often used by her father. She was convinced that the man speaking was the murderer of Grady O'Lang.

"You got a number for the management company?"

"You'll find them in the directory," replied the Professor, now tiring of having his time wasted.

"Okay, thanks."

"That was him," whispered Mary Beth once they reached the street."

"Are you sure?" asked Detective Hart.

"It was definitely him!"

Out of curiosity, the Professor looked through his window at the couple after they left. It seemed to him that the woman was walking stiffly. When Mary Beth started to cross the avenue, the Professor noticed something very peculiar—she didn't look toward the oncoming traffic. Not knowing what to make of it, the Professor locked the door and pulled down the shades.

The Professor wondered if the woman could possibly have been the blind woman on the subway platform. Unsure as to the accuracy of his recollection, the Professor wasn't about to take any chances. He opened the safe located under his desk and removed his passport. He also removed the gun, shield, and wallet of Grady O'Lang. After securing the safe, he set out to Philadelphia without looking back.

##########

THE DETECTIVES REGROUPED WITH their witness at police headquarters. While Mary Beth was having her disguise removed, Markie sat in his office with his detectives.

"She was great, Sarge," complimented Detective Hart.

"No problem with the identification?"

"Mary Beth couldn't have any been more definite in her identification," assured Hart.

"Beautiful."

"Do you want me to go out and make the pinch, Sarge?" asked Detective Hart.

"Let's take the witness back to her job. After that, we'll all go out and dig up the Professor."

The detectives took a moment to chat with Mr. Wozenkroll after dropping off Mary Beth at work. "I just want you to know that Mary Beth came through like a champ out there, Mr. Wozenkroll," advised Markie.

"Yeah, the woman is simply amazing. Are you gonna go pick up this bum now?" asked Wozenkroll.

"We're taking him down as soon as we leave here."

After leaving the trucking company, the detectives proceeded to the bookshop with their handcuffs at the ready. When they arrived, they were disappointed to find the store closed and the professor nowhere to be seen.

"We must have just missed this bastard," commented Detective Hart.

"We'll find him," said Markie. "Tell you what, Teddy, why don't you go back to your command and do what you have to do regarding the paperwork on the identification. Ollie and I will hunt down the Professor. When we catch up to him, we'll put him on ice and then call you to come and make the pinch."

"No problem, Sarge."

Markie realized he made a mistake in not moving in with Von Hess and apprehending the Professor immediately after the identification.

"He who hesitates is lost, Ollie," said Markie, acknowledging his tactical error.

26

Treachery Afoot

SAMSON BELLO, THE NEPHEW OF A MOBSTER, WASN'T YOUR typical attorney who adhered to standard ethical practices. Influenced by his uncle, who paid for his education, he gradually evolved into a fearless problem solving resource who prospered handsomely by doing whatever it took to achieve a favorable outcome for his clients.

His willingness to enter into illegal, immoral, and unethical practices, earned Bello a strong following among Philadelphia's unsavory element. The attorney was no stranger to bribing officials, tampering with witnesses, and orchestrating the most serious acts of lawbreaking imaginable without compunction.

The attorney was sitting in his office reviewing some paperwork when his secretary notified him that Diamond Joe Ormento had arrived.

"Send him in," directed the lawyer, rising from his chair.

"*Come va?*" said Bello, asking Ormento how it was going.

"*Va bene,*" replied Diamond Joe, indicating things were good.

"Take one," said the attorney, pointing to the cigar box on his desk." Ormento declined the offer, preferring his own brand. "So, what's the story, Joe?"

Sparing no details in his account, Diamond Joe articulated the situation concerning Ella, the Professor's Philadelphia wife. Bello was excited over what he viewed as an opportunity.

"Yeah, Sammy, it's like I said—her husband's got one hundred million."

"What's this woman to you, Joe?"

"She's just a friend. She used to work for me."

"I see," said Bello, nodding. "Look, Joe, we're talking serious money here. I know exactly the way to handle this, but before I sign on, I want to know—are you sure this girl can be trusted?"

"Don't worry about that, she's been around the horn."

"Does the husband have a will, Joe?"

"*Aspetta*," said Ormento, telling the lawyer to wait while he made a phone call. "Ella, your husband, does he have a will?"

"He always said he did,"replied Ella.

"Yeah, he's got a will someplace, Sammy," Ormento informed the lawyer.

"Okay, you better hang up the phone now, Joe."

"Ella, I'll call you back."

After Joe got off the line with Ella, the lawyer resumed.

"Let me make it simple for you, Joe," said Bello. "To cash in, we have to come up with a more recent will naming your friend as the sole beneficiary. That way, it's the first wife who gets the short end of the stick."

"You mean the husband's gotta get…"

"It's the best way to go Joe. With him around things can get complicated."

"How am I supposed to accomplish this?"

"That's my department, Joe. All you need to do is get me a

few things. I'll need the husband's picture, a sample of his handwriting and his schedule. Oh, and something that'll show how he writes numbers."

"Okay."

"You're gonna have to spend a little money up front, Joe," warned Bello.

"Don't worry about it, we're going after a big pot over here, Sammy."

"Alright, then, I'll need some cash to get the ball rolling."

"Okay, but tell me, what's the plan?"

"I'm gonna make out the husband's will."

"How do you do that?"

"I'll tell you exactly how, Joe, but first you have to give me some money."

"How much do you want?"

"Give me thirty grand in cash."

The restaurant owner was taken aback by the large sum. "That's pretty steep, Sammy. What do you have to do?"

"I have to spread money around to get things done. You just leave it to me, and I'll guarantee you that your friend gets practically *all* the money."

"Do me a favor, explain this to me."

"Alright, your friend is gonna give me two thousand in cash to draw up wills for her and her husband. She'll get a recently dated receipt from me in return for that money. She's also gonna get a copy of a signed contract from me and a copy of the will I draw up."

"How are you gonna get him to sign?"

"Like I said before, all I'll need is a sample of her husband's signature and how he writes numbers. I also want a picture of him. You get me that—and the thirty grand—and I'll put things in motion. Okay?"

Diamond Joe nodded in the affirmative. "Okay."

"Good. I'll take care of preparing the will. It'll reflect her husband's signature and date. The husband's signature has got to look perfect, Joe. Some of the thirty grand you give me will go to pay the mechanic who can do that."

"That's still a lot of money just to write a name...."

"Look, Joe, there are other expenses you really don't want to know the details about." The seriousness of the attorney's face made it clear to Ormento that he didn't need to hear more. "I want you to tell your friend—what's her name again?"

"Ella."

"You tell Ella that if anyone ever asks, she and her husband came here to my office to draw up their will. They signed a contract and paid me a fee of two grand in cash, and I gave them a copy of the contract, a copy of the will, and a receipt for the money. *Capisce*?" Diamond Joe nodded. "You're gonna be the witness on the paperwork, Joe. Okay?"

"Okay."

"With his money, I guess the husband don't work . . ."

"Sure he works. The son of a bitch owns a bookshop opposite my restaurant."

"That's perfect. Once we get the papers signed, all you have to do is let me know when he's at work. I'll take care of the rest."

"You're gonna fix his wagon *real* good," commented Ormento in a grave tone.

"It's the only way, Joe. You get me what I need, and this'll work out good for everybody."

"I'll get everything to you today, Sammy."

"Oh, one last thing," said Bello, smiling. Diamond Joe raised his chin as if to ask what. "When Ella comes into the money, my end is one-point-five million."

"You gonna want a receipt?"

255

"C'mon, Joe, this is serious."

The restaurant owner suddenly took on a very serious appearance. "There's gonna be one change Sammy. You get *five million* bucks from her, and half you're gonna give to me. Capisce?"

"Capisce, my friend," said Bello, who was now smiling broadly. "Are you sure you don't want a cigar?"

############

WHEN ELLA WAS APPRISED OF BELLO'S plan, she began to have second thoughts. Her wariness didn't stem from an aversion to breaking the law—she was well used to that. Ella's concern was rooted in her not being fond of entering into a murder plot, a crime that came with abrupt finality.

When Diamond Joe sensed that Ella was balking, he reminded her that by going along with Bello's scheme she'd be in line to inherit the Professor's fortune, less the five million dollars for the lawyer and whatever money awarded the first wife.

"But that still means my husband dies" said Ella.

Diamond Joe shrugged after hearing her statement. "Ella, listen, you're never gonna another shot at a score like this."

Unable to resist the temptation of such a staggering payout, Ella entered into the agreement. "I suppose you're right, Joe," she said, taking the blank document Diamond Joe handed her.

"Just sign the paper," instructed Diamond Joe.

"What is this supposed to be?"

"It's the will for you and your husband."

"But it's not filled out . . ."

"Relax, it's all gonna be beautiful," assured Ormento. "Now go get what the lawyer wants. I need a picture of your husband, a sample of his signature, and how he writes numbers."

"I have all that, Joe."

"This is perfect," said Joe approvingly after receiving what he requested. "When does your husband going back to work in the bookshop?"

"I'm not sure yet."

"Don't forget to call me when you know for sure, okay?"

"Sure, Joe, I won't forget."

"And don't worry about any cops—and don't tell them anything. *Il Professore* ain't gonna be around to see no cops," said Diamond Joe.

"You know something, I still can't figure out why I fell so hard for Grady."

"That guys yesterday's news. With the money you're gonna have, you could afford a hundred guys like him."

############

A GROUP OF DRUG ADDICTS MET each day early in the morning to congregate in front of a methadone clinic. Joining forces, they'd figure out ways to burglarize or rob in order to make money to support their addiction.

Samson Bello's resource was a tall, tattooed man in his early thirties. Although his cheekbones were pronounced, his eyes sunken, and his coloring pale, traces of a once-handsome man existed. He had been a charity case taken on by Samson Bello, who defended him on minor drug charges.

Bello's munificence wasn't a heartfelt act of kindness. It was a calculated strategy designed to make the dope addict beholden to him. Bello had need for a substance abuser in his rolodex. For a fee, a desperate druggie could be relied upon to agree to perform whatever unpleasant work necessary.

"How have you been?" asked Bello.

"I'm okay," replied the addict, who promptly responded to the attorney's office when summoned.

"I have a big paying job for you, if you're up for it."

"I'm up for it," immediately answered the druggie. "What kind of job is it?"

"It'll mean big money for you, kid."

"What do I have to do?"

"Have you ever committed a robbery before?"

"I broke into places—you know that."

"I don't mean burglary. I'm talking about sticking up a small business with a gun."

"I've done that," admitted the druggie. "You want me to rob a store?"

"Not exactly, but it's something along those lines. I want you to go into a small business and shoot a guy."

"You mean dead?"

"Yeah, I mean dead. What do you think I mean?"

"I don't know . . . I never killed anybody. I can't—"

"Look, my friend, you have a chance to pocket fifteen grand on this job. Need I say more?"

"That's a lot of money," said the junkie, now more amenable to the proposition.

"You bet it is," said the lawyer, "for just two minutes of work."

"But I—"

"And I'll throw in a five-grand bonus if the job goes off without a hitch."

"You're paying twenty thousand?"

"That's the payday. What do you say?"

"I'm in."

"Good, let me lay out the proposition. I'm gonna give you a gun with a silencer and a picture of the guy who has to go.

When the time is right, I'll call you and tell you exactly where to find him. All you have to do is go into his small business and put the guy to sleep. Just make sure no one else is in the place when you pull the trigger."

"Then what do I do?"

"Then you bring me back the gun when it's over. Do you think you can manage that?"

"Yeah, I can do it. When do I get the money?"

"As soon as you give me back the gun, you'll get the money."

"What happens if I get caught?"

"You keep your trap shut, that's what happens. Don't sweat it—I'll defend you. So are we in business, kid, or what?"

"Yeah, we have a deal. Can I get some money now?"

Bello looked at the future assassin and nodded. He pulled two hundred-dollar bills off the roll of money he had in his pocket. "Here, take it. Just stay straight. The call to move on it can come anytime."

"Don't worry—I'm good. I just wanted money to get something to eat."

"Yeah, you do that. Come by later this afternoon. I'll have the gun for you."

"Can I ask you a question?"

"What is it?"

"Why do you want me to give you the gun back?"

"So I know it'll be gotten rid of for sure."

27

Fishnet Makes a Friend

FISHNET MILLIGAN STEPPED INTO THE BACKYARD of Sally Belle's townhouse. The front half of the ground consisted of large, jagged cuts of gray slate. After a small step up, a bed of gray brick led to a pond at the rear of the yard. With the powerful waterfall not activated, the water remained calm. A wooden fence encased the yard to provide privacy.

Although it was fall, the sun did much to alleviate the coolness, making the day unusually warm. Fishnet placed his morning coffee and newspaper atop an iron yard table. Before taking a seat, he opened the table umbrella to block the glare of the sun. Once seated, he looked at his surroundings with satisfaction, believing that soon it would all be his.

After having coffee, Fishnet tended to the half-dozen koi that swam in the pond's clear water. Sensing his presence, the koi anxiously swam to the top, waiting to be fed. Fishnet reached into his pocket and removed a small plastic bag containing pond sticks.

"Time to eat, you guys," the ex-detective said cheerily to the fish.

Fishnet sprinkled the pond sticks across the top of the water. He enjoyed watching the koi race to the surface, competing for their breakfast. To his amusement, Fishnet gave each of the fish a name.

"You're getting to be a real piggy, Pascal," he said to the largest fish, who he named after his wife's former lover. "C'mon Maestro, put a move on if you want yours," he encouraged the yellow, white, and orange one. "What are you waiting for?"

After feeding the koi, the former detective sat down to resume reading the newspaper over a second cup of coffee. He was reading about the bankruptcy filing of the New York Giants linebacker Lawrence Taylor when a voice from above broke his concentration. It was Sally calling down to him from the second-floor deck just outside her bedroom. Due to Sally's insistence on privacy, she maintained the same living arrangement she had with Pascal. They slept apart, each having their own bedroom and bath.

"There is someone ringing at the front door, Shepherd. Please go and see who it is," said Sally.

"Alright," he answered. Fishnet mumbled something under his breath as he rose slowly to his feet. He took a gulp of coffee before heading inside the house.

"Hurry up, dear. It's probably Estelle and Andre. Don't keep them waiting."

Annoyed at being rushed along, Fishnet muttered, "What, am I living with a damn cripple?"

"What did you say, darling?" asked Sally, from above.

"I said that I'm going."

Needing to vent, Fishnet turned to look at the pond where the helpless koi resided. He flipped the switch that activated the powerful waterfall. The torrential downpour struck the water harshly, causing the koi to seek refuge at the bottom of the pond. Watching the traumatized koi scurry provided Fishnet with the satisfaction that only a sick mind would enjoy.

Leaving the koi to suffer, Fishnet went inside the house to admit Estelle Hatton and Andre Eastman, a writer for a theatrical publication. Eastman was there to interview Sally regarding the upcoming play she was to appear in.

"C'mon in—my wife is expecting you both," said Fishnet. His greeting was neither warm nor cold.

"Andre!" called Sally, making a grand entrance from the top of the stairs. "How simply delightful it is to see you, darling!"

Sally's enthusiasm went far in pissing off her husband further.

"I told you how thrilled Sally would be to see you, Andre," said Estelle, buttering up the writer.

The visitors continued conversing with Sally as she made her way down the steps. As they chatted freely, Fishnet stood by feeling alienated. His feeling of invisibility didn't sit well with the former detective.

"Shepherd, offer our guests refreshments," instructed Sally, without looking at her husband.

Fishnet took their orders and rustled up the beverages. Feeling totally disrespected, Fishnet made his exit after providing the refreshments.

"I'm stepping out for some air, Sally," he said.

Sally raised her hand to wave goodbye, barely looking at her husband. The others nodded their farewell politely.

Fishnet, needing to feel important, went for a drive in the black Mercedes that Sally gave him as a wedding present.

Finding Manhattan littered with people in nice cars, he needed a new venue where he could feel special. Fishnet drove to a Brooklyn neighborhood where he knew his fancy wheels would surely draw attention.

As he proceeded over the Brooklyn Bridge, the former detective's mind was operating feverishly on all cylinders. As a result of his intense thinking, he finally came up with a way to free himself of Sally and Estelle.

I'll lure them to the Pennsylvania quarry on an adventure, he thought, *and then, BANGO! They'll never see it coming!*

Satisfied with the formula he came up with to eliminate the two women, Fishnet thought a drink was in order. The ex-detective celebrated his brainchild by stopping at Roache's Four Leaf Clover, a neighborhood tavern that catered to the working-class crowd.

"Look who it is!" greeted Jackie the bartender, a blunt woman in her late thirties. "We all thought you were a vegetable!"

"I'm no vegetable, baby," said the ex-detective. "Take a look out that front glass."

The bartender did as directed. "What am I looking for?" she asked.

"Don't you see that car?"

"Are you talking about the Mercedes?"

"Yep—it's mine," he said proudly.

"Get away!" Jackie replied in disbelief. "That's not *your* car." Fishnet chuckled at her reaction.

"It certainly is my car. It took my getting married to get it!"

"C'mon—who did you marry?"

"On the level, I tied the knot with a bankroll."

As the two chatted, a short man entered the bar quietly, going directly to the restroom. It was Mitchell Emery, the man Markie's girlfriend nicknamed Little Creepy.

263

Mitchell waved at the bartender as he passed her. When he came out of the restroom he took a seat at the bar not far from where Fishnet was.

"What will it be?" asked Jackie.

"Let me have a beer," replied Mitchell.

After a while, Fishnet and Mitchell began chatting. It soon became apparent to the bartender that the two men were getting chummy enough for her to leave them to themselves. Fishnet noticed that Mitchell seemed to be staring at Jackie, giving the ex-detective the impression that interest existed.

"Do you like her?" asked Fishnet, referring to the bartender. "I can fix you up—I know Jackie good."

"You do?"

"Sure. I even know where her birthmarks are."

"Do you still see her?"

"Anytime I want—we go back a long time. I can put in a word in for you."

"Nah, I got my sights on one special lady," said Mitchell. "She's the only one for me—she's the ideal of my dreams."

"The ideal of your dreams?" asked Fishnet, raising his eyebrows. He began to wonder if his drinking companion had a mental disorder.

Mitchell removed a photo from his wallet. He then proudly held it out for Fishnet to see. "Here, take a look at her."

"This is *your* ideal?" asked Fishnet, recognizing the photo of Alley.

"Yeah, she's beautiful, ain't she?"

"Yeah, she is." *She's got a big set, I'll give you that,* thought Fishnet.

"We're gonna get married one day."

Fishnet began to formulate a profile on his new friend. His instincts were telling him that Mitchell was a tad off. "Let me

264

ask you something—does this gal have any idea of how you feel?"

"I think so. I've been dropping little hints that I got feelings for her."

"I see," said the former detective, taking a closer look at the photograph. "Say, where was this picture taken?"

"It was taken in the bar where she works."

"Where is that?"

"Fitzie's over on—"

Fishnet cut off Mitchell before he could finish his sentence. "Is her name Alley?"

"You know her?"

"I hate to bust your bubble, pal, but this gal is spoken for," replied Fishnet, who previously met Alley at a police function Markie had once taken her to.

"She *is* spoken for—by *me*," advised Mitchell in all seriousness.

Fishnet snickered at that statement. "Good luck, my friend." He was thinking of what Markie would have to say about that.

###########

WHEN FISHNET RETURNED TO THE TOWNHOUSE, he knew something was amiss as soon as he walked in the door. Based on the body language displayed by his wife, he knew she was awaiting his arrival. Sally Belle was sitting in a chair, grim-faced, her arms folded and her legs crossed tight. Seated nearby, her smile crooked, was the couple's occasional bedmate, Estelle Hatton. Sally didn't procrastinate in revealing her ire.

"Do you realize what you did, Shepherd?"

"What?"

"You left the waterfall going, that's what!"

"I did?" he asked, trying to sound innocent.

"When are you going to understand how such turbulence upsets the poor koi?"

"I must have accidently hit the switch when I rushed to let Estelle and Andre in," said Fishnet, trying to explain.

"You simply *must* be more focused on what you are doing!" scolded Sally.

"Aw, don't be so hard on him, Sally," said Estelle, smiling softly. "He didn't mean it."

I need this one's sympathy like I need a second asshole, thought Fishnet, fighting off his urge to speak his mind.

"I know, but this isn't the first time, Estelle."

"Oh, well, what's done is done. He'll be more careful," said Estelle, as if she were speaking of a naughty boy. "Didn't Pascal do the very same thing once?"

"He did, *once*," confirmed Sally. "But there was one thing about Pascal—"

Listening to the two women comparing him to Pascal only served to rile Fishnet. More than anything he wanted to put an end to his subservience. He saw disposing of his wife and Estelle as the only path to freedom. This belief caused Fishnet to act with urgency.

"How about you two letting me make it up to you?" asked Fishnet. "I've got an adventure for us to go on."

The two women looked at each in a puzzled way, wondering what he had in mind. Sally, who was still miffed, said nothing. Sensing the lingering chill, Estelle was the one to speak up. "Sally and I are always up for a new thrill, darling. Tell us more."

"I got on good authority that there is a classified government report hidden under a rock in a quarry in Pennsylvania. Supposedly, the report blows the lid off UFOs."

"What kind of quarry?" asked Estelle, who exhibited a degree

266

of interest.

"It's an abandoned quarry."

"Who told you this?" asked Sally skeptically.

"I got it from a guy I arrested years ago for rape. He told me that he got away with burglarizing the home of a government scientist and took the guy's diary."

"Why on earth would he be willing to admit that to you?"

"He wanted me to let him off the hook on the rape charge in exchange for the diary."

"And you believed him?"

"He was too detailed to be lying. He told me exactly where he hid it. I've always meant to go and get it, but then I got shot."

"Why didn't he go get it himself?" questioned Sally.

"He got sent up and died in jail of AIDS," replied Fishnet, without missing a beat.

"Are you sure that all this is true?" asked Sally.

"Definitely—why would I make this up? C'mon, let's go for it! It'll be great fun. It'll be sort of like a treasure hunt. What do you say?"

"Oh, I don't know. This cloak-and-dagger business doesn't interest me. Besides, I have rehearsals coming up."

"I'm not sure I like the idea either," interjected Estelle.

"You're missing the rest of the upside," assured Fishnet. "We can make a weekend holiday of it."

"Even so—"started Sally, but her sentence was interrupted by her husband.

"We'll stay overnight in a hotel that has a heart-shaped tub and a pool in the room. Think about the fun we could have."

The thought of nocturnal maneuvers went a long way in neutralizing the objections of the women. "Well, it might make for an interesting time, Sally," said Estelle.

"Perhaps . . ."

"C'mon, Sally, listen to Estelle. I'll dress up like a fireman again, how's that?"

"Oh, no, we did that already."

"But we've never experienced an Indian chief," suggested Estelle. "Just think of it, Sally—he could wear war paint!"

"Sure," said Fishnet, adding, "I'll tie you down and—"

"Yes! Yes! Yes!" enthused Estelle.

Fishnet, now knowing that he already won over Estelle, began dancing in a circle. He shook his head up and down as he tapped his lips with his fingers. When Fishnet began whooping, the two women laughed hysterically at his theatrics. Their guffaws prompted his own chortles as he envisioned the look on their face when they realized they were facing their final curtain.

"Alright, an Indian chief played by our Gable, it is," agreed Sally.

28

<u>Surprise!</u>

THE CHIEF OF DETECTIVES WASTED NO TIME in calling Police Commissioner Randolph after learning of the positive identification made in the Grady O'Lang homicide. Conveying positive news up the chain of command was always a good thing politically. As McCoy expected, the news made the commissioner very pleased.

"That's great, Harry," said the top cop.

"As it turned out, the Philly cop was shaking down a bigamist who had a wife in Brooklyn and one in Philadelphia," explained Chief McCoy.

"He had two wives? How did he manage that?"

"He had money. The bigamist was a lotto winner to the tune of a hundred million bucks."

"Where does the Philly cop fit in, Harry?"

"The cop was in cahoots with the guy's wife in Philly. He apparently underestimated his mark because the guy he was shaking down ended up killing him."

"So the dead cop was fooling around with the Philadelphia wife . . ."

"That's about the size of it."

"Alright, Harry, that's good," said Randolph, satisfied that he had enough information to update the Piladelphia police commissioner. "Did you pick up the perp yet?"

"He's being hunted now, John."

"Alright, let me know when they nab him. In the meantime, send me a report. Keep it brief, though—give it to me in bullets."

"You got it, John."

After hanging up the phone, McCoy called Lieutenant Wright into his office. He directed the lieutenant to prepare the bullet point report requested by the police commissioner. With everything under control, the chief of detectives took advantage of the lull. Now in the relaxed mode, he summoned Detective Silverlake.

"Get the Dixie cups—we're takin' a coffee break," said the chief. Silverlake didn't need to be told twice.

########

THE PROFESSOR WAS ALWAYS COGNIZANT that the day would eventually come when he'd have to flee the United States to avoid prosecution on bigamy charges. In preparation for that day the Professor had the foresight to install safeguards to avert a jail sentence. The first thing he did was to get a passport. He then placed ample funds in several locations overseas where he could live comfortably without worry of extradition. Now, after having committed a murder, he was more than glad he took these precautions.

Unsure of what the New York authorities might have pieced together, the Professor thought it best to stay away from New York for awhile. He hastily retreated to Philadelphia where he believed he would be safe in the short term. Comfort in knowing Rebecca would immediately notify him if the police showed up at their Brooklyn Heights home, he felt assured he'd remain one step ahead of the law. If need be, the Professor's plan was to hightail it to Arizona and stay with Concetta until he could make arrangements to flee to the Mediterranean beaches of Tunisia or the hot springs of Iceland. Once there, he had every intention of sending for his first wife and their son.

Upon arriving in Philadelphia, the Professor went directly to the home he shared with his second wife Ella. Upon seeing the Professor, Ella struggled to heed the instructions she received from Joe Ormento. Controlling her emotions, she put aside her venom and gave no indication of anything being wrong.

Being home alone with Ella went far in putting the Professor in a positive frame of mind. Although Ella appeared worn out, it did not diminish her husband's desires. Being alone with his second wife, the Professor intended to receive what Ella promised. Ella stiffened when the Professor began to make amorous overtures. She closed her eyes when she felt his hands going up and down her body.

"What the matter, Ella?"

"Nothing is the matter."

"You're all tense."

"I'm just a little tired."

"You didn't forget about my *special*, did you?" asked the Professor.

"No, I remember."

Ella's participation was mechanical. She performed with the same ardor as when servicing clients for Tootsie Roll Brown.

"Can we go for dinner at Ormento's?" Ella asked when their session was over.

"If you like," replied Fishnet.

Ella's straight-line smile was taut. She projected the same tolerant look she had given to those who fished for their money before being serviced.

That evening at the restaurant Diamond Joe seemed to be particularly animated. "*Il Professore!*" announced Ormento, using a booming voice to greet the Professor.

"Hello, Joe, how are you doing?"

"*Very* good, thank you."

"Hi, Joe," said Ella.

"I'm gonna fix you both something special."

"You don't need to go to any trouble for us, Joe."

"Don't worry, it's my pleasure," said the restaurant owner before leaving their table. He returned a short while later with a specially prepared appetizer. He then left, only to come back in the middle of their main course. "Did you like what I gave you?"

"It's great, Joe. Thank you," replied the Professor.

"It's terrific," added Ella, looking at the restaurant owner curiously. She wasn't quite sure what he was up to.

"*Mangia*—I want you to eat like it's your last meal," said the smiling Ormento, telling the Professor to eat up.

"You bet, Joe."

"Are you working here tomorrow?"

"I should be in tomorrow."

"What time?"

"I'll probably open up about 11:00 a.m."

"Good, come by for lunch. I'll make you something."

"Will do, Joe, but why are you being so nice to me?"

"Eh, you're a nice guy, that's why. And your nice to Ella, right, Ella?" Ormento asked, winking at Ella.

"A prince," she replied.

########

MARKIE AND VON HESS WENT TO THE Professor's residence in Brooklyn Heights. The detectives were greeted by a youth who came to the door.

"Is your father home?" asked Von Hess, flashing his shield. He correctly assumed the youth to be the professor's son.

"No, he's not home."

"Is your mother home?"

"No, she's at her friend's house."

"Do you expect your father home soon?"

"No, I don't think so."

"Do you know where your father is?" asked Markie, jumping into the conversation.

"I don't know." replied the boy, now growing wary.

"Look, son, we need to speak to your father," advised Von Hess.

"I don't know where he went—do you want me to call him?"

"How about you call your mother instead? Can you do that?" asked Markie.

The youth telephoned his mother. After advising her that the detectives wanted to speak to her, the boy passed the phone to Von Hess.

"Hello, this is Detective Von Hess. Are you Rebecca Blount?"

"Yes, I am. What's going on?"

"Everything is fine at the house here. We just need to speak to you about a matter."

"What?"

"I think it's something we need to discuss in person. Will you be coming home soon?"

"Well, I wasn't planning on it, but if I must, I will."

"If you like, we can come to where you are."

"Hold on a second," Rebecca turned to address Sally Belle. "Sally, these detectives need to talk to me, they're at my house."

"Oh, dear—what happened?"

"They aren't saying. They said they wanted to talk to me face to face."

"Tell them to come here. I'll call my husband and tell him to come right home. Shepherd will know what to do—he was a detective."

"Thanks, Sally. That's a good idea," agreed Rebecca, returning the receiver to her ear. She provided Von Hess with the address of Sally Belle's townhouse. "They'll be here in half an hour, Sally."

When Sally reached out to her husband, Fishnet was on his way to Pennsylvania to do the advance work necessary prior to the executions he intended to carry out.

"I need you to come right home, Shepherd," advised Sally.

"You want me home now?"

"Yes, right now,"

"Why? I'm kind of busy—"

"I need you home NOW. The police are coming to the house."

"What happened?"

"My friend Rebecca is here with me, and apparently they want to speak to her about something. She needs you."

"When are the cops supposed to get there?"

"They're supposed to be here in half an hour."

"I'll never make it back in time, Sally."

"Where are you?"

"I'm on Long Island visiting an old friend I used to work with," said Fishnet. "Just call me when they get there. I can talk to them over the phone."

"I suppose that'll have to do. I'd wish you would tell me when you're off on your little excursions."

"Yeah, I'll have to start doing that," Fishnet replied, rolling his eyes.

##########

WHILE THE PROFESSOR AND ELLA were having their dessert, Diamond Joe Ormento telephoned Samson Bello, the attorney.

"Sammy, our friend is gonna be at work tomorrow," whispered Joe into the phone.

"What time?"

"He'll be there just before lunch."

"Okay, got it."

After getting off the line, Ormento was forced to face his waiting wife. Mrs. Ormento, raising her hand, held her index and middle fingers to her thumb. She then began shaking it, palm upward. It was her way of asking her husband what he was up to without speaking. Mrs. Ormento's gut suspicion was that her husband was taking up with another woman. Diamond Joe hunched his shoulder as if he had no idea what she meant by her gesture.

"Who is she?" Joe's wife demanded to know.

"What are you talking about? I was talking to nobody."

"Chi è bugiardo in una cosa, è bugiardo in tutte," she snapped, walking off in a huff. She told her husband that a liar in one thing is a liar in all.

##########

MARKIE AND VON HESS PARKED in front of Sally Belle's

townhouse. They were impressed by how well maintained the property was. Scanning the front of the building, they noted the wrought iron gate and window bars were freshly painted black and free of blistering. The windows were new, and the cornice was without imperfection.

Appreciating the high-end neighborhood in which the property was located, the investigators assumed the building was owned by someone of means.

"We're talking big bucks over here, Ollie," commented Markie.

"Yeah, these houses are a fortune," agreed Von Hess. "Are we ready to go ring the bell, Sarge?"

"Yeah, let's go ahead."

Von Hess gave the button two quick pokes. A shrill ringing sound could he clearly heard from a distance.

"Jeeze. This bell could wake up the dead," commented Markie.

"Yeah, they must be deaf inside," added Von Hess. "Hold on, I hear somebody on the other side of the door."

The doorbell was answered by the owner of the townhouse.

"May I help you?" asked Sally Belle.

Von Hess thought the woman at the door looked familiar. Markie, a film buff, immediately recognized Sally as an actress but was unable to recall her name.

"I'm Detective Von Hess," said the detective, displaying his credentials. "And this is Sergeant Markie. We're supposed to meet Ms. Rebecca Blount here."

"We've been expecting you. Come in."

"Thank you, Ms. Belle," said Markie, finally recalling Sally's name. "I'm a big fan of yours."

Sally looked at the sergeant and smiled. Being primarily a stage actress, being recognized by the public always made her feel good. The actress led the detectives into the living room.

Markie, who was trailing behind, suddenly stopped dead in his tracks. Looking at the photographs prominently displayed atop the piano, he began rubbing his eyes in an effort to see clearer. He stepped closer to the piano to confirm his suspicion. After doing so, he turned to Von Hess.

"Ollie," summoned the sergeant, pointing to the framed photograph.

Seeing Fishnel's picture grace the top of the baby grand piano caused Von Hess to lock eyes with Markie. No words were exchanged.

"Is something wrong, gentlemen?" asked Sally, noticing the men seemed to be distracted.

"The man whose picture is on the piano reminds us of someone," advised Markie, playing it close to the vest.

Sally chuckled before commenting. "No, that's not Clark Gable, it's my husband, Shepherd. The resemblance is quite striking, isn't it?"

"*Shepherd*—what's your husband's last name?"

"Fish. My husband's name is Shepherd Fish. Why?"

Sally's answer didn't make sense to the investigators. "His resemblance to a detective we know is incredible," said Von Hess.

"Oh, I see," said Sally, now understanding. "My husband is a retired detective. Your paths probably have crossed in that world. He was nearly killed in the line of duty while apprehending some notorious gangster named Red something or other."

"Is your husband Bruce Milligan?"

"Why, yes! So you *do* know him."

"Yes, we do," replied Von Hess, "but not as Shepherd Fish."

"That's his professional name. My husband was quite the hero, wasn't he?"

"Yeah, quite," answered Markie, caustically. "But where does the name Shepherd Fish come from?"

"He uses it in his charitable work."

Markie couldn't bring himself to ask another question. It was Von Hess who stepped in to move things forward. "Is Ms. Blount here?" asked the detective.

"Yes, Rebecca is in the yard. I was showing her our koi in the pond. You know they live underwater out there all year round, even when the water freezes over. You'd be amazed at how well they do in terms of growth over the course of a winter."

"That's interesting," commented Von Hess, being polite.

"I'll get Rebecca for you," said Sally, sensing that the detectives could care less about her koi.

After a few minutes, Ms. Belle returned with Rebecca and introduced her to the authorities.

"What's this all about?" asked Rebecca. The concern in her voice was evident.

"Please, let's all sit down," injected Sally, directing the four to take seats in the living room.

"Go ahead, Ollie," said Markie, "you start."

"Ms. Blount, we need to speak to your husband. Do you know where he is?"

"What do you need to speak to him about?" countered Rebecca.

Von Hess looked toward Markie for guidance. "Give it to her straight, Ollie."

"Ms. Blount, I'm very sorry to have to tell you this but . . . you are married to a bigamist."

"That's absurd," said Sally, responding for her stunned friend.

Markie found the certainness in Ms. Belle's voice to be annoying. "Let me assure you that there is nothing absurd about this, Ms. Belle. Henry Harrison Blount has got a second wife tucked away in Philadelphia."

"There must be some mistake . . ." said the stunned Rebecca.

Sally put her arm around Rebecca's shoulder in support after seeing her eyes fill up. "Of course there is some mistake," consoled Sally.

"I know that was hard news to receive," said Markie softly, "but what we have to say next is gonna be even tougher to hear," he warned. "Go ahead, Ollie."

Detective Von Hess went on to convey some of the details concerning the Grady O'Lang homicide. The narrative the detective provided left Rebecca in denial of the allegations being made against her husband. She refused to accept that the Professor was living a double life and was suspected of murder.

Seeing beyond her hurt, Rebecca made the decision to face the issue head on. She steeled herself for the bumpy ride that was to follow.

"I'll cooperate fully with you," declared Rebecca, surprising all in the room.

"You need to talk to an attorney immediately, Rebecca," suggested Sally. "This is a very serious matter, so don't answer any questions."

"I know it is, Sally," said Rebecca. "But I'll not hamper the police in doing their duty. If what they say is true, which is highly doubtful, my husband will have to answer for his actions. I'm not worried—Henry will surely be able to clear this misunderstanding up," stated Rebecca, putting on a brave front.

Sally Belle looked at Rebecca with her mouth agape. For someone like Sally, who from her earliest age was conditioned to rely on lawyers to partition her from things unpleasant, all this was beyond comprehension. The actress was temporarily speechless.

"You might find my husband at his Philadelphia bookshop,"

said Rebecca. "I believe he either sleeps nights in the bookshop or takes a room in a nearby hotel when in Philly."

"Rebecca, please let me call Shepherd before you take this any further," pleaded Sally. "He can talk to the detectives."

"I'm sorry, Ms. Belle, but we're not interested in talking to anyone other than Ms. Blount right now," advised Markie, taking a hard line. The sergeant then turned to address Rebecca. "Do you have the key to the Manhattan bookshop?"

"I do—at home."

"Would you mind opening the bookshop up and looking around for us?"

"*Rebecca!*" blurted out Sally. "You need to confer with an attorney."

"I know my husband is innocent, so there is nothing to hide," said Rebecca, staunchly standing by her decision to cooperate. "Let's go, Sergeant."

The detectives drove Rebecca home to Brooklyn Heights so she could pick up the spare key to the Manhattan bookshop. After parking, the investigators accompanied her inside her home. Markie noticed the vanishing ace card trick atop a coffee table.

"Your husband likes his card tricks," commented Markie.

"Yes, it's his hobby."

"Does he have other hobbies?"

"Yes—he also likes to collect knives."

"He collects knives?" questioned the sergeant, recalling that the Philly cop Grady O'Lang was knifed to death.

"He does."

"Does he carry a knife?"

"He's never without one of his knives on him. It's his protection."

"That's very interesting. Where does he keep his collection?"

"Everything is in a special room he keeps."

"Can I take a look?" asked Von Hess.

"I'm afraid not—only he has the key to that room."

Markie had Von Hess drive them to the Manhattan bookshop. Finding no evidence in plain view, they returned Rebecca to her home. Before leaving, Markie advised the first wife that it would go easier on her husband if he surrendered to the law. Before parting company, Von Hess gave Rebecca his business card. He instructed her to have her husband or his lawyer contact him if and when she heard from him.

Once alone in the privacy of her home, Rebecca fell apart. Seeing her distraught condition, her son telephoned his grandmother asking if she would come over.

##########

DIAMOND JOE ORMENTO WAITED FOR THE Professor to leave the table. After paying his bill, the Professor proceeded to the restroom. His absence gave Ormento time to chat with Ella privately.

"It's all set. After tomorrow, your husband will be no more."

Ella nodded without responding. Attempting to avoid the ugliness of the matter, she preferred to think about the things she was going to do with the money she'd be receiving. She pictured her life without the Professor as a dream come true.

Mrs. Ormento watched her husband with uncertainty from afar. A controlling sort, she was miffed at not knowing what her husband was up to. The attention Diamond Joe was now paying Ella only fueled her suspicions.

"What's going on with that one, Joe?" asked Mrs. Ormento, after her husband left Ella's table. "I don't go for this baloney!"

"Will you stop, already," snapped her husband, "this is my business."

"Never mind, you better just watch your step!"

"*Fanabla*!" answered Joe, throwing up his hands in frustration as he walked away from her.

"Fanabla yourself," she barked at his back, telling him to go to hell.

##########

MARKIE AND VON HESS WERE IN THEIR CAR heading back to their office over at police headquarters.

"It looks like we're going back to Philly, Ollie."

"I figure we'll probably catch up with him there, boss."

"I think so," agreed Markie. "What do you make of Fishnet being married to that celebrity?"

"That guy never ceases to amaze me," replied Von Hess. "He really hitched his wagon to the gravy train this time."

"Do you really think he'll be satisfied? I'd bet my ass his sights are set on something higher."

"He's got plenty of money coming in, Sarge. Between social security, his disability pension, the money from the fundraiser, and whatever he milks out of the marriage, he should be set."

"He should be, but we're talking about a predator. Evil is in the prick's blood."

"Maybe he's in love—it's possible, Sarge."

Markie scoffed at the very idea. "Forget it."

"Who could tell when it comes to love?" commented Von Hess, inadvertently pushing Markie's buttons.

"Don't get me started, Ollie. Trust me—we'll be reading about that crooked son of a bitch one day. He's beyond redemption."

29

<u>Bye, Bye, Love</u>

SINCE SALLY AND ESTELLE LEFT MINOR DETAILS to others, Fishnet knew it would never occur to them to monitor the weather forecast. The prediction of inclement weather in the early afternoon fit perfectly into his plans. Sally's husband couldn't have hoped for anything better than on and off heavy winds and showers.

In preparation for the excursion to the Pennsylvania quarry, Fishnet got up early and drove to a notorious Brooklyn corner known for early morning drug trafficking. The location was just a few blocks away from the criminal court. When called to appear in court during his law enforcement days, and funds were low, Fishnet would shake down the nearby Smith Street drug dealers prior to reporting at the courthouse.

Fishnet parked his Mercedes a couple of blocks from where addicts roamed the street looking to score drugs. He approached the intersection in question on foot with his eye out for a familiar face. The ex-detective smiled when he spotted

Teo, a small-time drug dealer who pushed heroin, cocaine, and an assortment of pills.

Having been recently released from jail after serving a year, the six foot Teo looked healthier than most thanks to his incarceration. A steady regimen of exercise, jogging, regular meals and plenty of rest served him well.

The neatly dressed drug dealer stood in front of the building where he lived, making himself visible to transients visiting the area to cop drugs. His neatly trimmed black mustache; long curly hair; and cool facade made him stand out among the others frequenting the area.

Fishnet enjoyed sticking it to this particular drug dealer because he disliked Teo's arrogance. When high, the cocky Teo was in the habit of taunting police officers by grabbing his testicles as the cops passed by in their radio cars. Teo's luck ran out when Fishnet observed him doing this. Ever since Fishnet witnessed that disrespectful gesture, Teo was on Fishnet's get-even list, which was a compilation of people slated for persecution.

When Teo saw Fishnet approaching him, he abruptly retreated into his building. Realizing the building's second entry door was locked, the drug dealer fumbled for the key in his pocket.

"Hey, man, where you going?" asked Fishnet, after passing through the first door. "I wanna talk to you, my friend."

"What do you want with me, man?" asked the drug dealer, looking down and away from the one cop who could be depended on to shake him down.

Fishnet held Teo's chin up with his hand, forcing the drug dealer to look him in the face. "What happened? My little petunia is shy all of a sudden? Don't you wanna shake your one-eyed snake at me?"

"I ain't done that shit to you, man. I ain't looking for trouble," said the drug dealer humbly. "Why are you always picking on me for?"

"I'm not here to pick on you—I want us to be friends."

"I don't wanna be friends with no cop, man."

"Maybe you should rethink that position," advised Fishnet firmly. "Did you forget already?"

Teo touched his crooked nose. He then nodded slowly, signifying he remembered being smashed with a blackjack a couple of years prior.

"Nah, I didn't forget you, man," Teo said, adding, "but I got no money on me, man."

"Relax, Teo," said Fishnet. "I'm not looking for money. I'm out of the police business. I'm retired now."

"You ain't a detective no more?"

"No more, so we could be pals."

"Then why are you rousting me, man?" asked Teo, suddenly turning aggressive.

"Easy—" warned Fishnet.

"What do you want, man? You got no right to be in my face!"

Fishnet smiled an unmistakably cruel smile. "I need you to do me a favor."

"I ain't doing *you* favors. You got no badge, man, so we got nothing to talk about."

"I think you'll reconsider," said Fishnet, drawing his gun and punching the barrel into Teo's stomach.

Teo, winded by the blow, doubled over. The pain inflicted was sufficient enough for Teo to adjust his attitude. "What do you need from me man?" he asked, holding his forearm against his abdomen.

"All I need is two mushrooms," advised Fishnet, referring to hallucinogenic pills. "And you know what? To show there ain't any hard feelings, I'm even gonna pay you for them."

Fishnet's offer to pay drew a surprised reaction from Teo, who remembered well how the former detective would steal his drugs and money.

"No shit?

"No shit," echoed Fishnet. "Here, take this for your trouble."

Fishnet handed Teo a fifty-dollar bill. The dealer took the money and examined it closely. "This ain't a phony, is it?"

"No, it's legit. So, why don't we go get what I need?"

"Upstairs. I'll be right down."

"I'll go up with you."

The two men proceeded up the stairs to the roof landing where Teo had his products stashed. He reached into a small paper bag and removed the two mushroom pills. He turned the pills over to Fishnet along with the fifty-dollar bill he had been given.

"What's this?" asked Fishnet.

"I don't want your money, man."

"Why is that?"

"What can I say?" said Teo, "I don't take anything from cops."

"That's a good practice," replied Fishnet, feeling entitled to the consideration he received.

Fishnet wanted the mushrooms for a specific reason. He wanted the medical examiner to find that his wife and Estelle had drugs in their system at the time of death.

##########

FISHNET, WHO WAS FAMILIAR WITH the Lehigh area, knew that many of the local youths would visit an inactive quarry to swim illegally. What particularly stuck in his mind was the time he read about rescue crews along the banks of the quarry searching for the body of a youth who fell off a ledge that surrounded the deep water. Fishnet found this tragedy to be inspirational for a man seeking a way to kill off two mature women.

During the drive to Pennsylvania, Fishnet put on classical music for his passengers to listen to. He was hoping that the compositions would serve as a distraction from the iffy weather.

"Isn't it rather dark out?" asked Estelle, who was the first to take notice. "And look at the trees—the wind is awful."

"Perhaps we should turn back and visit the quarry another time," suggested Sally.

"It's supposed to brighten up," said Fishnet.

"Put on the radio so we can hear the weather forecast, dear."

"I listened to the forecast just before we left, Sally. It's supposed to get better."

"Perhaps the forecast changed," noted Estelle.

"So even if it did, I do my best teepee work in the rain," said Fishnet, trying to keep the women's interest up. "Anyway, why bother worrying about it? We're just a few minutes away from where we're going. Relax and enjoy the rest of Bach."

"That's not Bach," Sally pointed out. "The piece is Messiah by Handel."

"Oh, that's right, my mistake," acknowledged Fishnet. Being corrected only made the decision to kill his wife easier.

Fishnet's mind drifted as Sally and Estelle began reminiscing about having gone apple picking in their youth. Thinking of apples, the ex-detective pictured a large tin utility tub containing apples. The tub was filled with water, causing the apples to float. As Sally and Estelle dunked for a bite at the apple, Fishnet placed a hand over the back of their heads and dunked them. He began counting the surfacing bubbles as the women struggled to raise their heads above water."

"Shepherd!" shouted Sally. "Where are you?"

"What are you yelling about? I'm right here."

"Didn't you hear what I said?"

"No, tell me. I was listening to the music."

"Estelle and I think we should go straight to the hotel. The weather is simply too awful for this type of excursion."

"Let's stop for lunch first," said the former detective. "There's a place to grab a bite not far from the quarry."

"Well, alright. We might as well eat something," said Sally. "Just slow down—these roads are narrow."

"No problem, Sally, I'll slow up," he said. "We're in no hurry."

##########

FISHNET PULLED INTO THE PARKING LOT of the restaurant. "Look out the window, it's just drizzling lightly now," he said to the passengers before getting out of the car. It would be a shame to come all this way and not go to the quarry."

"We could go tomorrow," suggested Sally.

"Tomorrow we'll want to get home. We're here now, so let's just do it. It's not gonna take us long to do what we need to do."

"Do we even know where to look?"

"Of course—I know the place well."

"Well, I don't know. What do you think, Estelle?"

"We might as well get it over with."

"That settles it," said Fishnet. "Let's eat, and then just do it."

The two women subsequently went along with Fishnet's suggestion. As they got ready to leave the restaurant Fishnet gave each woman a mushroom pill.

"What's this?" asked Sally.

"Just something that will get you in the mood for later."

"I don't do drugs, dear."

"I know that, but I can see that you're both wound tight.

288

Besides, this is what *Chief Big One* wants," he said, flashing a devilish look.

The thought of Fishnet dressing up as an Indian chief convinced the two women to play along. After consuming the pills, the bill was paid, and the three left the restaurant.

"Get in the car—I need to use the restroom," said Fishnet. "I'll be back in a minute."

"Did you forget something, sir?" asked the manager, a young man of about thirty years of age.

"We had a change of plans—can you hold that table for me? I'm coming back in a few minutes for coffee and cake." Fishnet slipped the man a twenty-dollar bill.

"No problem sir, I'll hold the table for you," replied the manager, pocketing the cash. Will you be returning alone?"

"No, we'll be three. The women will be joining me later."

On the way to his car Fishnet felt for the black marker he carried in his pocket. When Fishnet, Sally, and Estelle arrived at the quarry, the ex-detective was surprised to see that there weren't any signs posted indicating that there was no trespassing.

"C'mon, follow me," urged Fishnet, getting out of the Mercedes. "We have to go where the local kids swim when the weather is nice."

Fishnet led the two women along a road that zigzagged through the quarry. Fishnet pointed to a cliff approximately 150 feet above the water. "It's up there," he said.

"Way up there?" asked Estelle.

"Yeah, it's under a big rock. I guess he felt nobody would look there. Anyway, the view must be something from up there."

"What is all that scribble up there dotting the cliff?" asked Sally as they neared the top.

"Just graffiti, I suppose. C'mon, we're almost there."

"Oh, no," said Sally when she reached the top. "There is no big rock here!"

"Jeeze, I'm sorry," said Fishnet, feigning remorse. "The guy really had me fooled."

"Oh well, let's head back," said Estelle.

"So it's not a total loss, how about we make our mark? I have a magic marker, so let's write our names and show we were here. Look at all the names—people do it for luck."

"Oh, Shepherd, you can be so juvenile sometimes. I don't know how steady I am."

"Oh, let's do it, Sally," said Estelle. "We could always use luck."

"Atta girl, Estelle, you tell her," encouraged Fishnet.

When they stared out from the top of the cliff, Sally and Estelle had to admit that the view was breathtaking.

As Fishnet embraced his wife, he slipped the car keys into her coat pocket. "Here, write your name on the rock," he said, handing Sally the marker. After writing her name, she gave the marker to Estelle. After the two women made their mark, Fishnet asked them to pose for a photograph.

"Step back and face me—I'll take your picture," directed Fishnet, reaching into his jacket pocket as if feeling for a camera.

"Did you say that you swam here?" asked Estelle, who appeared a bit more unsteady than Sally.

"No, I didn't, sweetheart . . . but you will!" said Fishnet, suddenly shoving Estelle off the cliff.

Sally stood frozen, aghast at what she witnessed. Paralyzed with fear, she managed to step several feet away from the edge. Taking her arm, Fishnet whipped her over the cliff the way a wrestler would throw an opponent into a ring turnbuckle. Fishnet looked down into the water at the two women he sent to their doom. Convinced they were done for, the former detective made his way back to the restaurant on foot. When he got to the eatery, he assumed a seat at the table he had reserved. Upon seeing the manager, he waved him to the table.

"Do you want to see the dessert menu?"

"Yeah, I do, but when the women get back. They went to look at something. They won't be long. Let me have a scotch and soda."

"No problem, I'll get the waitress."

After placing his order with the waitress, Fishnet began thinking of how he was going to spend his inheritance. While working on his third scotch and soda, Fishnet thought it time to express concern to the manager as to the whereabouts of Sally and Estelle.

"Where is the quarry around here?" asked Fishnet "Is it far?"

"Not very—it's actually very close."

"My wife and her friend went to look at it. I'm starting to wonder what's taking them so long."

"The quarry is off limits," said the manager. "Why would they want to go there?"

"They wanted to see the blueness of the water."

"I see," said the manager, nodding understandingly. He was aware that when the water in a quarry pit is exposed to the air the minerals remain suspended in the water column, giving it a unique blue coloring.

"I don't think they'd trespass. They must have warning signs posted."

"That's not always the case around here. Do they have a cell phone? Have you tried calling them?"

"I did, but I'm getting no response."

"Do you think you should go look for them? They could have gotten lost."

"They have the car—"

"Oh, then I don't know, sir," said the manager. "If they aren't back soon, maybe you should call the police, they may have gotten lost."

"I'll give it a few more minutes and do that."

When the police were called in, Fishnet played the role of a distraught husband to the hilt. When the authorities found the bodies of Sally and Estelle, Fishnet convincingly expressed the anguish that would be expected. He wept, hung his head, and blamed himself for not questioning the women on what he described as their inexplicable interest in seeing a quarry. His performance was as good as any that could have been given by his dead wife on the stage.

The account Fishnet provided to the authorities concerning the unique blueness of the water was perceived as credible. As expected, his history as a law enforcement officer helped the former detective avoid suspicion. It didn't hurt his credibility when the toxicology report revealed that Sally and Estelle had a controlled substance in their system.

30

Spaghetti And
Bullets

HAVING TO FULLFILL HER PROMISE OF providing *something special* for her husband made it easier for Ella to justify his execution. Down deep she saw murdering her husband purely for money as being too icy. Eliminating him for his perversions was far more palatable to her. She convinced herself that ridding the earth of the Professor was a public service.

When the Professor announced that he was leaving for work, she found relief in the knowledge that she would never have to endure the ordeal of engaging with him.

"Why don't you come by the bookshop and join me for a late lunch today?" asked the unsuspecting Professor.

"I have some errands to run," she replied. "Let's talk later."

"Take care of what you have to, we'll do dinner. Are you feeling okay?"

"I'm fine."

"You look run down, you have to take better care of yourself," said the Professor, as he wondered how his rose had begun morphing into a weed.

Once the Professor drove off, Ella wasted no time in alerting Diamond Joe Ormento that her husband was on his way to the bookshop. Diamond Joe waited until he saw the Professor physically arrive before passing word to the attorney Bello. Bello, in turn, reached out to his drug-addicted assassin. The lawyer became agitated when his call went unacknowledged.

"Where the hell is this junkie bastard?" asked the attorney aloud as he dialed the line again. "Don't tell me he's nodding out someplace . . ."

"Hello," answered the nasal-sounding voice after picking up on the third ring.

"Are you okay?" asked the somewhat-relieved lawyer.

"Yeah, I'm good," replied the junkie. "I was taking a dump."

"Where are you?"

"I'm at my mother's house."

"It's time to clean up," announced the attorney, speaking cryptically.

"You want me to go do it right now?" asked the addict.

"Yeah, get it done."

After getting off the line, the doper stared at the photographs of himself sprinkled about his room. They depicted him as an innocent young boy. He snickered as he recollected how adult like he felt when wearing the brown leather pen holder that hung from his belt. It was a gift from an uncle who always wore one.

Sighing, the drug addict proceeded to prepare himself for the job he was committed to do. He opened the brown attaché case containing the gun and silencer that the lawyer gave him.

Letting out a deep breath, he jammed the weapon in his waistband. He then put on a loose blue sweater and weathered black leather jacket to conceal the weapon.

The paid assassin went downstairs to the kitchen where his mother, an evening waitress at an all-night diner, was having a cup of coffee. She was a thin brunette nearing sixty. The heavy bags under her eyes and wrinkled brow reflected a woman plagued with years of worry over a drug addicted son. She was at a point where she considered not having her son arrested in months, for stealing from her home, as a promising sign.

Her husband, a retired auto mechanic of seventy, sat in another room tinkering with a vacuum cleaner that he was repairing. He was a tall, soft-spoken man with a small mustache. The little use he had for his son was evidenced by the silence between them. He long ago resigned himself to the fact that his boy was a lost cause.

"Do you want something to eat, Freddy?" asked the mother.

"No, ma," he replied. "I gotta head out."

"Where are you going?"

"Uhh, I got a job to do."

"Really?" she asked, perking up. "What kind of a job?"

"I'm working for the lawyer that handled my last case."

"Doing what?"

"He needs me to clean up his office," the junkie answered abruptly. Not wanting to be questioned, he left the room.

###########

THE PROFESSOR PARKED HIS CAR CLOSE to his bookshop in Philadelphia. He looked around the immediate area before removing a brown paper bag from the trunk of his vehicle. Inside the bag were the gun, shield, and wallet of the

Philadelphia police officer he murdered on the Manhattan subway platform.

The Professor saw some value in holding on to these items. In the event he needed to get make a hasty getaway, having police credentials would be helpful. The Professor was acutely aware of the risk he was running should the authorities ever catch him with Grady O'Lang's possessions, yet he still respected the upside to keeping the items. He locked the property inside the center drawer of his desk for safekeeping.

The Professor picked up the phone to check in with Concetta in Arizona. Their conversation was an upbeat one.

"I've found two beautiful palomino horses for us!" advised Concetta, with great enthusiasm. "I think I can get them at a bargain because we're buying two."

"What's a palomino again?" asked the Professor.

"In Spanish, palomino means young dove."

"I'm asking what kind of horses they are."

"They are Quarter Horses. Is that okay?"

"Sure, that's fine. What color are they?"

"The one I want for me is a mare with a gold coat and white mane and tail."

"And mine?"

"Yours is a gelding, a beautiful chocolate with white mane and tail. And I have to tell you . . ."

The Professor began going through his mail as he pretended to be listening to Concetta talk.

##########

FREDDIE THE DRUG ADDICT SAT IN THE PASSENGER side of his girlfriend's gold Toyota. To most observers, the two made for an odd mixture. People couldn't fathom what such an attractive young woman was doing in the company of such a loser.

Freddie's girl worked evenings selling cosmetics in a Philadelphia department store. Her job demanded perfect grooming and fashionable attire. These requirements served to enhance the physical disparity between her and the unshaven, clammy-faced Freddy. Even the emergency room nurses who knew the couple due to his drug overdoses were bewildered as to the inexplicable attachment. Maybe it was chemistry, or perhaps her need to standby a sad case. Whatever the reason, there was no question that she was devoted to a junkie who loved to shoot dope and eat spaghetti.

When Freddy, out of the blue, suggested that they drive to Diamond Joe's so that he could treat her to a nice lunch, his girlfriend was genuinely surprised.

"You don't need to treat me," she said. "It'll be expensive."

"I know, but I want to. I came into a little cash, so I can afford to spend some money on you."

"Maybe you should save it."

"Save it for what? Look, this is important to me, so come on and stop giving me a hard time."

She couldn't resist. "Well, Freddy, if you really want to, let's."

Even though Freddy was satisfied that the plan he worked out was a good one, he was nevertheless on edge. He reassured himself thinking, *It'll be an in and out job—pop and go!*

After parking, the couple walked hand in hand by The Professor's Used Bookshop. Glancing through the shop window as he passed, the soon-to-be assassin could see the Professor sitting at his desk. *He looks just like his photograph*, thought the junkie, *right down to the point of his whiskers*.

Once inside the restaurant, the drug addict asked for a table at the far end of the eatery, which was a distance away from the restrooms. He made sure his girlfriend sat with her back to the front entrance.

"Why don't you take off your coat? It's warm in here, Freddy."

"Nah, I'm good," he replied. "Order me my food—I gotta go to the bathroom."

"You want the usual spaghetti and meatballs?"

"Yeah, and get me a bottle of beer," he said.

"What's wrong? You seem to be all nerves."

"I gotta go take a massive crap," he replied, rising from his chair, "so I'll be a few minutes."

"That's really way too much information," pointed out the girlfriend, shaking her head.

"I just wanted to let ya know so you don't think I fell in."

"Are you sure you don't want to try something different?"

"Nah, get me the spaghetti. I gotta go."

"So go."

Freddie looked over his shoulder to make sure his girlfriend wasn't looking. He then slipped out the front door, put on a pair of light gloves, and walked the short distance to the bookshop. When he got there, he looked in the window. "Finally, I caught a break!" he said under his breath, seeing the Professor was alone in the shop. After looking around to make sure no one was in the area, he unbuttoned his coat and entered the business.

"May, I help you?" asked the Professor.

"You're the Professor, right?"

"I'm the Professor. How may I help you?"

"I got something for you, Professor," announced the assassin, producing the weapon he removed from his waistband.

Seeing the gun, the Professor went for the knife he carried on his hip. It was to no avail. Freddy fired three times—two more than was necessary. The sound of the gunfire drew no attention thanks to the silencer attached to the barrel of the gun.

Moving quickly, Freddy stuffed the gun back into his
waistband. The shooter then went behind the desk and pulled
the Professor off the chair and onto the floor. Intent on making
the murder appear as a robbery, he went through the pockets
of the dead man. He removed a set of keys and the Professor's
wallet. He then looked for a cash register. Not seeing one, he
confiscated the Professor's knife, using it to force open the desk
drawers. Seeing a revolver in the center drawer caused the
assassin to back off. Not wanting to waste any more time, he
put the cash he removed from the wallet in his pocket. Tossing
the wallet to the ground, he then left the shop. Once outside,
he locked the front door with one of the keys on the ring. He
then stuffed the keys and gloves he wore into his pants pocket.

When he returned to his table at Joe Ormento's restaurant,
Freddy took his seat opposite his girlfriend as if nothing
happened.

"Did you order the food?" he asked, seeing his beer had been
brought to the table.

"Yes, I did."

When the couple finished their lunch, the drug addict used
the Professor's money to pay the bill. He and his girlfriend
walked by the bookshop on their way to the car. Everything
seemed to be cool.

"Do me a favor and stop by Samson Bello's office," said
Freddy, who seemed much more at ease than earlier.

"Why? Did you get in trouble or something?"

"Nah, everything is cool. He owes me more money for some
work I did for him."

"What kind of work?"

"I did some painting for him."

"Oh, okay. I didn't know you did that work."

As the car was in motion, Freddy discreetly dropped one of

the gloves he wore out the window of the moving vehicle. After a few blocks, he dropped the second glove. Last to go out the window, one by one, were the Professor's keys.

When Freddy's girlfriend pulled up in front of the attorney's office, the drug addict jumped out of the car with alacrity. She had never seen him exit her vehicle with such expediency before. When he returned, she noticed a bulging square in the front right pocket of the jeans he wore. She correctly suspected that the pocket contained money.

"Is that money in your pocket?" she asked out of curiosity.

"Yeah," he answered honestly. "You scoped that out pretty fast."

"I couldn't miss it—it sticks out like a sore thumb," she said. "What did you do, paint his house?"

"C'mon, stop with the questions, will ya?"

##########

DIAMOND JOE, WHO HAD BEEN KEEPING AN EYE ON THE BOOKSHOP from his restaurant, knew the customer who had just left his eatery was the assassin assigned to take out the Professor. As far as he was concerned, no one who was up to any good ever looked in every direction before entering a location.

Once Diamond Joe saw his customer return without a book, he was confident the dastardly deed was done. He wanted to go over to the bookshop to satisfy his curiosity, but he dared not to. He only went as far as the restaurant's front sidewalk.

When he went back inside Joe noticed that Mrs. Ormento was staring at him from across the room. His wife approached him with her arms folded under her breasts. This position was a familiar one to her husband. It indicated she wanted to know

300

what he was up to.

"I just stepped outside for some air," said Diamond Joe defensively. "That's no good now?"

"Ahhh, you shut up!" said Mrs. Ormento tartly. She quickly dropped her right hand, palm downward, toward the floor.

When his wife walked off, Diamond Joe Ormento went to the men's room for the privacy he needed to call Ella. After being updated, Ella's first instinct was to go out and buy a bottle of scotch. She fought off this urge after taking into consideration the importance of her maintaining sobriety.

31

New Fish

MARKIE AND VON HESS went to Philadelphia in search of the Professor. Their first stop was the residence the suspect shared with his second wife, Ella. As they approached the front door, they could hear the blasting of Elton John's singing coming from within the home.

Inside the house Ella was sitting on a couch looking into a large round hand mirror. Wanting to look her best for her debut as the grieving widow, she was searching for hairs in need of plucking.

"Whoever is inside must be either deaf or dead, Ollie," said Markie.

In anticipation of facing off with the Professor, the sergeant drew his five-shot snub nose .38 caliber revolver and placed it in the pocket of his sport jacket. Von Hess held his Colt revolver at his rear, pointed at the ground. The two investigators were among the few remaining police officers on the force who hadn't switched to automatic weapons.

When the doorbell rang, Ella turned down the music. When she answered the door, her mouth dropped. The sight of Markie and Von Hess caused her guilty mind to race.

"What are you doing here?" Ella asked the detectives.

"We're looking for your husband, Ms. Blount," advised Von Hess. "Is he here?"

"He's not home," answered Ella.

"Is he still living here?"

"Sometimes," she replied.

"Do you know where he is now?" asked Markie.

"I think he must have gone to work."

"You don't know?"

"How can I know for sure where he goes?" she asked, getting aggressive. "He'll be home later."

"Are you *sure* he's not in the house?" asked Von Hess.

"Come in and search if you like. I'm telling you the truth." The investigators took Ella up on her offer and went through the house in search of the Professor.

"Now are you *satisfied*?"

"Yes. Did you ever retain an attorney?" questioned Von Hess, finding it hard to believe that she was still living with a husband she knew to be a bigamist.

"No, we've been trying to work things out."

"C'mon, Ollie, let's get going," said Markie, thinking that her answer was less than truthful.

After the detectives left, Ella telephoned Diamond Joe Ormento's cell phone. Seeing it was Ella, the restaurant owner immediately took the call. Covering his mouth with his hand, he spoke into the receiver.

"What's up, anything the matter?"

"The New York detectives just left my house. They were here asking for my husband," advised Ella nervously.

"What did ya tell them?"

"I told them I don't know where he is."

"Good, you did right," said Ormento before hanging up the phone. "Sit tight, things will be breaking soon."

Diamond Joe was positioned by the front glass of his restaurant, where he had an unobstructed view of the bookshop. When the restaurant owner spotted the arrival of Markie and Von Hess, his deep focus caused his mouth to open. Once again, Joe's keen interest in something happening outside their restaurant raised the suspicion of his wife. When she questioned him regarding who he had been talking to on the phone, his reply was vague, informing her that had been talking to a friend.

"The joint is closed, Sarge," said Von Hess, as the two investigators stood outside the bookshop.

"Don't tell me this guy went back to New York," declared the frustrated Markie, trying the front door. "He may be in the back someplace—the light is on. Ollie, run the plates on the cars around here," directed the sergeant.

"Righto," replied Von Hess.

The investigators subsequently determined that the Professor's BMW was parked near his bookshop.

"If his car is here, he's gotta be around someplace, Sarge. He'll be back."

"Yeah, let's sit on his car. Do you want to get something to eat?"

"We might as well."

"Keep an eye on things. I'll go pick us up something."

Markie went to Diamond Joe Ormento's restaurant. The restaurant owner greeted the detective graciously, pretending he was glad to see him.

"Can I order food to take out?" asked Markie.

"Sure," replied Ormento.

"Let me have two meatball specials to go."

"Drinks?"

"Two sodas—give me whatever is cold. Did you see the bookshop owner today?"

"No," replied Diamond Joe, shaking his head.

"His car is outside."

Ormento shrugged his shoulders. "I didn't notice."

"Does he ever leave his car at work overnight?"

"I don't know."

"Do you know who owns the building over there?"

"Santo—he owns this building too," replied Diamond Joe.

"Do me a favor—let me have Santo's number. I may need to talk to him."

After Markie left the restaurant with his food, Diamond Joe telephoned the building owner.

"Santo, Joe Ormento here."

"Yeah, Joe, is everything okay?" asked the property owner.

"Some cops from New York maybe calling you."

"Why would they be calling me?"

"I think they wanna go in the bookshop. You got the key for over there, right?"

"I do . . . but why do they want to go inside the bookshop? What's wrong?"

"What do I know what for? You're gonna have to let them in."

"I suppose I'll have to."

When darkness set, the detectives decided to telephone Santo, who agreed to respond to the bookshop with a spare key. What the three men found wasn't a pretty sight.

##########

ON THE RIDE BACK TO NEW YORK CITY, Markie and Von Hess discussed the homicide of the Professor. His murder was a development that they hadn't seen coming.

"This is one for the books, Sarge," commented Von Hess.

"Yeah, that's for sure," agreed Markie. "I wonder who clipped him—and why."

"There has to be some shady stuff going on here in Philly."

"I'm thinking Grady O'Lang might have had a crime partner we don't know about, Ollie."

"That could be, Sarge."

"Well, whatever it is, it's not our headache. Our case was cracked once the Philly detectives found Grady O'Lang's gun in the Professor's desk drawer."

"And don't forget the knife. I wouldn't be surprised if that was the knife used to take out Grady."

"We don't need more proof, Ollie. We got more than enough. Let me tell you, everybody is gonna be happy when we tell them that this case can be put to rest."

"Do you want me to notify Teddy Hart, Sarge?"

"Yeah, you do that. I'll post Lieutenant Wright."

##########

FISHNET GENTLY DROPPED THE TWO recently purchased koi in the pond. He watched them for a few seconds as they acclimated themselves to being among the other fish. Finding the single red spot on the head of the Tancho unique, Fishnet named the koi Sally, after his late wife. The gold metallic Hikari Muji was dubbed Estelle.

"*Hail, hail, the gang's all here,*" sang Fishnet as he sprinkled fish food atop the water. Looking down at the pond he addressed the koi. "Boys, you got company," he playfully shouted into the pond. "Better eat up, Pascal—you're in with a couple of real barracudas so you'll need your strength. They're gonna probably want you to dress up like a frog!"

After having his laugh, the former detective dropped some more pond sticks into the water. He then lit a cigar and sat in a yard chair. With Sally gone, he now had the full run the townhouse. Seemingly carefree, he was the picture of contentment as he blew smoke rings into the air.

As he enjoyed his cigar he began thinking about the Pennsylvania newspaper accounts regarding the Lehigh Valley deaths of his wife Sally and Estelle Hatton. The general consensus in the press was that the two women met their doom as a result of an accidental fall from a slippery cliff while under the influence of drugs. The one question being harped on by a couple of reporters was *why* two mature women would venture into a quarry that was off limits to the public. They didn't buy the blue water story.

The saps, thought Fishnet, who was confident that the answer he provided to the law when asked that question was sufficient. "If not to see the blue water, then only the good Lord knows," he had said.

Right after the quarry deaths, Fishnet took the precaution of muting Marvin Butterworth, his late wife's attorney. As the family attorney, Butterworth represented the one person who could ignite further probing should he voice any suspicion.

Cognizant of the sway that came with money, Fishnet put his inheritance to good use. He put Butterworth on the payroll at a healthier rate than the attorney had been receiving from Sally. Pleased to have his fingers deeper into the pie, Butterworth quelled any suspicions he may have harbored. As far as Fishnet saw things, fattening up Butterworth was a worthwhile insurance.

########

EVEN THOUGH FISHNET ATTAINED THE financial wealth he always dreamt of, he began to feel as though something were missing. The nice car, slick wardrobe, and fancy jewelry only went so far. What Fishnet lacked was the stimulation necessary to excite him. Sure, he had his excursions into his fantasy world, but that wasn't live action.

As he sat in the yard smoking, his thoughts drifted to Scotland. As the koi swam peacefully in the pond, Fishnet pictured himself in Scotland's West Central Lowlands on the River Clyde. He was cavorting in a Glasgow night spot known as The Merry Coach, a venue frequented by tourists. Boldly attired in a plaid kilt and carrying bagpipes, Fishnet was someone to be noticed.

"Are you going to play?" asked a Canadian woman, pointing to the woodwind instrument he carried.

"Perhaps," replied Fishnet, sounding aloof.

"Are kilts drafty?" she asked, trying to be amusingly lighthearted.

"Sometimes . . . but they're convenient," he replied. The thought of his remark caused Fishnet to chuckle, snapping him out of his daydream.

Reflecting back on his days as a detective, Fishnet experienced an epiphany. He came to appreciate that his tenure in law enforcement provided him the opportunity to steal, connive, and scheme with little risk. This was something that, even with all his newly acquired wealth, was now beyond his power. As Fishnet puffed on his cigar, he began to deeply ponder this reality. It was at this point he knew that he needed to search for an activity that would satisfy his unusual needs.

32

One Case Closes, Another Opens

DETECTIVE VON HESS WAS FOOD SHOPPING at the supermarket with his wife. Not finding shopping a particularly enjoyable thing to do, the well intentioned detective nevertheless volunteered to go along with his spouse in order to make things a little easier on her. Armed with coupons, they sought out items on sale and checked the expiration dates on the things they purchased. After a bit, the detective grew bored and just stood behind their shopping cart while his wife made the selections.

Von Hess grew irritable as he began crossing paths with some of the shoppers. Particularly disturbing to him was the congestion they created in the aisles they blocked. The detective found it mind boggling how a family could form a circle around a single cart discussing the merits of string beans, while failing to realize the inconvenience they were causing.

"Jeeze, can't some of these people wait in the car?" Von Hess asked his wife.

"What did you say?" asked Mrs. Von Hess.

"I'm gonna wait in the car. Call me when you're checking out."

"Oh, alright." Mrs. Von Hess actually welcomed the news—she didn't have to worry about being rushed.

Once inside his car, Von Hess pushed back his seat, turned on the radio, and closed his eyes to nap. Von Hess jumped up in his seat when the radio announced the death of the actress Sally Belle and her agent, Estelle Hatton. Knowing this would be of great interest to Markie, he wasted no time in conveying the news telephonically.

"Sarge, listen to this," said Von Hess. The excitement in his voice indicated big news was coming.

"What happened?" asked Markie.

"That actress Sally Belle and a friend of hers were found dead in a Pennsylvania quarry."

"No shit!" blurted Markie.

"I just heard it over the radio."

"How did they die?"

"They're saying the two of them took a header off a cliff. They figure it to be accidental."

"Accidental? What the hell were they doing on a cliff in a quarry?"

"That's a good question, Sarge. According to the radio, Sally Belle comes from one of the richest families in the country."

"What else did they say?"

"They reported that Belle had no family, other than her husband, a former NYPD detective. It looks like Fishnet is in the chips."

Markie shook his head slowly. "That son of a bitch...I'll bet my ass he had something to do with the death of those two, Ollie."

"You figure he was out for the money?"

"What else?"

"That's a big accusation to make, Sarge, without proof."

"I got no proof, Ollie, but I don't need any. I know how that bum thinks."

"What can *we* do? Remember, it's a Pennsylvania case."

"We'll do our part."

"I don't follow you, Sarge."

"We're gonna do a little nosing around to see what we can find out."

"Where do you want to start?"

"Let's pull all the newspaper articles that mention Sally Belle. That might lead us to some of her friends. We can start by talking to them."

"Maybe we should first clear this with the powers that be," suggested Von Hess.

"We probably should, but they'll only say we should mind our business." Von Hess could see there was no way to discourage the sergeant. "We're between cases anyhow, so this will give us something to do when we're back in the office.

"Okay, Sarge. I've been anxious to use that new search engine we got."

"What's that called again? Giggle?"

"No, they call it Google."

"What the hell kind of a friggin' name is that?" asked Markie, shaking his head.

When they returned to work, Von Hess spent a couple of hours conducting online research. He identified several people he felt might be closely aligned to the deceased Sally Belle.

"So which one do you want to start with, Sarge?" asked Von Hess, showing Markie the list of names.

"Let's start with this lawyer, Butterworth."

MARVIN BUTTERWORTH WAS A MAN who believed in dressing for success. He favored three-piece suits and imported ties from Italy, and he sported a diamond pinkie ring. His sparse hair consisted of a horseshoe fringe that touched the top of his ears. The unmarried lawyer had just one passion: making money.

Butterworth's professional focus had always been on high net-worth clients with an interest in the theater. For decades, such a client was Sally Belle's father, who on occasion invested in Broadway productions.

Butterworth was basically a frugal man who conducted business out of a small Broadway office that he shared with his nephew, a ticket broker. Part of his client base included some labor unions. These ties rendered him a valuable resource to those with an interest in the theater. A phone call from the attorney to the right person could grant a favor. Such a call could also quell or create workplace turmoil. Unbeknownst to Sally Belle, it was at the behest of her father that Butterworth stepped in more than once to secure a coveted role for her.

"There are detectives here who want to see you, Mr. Butterworth," informed the receptionist.

"Did you say detectives?"

"Yes, sir, I did."

"Well, what do they want?"

"Mr. Butterworth wants to know what you gentlemen want," conveyed the receptionist.

"Tell him it's a sensitive matter," replied Von Hess.

"I'm being told it's a *sensitive* matter," reported the receptionist.

"Very well, send them in," directed the lawyer. When Markie

and Von Hess entered the office, the attorney was the first to speak. "Sit down, gentlemen."

"I'm Detective Von Hess," said the investigator, "and this is Sergeant Markie."

"What can I do for you boys?"

"You were friendly with Ms. Sally Belle, weren't you, sir?" asked Von Hess.

"Why, yes. I've represented the family for many years. Why?"

"You represented *Sally* Belle?

"I've represented the entire family."

"What kind of person was Ms. Belle?"

"She was an absolutely lovely person. I'll have you know I was instrumental in helping Ms. Belle gain traction on the stage."

"Is that a fact?" injected Markie.

"Yes it is. I never fabricate, Sergeant."

"Of course not," said Markie, who was beginning to form an unfavorable impression of Butterworth.

"Was Ms. Belle the adventurous type?" asked Von Hess.

"In some things she was; in other things, not very."

"Would you say that she was the type who could fall off a cliff in a Pennsylvania quarry on a lousy day?"

Butterworth paused before answering. "Who knows what people have a notion to do at any given moment?" he answered. "Theater people can be quirky at times. Why are you asking me these questions?"

The investigators ignored the attorney's question. "To your knowledge, has Sally ever done anything like that before?"

"I'm not really sure. She may or may not have. Wouldn't all this be a Pennsylvania matter?"

"In your estimation, was Ms. Belle a woman who could be easily influenced by her new husband?" questioned Markie.

The mere mention of Sally's new husband in this context was

the beginning of the end of their dialogue. Caught between his suspicions and his income, Butterworth opted to protect his financial status.

"Before we go further, can you tell me what all these questions are about, Sergeant?"

"It's about making sure the death of Ms. Belle was accidental," replied Markie bluntly.

"Do you have evidence to suspect otherwise?"

"No. The only thing I have to go on is that two mature Broadway women falling off some cliff in Pennsylvania smells to high heaven."

"Just so you know, Sergeant, as I already said, I've handled the affairs of the Belle family going back a very long time," advised Butterworth. "Sally's death is most unfortunate, of course. However, for me professionally, nothing changed. Sally's husband is now my client. With that said, there is little I'm at liberty to discuss with you gentlemen."

Markie and Von Hess were no more than two minutes out of the attorney's office before Butterworth picked up the telephone to call Warren Watkins, the top security consultant for the theater district.

"Warren, its Marvin Butterworth speaking. How are tricks?"

"Busy. I've been busy coordinating with the police department over the upcoming parade."

"Making any money?" asked Butterworth.

"Heh, heh," laughed the former police inspector. "What do you need, Marvin?"

"I need the legs cut out from under a couple of detectives."

"What did they do?"

"Never mind what they did—I need them called off a case."

"Well, can you tell me what kind of a case at least?"

"They're looking into an accidental death that occurred in

Pennsylvania and trying to make more out of it."

"This definitely happened in Pennsylvania?"

"Yes. Is this something you can you handle for me or not?"

"I think so, but since this is out of state, it's gonna cost you a few bucks."

"How much do you want?"

"Let's say twenty-five thousand."

Butterworth went ballistic after hearing the price. "Are you crazy? I'm not asking to make them disappear. All I want done is for them to go save some poor cat stuck in a car engine. I'll give you five grand."

"You gotta understand something, Marvin—my man in police headquarters has to be taken care of, and he's not gonna come cheap. And then there is my fee to factor in."

"Look, I'll tell you what. I'll spring for ten grand, tops. You carve up the money whatever way that suits you. Is it a deal?"

"Add another twenty-five hundred, and you got a deal," replied Watkins.

"I'll go for twelve and that's it."

"Alright, we're in business, Marvin."

##########

WARREN WATKINS CALLED THE OFFICE of Police Commissioner Randolph. The two men had been radio car partners back in the day when there were very few Black and White cops working together on patrol as a team.

"Who may I say is calling?" asked the captain who monitored all of the commissioner's calls.

"Tell him Warren Watkins."

"Hold the line please."

After a minute, Police Commissioner Randolph got on the line with Watkins.

"Hey Warren, how is it going?"

"All is good, John. I'm calling to give you a heads-up on something that might lead to trouble."

"What is it?"

"You got a couple of detectives out there looking to turn Pennsylvania into a sixth borough."

"What do you mean?"

"Well it seems like they're poking their nose into a case out of their jurisdiction. They're making more out of a couple of accidental deaths in Pennsylvania than needs to be.

"Who are they?"

"Sergeant Markie and Detective Von Hess."

"Hmmm, I know those two. Why would they be doing that?"

"For a payday would be my guess, John."

"Where did you get this information from?"

"I got it from my sources in the theater district."

"Are they reliable?"

"They're solid as a rock."

"Thanks for the heads-up, Warren. I don't need a couple of cowboys in business for themselves. I owe you one."

"No problem. I thought you should know."

"Say, before you go, could you swing a couple of seats to a Broadway show?"

"Sure, John, which show?"

"I like to get tickets to Cabaret."

"No problem, John. You'll have them by tomorrow."

After hanging up with the police commissioner Watkins telephoned Butterworth.

"I took care of that thing for you, Marvin," advised Watkins.

"Good, come by whenever you want and we'll straighten out."

"I had to sweeten the pot by promising two tickets to Cabaret to put it over."

"Okay, I'll get them from my nephew."

After hanging up the phone the former police inspector began wondering how he was going to spend the twelve thousand Butterworth was going to give him.

##########

POLICE COMMISSIONER RANDOLPH reached out to the chief of detectives to get to the bottom of what Watkins told him.

"Harry, what's Markie and Von Hess been up to?"

"What do you mean, John?"

After filling in Chief McCoy, the commissioner asked, "Are they in the office?"

"Let me find out, I'll get right back to you." Chief McCoy called the office of Lieutenant Wright. "What are Markie and Von Hess doing?"

"They're in the field, Chief."

"Where in the field are they?"

"Let me take a look at the movement log." Wright noticed the log reflected the investigators had been vague, indicating their destination was the vicinity of Manhattan.

When located, Markie and Von Hess were ordered back to the office forthwith. They were called on the carpet to answer questions as to who gave them permission to devote time to a matter outside of their jurisdiction. Once it was established that the detectives had none, Chief McCoy placed them under house arrest. The investigators, now relegated to the confines of their office, took their medicine stoically. They may have been bloodied, but they were far from bowed.

33

Squaring Off

MARKIE AND VON HESS WERE UNDER STRICT ORDERS not to leave their office at headquarters. The veteran detectives suspected the attorney Marvin Butterworth had something to do with their being sidelined.

As he sat bored in his office, Markie began reading *The Black Camel*, a Charlie Chan mystery by Earl Derr Biggers. Prevented from doing his own investigating, he found the novel to be as close a substitute as he could get to the real thing.

While the sergeant was reading about a Hollywood star who was murdered in Waikiki, Von Hess passed the time by muddling through a newspaper crossword puzzle. Their humdrum finally concluded when Lieutenant Wright summoned the investigators to accompany him to Chief McCoy's office. Wondering what they had done wrong, they met Wright at the chief's door.

"The chief has a special job for you," advised the lieutenant prior to entering the office.

"Sit down," said Chief McCoy. "I want you two to accommodate a reporter who wants to tag along on a search warrant. It's for some kind of story she's doing. Find out what squad is going to be executing a warrant and pick one to accompany. Just make sure you don't make arrangements to go out on anything too heavy."

"Is the reporter a friend of yours, Chief?" asked Markie, trying to establish just how nice he had to be.

"No, she's nothing to me. The contract came from someone out of the Mayor's office. Here the reporter's number. Her name is Beverly Afflis."

"No problem, Chief."

Thirty minutes later, the sergeant ascertained that the Seven-Nine Squad was intending to execute a search warrant at a Bedford Stuyvesant drug den.

"What do you think about a narco raid, Loo?" Markie asked Lieutenant Wright.

"Forget it, Al, things could get dicey over there," replied Wright. "Make some more calls and try and find easier pickings." Markie's further efforts identified a less dangerous opportunity.

"I checked with Public Morals. They're knocking over some wise guy's gambling joint on Staten Island," informed Markie. "They got no problem with us tagging along."

"Okay, that sounds more like it," said the lieutenant. "I'll let Chief McCoy know."

When Lieutenant Wright returned, he informed Markie that Chief McCoy decided to join them on the raid.

"The chief wants to come along with us?" asked the sergeant.

"That's what the man said," replied Wright. "Call up the reporter and let her know the particulars.

"Are you going, Loo?"

"No, the old man wants me to hold down the fort here."

On the morning of the raid, Markie, Von Hess, and Chief McCoy met with the reporter. Their role as observers in the raid called for their positioning themselves in the rear yard of a private house until the entry team secured the location in question. A five-foot-high chain link fence prevented their entry into the yard.

"For safety reasons, you'll have to remain on the other side of this fence, ma'am," instructed Chief McCoy, addressing the reporter. "Once the apprehension is made and the scene secured, you'll be granted full access to witness the actual search and so on."

Each of the men began to climb over the fence. Von Hess was the first to make it over, doing so easily. Chief McCoy, who was dressed in a suit and long white raincoat, ran into some difficulty making it over the barrier. The chief straddled the fence, struggling to get one of his legs over the top. Markie, who was atop the fence and set to jump to the ground, waited patiently until the chief made it safely over. Only then did he jump down off the fence. The sergeant's hesitation did not go unnoticed by the chief.

When their assignment was completed without incident, the chief and his detectives returned to police headquarters. Shortly after arriving at his office McCoy called in Lieutenant Wright.

"Loosen the screws on Markie and Von Hess," said the chief.

"Very good, chief," answered the surprised Wright.

"I want you to prepare a memo for me that I want sent out to all the squads."

"What about, Chief?"

"It'll be about physical fitness. I want to remind our detectives that they have to stay in shape. They have to realize that they could be called upon to do something strenuous at any time.

We had to go over a fence earlier that was demanding. *We* met the challenge of course, but a lot of others would have never been able to."

After the memo was prepared and distributed, Von Hess read it. Finding the contents of the memo odd, he asked Markie about it.

"What do you make of this memo, Sarge?"

"That's just the chief," replied the sergeant. "Since he climbed a fence, everyone has to be able to do it."

"He just made it over by a whisker," said Von Hess. "Did you find that fence to be difficult?"

"Nah, it was easy. Why?"

"I saw you hanging on top of the fence next to McCoy."

"That was intentional, Ollie."

"It was? Why?"

"There was no way I was going to have McCoy looking up at me from the ground after he fell on his ass," explained Markie. "If he took a flop, I was gonna come tumbling down right alongside him—and say that was the most difficult fence ever erected."

"You think he realized that?"

"You bet he did. He took the chains off us, didn't he?"

"So that's why."

"Yeah, now we can go out tomorrow and do some work again.

###########

ON HIS WAY HOME FROM WORK, MARKIE stopped off at Fitzie's to see Alley. The place wasn't crowded, so he and Alley had ample time to spend chatting while he had a drink.

"Did you talk to your mother?"

"I did! She was simply thrilled, Al."

"I'm looking forward to the trip. I was never in England."

"You'll love it. You'll get to meet everyone."

"I want to see everything—where you grew up, the school you attended . . . the works."

Alley Cat was impressed that Markie took such an interest. Making a person feel special was one of Markie's greatest qualities—*if* he liked you.

It was 10:00 p.m. when the sergeant decided to head home. By this time he had consumed enough alcohol to, as they say in police jargon, get his beer balls up. As he made his way to his car, thoughts of Fishnet Milligan crept into his mind. His suspicion that foul play took place at the quarry gnawed at him. *Accidental death? In a pig's eye*, he thought. Fueled by alcohol, the urge came upon him to drive to the townhouse where Fishnet resided.

Being a seasoned drinker, the sergeant had built up a tolerance that could handle his alcohol intake. If stopped en route, he'd be able to speak without slurring and walk a straight line if he had to. However, taking a breathalyzer test would be another matter.

#########

FISHNET HAD BEEN SPENDING a quiet evening at home. Relaxing in a black silk robe, he leisurely watched television. He liked to wear the monogrammed robe around the house in the evening because he felt elegant in it. When donning the robe, he pretended to be the man he was credited with looking like, Clark Gable.

Fishnet had just prepared for himself a tall Coke with plenty of ice cubes. As he stirred his beverage with a plastic straw, his mind drifted off to that faraway place he frequently visited.

Fishnet envisioned himself as Gable, sitting at a table poolside. He was enjoying a tropical drink as he gazed at several of his famous leading ladies frolicking in his pool. This pleasant fantasy was interrupted by someone banging on his front door.

It wasn't a typical knocking that distracted Fishnet from his fantasy. It was more of a heavy-handed pounding that rocked him to reality. Considering the hour, the former detective decided to play it safe. He removed a derringer from the end table drawer and slipped it in the pocket of his robe. The gun was one of the many illegal weapons he confiscated from criminals and kept. Fishnet believed stashing a gun a gun in every room of the house was the best way to protect against a home invasion. Since all of these ill-gotten weapons had their serial numbers filed off, he would have no compunction in shooting a home invader and later claiming that he wrested the weapon from the intruder.

Gripping the derringer in his pocket, he answered the door. His gun rested just below his belly button and was pointed ahead. He was more than a little surprised to see Sergeant Markie standing before him.

"Hey, Sarge, what brings you here at this time of night?" said Fishnet, in a cheery voice.

"You do," replied Markie, using a confrontational tone. "I have words for you, Fishnet."

"You have words for *me*?" asked Fishnet, genuinely baffled. "Come on in. I'll fix you a drink," he said casually.

"I don't want a drink," said Markie, entering the townhouse.

"Chill out will ya, Sarge? I thought you were somebody trying to break down the friggin' door." Fishnet removed the derringer from his pocket and returned it to the end table drawer. "That's a good way to get shot up." Seeing the gun was a reminder to

Markie that Fishnet could be dangerous. "Take a seat, Sarge, and tell me about the bug you got up your ass."

"What I have to say to you ain't gonna take long."

"Alright then, have it your way," said Fishnet, doing away with all pretense of politeness. "What's the beef?"

"I'm putting you on notice."

"You're putting *me* on notice?"

"You got a lot of people bullshitted, my friend . . . but not me."

"What the hell are you talking about?"

"I see the set up you got over here. Those were no accidental deaths in that quarry. You orchestrated the whole shooting match," accused the sergeant.

The remark hit home for Fishnet, reddening his face. "You gotta be fuckin' drunk!" shouted the now highly agitated former detective.

Fishnet's reaction was a dead giveaway for someone as experienced as Markie. The sergeant now felt certain of Fishnet's guilt. "Yeah, I'm drunk alright—drunk on the knowledge that y*ou* killed those two women!" accused Markie, pointing his finger at Fishnet.

"You know what, try getting off the angel dust or whatever shit you're on!"

"I'm not on anything, I'm just on to you. I don't know exactly *how* you did it, but I *know* you did it."

"Yeah, and I suppose you got proof to back up your hallucination?"

"Trust me, my friend. I'll get the proof and bring you down with it. *That*, you can take to the bank."

"You know what? Just get your ass out of my house," shouted Fishnet, pointing to the door. "Go out and sleep it off."

"I'm going—but not forgetting."

"As far as I'm concerned, you're a fucking burglar, so get your ass out of here before I call the cops or put one in ya," shouted Fishnet, walking toward the end table.

Markie, who was now beginning to fully sober up, felt more certain than ever that Fishnet killed the two women in the quarry. Recognizing the potential for gunplay, the off-duty sergeant knew enough to back off at this point.

"I'm going, Fishnet. But remember this. I'm coming for you," warned Markie. "You know me, and you know I'm capable of putting a case together. I'm gonna get the goods on you for killing your wife and that other woman." he threatened.

"What is this, some kind of a shakedown? If it is, just say so."

"No, this is no shakedown. It's just a case of every dog having his day."

"Yeah, yeah, yeah," answered Fishnet dismissively. "You and nobody else in this life is *ever* gonna get me for killing anybody. Now get your drunken ass out of here!"

Markie categorized Fishnet's words as being practically a confession. "I got you running scared, Fishnet, and you should be. I'm gonna be on you like stink to shit."

"You got me shaking in my slippers, chump. Now get out of here, and don't let the door hit you on the ass," ordered Fishnet.

"I'm going," answered the sergeant.

"Then shut the fuck up and go already!" roared Fishnet.

Once on the other side of the entrance door, Markie turned to address the man he accused of murder one final time. "And keep this in mind in case you start getting any bright ideas: I'm not some over-the-hill actress."

Furious, Fishnet slammed the door shut. He returned to his chair and gulped down his Coke. Knowing Markie was too honest to be bought off, Fishnet began to worry. He mixed himself a stiff drink to calm his nerves. He then took a seat on the couch, where he returned to his other world. Now in an environment in which he was able to control the action, he was at ease.

The stage he set was in the townhouse basement, where he had each of Markie's arms tied to brick posts a short distance apart. Virtually helpless, the sergeant stood shirtless with his arms spread wide apart.

"What are you going to do?" asked Markie, his voice trembling before his captor.

Fishnet snapped the whip he was holding against the cellar floor. "Heh, heh, heh," laughed Markie's captor. "*You* need a lesson so that in the future, you know where the power lies."

Fishnet began viciously whipping Markie. The rawness created by the lash marks soon became a hideous sight to behold. After numerous lashes, Fishnet tired, stepping back to catch his breath. Finding the whipping to be labor intensive, Fishnet came up with an alternative torment.

"Since you don't listen to me, I'm gonna give you a reason why you don't," said the former detective.

After stroking Markie's ear, Fishnet removed a straight edge razor from his pocket. Fishnet drifted out of his daydream just after lopping off the sergeant's ears. When reality returned, he was left with but a single thought: *What in the hell am I really gonna do about this guy?*

Fishnet glanced at the drawer that contained his gun. "There's got to be another way," he said, making it clear he was conflicted. Bad as things were, he didn't want to kill a fellow cop unless it was absolutely necessary.

34

Life Without The Professor

SAMSON BELLO WASTED NO TIME IN ARRANGING for Ella to wake the Professor. His connections to a friendly Philadelphia funeral parlor facilitated the handling of all the arrangements. It turned out to be a bare-bones affair, complete with the cheapest casket available, few flowers, and no religious involvement.

Of the half dozen people who attended the one-day viewing, the only people Ella knew were Diamond Joe Ormento and the attorney Bello. The others present were people paid by Bello to attend and look sad. Amidst this false remorse reposed the Professor, who looked at peace in his coffin as he held on to the black rosary beads Diamond Joe placed into his hands.

"The mortician did a nice job on him," commented Bello, as he stood over the corpse.

"I added the rosary beads," pointed out Diamond Joe, who stood beside the attorney. "Even though he was a prick, I thought it was a nice touch."

Keeping her distance from the casket, Ella stood at the far end of the room. She remained quiet throughout the viewing, preferring not to converse with anyone. At the cemetery she maintained her silence. She watched the Professor's casket as it was lowered into the ground without expressing any signs of emotion. It was during the ride home from the cemetery that she finally decided to speak.

"Well, that's that," she declared coldly to Bello and Diamond Joe, anxious to embark on a life of affluence.

##########

COMING TO TERMS WITH THE BIGAMOUS behavior of the man she loved was traumatic for Rebecca. While still reeling from that reality, the Professor's first wife learned of his assassination. The news crumbled her emotionally, leaving the loyal Rebecca with little interest in maintaining her appearance, eating regularly or assuming everyday responsibilities. Faced with her daughter's zombielike condition, Rebecca's mother had no choice other than to step in and take charge of the situation.

When Rebecca's mother inquired in Philadelphia about the Professor's body, she learned that arrangements had already been made by Ella, the Professor's other wife. When she communicated this to her daughter, Rebecca's initial reaction was to turn her head away to stare blankly at nothing in particular. Then, after a few minutes, Rebecca rose slowly from her chair and retreated to her bedroom. She emerged a couple of minutes later holding papers in her hand. It was the will the Professor had prepared years prior. After handing her mother the document Rebecca then returned to her seat to once again disengage.

Rebecca's mother read the will and immediately contacted the Manhattan based attorney involved in preparing the document. Once notified that the Professor was dead, the attorney called for a meeting with the family. After gathering the facts from Rebecca's mother he began taking steps.

Once the New York lawyer was made aware that the Professor had drawn up a more recent will in
Philadelphia, he immediately telephoned Rebecca, who handed the phone off to her mother.
Arrangements were subsequently made to once again meet with the attorney at his office.

Rebecca's mother arrived at the attorney's office with her daughter in tow. The older woman's intention was to use the inheritance to send her daughter to a place where she could receive proper treatment for her condition. This recipe for normalizing Rebecca fell apart after the mother was informed that her son-in-law had prepared a more recent will in Pennsylvania, naming his second wife Ella as his sole beneficiary.

Rebecca's mother collapsed back into her seat, frustrated by this additional complication. After taking a moment to digest the disturbing news, she went on the offensive.

"We'll settle this in a courtroom if we have to in order to collect." said Rebecca's mother. "We probably should give the wife in Philadelphia a little money—after all, she was victimized as well."

"Well, I'm afraid the emergence of a more recent will slightly changes things," advised the attorney.

"What do you mean?"

"The presence of a more recent will means that our side gets less," advised the attorney.

"How can that be? Rebecca is his *first* wife."

"Unfortunately, in most cases it's the most recent will that carries weight," advised the lawyer.

"You mean that we're out the money?"

"Well, no, you'll get something. You have to understand that we're in for a fight with this wrinkle."

"How much is something?"

"We'll shoot for the full third."

"You mean we don't even get half?"

"I'm afraid not."

"Who the hell drew up this other will?" asked Rebecca's mother, making her annoyance obvious.

"It was an attorney in Philadelphia.

"Do you know him?"

"No, I have no prior knowledge of him. But I know of someone who does."

"What a mess that son of a bitch left behind!" shouted the mother-in-law in disgust. "I should have let my husband beat the hell out of him years ago!" she said with regret.

"I'm sorry about this," said the attorney trying to console his client's mother.

"This whole thing stinks to high heaven! You have to do something about this!"

"I'll do my best to get what we can."

Rebecca sat quietly throughout the exchange. Finally there came a point where she spoke. "What's done is done, ma," was all the widow could think to say.

"Will you just listen to her," directed the mother, pointing to Rebecca. "What am I supposed to do with her?"

"What's done is done," Rebecca again repeated.

"You think so?" questioned the mother. "Well I'm not done! If I get sick what's gonna happen?"

Rebecca had no answer for her mother. She simply stared off, resuming her place among the lost. The one upside to Rebecca's condition was that she was beyond worry. That couldn't be said of her mother.

##########

THE AMOUNT OF WINE BEING CONSUMED BY her husband at Diamond Joe's Italian Garden disturbed the restaurant owner's wife. Mrs. Ormento was unaware as to why her husband Joe, his lawyer, and their former employee Ella, were in such a jubilatory mood. She had been married to Diamond Joe long enough to know that he only drank when he came into good fortune—and that usually meant lots of money.

The cause behind the joviality rested with the attorney Bello. With the help of some under-the-table money and promises of future business referrals, he had induced the attorney representing the Professor's first wife to settle out of court for an amount favorable to Ella's side of the equation.

Mrs. Ormento, her curiosity getting the best of her, summoned her husband from across the room after making eye contact. Excusing himself, Diamond Joe rose from the table to see what his wife wanted. He pushed his chin upward when he reached her. It was his way of asking what she wanted.

"What's the big celebration about?" Mrs. Ormento asked.

"Ella and Sammy settled their case, so their having a party."

"She's having a party when her husband isn't even cold yet?"

"He was a bum—what do you want from me?" asked Joe.

"But he was still her husband," pointed out Mrs. Ormento.

"Let's talk about it later. I gotta go back and sit with them, they asked me to join them."

"Why? What does all of this have to do with you?" Mrs. Ormento asked under her breath, as she looked suspiciously at the table where her husband joined Ella and her attorney.

Mrs. Ormento's antennae elevated further after seeing Samson Bello begin to whisper in his client's ear. When Ella's neck snapped back as if surprised by his words, Diamond Joe's wife could tell that Bello had been flirtatious. Ella's wide grin made it apparent that she didn't disapprove of the lawyer's advances. Mrs. Ormento shook her head in disgust.

At the table Samson Bello said something to Diamond Joe in Italian that Ella didn't understand.

"Sure, why not, if that's what she wants," commented the restaurant owner in answer to what Bello said.

"So how about it, Ella?" asked the attorney.

"You made your money, Sammy," she reminded. "What do you want, everything?"

"I'm thinking of Joe."

"Here, have some more wine, Sammy" said Joe, filling his glass. "What about you, Ella, another soda?"

"No thanks, Joe," replied Ella, who made up her mind to stop drinking.

Mrs. Ormento continued to monitor the goings on at the table. Getting the drift of what was happening, she walked over to her husband in a huff. A silence came over the table.

"Giuseppe, I need you in the kitchen right NOW!" she declared authoritatively. "Come with me."

Whenever his wife called him Giuseppe, the restaurant owner knew that the best thing for him to do was to comply in order to avoid a scene. Once alone, Mrs. Ormento unloaded. Joe sucked up the verbal lambasting she administered without offering a counterargument. Experience taught him that when his wife's ire reached this point, talk would only aggravate the situation. While Diamond Joe wasn't particularly afraid of his wife, he did have concerns regarding her two brothers. Both men were known to be capable of doing nasty things.

Mrs. Ormento concluded her diatribe by stating, "*è una puttana,*" in reference to Ella.

"Eh, c'mon, she's not a whore," replied Joe softly, trying to defend Ella's reputation.

"*Stai zitto!*" Joe's wife shouted abruptly. Diamond Joe did as he was told and shut up.

Joe shrugged and returned to performing the duties of a restaurant owner. He knew that it was the best thing for him to do at this point.

With his end of the money, Diamond Joe intended to make peace with his wife by treating her to a trip to Italy. He felt certain that sending Mrs. Ormento off to the old country to visit her family on the other side was a good strategy. Historically, she usually returned from such visits in a forgiving mood.

"Goodbye, Joe," said Bello, "we're heading out." The attorney was smiling rakishly as he departed the restaurant with his arm over Ella's shoulder.

"*Arrivederci,* Sammy," replied the restaurant owner, saying goodbye.

"So long, Joe" echoed Ella. "Thanks for everything."

Joe nodded and smiled as he waved farewell. Diamond Joe watched sadly as they exited his restaurant. He then turned to see where his wife was. When their eyes met, he let out a sigh. He could only imagine what he was missing out on.

##########

WHEN ALL WAS SETTLED ELLA USED HER INHERITANCE to

relocate to Florida, where she began investing in real estate. At her side advising her was her new husband, the now retired Samson Bello, who had left his wife and two children for Ella. The couple relocated to Florida where they purchased a penthouse apartment in Fort Lauderdale.

At Bello's urging, he and his wife began taking golf lessons. Finding she had a natural aptitude for the sport, Ella purchased a condo in Myrtle Beach so she could further enjoy her newfound passion. As they progressed at the game, Ella and Sammy began taking overseas golf vacations in places such as Ireland and Scotland.

A few years later, Ella happened to read an article concerning Netflix, a relatively new subscription streaming service. On a lark, she decided to purchase some stock in the entity. When the stock skyrocketed, Samson Bello became so impressed with his wife's insight that he encouraged Ella to begin reading the newspapers in search of other winning opportunities. As it turned out, Ella came to enjoy knowing things. After becoming a voracious reader, she proved herself a valuable resource in identifying similar stock opportunities.

Sammy and Ella used some of their gains to establish a reputation as benefactors to worthy charitable causes. There was even an Ella and Samson Bello wing at a small Florida hospital they supported. With all memory of the Professor erased from their mind, the couple couldn't have been happier during this period.

When not busy identifying stocks to purchase, Ella threw herself into improving her golf game. She began taking lessons from Romolo, a handsome golf pro. These frequent sessions enabled the student and pupil to grow close.

Samson, as he aged, let himself go. Unbridled when it came to his eating habits, he packed on poundage that couldn't be offset by the rigors of golf. His dietary indulgences led to a serious stroke. Wheelchair-bound and unable to speak clearly, the once high-powered attorney had morphed into a domestic eyesore for Ella.

Finding the situation depressingly untenable, Ella placed her husband in a home where Sammy would be someone else's problem. With Ella's husband safe in storage, Romolo transitioned smoothly into Sammy Bello's Bentley and double-jointed wife.

##########

WHEN CONCETTA IN ARIZONA, the Professor's intended third bride, stopped hearing from him, she didn't know what to make of it. Since her calls and messages weren't being answered, she began fearing something terrible might have happened. Concerned, she recruited a Manhattan based friend to visit the New York City bookshop. When Concetta's friend reported back that a sign was posted in the bookshop window advertising the store was for rent, Concetta began experiencing a sick feeling in her stomach.

After telephoning the hospitals in the New York area with no results, the worried Concetta conferred with the New York City Police Department. When she was told that there was no report of the Professor being in an accident or his being the victim of a crime in New York City, she began to wonder if he was dead. She came to the conclusion at this point that his status made no difference, finally admitting to herself that the Professor wasn't coming back.

Concetta got over her disappointment after meeting an Arizona man at a church sponsored singles event. She and the man, who once worked as a rodeo bull rider, clicked. Within a year she had the husband and palomino she always wanted.

##########

THE LIFESTYLE OF PASCAL HAD BEEN IN DECLINE ever since Sally Belle severed ties with him. After having lived off Sally's largesse for many years, the aging lothario's finances had dwindled to the point of desperation.

Pascal's meager budget left him no choice other than to secure the cheapest possible lodging. With great apprehension he entered the Blackbird Hotel, a lower Manhattan flophouse. Not realizing how awful the hotel was, he was shocked after entering the building. The interior lobby, while hardly clean, was ancient in appearance. The floor was made of a chipped black-and-white tile that is usually now seen only in old tenement bathrooms. The wooden furniture lacked luster. Carve marks in the wood were visible on the arm rests of the chairs. A cobweb could be seen on the singular overhead light. After spotting a roach creeping along the floor, Pascal winced and shook his head slowly.

Pascal forced himself to believe that this was just a temporary stopover and that he'd be fine once he found himself another well-heeled person to take care of him.

The unshaven hotel clerk was a slightly built man who looked old for his years. He sat behind the lobby desk squinting as he struggled to read the small print in the newspaper he held. He only looked up after Pascal cleared his throat to gain his attention. After paying for the night, Pascal was handed one of the keys that hung from a plywood board behind the desk.

Before going to his room, which was a caged cubicle, Pascal turned to his right for a final look at the lobby sitting room. A television sat on a high shelf for the residents to watch. Present were a half dozen men, all who appeared sober. They sat quietly and kept to themselves as they watched the overhead screen. Being between benders, some of these residents had cleaned up nicely. Based upon their clothing, Pascal presumed they were receiving social security checks, a pension or some other form of revenue.

Pascal's wire cubicle was much worse than he anticipated. Once behind the wire door he found himself in a cramped space that contained a bunk bed and a tall, narrow metal dresser. The attached cubicles shared wire walls and ceilings. Green army type blankets covered the walls, providing minimal privacy. The top of the cubicles were bare and receptive to exterior light and noise.

After dropping his grip, Pascal sat on the bed for a moment to gather his thoughts. Needing to use the restroom, he made sure to lock the door to his cubicle when leaving. There was a community bathroom on each floor of the hotel. Pascal let out a low groan after seeing the poor condition of the urinals, bowls, sinks, and showers. His dismay almost caused him to scream.

Pascal's real nightmare came overnight. The nocturnal activities that prevented him from sleeping were varied. The snoring of those sleeping off their drunkenness, eerie rants of the seemingly demented, and the endless talking jags of the intoxicated all kept him from slumber. Pascal knew he could never spend another night there.

When the inevitable arguments and fighting occurred, it all became too much for Pascal. He feared that it would only be a matter of time before he'd be taken advantage of by someone with abusive tendencies.

Pascal was compelled to make the call he thought he'd never make. He swallowed his pride and telephoned the Maestro the following morning. The elderly musician was more than receptive to Pascal's overture.

"Things haven't been good since I was put out by that brute Sally married. Can I come and stay with you awhile?"

"Where are you, Pascal?"

"I've taken lodging in a flophouse on the Bowery."

"That is so beneath you, my dear friend. Of course, come home—you belong here with me."

"Thank you, Maestro."

"Have you eaten?"

"Not since yesterday."

"Come now, and bring your things. We'll breakfast in the park. It's warmed up to be a lovely day."

The much-relieved Pascal immediately packed his bag and checked out. He then proceeded to where the Maestro lived in the West Village.

"So you've finally come back, Pascal—it's so good to see you," said the Maestro, with the look of a man who possessed a winning hand.

"You're looking well, Maestro," lied Pascal, feeling a little sad how poorly the much-older Maestro had aged.

"I'm getting a little old, but other than that, I'm doing fine. It's going to be like old times, isn't it?"

Pascal stared into the old man's face. Trying to overlook the wrinkles, he responded softly, "Yes, Maestro, like old times."

"I've been planning on preparing a magnificent meal for us this evening."

"You don't need to trouble yourself by cooking anything special for me. Anything will do as long as you have some scotch. You do have scotch, don't you?"

"Of course I have scotch. But, come, let's pick something up to eat and go to the park."

The two men entered Washington Square Park to eat their

coffee and cake. The Maestro signaled a young man in his twenties to come to him.

"Can you accommodate me?"

"The usual?" asked the young drug dealer.

"Twice that—I have company," replied the gloating Maestro.

After scoring the cocaine, the Maestro and his houseguest finished their food. They then took a stroll before returning to the older man's apartment. That evening, as they got high, they discussed the death of Sally Belle and Estelle Hatton.

"I heard that the cop inherited Sally's money," said the Maestro.

"I never trusted that poor man's Clark Gable from the beginning," said Pascal bitterly. "I'll bet my life that he was the one who sabotaged my relationship with Sally."

"How did he accomplish that?"

"Trust me, Maestro, he has two sides, that man—both evil. He's the one who set me up. He made it look as if I stole from Sally. He's a diabolical brute!"

"That hardly surprises me. I never for a moment believed that line he gave everyone. He didn't strike me as someone dedicated to doing God's work," noted the Maestro.

"Talking about a line, how about it Maestro? Shall we?"

"Let's—and then I'll play my favorite instrument for you, Pascal."

Pascal's smile was forced. "We might as well break out that scotch as well," he said.

35

A New Mission

AFTER SHOWERING, MITCHELL EMERY STOOD IN FRONT OF HIS
bathroom mirror, doing all he could to enhance his appearance.
Satisfied his hair was precisely the way the barber left it, he
then shaved. After applying his favorite balm, he dabbed
cologne behind his ears. All of this was in preparation to see
Alley, the woman he had an incredible thirst for.

Mitchell secured the day off by calling his job and claiming to
be sick. His plan was to intercept Ally on the street when she
left her building for work.

When he arrived on Alley's block, an edgy Mitchell carefully
searched the immediate area for the vehicle he had vandalized.
Once confident the man who took Alley home that upsetting
night wasn't around, Mitchell felt relieved. He waited patiently
on the street for Alley to depart her residence. When Alley
finally exited her building, the stalker reacted by licking his
fingers and patted his hair down.

As Alley walked down the street, she noticed that the people walking in the opposite direction seemed to be looking over her shoulder at something to her rear. Curious as to what was so interesting, Alley turned to see for herself. Startled to see Mitchell, Markie's girlfriend wasted no time in reacting.

"Are you following me?" she asked in a harsh voice. "You must be looking for more of what you got at the bar," she said, referring to the beating Mitchell received after harassing her at work.

"I . . . uhh, just wanted, err...what I wanna say is, that I'm very, very sorry for my ungentlemanly behavior," awkwardly stated Mitchell, who was having a difficult time finding the correct words to express himself.

Alley, taken by surprise, was terse in her response. "Well, as long as you got the message, let's just forget it."

Mitchell interpreted her words as a sign of encouragement, bolstering his confidence. "Let me make it up to you."

"Look, all I want you to do is stay away from me. If you do that, we'll get along just fine."

"How about we go for some coffee?"

Alley rolled her eyes in frustration. "Look, I'm not going out with you! Besides, I have to go to work."

"You have plenty of time. You always go in early," said Mitchell, his persistence going unabated.

His knowledge of her routine concerned Alley. "And how do you know what time I leave for work?"

"I know all about you, Alley."

Mitchell's statement freaked Alley out, causing her to lash out. "Listen, you little creep—you better just leave me the hell alone if you know what's good for you," she warned.

"But Alley, can't you see that we belong together?"

"For your information, I'm getting married. So just back off.

My fiancé is the jealous type, and he isn't someone to trifle with."

"He doesn't frighten me. I *know* who he is."

Alley was shocked by Mitchell's statement. "You *know* my boyfriend?"

"I've seen him leave your house."

"What?" she asked, now realizing that it must have been Mitchell, who vandalized Markie's vehicle.

"Like I said, I know all about you, Alley. All you need to do is give me a chance. I promise you, you'll forget all about him."

Alley couldn't believe what she was hearing. "You must be totally out of your mind! Why, compared to him, you're . . . you're just a *squirt!*"

Alley's remark wounded the stalker. Being called a squirt brought back unpleasant memories of Oswaldo, his abusive brother. Outrage over the insult now overshadowed the advice he heard over the radio from the talk show host. With a sneer, he held his chin up as he stared at the taller woman.

"Well remember this—I'm the *squirt* that created Alleytown for you!" said Mitchell, in a way that made it sound like he accomplished something big.

"What the hell is Alleytown?"

"I'll show you," replied Mitchell, grabbing Alley's forearm. His grip was strong, much stronger than Alley could have imagined.

"Take your hands off me," shouted Alley, trying to pull away from him. "I'm not going anyplace with you. You're nuts!"

"You *are* coming with me," said Mitchell, who reached into his pocket to remove a box cutter.

Now being truly menaced, Alley understood that Mitchell wasn't going to take no for an answer. Her efforts to pull away were to no avail; his hold was vice-like. Alley's only hope rested with people on the street. To her dismay no one was in the area other than an elderly man who paid her no attention. Alley had to think fast.

"Maybe I've misjudged you," she said, stalling for time. I have to go to work now, so why don't you walk me? We could talk on the way."

"What I want to show you won't take long," insisted Mitchell, yanking her forearm to his chest. "You can go to work afterward if you want." Mitchell then pressed the blade of the box cutter against her wrist.

Fearing that he would slice her, Alley had little choice other than to go along with the abduction. Once they began walking, Mitchell pocketed the box cutter. After arriving at Mitchell's house, Alley was reluctant to enter. When she tried resisting, Mitchell again took out the box cutter. This time he raised the blade to her cheek as an inducement for her to accompany him inside. Rather than face disfigurement, she capitulated and went along with her kidnapper's wishes.

Alley couldn't believe her own eyes when she entered the house. Seeing her expression of awe, Mitchell smiled proudly at what he considered a triumphant moment.

"Welcome to Alleytown," he declared. "It's the city I created in your honor. The Alley Express runs throughout the first floor of the house."

"You did all this?" she asked, finding the whole scene frighteningly bizarre.

"I did. I knew you'd love it once you saw it."

"This is . . . incredible," said the stunned Alley, who was now convinced the man she labeled Little Creepy was a lunatic.

Mitchell began stroking the top of Alley's head as though she were a puppy. The abducted woman bristled at his touch. As his hand traveled down the back of her head, she stiffened. The feel of his fingers infiltrating the strands of her tresses caused a chill to go up her back.

I've got to do something! Alley thought, as the panic began to set in. Just then Mitchell's hand shifted to the back of her neck, which he began to gently massage.

"Why are you shaking?" asked Mitchell softly. "I'm not going to hurt you," he assured her. "I love you. C'mon, we'll start the tour at Alley Station."

In a trancelike state, Alley accompanied him. Mitchell donned his engineer's cap before activating the train. "All aboard," he shouted, as usual. "Let's follow the locomotive as it makes it way along the track," he added, leading her by the arm. "My plans are to erect Alley Airport for you."

When Mitchell's prisoner entered the room that was papered with her photographs, her heart began racing dangerously. The stalker's captive grew desperate.

As Mitchell admired his handiwork, Alley decided that her only course of action was to make a fight of it. She looked about her immediate vicinity to see what she could use as a weapon. *The tracks!* She thought, as she stared at some loose tracks that rested near the transformer. *If I could grab one of them, I could poke him in the eye and run out of the house!* Alley's opportunity came on the train's return trip.

"So now you know just how I feel about you," said Mitchell softly as the train pulled in.

"I do," she said, trying her best to sound flattered. "How does the transformer work?" Alley asked, hoping to get close enough to the loose track to use it as a weapon.

Mitchell was delighted by the interest she expressed. He saw it as a sign that she was thawing out. "It's easy, Alley. Let me show you how things work."

When they got close to the transformer Alley was prepared to make her move. "Are those tracks heavy?" she asked. "Can I hold one?"

Her request further delighted Mitchell, who felt he was making great strides. "Of course—here," said the abductor, releasing his grip on her. He then passed a piece of track to Alley.

Alley juggled the piece of track in her hand evaluating its weight. She then suddenly let out a scream and jabbed the metal track into Mitchell's face, aiming for his eyes. As Mitchell reeled backward, Alley rushed to the front door and ran into the street.

Alley's blow landed high and struck Mitchell's eyebrow, which began to leak a steady flow of blood. Recovering quickly, he chased after her, stopping short at the front door. He used his sleeve to wipe away the blood that flowed freely down his face.

When Alley reached the corner, she halted for a second, unsure of which way to flee. Assuming that Mitchell was hot on her trail, she bolted across the avenue without looking. Her haste proved fatal. Alley was struck by a racing city bus whose driver was behind schedule.

The bus driver subsequently told the police that the woman ran in front of his bus for reasons unknown to him. With no evidence to the contrary, the police didn't view this as a criminal matter. They looked upon Alley's death as an accident or possible suicide—a conclusion that wasn't going to sit well with Al Markie.

###########

MARKIE NEEDED TO TAKE TIME OFF after learning of Alley's death. It took two weeks of vacation time to normalize him. The first week saw him occupied with notifications and making the necessary unpleasant arrangements for Alley. The first half of following week he turned to drink to deal with his grief. The final half was spent recuperating from the physical abuse he subjected himself to with alcohol.

Once back at work, Markie and Von Hess discussed the matter of Alley's death with the detectives who investigated the fatal accident. While unhappy with what he was told, the sergeant nevertheless understood how they arrived at their conclusions.

"There has to be more to this, Ollie. I can't see Alley intentionally running in front of a bus to cross an avenue anymore that I can see her committing suicide. She had to be running away from somebody."

"But who was she running from, Sarge?" Von Hess asked. "The bus driver didn't see anyone near her."

"I have no idea who. But someone had to have made her run in front of that bus. And whoever that was had someplace nearby to hide."

"The detectives said they did a canvass of the area."

"That's what they said. But you know how that goes, Ollie. How much effort did they really put into it?"

"If you want to do a canvass, Sarge, I'm game."

"Thanks, Ollie. But first, I'm gonna go to the bar where Alley worked. I want to talk to Fitzie. Maybe he can shed some light on this."

"Let's go."

"Don't feel obligated to come along, Ollie. I can handle it."

"I know you could handle it, but I'm sticking with you." Markie just nodded his appreciation.

###########

WHEN MARKIE AND VON HESS entered Fitzie's, the bar owner was behind the stick pouring beer for a customer. After spotting the detectives, Fitzie came out from behind the bar to embrace the sergeant.

"I'm sorry, Al. I didn't get a chance to really talk to you at the wake. This whole business devastated me. I just can't believe what happened to Alley."

Markie was unable to speak. All he could manage was a nod of understanding. It was up to Von Hess to take the lead.

"We're all having a hard time making sense of this," said Von Hess.

"I can't imagine what would drive her to suicide," said the bar owner.

"That was no suicide, Fitzie," said Markie. "They're calling it that or an accident, but there had to be more to it. And we're gonna find out what."

"You suspect foul play?"

"Can you picture Alley running anyplace?" asked the sergeant bitterly. "She had to be running from someone or something."

"Fitzie, was anybody bothering Alley?" asked Von Hess.

"No—everybody loved Alley," replied the bar owner.

"Did she have any ill will toward anyone or have words with a customer, perhaps?"

Fitzie thought for a moment before responding. "Now that you mention it, there was this one guy . . . a little shit who used to come in once in a while."

"What guy was that?" asked Markie, his interest stirred.

"I don't know his name, but he was a lecherous little prick."

"Did Alley have a problem with him?"

"Sort of—she used to complain that he was creepy. Matter of fact, that's what Alley called him: Little Creepy."

"She never mentioned any of this to me," said Markie.

"Nah, she was always afraid you'd overreact and do something crazy. She didn't want to see you getting into trouble."

"You don't know his name?"

"I don't know—he was just a guy who came in once in awhile."

"What was the story with him?"

"He was thinking with his little head, you know the type. He had a thing for Alley."

"Why was he creepy?" questioned Von Hess. "What did he do to make you figure him for a pervert?"

"He used to come in here and flick his tongue at her, stuff like that. I corrected that shit fast," noted Fitzie.

"You did?"

"Yeah, I sent a couple of convincers to show him the error of his ways."

"When was all this?" asked Markie.

"I don't know—not too long ago."

"Did he ever touch her?"

This was a question Fitzie felt awkward in answering. "I don't know, Al. The guy was just a creep."

"So did he ever touch her?" repeated Markie, seeking an answer to his question.

"He'd rub her hand when she placed his drink down. Shit like that."

"You saw him do this?" asked Von Hess.

"Yeah, that's one of the reasons why I had him worked over."

"What does this guy look like?

"He was short, sort of muscular, like a guy who works out. I don't think he was forty years old."

"Any distinguishing features?"

"Other than being short, nothing I could see. Maybe his teeth were a little crooked. He's probably still banged up from the beating he got. The boys gave him a good tune up."

"Does this guy work?"

"I don't know anything about him."

"Thanks, Fitzie," said Markie, preparing to leave with Von Hess.

"Hey, where are you going, Al? How about having a shot on the house?"

"No, we got things to do."

Once back in the car, Von Hess could tell Markie was in a foul frame of mind. This caused the detective some concern. "What do you think?" he asked.

"We're gonna go find this guy, Ollie. I'm getting the feeling this could be the same guy who messed up my car."

"Where do we start looking?"

"Let's go to the scene of the accident. We'll give the area a good canvass. If he's still banged up, we should be able to get a line on him."

The sergeant worried Von Hess. Since this was personal to Markie, the detective wasn't sure how his boss was going to react to seeing Little Creepy. If the sergeant believed him as the cause of Alley's death things could get ugly fast.

"Sarge, I think we should probably get the okay from Lieutenant Wright if we're going to be working this case," said Von Hess. "At least if we're on record, we'll be covered if things happen to turn shitty."

Markie thought about what Von Hess said before replying. "You're probably right, Ollie," answered the sergeant. "I just hope he doesn't think I'm too close to the situation."

"I'm glad you agree, Sarge. It's best that we watch our step right now, especially on the heels of the Fishnet mess."

"Fishnet ain't important anymore, Ollie. I got other priorities. Anyway, approval or not, I'm working the case."

"I hear you, Sarge."

The following day Markie received approval to look into

Alley's death, with one stipulation posed by Lieutenant Wright: if a more pressing matter arose, Markie and Von Hess would have to stop what they were doing and work the new situation until it either was resolved or under control.

Markie knew that Wright didn't make this call on his own. Permission had to have come from Chief of Detectives McCoy, who decided to give the sergeant a gift. It was further reward for his hanging on top of a fence a few seconds longer so as not to embarrass his boss.

36

The Neighbors

MARKIE'S HEART WAS HEAVY AS he stood at the intersection where Alley was killed. Gazing at the accident scene brought him unpleasant thoughts of Alley's last moments. He visualized the oncoming bus, Alley's face just prior to being struck, the screech, the horn blowing, and her sailing high in the air upon impact. It was all so vivid to him. The only thing unclear was the circumstances that caused Alley to run in front of the bus.

"Where do you want to start, Sarge?" asked Von Hess.

Markie turned slowly to look at the detective. "With the pedestrians," he answered.

The investigators commenced their inquiry by randomly stopping people walking on the street. Of particular interest were those who were carrying packages, believing them to be primarily area residents. Their questioning wasn't encouraging in terms of results.

The detectives next focused on the residential houses located within a three-block radius of the scene of the accident. Once again, their efforts proved unproductive. Sympathizing with his supervisor, Von Hess thought a cocktail after work might be in order.

"Tomorrow's another day, Sarge. There are still lots of houses to hit. How about coming home with me for dinner? I feel like having a couple of pops."

"Tonight?" asked the sergeant.

"Sure, come home with me. We'll have a couple, the wife will cook dinner, and when you're ready, I'll drive you home. Or you could even stay over in the spare room if you want."

"Nah, I don't think so, Ollie. Let's save that for another night, but thanks anyway."

"C'mon, you have to eat. I'll call the wife, and she'll set another plate. Besides, you never saw the new bar I built in the basement."

The prospect of seeing the bar interested Markie. "Well, maybe a shot or two will do me some good."

"Great. I'll call the wife."

On the way home, Von Hess pulled the car over to a convenience store where he picked up two six packs of beer. After paying for the beer he thought to call his wife.

"I'm bringing Al Markie home for dinner," he advised. "Do you need me to pick anything up?"

"He's coming tonight?"

"Yeah, the guy is pretty low since his girlfriend died."

"I hate when you pull this last-minute stuff," said Mrs. Von Hess, who was a bit put off.

"Look, we can order take out if it's too much work—"

"No, I have enough food in the house. I just don't like last-minute calls like this."

"It doesn't have to be anything fancy."

"It'll be fine, Oliver. Drive slow though—it'll give me some time to straighten out the house."

##########

WHILE MRS. VON HESS WAS PREPARING DINNER, Markie sat at the bar in the finished basement. As Von Hess stood behind the bar pouring drinks, Markie stared at the imposing picture of Teddy Roosevelt that hung on the wall behind him.

"I glad you came to terms with Crappy Erwin over that picture, Ollie," said Markie, referring to the Manhattan store owner who sold secondhand clothes. "The Rough Rider looks great. Based on the size of it, that picture must have once hung in a library or a private club someplace."

"Everybody loves it. They all want to know where I got it."

"It looks much nicer hanging down here that it ever did in the back of Crappy Erwin's joint."

"That's because I had the frame redone. This picture must have been in the back of that store for I don't know how long, Sarge. If you remember, there was an inch of dust on the frame."

"I remember. I knew Erwin would eventually come down in price rather than lose a sale."

"Here you go, Sarge," said Von Hess, placing a double whiskey in front of Markie. "I got you Bud for a chaser, okay?"

"Anything you have is good with me, Ollie."

"Bottoms up," said Von Hess after pouring the beer. "Did Erwin ever get you that sport jacket you wanted?"

"Yeah, he did. You've seen me wear it—it's the black one with the black buttons I wore the other day.

"Jeeze, I thought you had that one awhile. It really looked broken in."

"What do you want, Ollie? Don't forget, it's secondhand."

353

"That's right, I forgot."

"So what do you say, we continue our canvass tomorrow?"

"No problem. Have another blast?"

"A man can't travel on one leg," replied Markie, pushing his glass forward. "Balance me."

##########

THE FOLLOWING DAY, THE INVESTIGATORS resumed their canvass near the scene of the accident. They began knocking on the doors where no one was home the day prior. They came upon an elderly homeowner who stood outside his house barking at several small children. He was a leathery skinned, angry-looking man of about ninety who walked with a wooden cane. The brown wide brimmed hat he wore was pulled down in front, stopping just above his eyebrows. A heavy button-down sweater covered his black and yellow flannel shirt. A tiny hole could be seen near one of the buttons on the tan sweater.

Solidly built for a nonagenarian, the cranky homeowner ceased shouting when the detectives appeared. "These kids are too much," he complained to the strangers. He then turned his attention to the children. "Go on, I said get outta here!" he yelled in his gravelly voice. "Go play in front of your father's house!" To the old man's further annoyance, the children ignored him. "GO HOME, I SAID!" he shouted at the top of his lungs. He seemed bewildered when the youngsters failed to pay him any mind.

"Go on, kids, go find someplace else to play," said Markie, placing his hand on the back of one of the youths to move him along.

"These damn kids," muttered the old man, after making eye contact with the detectives. The homeowner asked what they wanted by lifting his chin.

"We're detectives," said Von Hess, flashing his tin.

The old man nodded. "Where's *your* badge?" he asked, addressing Markie. He squinted as he examined the sergeant's shield Markie produced. "You guys got any ID cards to go with those badges?"

"Sure we do," answered Von Hess. "Don't you trust us?"

"Why should I? This could be a pottsy you're showing me."

Von Hess chuckled at hearing the term *pottsy*, a slang term for a duplicate police shield he hadn't heard used in years. The detective smiled as he presented his police photo identification. "Satisfied?"

"You know, you gotta be careful these days," said the homeowner.

"That's right—you can never be *too* careful," concurred Von Hess. "Let me ask you something—have you seen a short man who looked like he was recently beaten up around here?"

"What are you talking about, beaten up?" asked the old man indignantly, misunderstanding the question. "I never touched one of those squeaky-voiced little brats!"

"Hold your horses, pop," injected Markie. "We're not talking about the kids, and we're not accusing you of anything. We're looking for a guy in the area who got cuffed around. You know, somebody with bruises on his face, like he had been in a fight."

"I don't know anything about that. All I know is that I got a bunch of dopey people around here who don't know how to keep their kids quiet for five minutes."

"I hear you," said Von Hess. "Kids do make a racket sometimes."

"It's these parents! All they do is stand around blocking the sidewalk while their kids do what the hell they want. Look down the block—there they are! Look, there's even a man standing with all the women! Why the hell ain't he out working?"

"I don't know," replied Von Hess, scratching his cheek.

"Maybe he works nights."

"So have you seen anyone with injuries that could have been the results of an assault?" questioned Markie, bringing the conversation back on topic.

The senior citizen was thinking about the question when his wife came outside to join the men. She had been listening in from the doorway. For her age she had very few wrinkles. Her skin was clear and her teeth perfectly aligned. She was a soft-spoken woman who looked about ten years younger than her husband. Her snow-white hair was long and worn with a part.

"You should talk to the president of the block association," she said, smiling politely.

"Who might that be?" asked Von Hess.

"Her name is Rene. She knows about everybody on this block."

"Where can we find her?"

"She lives in the house up the street with the lit gaslight."

"Who are you talking about?" asked her husband. His abruptness made it clear he was a handful to live with.

"Rene Gilbert, her husband is Jeremy. You know them—they're teachers," answered his wife.

"Those are the ones with the damn kids!"

"Thank you," said Von Hess, shaking his head with an amused look on his face.

The Gilbert family was at home when the detectives knocked on their door. After explaining their purpose they found the couple amenable to helping them.

"I think they're talking about Mitchell," Rene said to her husband. "You know Mitchell—we used to talk to his grandmother whenever she passed by the house to go

356

shopping."

"I know who you mean, the two brothers—which one is Mitchell again?"

"There is only one brother now. The taller brother was the one who got killed."

"Oh, that's right," said Rene's husband.

"Mitchell was bruised up?" asked Markie.

"Yes, he must have gotten into a fight or something," advised Rene. "He was starting to heal, but then I think something else must have happened."

"What do you mean?"

"He's got a new bandage over his eyebrow. He didn't have that before."

"Let me ask you something—how tall a man is Mitchell?" asked Markie.

"Mitchell only comes up to my shoulders, and I'm not all that tall."

"How old is he?"

"It's hard to say. He's not old, and he's not exactly young."

"Do you know Mitchell's last name?"

"Emery, that's spelled E-M-E-R-Y."

"And he lives on this street?" asked Von Hess.

"Yes, in the rundown house. It's the only eyesore on the block."

"He owns the house?"

"Yes, his grandmother left it to him."

"I see. Do you know if he has a tenant?"

"He does. The tenant's a retired fireman. He's divorced—I think he likes to drink."

"Is Mitchell in some kind of trouble?"

"No, we just want to have a word with him about something."

"Oh, I'm curious—is there something we should know?"

"Not really," replied Von Hess. "It's a police matter."

After Rene provided the investigators with the name of the retired fireman, the investigators returned to their vehicle. Markie was more determined than ever to forge ahead.

"Let's swing over to headquarters, Ollie. I want a background check done on this guy Mitchell to see what we're up against."

########

WHEN VON HESS RESEARCHED Mitchell Emery, he found the subject seemed to live life under the radar. Mitchell was never arrested, had no driver's license, and was never involved in any civil litigation. His only property ownership was the house he lived in. According to the available information, Mitchell had co-owned the property with a man believed to be his brother, the late Oswaldo Emery. Based on a review of the work up, Von Hess noted that Oswaldo Emery died at a relatively young age.

When Von Hess checked the name Emery in the media, he came across information of interest. The detective learned that Oswaldo, who was reported to be Mitchell's older brother, met an accidental death on the subway. There was also a photo in one of the papers of a distraught Mitchell. Von Hess rushed to inform Markie of his findings.

"What the hell is going on?" asked Markie after reading the newspaper accounts. "First we got an out of town cop whacked on a subway platform, then Fishnet turns up with two dead women in a quarry, and now this Oswaldo gets hit by a train after his brother trips into him," said the sergeant, his voice laced with skepticism. "How does this shit sit with you, Ollie?"

"I don't know, Sarge," replied Von Hess, who was not a man to rush to conclusions. "I guess the deaths could've all been accidents. But let's face it, there are red flags."

"Of course there are. C'mon, let's make a copy of this Mitchell's picture. We're gonna show it to Fitzie over at the bar."

########

AFTER FITZIE IDENTIFIED MITCHELL EMERY as Little Creepy, Markie reported his results to his boss, Lieutenant Wright. In doing so, he tried his utmost to project the calmest façade possible. He worried that failure to display anything other than a composed demeanor would result in his being denied permission to continue investigating.

"Lieutenant, we made some headway," the sergeant advised. "There's more to Alley's death than meets the eye."

"What have you got?" asked Wright.

Markie detailed the facts he gathered in a methodical fashion. He explained how Mitchell Emery had a history of sexually harassing Alley at work. He spoke of Mitchell getting beaten up, though without revealing Fitzie's involvement. Markie then pointed to the more recent injury sustained by Mitchell under undetermined circumstances. Finally, he emphasized the unusual subway death of Mitchell's brother.

"The arrows all seem to be pointing in one direction, boss," said Markie.

"The death of the brother could be a coincidence, couldn't it?"

"It could."

"Go talk to the investigator who handled the bus accident investigation," instructed Wright. "Fill him in, and keep him abreast of what you're doing."

"How about I do a little more digging before I do that, Loo?"

"Alright," said Wright, after thinking about it. "See what else you can find out. But keep in mind that everyone knows you got

359

a personal interest in this, so tread lightly."

##########

LIEUTENANT WRIGHT HAD BEEN on the money. Conducting an investigation into the circumstances surrounding Alley's death was something personal for Markie. Nothing was going to prevent him from getting to the bottom of things, even if that meant tossing the rule book out the window.

When it came to Detective Von Hess, Markie felt obligated to be protective of him. The last thing he wanted was to see the loyal Von Hess get into trouble on his account. He broached the subject with Von Hess in their office.

"Look, Ollie, I got no problem tackling this situation about Alley alone," advised Markie.

"What makes you say that, Sarge?"

"I'm sticking with this on my off-duty time."

Von Hess didn't hesitate in stepping up. "I got nothing better to do in my off time. Either I work with you or do the chores my wife gives me. Running with you will be a break."

Markie smiled warmly. "Thanks, Ollie, but I don't want you mixed up in my mess."

"How long have you known me, Sarge? You honestly think I'd run out on you at this stage of the game?" Markie just nodded in appreciation. "Don't sweat it, Sarge. What's our next move?"

Markie knew there was no sense in arguing about it. "We go talk to the fireman."

"You mean the suspect's tenant?"

"Yeah, let's figure out what kind of car he drives so we can sit on it. I don't want to risk giving Mitchell Emery a heads-up by showing up at his doorstep."

########

THE RETIRED FIREMAN WAS SITTING in his white Honda waiting
for the alternate side parking restrictions to expire. Fortunately
for the detectives, he was parked around the corner from
where he lived, minimizing the risk of Mitchell seeing anything.

The former firefighter was a strapping man with a full head of
red and white hair. The glow on his face suggested the look of a
drinker. Mitchell's tenant was more than willing to cooperate
with the law once made aware of some of the circumstances.

"Mitchell has always been a strange little fucker, that's for
sure," said the tenant.

"In what way?" asked Von Hess.

"He's a loner. I've never been downstairs inside his house
once, and I've been living there for years."

"Is he the nasty type?"

"Oh, no, I've had no problem with him, as far as that goes. The
guy hasn't even raised my rent in all the time I've been living
there, so I can't really badmouth him. He's never bothered *me*."

"Is he prone to get in scraps?"

"I think he must be. But I'd say that's a recent development."

"What makes you say that?"

"Lately he looks like a guy who has been getting into fights. I
think somebody tuned him up."

"Did he tell you that?"

"No, he never said a word. We don't have a confiding
relationship."

"Why would anyone want to do give him a shellacking?" asked
Markie.

"I got no idea. If I did ask him what happened, he wouldn't
give me a straight answer anyway."

"Did you ever talk to him about the death of his brother

361

Oswaldo?"

"I did, sort of. I extended my sympathy at the time and asked him how he was doing."

"What did he have to say?"

"He just shrugged his shoulders and said he was doing okay. To be honest, I don't think he really gave a shit. Like I said, he's a strange little fucker."

"And you got no idea what he's been up to that would warrant his getting a beating?"

"I got no clue. But, I'll tell you one thing—"

"What's that?"

"Whatever he's doing to piss people off, he's still doing it."

"What makes you say that?"

"Because I think someone must've popped him a good one over the eye. He had to have been opened up because he's wearing a big bandage that covers his eyebrow."

"Did you ask him about that?"

"You know, this time I actually did ask him what happened when I saw him outside the house."

"And what did he say?"

"He told me he ran into a door. Then he just scooted inside the house."

Von Hess took a second to look at the date and time Alley was struck by the bus in his notebook. He then pointed out the page to Mitchell's tenant. "Do you remember where you were at this specific time and date? We like to know if you were home."

The tenant looked at the paper and nodded in the affirmative. "I can tell you exactly where I was," he said. "I was in Maryland visiting my sister that whole week."

37

Bonita Baby

MITCHELL STARED BLANKLY AT the engineer cap hanging off the doorknob. He found it to be a depressing reminder of his losing Alley. Abandoned were his plans of expanding Alleytown. He no longer had the enthusiasm to construct an Alley Airfield or a monument along the train route paying tribute his passion's memory.

Mitchell's melancholy was interrupted by the doorbell ringing. When he opened the front door, he found that a large, square box had been left on his doorstep. Not expecting a delivery, he checked the address on the carton. Once he realized that the package was incorrectly delivered, he stepped outside to look for the delivery truck. Seeing that the UPS truck was still parked on his street, he walked over to the vehicle to return the package.

"Hey, lady!" shouted Mitchell as he approached the truck.

The UPS driver, who was just preparing to drive off, turned to see who was calling her. Seeing the man carrying the package, the driver put her vehicle in park. She then stepped down from her truck to join Mitchell on the sidewalk.

Mitchell's jaw dropped upon coming face-to-face with the young woman. She bore a resemblance, as did Alley, to Page Thirty-Seven, the magazine photo that kept him company many a night. As if struck by Cupid's arrow, Mitchell's spirits reversed. He smiled as he held out the package for her to receive.

"Did I deliver this to the wrong address?" asked the driver cheerfully.

"I think so," answered Mitchell, his eyes affixed on the driver's lips.

"Thanks," she said, taking the package to read the label. "I must need glasses," she said in a friendly manner. "I mistook the 694 for 894. Here, take a look at the number—see what I mean?"

The driver innocently brushed against Mitchell's chest as she held the package for him to read the label. Mitchell interpreted this in the most favorable light. In his mind, this slight meeting of their bodies was an indication of her desire for him. Now smitten, he sought to continue their conversation.

"Yeah, I see what you mean," he said. "The ink wore thin."

"Well, have a good day, sir."

"Are you new on this route? I've never seen you before."

"I just started a couple of weeks ago," she answered, trying not to stare at the bandage that covered his eyebrow.

"What happened to the old guy with the glasses who covered this area?"

"He retired," she replied.

"Oh. Well, I'm glad *you* replaced him," said the smiling Mitchell.

At this point the driver wasn't sure if Mitchell was just being friendly or had other ideas. She attempted to conclude their conversation without appearing rude.

"Well, have a great—"

"What's your name?" asked Mitchell, cutting her off mid-sentence.

"Bonita."

"That's a pretty name."

"Thank you," she replied politely. "Well, it's been nice taking to you—"

"What your last name, Bonita?"

"Why do you want to know?" Bonita asked curiously, wondering if Mitchell was someone she should be wary of.

"You're supposed to identify yourself to customers, aren't you?"

Being new at her job, Bonita felt she had to answer his question.

"My name is Bonita Daniels."

"I like that name fine," said Mitchell. "You remind me of a beautiful model I know."

Bonita was taken aback by this line of conversation. "Well I have to get back to work now, sir."

"Call me Mitch—" he said as she got behind the wheel of her truck.

Bonita shook her head as she drove off. Her thoughts of Mitchell were aligned with those of the late Alley. *What a little creep*!

When Mitchell returned to his house, he entered intent on converting Alleytown into Bonitaville. Before undertaking this work he needed to do one thing: order something to be delivered to his home.

##########

ACKNOWLEDGING HE MISHANDLED ALLEY, Mitchell was
determined not to make the same mistakes with Bonita. *This
time there will be no missteps,* he thought. *I'm gonna schmooze
Bonita right out of her uniform,* he confidently thought.

The love-struck Romeo stood by his window with his camera
in hand. This was the day that UPS was scheduled to deliver the
boxer trunks he ordered. The elevator operator wanted to be
sure that once the time for intimacy arrived, he wouldn't be
embarrassed by old underwear. Mitchell was sure that Bonita
would be impressed by the little lizards that adorned his new lily
white undershorts.

When Mitchell sighted the delivery truck on the block, he
focused his camera. His began snapping as many photos of
Bonita as possible before opening the door to greet her.

"Thank you, Bonita!" said Mitchell, smiling broadly. "You're
looking really great today."

Started by his sudden appearance, Bonita tried not to
encourage him. She just nodded and began to walk off.

"Hold up a second," he shouted after her. "I have a bottle of
water for you. I'll go get it."

Even though Bonita kept walking, Mitchell wasn't deterred. He
caught up to her by jogging to her truck, carrying a bottle of
water and a Hershey bar.

"I got you some candy, just in case you get the munchies,"
announced Mitchell, trying hard to gain her acceptance.

"Thank you," she said, taking his offerings. "My favorite is
Godiva," she expressed, figuring she might as well get whatever
she could out of such an ardent admirer.

"I love Godiva chocolates as well!" said Mitchell, seizing the
opportunity to step onto common ground.

Bonita found it astounding that someone like Mitchell could

ever have expectations of getting anywhere with her. Having a healthy ego, she considered herself among the nines and tens.

"Wait, Bonita, before you go, I have to tell you something. In a week or so, I'm gonna have a great surprise for you."

"What kind of surprise?"

"I'm gonna show you something that'll knock your socks off."

"What is it?" she asked out of pure curiosity.

"I can't tell you now because I'm still working on it. I don't want to spoil the surprise. When I'm finished, you'll come in the house and see for yourself. Trust me, you'll love it."

Bonita looked at Mitchell with wariness. Although very suspicious of his motives, she nevertheless was curious as to what his great surprise was. "I don't know about going inside your house, we're really not allowed to—"

"Oh, no, you don't," replied Mitchell, cutting her off. He thought she was being coy. "You're not going to make me tell you what it is now. You'll have to wait until next week."

Bonita frowned. "I have to get back to work," she announced, tired of the foolishness.

Mitchell watched Bonita drive off. He entered his house believing that the advice giver on the radio would be proud of him.

38

Fishnet On The Case

FISHNET ALWAYS EQUATED MONEY with happiness. Yet, after inheriting all the money he could want, he came to feel that he required more than money to be happy. In an effort to determine what this additional need was, he proceeded to analyze himself.

After objective self reflection, the ex-detective concluded that power was the missing ingredient to his happiness formula. Having authority over others, the very thing that drew him to law enforcement in the first place, was what was now lacking.

Fishnet came to recognize that being judge, jury, and potential executioner was the key to his achieving true bliss. The badge he once carried enabled him to determine fates and administer consequences. The power to reward or punish, be lenient or harsh, and choose to overlook or not had once been up to him.

When it came to money and possessions, Fishnet came to understand that there was a thrill stemming from *how* he acquired those things. As a cop, whatever Fishnet lacked in salary, he made up for on the street while working. As a rogue member of law enforcement he viewed every workday as an adrenalin-filled holiday that offered a multitude of opportunities. Every benefit derived from thievery was considered a present. Now having sufficient funds there was no need for him to steal, and thus, the kick was gone. For Fishnet, paying for something was the equivalent of scratching a place that wasn't itchy.

Fishnet examined this affluent chapter in his life as only he could. Acutely aware that he required stimulation, he picked his brain for an appropriate vehicle to meet his need. In evaluating his abilities, he keenly observed there were many toughs in the world, but few who had what it took to commit murder. He saw the ability to kill as what separated the men from the boys, so to speak.

In terms of recent thrills, nothing compared to the charge Fishnet received in successfully carrying out the double homicide of his wife and her friend. To justify such atrocious behavior he took the position that some people simply didn't deserve to live. *If a party was deserving of death, then taking a life would be a good deed,* he thought. It was an opinion he sought no counterargument for.

#########

FISHNET, AS HE STARED AT HIS REFLECTION IN THE POND, was uneasy knowing that Sergeant Markie might be coming for him.

Having the tenacious Markie breathing down his neck was not a pleasant thought. Complicating matters was the fact that the sergeant was beyond being compromised with money.

Aside from Markie, there was Von Hess to consider. The old sleuth would definitely surface as a threat if something unfortunate were to happen to his boss. Resolving the problem Markie and Von Hess posed was going to be difficult.

"I'm gonna have to do something, guys," said Fishnet, speaking to the koi as he sprinkled their food into the backyard pond. "But what can I do?" It was a question he asked the fish as he watched the koi compete for their food.

In order to think his problem out, Fishnet took a long walk after feeding the fish. Since it was a nice, windless day, he took along the morning newspaper with the intention of reading it in a small park. When he arrived at his destination, he sat on a bench next to a sleeping man who appeared to be down on his luck. As Fishnet made himself comfortable, he realized the man's snoring was going to be a distraction. The former detective, drawing back on the days when he was enforcing the law, took steps to relocate the man.

"Hey, pal, get up and park it someplace else to get your beauty sleep," barked Fishnet, after smacking the man's feet off the bench.

The man rose as directed without fully opening his eyes. "All right, officer, I'm going," said the disheveled man.

The unquestioned compliance of the down-and-outer couldn't have made Fishnet happier. For a few seconds he was able to once again enjoy the power trip that came with telling people what to do. *These winos can smell a cop a hundred yards away*, thought Fishnet.

Once taking control of the bench, Fishnet began reading the

newspaper. He did so without finding any content of particular interest. This changed when he noticed the photo of a familiar face accompanying the tragic story of a woman who met her death after being struck by a bus. The story was about Markie's girlfriend, Alley. The wide-eyed former detective read the article in the newspaper twice.

I wonder if that sawed-off runt had something to do with this, he thought, remembering the little man he met at Roache's Four-Leaf Clover. *What was his name again? Was it Mike? No, it was Mitchell!*

As Fishnet pulled on the tiny hairs of his Gable-like mustache, a mischievous smile crossed his face. If his suspicions were correct, he now saw a path to solve the Markie dilemma.

##########

FISHNET WAITED IN HIS CAR FOR JACKIE THE BARTENDER to conclude her shift at Roache's Four-Leaf Clover. A tall woman with short, dark hair, Jackie walked out of the bar lighting up a cigarette. She turned to the street at the sound of the car horn. Seeing Fishnet at the wheel of his Mercedes caused her to smile.

"Fishnet!" she yelled in a voice that was more than loud enough to reach the Mercedes. "What are you doing around here?"

Fishnet waved her over to his car. "C'mon, jump in. I'll give you a ride."

Jackie got in the passenger side of the car without being told twice. "So what do I owe this honor to?" she asked, loving every minute of riding up front in a Mercedes.

"I was just wondering what you were up to. I miss you."

Jackie wasn't easily joshed. "You miss me!" she exclaimed in a loud voice. "Hah! That's a hot one. What do you want?"

"I've been a little lonely since my wife died. You know she died, right?"

"Yeah, I know." Jackie looked at Fishnet seriously as she tried to gauge his sincerity. "So how are you doing?"

"I take it a day at a time. You know me."

"Yeah, I know you." The more Jackie looked at Fishnet the more she remembered why she went with him years ago when drinking heavily. She suddenly chuckled, thinking of something funny.

"What was that about?" asked the former detective.

"I was just thinking about when we used to go around together. I used to pretend that you were really Clark Gable when we made it."

"Tell you what—how about we go to put the feedbag on? Then maybe we go back to your place and get reacquainted?" he asked.

Since it had been awhile since Jackie's bones had been put to the test, she took him up on his offer. After dinner they went to Jackie's apartment. During the course of their time together Fishnet began to casually ask Jackie about the little man he met at Roache's.

"Who was that guy I was talking to that day?" asked Fishnet.

"What guy?"

"You know who I'm talking about, the little guy. He was real short and sort of muscular."

"Oh, you're talking about Mitchell."

"Yeah, that's the guy. What's the story with him?"

"There's no story with him. He's just a loner who comes in for drinks. I feel kind of sorry for him."

"What, does he live around there or something?"

"He lives in the neighborhood someplace. I don't know too

much about him other than he lost his only brother in a subway accident."

"Is that so . . ."

Jackie could see by Fishnet's reaction that there was something more to his inquisitiveness. "Why all the interest?" she asked.

"I think there may be a chance for him to make a few bucks," Fishnet fibbed. "What does he do for a living?"

"I think he works an elevator. I remember him mentioning that once."

"I see. When does he come around the bar?"

"He's got no special routine."

"Do me a favor—call me next time he's at the bar. Will you do that?"

"I can do that. What does he have to do?"

Fishnet smiled without answering as he took the back of her head in his hand.

##########

JACKIE WAS WORKING AN EVENING SHIFT when she telephoned Fishnet to advise him that Mitchell entered the bar.

"He just walked in," she whispered on the phone.

"Ahh, shit. I'm all tied up," said Fishnet, trying to sound disappointed. "I'll have to catch him next time."

"When are you coming around to see me?"

"Soon—right now I'm in the middle of something. I'll have to call you back later."

Fishnet rushed to the bar immediately after hanging up the phone. After finding a parking spot not far from the Roache's Four-Leaf Clover, the former detective telephoned Jackie.

"Sorry I had to cut you short," he said. "You busy?"

"Kind of, do you want me to give Mitchell your number?"

"Is he still there?"

"Yeah, I just poured him another beer."

"Well, forget about him," said Fishnet. "The opportunity went away, so I don't need to talk to him anymore."

"Oh, okay. So when are you coming by to meet me?"

"I'll call you, baby," said Fishnet, hanging up the phone.

Jackie shook her head and began cursing herself under her breath. The first time Fishnet dropped her like a hot potato she didn't know any better. This time she should have.

Fishnet waited patiently for his prey to leave. He ended up following Mitchell home on foot from a safe distance. Once armed with Mitchell's address, Fishnet returned to his car.

39

An Unexpected
Payoff

FISHNET SAT UP IN BED READING a book about Ferdinand Waldo Demara, Jr. The subject of Robert Crichton's *The Great Imposter,* Demara was a high school dropout who attained fame by acquiring professional credentials that enabled him to impersonate others. Fishnet found Demara's multiple deceptions, which ranged from a surgeon to a Benedictine monk, to be insightful. When Fishnet closed the book, he rested his head back on his pillow and began thinking of how easy it could have been for him to impersonate Clark Gable had the actor still been alive.

Once his thoughts of Demara passed, Fishnet concentrated on how to go about dealing with Markie. Mitchell's infatuation with Alley made him a perfect patsy and lifeline for Fishnet. If he could show that the freight elevator operator had something to do with Alley's death, or at least make it seem that way, he was certain Markie would feel obligated to him. As Fishnet saw it, once indebted, a man like Markie couldn't bring himself to put him behind bars. Hence, the double homicide of Sally Belle and Estelle Hatton would remain buried along with other closed cases. Fishnet went to sleep believing this.

The following morning Fishnet set out to establish that Mitchell had something to do with Alley's death. Since snatching Mitchell off the street was a too risky a tactic, Fishnet decided to ambush his prey at home. Fishnet parked his car a safe distance from Mitchell's house. He proceeded to Mitchell's home on foot while armed with a small leather case containing lock-picking tools. Concealed in his coat pocket was a pint of bourbon he laced with a deadly poison. Fishnet had lifted the lethal substance from a burglarized lab years prior.

Fishnet rang the doorbell and knocked on the front door of the house. When no one came to the door, he rang the bell to the upstairs apartment. Again there was no response. Fishnet, who was skilled at picking locks from years of practice when in the department, gained entry to the house with little trouble. Once inside he began exploring the premises.

Fishnet couldn't believe his eyes when he saw the massive train display. Following the track, his eyes widened when he came to the photos of the two women that adorned the walls. *This friggin' guy is crazier than me!* Fishnet thought, shaking his head with amusement. *He must be an out-and-out psycho!*

While Fishnet recognized the pictures of Alley, he had no inkling as to who the other woman was. The only clue was that she was wearing what he believed to be some type of uniform. Next to the transformer, Fishnet came upon a newly painted sign that read, *Welcome to Bonitaville*. Prominently posted was one that reflected the name Alleytown.

376

"Jesus Christmas—they ought to give me a medal if I'm right about this nutty bastard," he said.

Once Fishnet got over being blown away by what he was seeing on the first floor, Fishnet went up to inspect the second floor. The search upstairs netted him a pillowcase filled with goodies he intended to take home. Among these items were watches, cufflinks, and tie clips that had belonged to Oswaldo, Mitchell's late brother.

When he finished treasure hunting upstairs, Fishnet returned to the first floor, where he made himself comfortable in an easy chair. While waiting for Mitchell to return home from work, he passed the time by mentally transporting himself in and out his fantasy world.

Fishnet sprung to his feet after hearing noise coming from the other side of the front door. With his revolver drawn, he concealed himself behind a couch. As expected, it was Mitchell returning home from work. At the sound of the door closing the intruder emerged from behind the furniture brandishing his weapon. The sight of an armed home invader caused Mitchell to freeze. The homeowner's mouth was agape as he faced the business side of the handgun.

"Don't do something stupid," warned Fishnet, using his most thuggish voice, "unless you want your brains spattered all over the living room."

"What do you want from me, man?" asked Mitchell. "I got nothing in this house worth a shit other than my trains."

"Start heading toward the kitchen," ordered Fishnet. "Now take a seat," he directed, once there.

"It's you!" exclaimed the victim, finally recognizing Fishnet from Roache's Four-Leaf Clover. "What's all this about? You remember me..."

"Sure I do, we're pals. You and me are gonna have a heart-to-heart talk."

"Talk about what?"

"I want to know what went on with you and your *girlfriend*, the one who got hit by the bus."

"I don't know what you're talking about . . ."

"Listen, Shorty, you're gonna come clean, or you're gonna get hurt. I happen to know that Alley's boyfriend is gunning for you," claimed Fishnet. "He's a friend of mine and a very dangerous guy when pissed off. He thinks you had something to do with Alley getting killed. I'm here to do you both a favor before he comes over here to see you."

"He knows where I live?"

"Yeah, that's what I'm trying to tell you, pal!" said Fishnet. "I'm here to prevent things from getting out of hand, so let's get together on this."

"How does he know where I live?"

"Forget about how he knows—I'm here, ain't I?" Fishnet replied. "If I figured it out, he will. You ain't exactly invisible, you know."

"So what do you want?"

"I know that shit happens. You seemed like a decent guy when we met—that's the only reason I even give a crap. Just tell me the truth, and I'll do what I can to square this mess for you. I can talk to my friend once I get the full story."

"Why didn't you just knock on the front door instead of breaking in?"

Fishnet had no good answer for the question posed. "I'll ask the questions," he said. "Just consider yourself lucky that we met before. I'm gonna run a little interference for you."

Mitchell, not being the brightest of men when on the defensive, bought it. "The accident was her own fault. I didn't do anything to that girl."

"But you were with her that day, right?"

"Yeah, but we were just talking in the house. All of a sudden she got nuts and ran away from me. I didn't even go after her after she slugged me with a train track."

"Whoa—hold it right there. You better write down exactly what happened. Here, put it all down on this spiral," instructed Fishnet, removing a pad and pen from his jacket pocket. "I won't be able to remember all the details. Make sure you put down the date and time."

"Are you a cop or something?"

"Just write," replied Fishnet. "Like I said, shit happens. Trust me, if your story is a good one and it was really an accident, I'll make my friend understand. He won't be happy, but he'll understand."

"I can explain it to him—"

"Forget that idea—he's liable to flip out and kill you on sight."

"But why do I have to write it down?"

"Just friggin' write," ordered Fishnet. Seeing Fishnet cock his gun made a huge impression on Mitchell, who was persuaded to write down his version of what occurred.

After reading what Mitchell wrote, Fishnet smiled with satisfaction. "This is good," he declared. "Now, just add this before you sign off," directed Fishnet, dictating what he wanted written. Mitchell did as he was told. "Okay, now read that last line back to me," ordered Fishnet.

"Forgive me, but this is the best I can do to right things, I'm sorry. Mitchell Emery."

"Perfect. Now write it all out the same exact way once more."

"Why do I have to do that?"

"I want you to keep a copy for your own records," Fishnet lied.

"Now what?" asked Mitchell, after duplicating the note. "Are

379

you gonna go to the cops?"

"No, no, no. The cops will gum everything up, so forget the cops. My friend just wants closure, and this is gonna give it to him."

"He'll be okay with it?"

"Sure, he'll come around. This worked out pretty good, didn't it, Shorty?"

"Stop calling me *Shorty*, will ya?"

Fishnet backed off, realizing how offended Mitchell had become. "Alright, don't get so touchy. The hard part is over. Now, to show you there are no hard feelings, I want you and me to have a little drink," said Fishnet. "Here, you can take the first swig," said Fishnet, passing him the pint of doctored bourbon.

"Make it a big one."

"But . . . I don't drink bourbon."

"What, after I do you a favor, you're trying to insult me now?" asked Fishnet, turning foul. "Drink the drink already!" he demanded. "I want to get outta here, so hurry up."

Mitchell had a sickened look about him soon after he consumed the bourbon. He began to double over as his mouth started foaming. It didn't take long before he could no longer be counted among the living.

Fishnet left the death note on the kitchen table for the police to find. Wanting to ensure the only fingerprints discovered on the bottle belonged to Mitchell, Fishnet wiped the bottle clean. He then pressed the dead man's fingers against the cleaned bottle.

Fishnet left the apartment carrying the pillowcase full of goodies. He saw it as a just reward for doing a good job,

40

Quid Pro Quo
And Nowhere To
Go

FISHNET LOOKED DOWN INTO THE POND, marveling at how the open-mouthed koi rose to the surface, awaiting their rations. As the fish prepared to compete for their food, he wondered how they were able to sense his presence. As the koi jockeyed for position, a cruel thought came to him.

Fishnet went inside the townhouse to fetch a piece of string. When he returned, he tied the string to a pond stick. He then enticed the koi by floating the food atop the water. Just before Pascal, the largest of the koi, was about to chomp, Fishnet suddenly lifted the string, preventing the fish from gobbling up the pond stick.

Fishnet got a hoot at seeing Pascal's bite falling short. When he tired of tormenting the koi he ruled over, he dropped a handful of the pond sticks into the water for all to feast on.

"Come and get it, my children," said Fishnet. "Now, now, Pascal, don't be a little piggy—give the old Maestro a chance to fatten up. Go on, Sally—go and get your own. There are no peons working for you now. Save some for your girlfriend Estelle."

After he finished amusing himself with the koi, Fishnet went in the house to have a cup of coffee. After finding comfort in his favorite chair, the time had come to dial up Markie at his office in police headquarters. His smugness was comparable to a card player holding four-of-a-kind in a poker game.

"Police Headquarters, how may I help you?"

"Let me have Sergeant Markie in the Chief of Detective's office," said Fishnet.

"Hold on, please, while I transfer the call."

"Chief of D's office, Detective Silverlake speaking."

"I'd like to speak to Sergeant Markie, please."

"Who is calling?"

"Fishnet Milligan," answered the retired detective.

"Is this *the* Fishnet Milligan?"

"In person," replied Fishnet.

"Hey, pal—how ya feeling? Everyone on the job was pulling for you after that Red Harris business," said Silverlake, referring to the now-legendary gunfight. "You did a great job. Everybody calls you the miracle man."

Fishnet took great pride in what he was hearing. "I was lucky," he said, feigning modesty. "Is the sergeant in?"

"Yeah, he's around. I'll send the call over to his line. Take care."

The transferred call was picked up on the second ring.

"Sergeant Markie's line," answered Von Hess.

Fishnet didn't expect to hear the voice of Von Hess. Since he wasn't sure of what Markie shared with the detective concerning their confrontation at his townhouse, Fishnet pretended as if everything was cool.

"Hey, Ollie, it's me, Fishnet. How are tricks?"

Von Hess was shocked to hear from the former detective. "Milligan?" he asked.

"Yeah, how many Fishnets do you know? I guess you're surprised to hear from me."

"Err, no . . . umm, actually, I am," replied the stammering Von Hess, who was at a total loss for words.

"Is Markie around?"

"He just stepped out of the office for a minute to see the lieutenant about something. Give me a number and I'll tell him you called."

"Tell you what, how about you just give him a message for me?"

"What's the message?"

"Tell him it's *very* important for him to come see me tonight at my townhouse. He's got the address. Tell him to come *alone* because I got important news for him."

Von Hess thought the message odd enough to probe a bit. "What's all the cloak-and-dagger about?"

"Don't get me wrong, Ollie, I'd love to see ya, but this is a personal matter. You can come to the house *after* we talk."

"The sergeant's gonna ask me what this is about."

"Just tell him I got some answers for him."

"What time?"

"Figure on about 7:00 p.m. Just remember to tell him to come in alone."

"I heard you the first time, Fishnet."

##########

WHEN MARKIE RETURNED TO HIS OFFICE, Von Hess filled him in on the call he received from Fishnet. Markie was stunned Fishnet wanted to see him. His first thought was that Fishnet was looking to set him up in some way.

"Is that all he said, Ollie?"

"That's it, Sarge."

"He was sober, right?"

"He sounded sober to me."

"I wonder what he wants."

"I got no idea. The only thing he made clear was that this was to be between you and him."

Markie nodded, thinking that once he got there he'd take one precaution. He'd let Fishnet know that Von Hess was waiting outside for him in the car just in case he was walking into an ambush.

"This is really strange," said Markie, shaking his head.

"Have you been speaking to him?"

"Well, to be honest, I paid him a visit at his house one night when I got a load on."

"You didn't—"

"I did. I confronted him over the deaths of his wife and her friend in Pennsylvania."

"What did you tell him?"

"I told him flat out that I was gonna figure out a way to nail him to the wall because I knew he killed them."

"Jeeze, Sarge—tell me this isn't true."

"I know it was a dumb move, but I had a few in me. I did it,

384

and what's done is done."

"So his good news probably has something to do with that," conjectured Von Hess. "Maybe he has proof of his innocence."

"Now that would be a kick in the ass for me. I guess we'll just have to wait and see."

############

DETECTIVE VON HESS PURPOSELY TOOK HIS TIME driving Markie to Fishnet's Manhattan townhouse. The silence in the car was due to both men being absorbed in their own thoughts. Finally, Von Hess initiated a conversation.

"Look, Sarge, I've been thinking. Maybe it's not such a good idea for you to be in there alone with Fishnet."

"Don't worry, it'll be alright. I'm gonna let him know you're sitting outside in the car waiting for me."

When they arrived at their destination, Von Hess pulled up the car in front of the townhouse to let Markie out. The detective turned on the radio to listen to the news while keeping a sharp eye on the townhouse. He watched as Fishnet opened the front door to admit Markie into his home. Before closing the door, the ex-detective waved at Von Hess, who remained behind the wheel of his car. Expressionless, Von Hess nodded his acknowledgment.

Fishnet let Markie into the townhouse without saying a word. He directed the sergeant into the living room by lifting his chin in the direction of the couch.

Alright, I'm here," said Markie, who remained standing. "What's the big bulletin you have for me?"

"Look, Sarge, I know you got it in for me," began Fishnet. "You made that clear enough. I don't know *why* you feel the way you do, but you do."

"How about you get to the point?" asked Markie coldly.

"I don't go for being falsely accused . . . and the thought of having you up my ass for the rest of my life isn't very appealing, so I took steps."

"What steps?"

"I took steps that would smarten you up."

"Make sense, will ya? Say what you gotta say."

"I found out exactly what happened to your girlfriend."

"Yeah? What happened?" asked Markie, assuming a dead serious look.

"I figured that would get your attention," commented Fishnet smugly. "I got it all in writing what happened to her. Here, read it for yourself." As be began reading Mitchell's written statement, Markie's expression turned to one of astonishment. "Take a seat, Sarge. You look like you could stand a drink. What's your poison?"

Markie sat down as directed. "Scotch," he replied, as he reread the statement.

Fishnet walked to the liquor cart that held bottles of whisky and rye. He poured a stiff shot into a four-ounce tumbler for the sergeant.

"I'll join you, *partner*," said Fishnet, pouring the second drink for himself. Although Markie cringed at the very thought of being Fishnet's partner, he was too stunned to comment. He simply nodded when Fishnet gestured good luck with his glass.

"How did you get this?"

"Relax, Sarge. Just remember this: you were looking for answers, and I'm the guy who went out and got them for you. The guy responsible for your girlfriend's death is some runt named Mitchell Emery."

"The squad that caught the case should have this confession," said Markie, regaining his composure.

"Don't you want to know who Mitchell Emery is?"

"I already know who he is. What about the squad detectives?"

"You already know?" asked Fishnet, not knowing whether to believe Markie.

"Yeah, I do. What about the case detective?"

"The cops are gonna find a letter, just like the one in your hand, on the little guy's kitchen table. They can't miss it."

"There are two copies?"

"Natch. The one you're holding is just for you. I want you to understand that it was me who got you satisfaction."

"Where is Mitchell?"

"They'll find him too."

Markie felt helpless, now realizing what Fishnet might have done. "So it definitely was this son of a bitch Mitchell Emery!"

"The little prick had a fixation, Sarge. He built a whole friggin' town inside his house in your girlfriend's honor."

"He built a town? What kind of a town?"

"Yeah—he calls it Alleytown, and quite a town it is. It comes complete with all the trimmings. He runs electric trains through the town."

"So what did you do with him?"

"C'mon, Sarge, stop with the questions."

"At least let me know how you found out about Mitchell."

"I read about Alley's death in the newspaper. Then I figured, with you on my back over some bullshit homicides you *think* I committed, it might be a good idea for me to do a little digging in order to level the playing field. Don't forget, I was a pretty good detective."

"Yeah, you *were* one in a million, but tell me how you found out about Mitchell."

Fishnet refused to provide further specifics. "All you gotta remember is that I was the one, nobody else, who did you a big favor," declared Fishnet, using a much more serious tone. "The way I see it, you owe me."

"What favor did you do for me?"

Fishnet shrugged. "I gave you *full* closure."

"Wait a minute . . . are you telling me—"

"What I'm telling you is that the little guy got himself depressed and cashed in his chips."

"Are you saying he committed suicide?"

"Yeah, that's right, suicide. The poor guy just couldn't take the guilt connected to what he did."

"But you were there with him . . ."

"Errrrrr, let's get that part straight. For our purposes, I think it's in both our interests if we keep it simple. Like, you and me never figure into this at all."

"You're taking a lot for granted, Fishnet."

"Cut the shit, Sarge. What the hell else do you want from me?"

Markie looked at Fishnet as if he were seeing him for the first time. "I intended to bring the son of a bitch before a judge," declared Markie, the anger in his voice most evident.

"Well, now you don't have to bother with that. C'mon, will ya—get off your high horse. You've been spared deciding whether or not to take him out yourself."

"You're wrong. I'd have never thought to do that," declared Markie.

"Whatever you say, Sarge, just remember one thing—it's a moot point now. Thanks to me, you're free of all that shit."

"How did you do it?" questioned Markie, wanting to hear the details of how Fishnet killed Mitchell.

"Whoa! There you go again! Look, get it through your head—I didn't do a thing, so stop jumping to conclusions. The jerk-off committed suicide, period! The note he left on his kitchen table will support that conclusion, so let it go already."

"You can be a pretty clever mother, Fishnet," stated Markie, "but there is one loose end."

"And what might that be?"

"You underestimate me. Do you honestly think I'll look the other way or something like this?"

"Yeah, well, it's more like *you* underestimating me, Sarge," answered Fishnet, pouring them both another drink. "I'm betting that a guy like you don't turn rat, *if* he feels obligated." Fishnet then took a step closer to the sergeant to click glasses. "And you, my friend, whether you want to admit it or not, are obligated."

"What makes you so damn sure?"

"Because I know people, and it ain't in you to forget someone who did you a solid by taking care of your dirty work." Fishnet took a healthy sip of his drink as he stared at the seated Markie. "No, you'll keep your yap shut about this, especially since there ain't any hard evidence to indicate anything other than a suicide."

Fishnet stood smirking as Markie let out a deep breath before responding. "I wouldn't count on that."

"I'm not only counting on *that,* I'm also counting on you forgetting all about that crazy notion you have about those accidental deaths in the quarry. You got no proof there either!"

Markie remained silent for a moment before responding. "You got it all figured out, don't you?"

"I think so, Sarge. This is sort of like that Hannibal Lecter movie, you know, Silence of the Lambs. What did he call it again? You know, when they scratch backs . . ."

"Quid pro quo."

"Yeah, that's it, quid pro quo. Beautiful words, ain't they? C'mon, drink up—you look like you need it."

Markie couldn't think of anything else to do other than swill down his drink and then hold out his glass
for another. Their meeting came to a conclusion when the sergeant's cell phone went off. It was Von Hess calling.

"Yeah, Ollie, everything is good. I'll be out in a minute."

"Oh, Sarge, before you go, I think you better give me that piece of paper."

Fishnet removed the document Mitchell signed from the sergeant's hand. He then lit a match and put it on fire as Markie watched grimly.

"I don't think it does anybody any good to clue in Ollie," advised Fishnet. "He might not understand."

Markie didn't disagree.

##########

ON THE RIDE HOME, MARKIE did very little talking, but lots of thinking. He found himself at a crossroad. He was a man who lived his entire life believing there was a clear distinction between right and wrong. Now, to his dismay, he found himself in an area that at best could be described as dark gray. On the surface, the righteous thing for him to do would be to go to his superiors with what he knew.

But what would that accomplish? He thought.

The Sergeant knew Fishnet had been clever enough to cover his tracks. Without evidence, there was no case to put together, just his word against the word of a hero detective. Even if Fishnet were to be arrested, he'd certainly be acquitted. As far as gathering the necessary evidence, Markie faced the fact that there would be no chance of Fishnet ever talking about Mitchell Emery or the quarry deaths again. The former detective was simply too smart for that.

390

Torn between his oath as a law enforcement officer and keeping a dark secret, Markie had no choice other than to consider the matter practically. Swallowing a bitter pill, the sergeant made up his mind to concede the round to Fishnet and move on.

Let the Philadelphia police worry about happened in the quarry, he thought. *As far as Mitchell Emery was concerned, the little bastard got what he deserved for doing what he did to Alley.*

"So, are you gonna tell me how it went in there, Sarge?" asked Von Hess, interrupting Markie's thoughts. "You spent a lot of time in there."

Markie turned in his seat to look at his loyal friend. "It went. That's about all I can say, Ollie."

"What was his big news?"

Markie just shook his head. "He said nothing worth repeating. Sometimes you just have to let things go."

After ten minutes of silence in the car, it was Markie who broke the ice. "Hey, Ollie, have you ever thought what you would do once you retired?"

"Not really."

"To tell you the truth, I'm starting to think of it now. I'm beginning to find this job harder and harder to do."

"Ahhh, you're just going through a rough patch."

"Yeah, maybe you're right. I still got one egg to fry, anyway."

"What's that?"

"If it's the last thing I do, before I pack it in, I'm gonna bury Fishnet."

"Are you going after him on the quarry case?"

"Nah, let's face it, that's a dead issue. We gotta look ahead. A guy like Fishnet is bound to trip up down the road, and when he does, I'll be there to throw the net over him."

"Time is on our side, I suppose. Oh, I forgot to tell you, Sarge—
I got a call from Detective Silverlake over at the office while you
were inside."

"What did he want?"

"He gave me a heads-up regarding a criminal court judge in
Queens who just got whacked. We're probably gonna be
assigned to it in the morning."

Markie nodded approvingly. If anything could take his mind off
things, it was a new case. He needed the diversion after being
outmaneuvered by Fishnet Milligan. Down deep, Markie knew
that the new case would serve only as a preliminary bout. The
main event with Fishnet was yet to come.

THE END

Ingram Content Group UK Ltd.
Milton Keynes UK
UKHW020625170323
418727UK00011B/1242